What people are saying about …

REINVENTING RACHEL

"A fascinating story of one woman's search for God, of falling and rising and finding that we're never alone. In Rachel's struggles, many readers will recognize their own."

Lisa Wingate, best-selling author of *Beyond Summer* and *Never Say Never*

"This honestly written book is a must-read for any survivor of 'churchianity.' Realistic and transparent, Rachel Westing will strike a familiar chord with anyone who's ever felt disenfranchised with contemporary 'Christian' culture. I lent this book to a friend—and she called it a life-altering story. Way to go, Alison!"

Melody Carlson, author of The Four Lindas series and 86 Bloomberg Place series

"*Reinventing Rachel* is one of the most emotionally powerful and insightful books I've read in years. The author's intimate understanding of spiritual truth and the frailties of the human heart is evident in this well-written story. The conflict was so genuine and believable that it took my breath away and moved me to tears. God is really going to use this book to reach the hearts of people who are floundering in their faith."

Michelle Sutton, author of over a dozen novels including *It's Not About Me* and the best-selling *Danger at the Door*

"*Reinventing Rachel* is the story of a young woman who finds herself questioning her faith and engaging in dangerous behaviors when her relationships are torn apart. Author Alison Strobel draws the reader into Rachel's world where, after spiraling into disbelief and brokenness, she begins the uphill, grace-filled journey back to God and a life punctuated by hope."

Tamara Leigh, American Christian Fiction Writers' "Book of the Year" author of *Splitting Harriet* and *Nowhere, Carolina*

"Alison Strobel delivers a tsunami of emotion in *Reinventing Rachel.* I haven't read another book that grew with as much intensity and depth. Deceptively innocent in its first chapters, *Reinventing Rachel* will grab your heart and hold it captive, leaving you breathless until the end. Novel Journey and I give it a high recommendation."

Ane Mulligan, editor of Novel Journey, NovelJourney.blogspot.com

"Alison Strobel's novel depicts the painful unraveling of a self-righteous soul—and her reascent up a daunting spiritual mountain. Strobel's passion for her character's journey and pursuit of truth comes through loud and clear on the page. For every reader who has doubted God through troubled times, this book is for you."

Rene Gutteridge, author of *Listen* and *Never the Bride*

reINVENTING raCHEL

reINVENTING raCHEL

alison strobel

REINVENTING RACHEL
Published by David C. Cook
4050 Lee Vance View
Colorado Springs, CO 80918 U.S.A.

David C. Cook Distribution Canada
55 Woodslee Avenue, Paris, Ontario, Canada N3L 3E5

David C. Cook U.K., Kingsway Communications
Eastbourne, East Sussex BN23 6NT, England

David C. Cook and the graphic circle C logo
are registered trademarks of Cook Communications Ministries.

This story is a work of fiction. All characters and events are the product of the author's imagination. Any resemblance to any person, living or dead, is coincidental.

LCCN 2010930765
ISBN 978-1-4347-6774-5
eISBN 978-0-7814-0566-9

The author is represented by MacGregor Literary.

The Team: Don Pape, Nicci Jordan Hubert, Amy Kiechlin, Erin Prater, Karen Athen
Cover Photo: iStockphoto, royalty-free

Printed in the United States of America
First Edition 2010

1 2 3 4 5 6 7 8 9 10

063010

Maggie, I dedicate this book to you. I will always treasure our friendship, regardless of how many miles and time zones away we might be. (But let's try to see each other soon, okay?) I love you, sister.

ACKNOWLEDGMENTS

Many, many, many thanks go out to:

• Matt, Linda, and Karin for bringing life to my characters by giving them their names. I hope you like how they turned out!

• Amber, for giving me a glimpse into the life of a coffee-shop manager.

• Maggie and Laura, for schooling me in the realities of alcoholism.

• Amy, Heather, and Elizabeth for sharing your psych-unit experiences.

• The folks at David C. Cook for signing a book that looked a little iffy at the start and ended up being very different (though I think we'd all agree *better*) from the original concept, as well as for extending both my deadlines and granting much needed grace as I wrestled with Rachel and her story.

• Nicci Jordan Hubert, who is really the one responsible for this story existing at all. Through three drastically different incarnations and some seriously bad writing, you persevered with me and walked me through the most heinous writing experience I've ever weathered. Thank you for your encouragement, your friendship, and for pushing me to be a better writer.

• My parents, Lee and Leslie, for making it possible for me to live my dream. I am the luckiest daughter in the world. I love you guys so much!

• Daniel, my partner in life and love. Without your willingness to play Mr. Mom, I wouldn't be writing, period. I am so blessed to be married to someone as encouraging and sacrificial as you. Thank you for being my cheering section, for protecting me from theological heresy, and for being such an amazing father to our girls. They are so lucky to have you, and so am I. I love you.

• My Lord and Savior, for whom my books are written and my life is lived, and without whom I would be nothing.

CHAPTER 1

Rachel Westing pulled into the parking lot of Beach Cities Church and finished the last sip of Ethiopian Harrar she'd been nursing. The exotic coffee had required a half hour detour up the coast, but she'd needed a break from the seminary application she had been working on that morning before frustration made her head explode. The traffic on Beach Boulevard had given her plenty of time to think, but she was no clearer on the essay she still needed to write. Rare coffee usually sparked her creativity, but as she left the cool cocoon of her car for the SoCal May heat, she resigned herself to the fact that she was no closer to starting her paper than she'd been over an hour ago.

The worship team was polishing their set in the sanctuary when Rachel arrived. Despite feeling like a raincloud of consternation followed her, she sang along with the leader as he came to the chorus. *The love of God is greater far, Than tongue or pen can ever tell....* Upon hearing the words, warmth spread through her, and the cloud began to dissipate. The concept of God's love would never cease to amaze her.

Rachel exchanged waves with fellow volunteers as they caught each other's eyes, basking in the familiarity and security she always felt when she entered the building. After setting her Bible in her usual spot, she headed back out to the foyer where the associate pastor's wife was preparing the refreshments table with coffee and cookies.

"Coffee, Rachel?" Lily was setting out the plastic cups and stir sticks on the flowery tablecloth.

Chasing Ethiopian Harrar with Folgers crystals was coffee sacrilege. "No, thank you, Lily. But thanks for asking."

"You're welcome. Oh—I have something to return to your mom, but she wasn't at the service this morning. Are your parents out of town?"

Rachel bit her lip, thinking. "No, they're around—or should be, anyway." That was odd. They never missed church.

Lily waved a hand. "Not a big deal. I probably just missed them. Anyway, how are you? How's the wedding planning coming along?"

Rachel smiled, hoping her eyes didn't betray her slight frustration. "Sometimes I feel like it's never going to be done."

Lily chuckled as she refilled the containers of packaged sweeteners. "I remember that feeling. Just keep in mind it's the marriage and not the wedding that matters in the end. Everything else is just fluff. Wonderful, beautiful, fun fluff, of course—but fluff nonetheless." Rachel felt herself nodding—she'd heard this advice many times before. "What's the date again?" Lily asked.

"Well ..." Rachel brushed invisible crumbs from the table. "We've been going back and forth on that. June, most likely."

"Next month?" Lily's eyes grew wide.

"No, no—June of next year."

"Goodness, that's a long time." Lily helped herself to coffee. "Certainly I can speak for the church ladies by offering to pitch in if you'd like to make it happen sooner. I'd be happy to do the cake myself, and I'm sure Gwendolyn Meyers would love to do the flowers. We may not be the biggest church in the world, but I'll bet we can get you just about everything you need. You just let us know what needs doing, and I bet we can have you two under the same roof by autumn."

Rachel gave Lily a hug. "You're so sweet. I'll talk to Patrick and see. Sooner rather than later would certainly be my preference."

"Absolutely," Lily said. "So where is that fiancé of yours, anyway?"

Rachel looked around. "He usually meets me right before the service starts." She caught sight of one of her girls in the parking lot. "Oh—there's Amanda Kline. I need to talk to her. Thanks again for the offer, Lily." Rachel jogged out into the late afternoon sun to greet the high school sophomore, whose head was bent over her cell phone as her thumbs moved over the keypad.

"Hey, Amanda."

"Oh, hey, Rachel!" Amanda gave Rachel a smile. "I was just texting with Macy. She said she'd try to come tonight, but she's got a lot of homework."

Rachel frowned. "Again? Someone has to help that girl with time management. She hasn't been here since Easter."

"Yeah, I know. If she could convince Jeff to come, I think she'd be here more often."

"Jeff? Whose that?"

"Her boyfriend—didn't she tell you? They started going out back in March."

"Oh. No, I didn't know about him." Rachel was surprised Macy hadn't told her about this guy. They'd e-mailed enough that it definitely should have come up. "Is he a Christian?"

"I think so, but I'm not sure. I know she's gone to church with him a few times."

Rachel made a mental note to call Macy this week and schedule some hangout time. Macy was a sweet girl, and Rachel didn't want to see some boy pulling her away from her church family when she was at such a formative age. "Anyway, how are you doing, Amanda? Classes going all right?"

"Yeah, they're okay. Only three weeks left until finals—I can't believe it! This year went fast. And then there's only six weeks until the Mexico mission trip. I'm so excited."

Rachel smiled. The girl's enthusiasm reminded her of herself when she was Amanda's age. She had fond memories of those same mission trips with her high school leader, Barbara, who was still one of Rachel's closest friends. She hoped Amanda—and all the other high school girls she worked with—would make the same choices she had made and still be faithful Christians when they were her age.

Rachel and Amanda talked about the upcoming mission-trip fundraiser while they waited for a few other girls to arrive. Olivia showed up a few minutes later, trailing her mother and sister who passed Rachel with a wave on their way into the sanctuary. Gracie, Natalie, and Jenny showed up in quick succession, and together they all trooped into the sanctuary to claim their row.

The worship band took the stage and began to play the first song. The aisle seat beside Rachel remained empty, embarrassing her. Where was Patrick? She was also disappointed to see that Macy hadn't shown up again. She was likely being led astray, Rachel decided, and Patrick was probably still buried under English essays that needed grading. She wished he taught something straightforward, like math, so she could help him grade. She hated when his whole weekend was consumed with work, especially since Sunday was the only day during the week when they both were off. Yet another reason why she couldn't wait until they were married—at least then they'd share a bed at night and breakfast in the morning.

The worship band was filing off the stage when Patrick finally slipped into his seat. "Sorry," he mouthed to her when she looked at him with eyebrows raised. She rolled her eyes and smiled, then gave his hand a squeeze. At least he showed up.

When the service ended the girls took off en masse for the bathrooms as was their usual practice, leaving Rachel in the dust. She and Patrick hung back in their seats as the sanctuary emptied. "What happened to you this morning?"

"Time got away from me. These essays are killing me—you'd never know we've spent the last three months discussing proper writing technique."

She rubbed his back. "I'm sorry, sweetheart. Just a few more weeks and you'll be done for the year."

He heaved a sigh and squeezed her knee. "Amen to that. You should get going before the girls decide to go AWOL."

She planted a kiss on his cheek, then stood. "See you after, then—think about what you want for dinner. I was thinking maybe Chinese."

Patrick sucked in a breath through his teeth, pulling a face that made her heart sink. "I don't think I can tonight, babe. I've got to get these papers back before Tuesday, and if I don't get through a bunch more tonight then it's not gonna happen with baseball tomorrow."

Rachel groaned. "But I haven't seen you all week."

He stood and wrapped his arms around her. "I know, I know, I'm sorry. This is always a busy time for me, with the coaching and everything. But like you said, just a few more weeks and then we've got the whole summer. I'll make it up to you, I promise."

"Okay, okay." She kissed him on the cheek, then picked up her purse and Bible. "Take a break and call me tonight, okay?"

"I will."

She fought off bitterness as she exited the sanctuary and headed for the classrooms across the courtyard. Lily's suggestion came back to her as she passed the cookie platters that were nearly picked clean. She decided to broach the topic of a this-summer wedding when Patrick called her that night. She knew that wasn't what he'd been thinking when he'd promised to "make it up to her," but it didn't hurt to ask.

After Sunday school let out and she'd given rides home to Natalie and Amanda, Rachel stopped at Dream Cream and picked up a pint of Caramel Craziness to bring to Macy's.

Armed with the ice cream, she rang the bell on Macy's front door. Macy's mother answered, smiling. "Rachel, hi. Come on in. Macy's upstairs—go on up."

"Thanks, Mrs. Bell. Mind if I grab a couple spoons first?" She held up the pint.

Mrs. Bell chuckled. "Sure, help yourself—there's bottled water in the fridge, too, if you'd like some."

Rachel held the waters, spoons, and ice cream in a precarious grip as she climbed the squeaky wooden steps to Macy's attic room, then bumped open the door with her shoulder. "Surprise, surprise—hope you're ready for a study break!"

Macy smiled, though it looked the way Rachel's own smile felt when people asked her about the wedding. "Hey, Rachel! Oh yum—thanks for bringing ice cream. I need some refueling." She stacked the textbooks that were spread on her bed. "Here, sit down. I've been working on this stupid study guide for AP History for, like, three straight hours, and I feel like my brain is melting."

"I remember that feeling." Rachel pulled the top off the pint. "Dig in. First bite is yours, you poor, suffering student, you."

Macy scraped her spoon along the smooth top of the ice cream. "How was church? Sorry I couldn't make it."

"It was good. Pastor Mark's doing a series on Ephesians. It's been really eye opening." Rachel took her own bite and let the ice cream melt in her mouth before continuing to talk. "But Amanda totally surprised me—she said you were dating someone. I had no idea—you've got to give me the lowdown!"

Macy's smile was authentic this time, and Rachel couldn't help but smile along with her at the memory of her own high school crushes. "Yeah, I'm dating this guy, Jeff Anders. He works with me on the yearbook committee. I think you'd really like him. He's such a strong believer, and he's been really challenging me."

It wasn't what Rachel had expected to hear, but it didn't ease her concerns, either. "Where does he go to church?"

"His family is in a house church."

Rachel frowned. There was the catch. "A house church, huh. Like a small group?"

"No, it's more than a small group. They don't go to a church building; they don't have all sorts of ministries and stuff like we do. They just take turns meeting in each other's homes, and they do dinner together and hang out and discuss theology and stuff. It's really cool."

Rachel concentrated on her next bite of ice cream, searching for a way to be diplomatic. "That sounds … interesting. But I'd be wary of a bunch of people meeting without any sort of leadership or trained pastor, Macy. That sounds like a recipe for shaky doctrine. Why don't you invite Jeff to come to our service next week? Maybe he'd enjoy it, and then you could be sure you're getting truly Biblical teaching."

Macy stabbed her spoon into the ice cream and slouched back against the pillows on her bed. "This is why I didn't tell you about this earlier, Rachel. I knew you wouldn't like it."

Rachel fought the defensiveness that rose in her chest. "I just want to make sure you're not being taught untruths, that's all. What do your parents think about it?"

Macy shrugged. "They don't care. They're just glad I'm going to church somewhere."

Righteous anger over the Bells' lack of discernment joined the concern she felt for Macy. "But if they're not associated with a particular church or denomination, how can you be sure they're not a cult?"

Macy let out a laugh. "They're totally not a cult, trust me. Seriously—they're the godliest people I've ever met. I don't know anyone at our church who has a relationship with Jesus that these people do." She leaned her elbows on her knees and stared at Rachel with an earnest face. Rachel was stunned—and slightly offended. But Macy continued, oblivious. "I've been a Christian my whole life, Rachel, and I've never felt like I really knew God. I always felt like there was this wall between him and me. But talking with these people, seeing how they approach the Bible, and prayer, and service—they're friends with Jesus, the way I want to be."

Red flags were flying all over the place in Rachel's mind. "Macy, I wish you would have told me that you didn't feel close to God. Everyone struggles with that after they've been a Christian a while. I've got a whole bookshelf of studies we could have done together—"

"No, no, studies wouldn't do it. Trust me." Macy pulled her hair into a ponytail, then let it fall back to her shoulders with a sigh. "You know, I really have to get this study guide done. It's due tomorrow. Thanks for coming by, and for the ice cream. Maybe I'll see you next week." She was obviously avoiding Rachel's eyes as she pulled a textbook back to her lap and began to leaf through its pages.

Rachel stood, feeling awkward at being given the cold shoulder by a sixteen-year-old. "Sure. Good luck with that. I'll pray the test goes well. Give me a call if you ever want to talk, okay?"

"I will. Thanks."

Rachel let herself out of the room and returned the spoons to the kitchen where Mrs. Bell was emptying the dishwasher. "Thanks for stopping by."

"Sure." She forced a smile. "See you later." But as she walked down the steps to the sidewalk, Rachel had a feeling it would be the last time she visited.

That night when Patrick called, Rachel vented about her conversation with Macy. "I mean, where is the accountability? You can't just decide, 'Hey, forget church—I'm going to go do my own thing.'"

"Sure you can."

"Well, you can, but it's not right."

"Rachel, I think you're taking this a little hard. You don't know anything about these people. How can you know that they're wrong?"

"It's just a feeling I have."

He made a noise of dissent. "Well, feelings can lie."

"True. But regardless, I feel like I need to do something."

"Keep your nose out of it, Rach."

"I'm not talking about crashing their meeting or anything. I'm just going to call Barbara and see what she'd do in my shoes."

"Now that is a good idea."

"Hey, speaking of good ideas …" Rachel sat up straighter on her bed. "I was thinking maybe we could consider moving the wedding date up."

"Up? Like, to the spring?"

"No, like, to August."

"This August?" He laughed. "Are you nuts?"

Rachel felt a sting, but she pushed through. "No, hear me out—I was talking with Lily before the service today, and she mentioned there's lots of people who would be willing to help out with the wedding. Like, she said she'd make the cake, and that Gwendolyn Meyers could do the flowers—"

"Whoa—Rach, honey." Patrick's voice held a note of condescension. "Think of what you're saying. Plan a wedding in three months? Do you really want the biggest day of our lives to be thrown together under the gun like that?"

"The wedding isn't as important as the marriage, Patrick. I'm tired of only seeing you a couple days a week. I'm tired of sleeping alone. I want to be married. Don't you?"

"Of course I do, but I don't want us to look back in ten years and wish we'd done things differently. We've only been engaged for five months. That's nothing compared to some people."

"I don't care about other people's relationships, Patrick. Who cares if other people stay engaged for longer. The point is, why should we?"

"Sweetheart, listen. We've only known each other a year. We still have a lot to learn about one another. I want to make sure we're both prepared, that's all. I don't want to rush anything and regret it later."

Rachel's stomach fluttered. "You're not sure you want to marry me? Is that what you're saying?"

Patrick muttered an uncharacteristic curse under his breath. "No, that's not what I'm saying, Rachel. I'm saying there's nothing wrong with taking things slowly, that's all." He let out a sigh. "Look—what if we compromised? This summer is too early, but yeah, maybe next summer is a little far off. What about this winter—like New Year's Eve? Yeah—big party for the reception, big countdown. Think of what our anniversary will be like every year."

The flutter in her stomach morphed to butterflies of excitement. "Seriously? Patrick, that sounds amazing. I love it! And you're totally cool with that?"

"Yes, totally cool."

"You're wonderful. I love you so much. What a great idea."

"And if you want to hit up the church ladies for a little help, go for it. Probably save your parents a bundle."

She laughed. "I'll talk to Lily next week and see what she says."

"Listen, babe, I need to get going—and you need to call Barbara."

"Yes, you're right. Okay." Rachel hung up with a smile on her face that made her cheeks ache. She pulled her organizer from her desk and flipped to the end, then wrote "Wedding!!!!" on December 31. "Thank you, thank you, thank you," she sang as she tossed the planner back to the desk and dialed Barbara's number. Her friend answered just as Rachel expected voice-mail to pick up. "Barbara, hey. It's Rachel. I'm not calling too late, am I?"

"No, no, this is fine. How are you?"

"I'm okay. Great, actually—we just set a date for the wedding. New Year's Eve!"

"Oh wow, that's really fantastic. Congratulations."

"Thanks. Hey, listen—could we get together this week? I'm concerned about one of my girls, and I'd like to get your insight on what I should do."

"Well, um, sure—that's good timing, actually, because I needed to talk to you too. How about tomorrow? Are you free?"

Rachel grabbed the planner again and flipped to the spot her bookmark held. "I work until three, but I'm free after."

"Great. Let me meet you at the coffee shop."

"Okay. I'll see you then."

Smiling so hard her cheeks hurt, Rachel hung up and went to the kitchen to throw together a belated dinner, which she ate in front of the television. She was just getting ready to turn in for the night when Trisha, her roommate, came in from work. Her red-rimmed eyes brought a frown to Rachel's face. "Hey, you okay?"

"No." Her expression made it seem like she had more to say, but instead she ducked her head and disappeared into her room, the door shutting behind her just a pinch short of a slam.

Rachel stared at the door for a moment, debating what to do before switching off the TV and heading for her room. There was only so much she could do for her backslidden roommate without getting pulled into her drama. She flung yet another prayer heavenward for Trisha before devoting her remaining waking moments to wedding plans.

Work always flew for Rachel. From the minute the first customer walked through the door to the time she pulled off her apron and logged out of the office computer, her head was immersed in the business of *Espress-Oh!* and her managerial duties. She loved what she did and knew how blessed she was to have a job she looked forward to every day. Ever since her first cup on a high school mission trip, coffee had been her morning eye-opener, her mood stabilizer, her hobby. The aroma alone was enough to perk her up and clear her head.

But when she crossed to the other side of the counter, she left the responsibilities of her position behind and became just another caffeine addict hanging out in the beachside shop. This week she needed to focus her extracurricular energy on her seminary application essay. She'd decided to go back for her master's in Christian education, and she was thinking about going into full-time high school ministry. Managing a coffee shop wasn't something she wanted to do forever, and working with young women on the cusp of adulthood as they navigated faith and life struck a chord. All she had left for her application was the essay, but creativity continued to elude her. She was supposed to write about her faith—when she had become a

Christian, the high and low points of her relationship with God—but for some reason she was stymied. "I've been a Christian all my life, and it's always been great" didn't strike her as master's-level writing, and embellishing a seminary application essay didn't seem like the best idea, but the statement was the truth. Church had been her second home since birth, and her life had always been blessed. A loving family, a happy childhood, health and financial stability, with a handful of life's unavoidable disappointments and sad moments, but no tragedies or life-altering events. Those without a belief in God might called it charmed, but she knew better. Obedience and faith had their rewards.

By the time Barbara showed up, Rachel had managed a decent opening paragraph. She shut the laptop when she saw her friend ordering a drink at the counter, and waved her over when she glanced around.

"Long time no see!" Rachel gave Barbara a hug before she sat down with her iced tea. "I don't think we've talked, except over e-mail, since—wow, now that I think about it, it's been nearly three months! How is that possible?"

Barbara gripped her iced tea tighter; the plastic cup buckled beneath her fingers. "Yeah, yeah—there's a reason for that, actually."

Rachel frowned as she noticed her friend hadn't yet met her eyes. She leaned in closer, arms folded over the laptop. "What's up, Barb?"

Barbara's eyes, when she finally met Rachel's, were bloodshot and red-rimmed. Rachel also noticed Barbara's skin was bare—no trace of makeup. And Barbara never left the house without lipstick or mascara. "I have something I need to tell you, Rach. Remember the knee surgery I had last year?"

"After your skiing accident last February—yeah, I remember."

"Right. Well …" She took a deep breath, then closed her eyes and blurted, "I've been addicted to painkillers ever since."

Rachel's jaw dropped. "Barb—my gosh, I had no idea."

"No one did. But I've been falling apart the last few months, and I couldn't hide it anymore. Devon found out, and tried to help me quit, but I couldn't do it." Her eyes began to tear and she dropped her gaze to the table. "He's taking me to a rehab clinic tomorrow."

Rachel couldn't think of what to say. "Barb … I'm so sorry," she said, incredulity stammering the words. "I wish I'd known. I mean, I wish I could have helped."

Her friend sniffed and took a long sip of her drink. "Thanks, Rachel. I wish you could have helped too—I wish anyone could. But it's way bigger than I ever thought it would get, it's totally out of control—*I* am completely out of control."

"That's hard for me to imagine."

"Tell me about it." She wiped tears from her cheeks. Rachel reached out and gripped her arm. "Anyway, I wanted you to know," Barbara continued, "and I wanted to apologize, because I haven't been a very good friend or mentor. I haven't been honest with you. And I know you called because you wanted to talk about one of your girls, but honestly, I can hardly put two thoughts together anymore, so I don't think my advice would be any good."

"No, no, that's fine, I understand," Rachel said, not fully believing her own words. "Listen—get better, okay? Call me when you come home and we'll catch up. I'll be praying for you."

Barbara's gaze drifted away. "Yeah, okay …" She licked her lips, her stare resting on a point somewhere over Rachel's shoulder. "God and I aren't doing so well these days. I'm kind of struggling with my faith … and with the concept of faith in general, I guess. So, yeah, I appreciate the prayers." She chuckled. "Though I don't really think they'll help."

Rachel was stunned. She didn't know how to respond, and she said as much.

"It's all right," Barbara said. "I wasn't expecting you to be able to make it better. I just thought you should know." She stood. "I need to go. Devon's waiting for me in the parking lot—he won't let me drive, which is probably good, actually."

"Oh—okay. Well …" Rachel stood, and they engaged in an awkward hug. "Like I said, give me a call when you return home, if you feel like getting together."

"I will, thanks."

Rachel watched her friend leave, wincing at the defeat that showed not only on Barbara's face but in her hunched posture and clumsy steps. Rachel sat down, intending to pray and then continue her essay, but instead she slipped into a haze of disbelief and sadness for her friend. It was Barbara's confession of faltering faith that shocked her the most.

Rachel never would have guessed Barbara was so weak.

CHAPTER 2

Rachel was on lunch the next day when her cell phone vibrated in her pocket. The readout on the caller ID brought some sunshine to her gloomy day. "Daphne, hey!"

"Oh good, you *are* still alive."

"Haha, right back atcha. What happened to 'call you next week'?"

"When did I say that?"

"Two days before Christmas."

Daphne groaned. "Okay, you win. Better late than never, right? How are you?"

"Pretty good. We moved the wedding to New Year's Eve."

"That's great! Well, then this is even more fitting. We need to celebrate. What are you doing the weekend after next?"

Rachel frowned, thinking to herself. "I don't have my planner, but off the top of my head I don't think I have anything big. I usually work Saturdays, but I can trade with someone. Why, are you coming back?"

"No. I won the yearly sales challenge, so we're going to Vegas, baby!"

Rachel let out a laugh that startled the coworker who was restocking the supply shelf beside her. "Are you forgetting who you're talking to?"

"Well, I will admit you weren't my first choice."

Rachel let out a snort. "I love your honesty."

"Well thanks." Rachel could hear Daphne's smile in her words. "Of course I'd want to do Vegas with my boyfriend, but Marc can't go because of his work schedule, and Carolyn is into the guy she's seeing right now and doesn't want to be gone for a whole weekend. And my other friends … eh, just not the kinds of people I'd want to share a hotel room with, you know?"

"I can understand that."

"So please, please, please? Free food, some gambling cash, a totally awesome suite at the Paris Las Vegas, *naturellement*—the closest I'll probably ever get to the *ville de mon coeur.* It would be so fun, and we haven't seen each other in so long."

Rachel had to concede that. And while she could think of better locations in which to catch up on their friendship, Las Vegas didn't have to be Sin City if she didn't want it to be. "Let me think about it. When do you have to know by?"

"That depends—if you want to fly, I need to know by Friday. But if you're going to drive, I can reimburse you for gas. Your choice."

"Ugh, I don't want to drive for four hours. I'll fly, thank you. If I decide to go, that is."

"Fair enough."

"Well, I'll let you know as soon as I've checked my calendar and considered whether my delicate sensibilities can handle the shock."

Daphne chuckled. "Okay. You do that. Kiss kiss, darling. *Au revoir.*"

"I'll call you Thursday or Friday, and *au revoir* to you, too."

Rachel shut her phone and smiled. She'd needed a boost to her spirits, and the fact that it had been Daphne who had brought that boost showed that God could use anyone for his purposes.

Still, her mood was overcast by the storm clouds of Barbara's bad news. She just couldn't get over it. She'd known Barbara for nearly fifteen years. How could she have missed that her mentor was in such a dark place? And how could Barbara have let herself slip so far? That was the part Rachel just couldn't fathom.

She finished her sandwich and swirled the remains of her Brazilian Santos in her mug before drinking it down. She had five minutes left of her lunch, which was just enough time to call her mother about dinner.

It rang six times before getting picked up. "Oh, Rachel. Hello."

"Mom, what's up? You okay?"

"Um … just not feeling well today, that's all."

"Aw, I'm sorry, Mom. Is that why you missed church Sunday—you were sick? Do you have a cold or something?"

"Uh, yeah."

"Well, I'm sure you don't feel like cooking tonight, so you'll be happy to know that Patrick and I can't make it anyway. Or rather, he can't make it—he got asked to sub in a softball game for a teacher friend of his. But we're free tomorrow. Do you want to move it or just cancel for this week?"

Her mother's silence lasted a long beat. "Well, actually, why don't you stop by tonight anyway, if you haven't made plans for yourself. We can do dinner, just the two of us."

"Two? Where's Dad?"

"He won't be here tonight."

"Oookay." Her mom sounded weird. *Must be the cold medicine.* "All right, then. Sure, I'll come by. Six still all right?"

"Yes, yes, that's fine."

"Great. See you then." They said their good-byes and Rachel hung up just as her lunch break was ending. She slipped her phone into her pocket and went back to the counter to check on the baristas.

Julia and Ben were lounging against the counter and talking during the break in business. "Everything good?"

"Yeah—slow, though," Julia said. "I'm off in five, but can I just go now? I need to get gas before I leave for class or I'll never make it."

"Sure, go ahead."

Julia pushed off the counter and said good-bye to Ben before disappearing into the back. Rachel followed her, saying a quick prayer in her mind, and catching her just before she left. "Hey, Julia—did you give any more thought to that study I told you about?" Rachel just knew if she could get Julia to the young-adult Bible study at church, she'd be hooked.

Julia bit her lip and gave Rachel a sheepish look. "Yeah … thanks again for inviting me, but I don't really think it's my thing, you know? I'm not really into all … that."

Rachel smiled despite her disappointment. "I understand. But the invitation is always open, just so you know." Not that she was going to give up that easily. Julia was a sweet girl, and Rachel was worried about the way she'd been describing her weekends lately.

"Thanks. You're sweet." Julia gave her a little wave before letting herself out through the back door.

Rachel went back to work, praying alternately for Julia, her mother, and Barbara. After work she stopped at home to change clothes before heading to her mother's. Trisha was just getting ready to walk out the door when Rachel walked in. "Hi and good-bye," Rachel said with a grin. "What is it today?"

"Hobby House."

"Have fun," Rachel said with a wave as her roommate passed her on the steps that led up to their apartment. Trisha worked three different jobs, all with crazy hours, and given how often she seemed to be running late and dashing out the door, even she couldn't keep them all straight.

She took an apple into her bedroom and opened her laptop. *I really think you want me at this school, God. So I could use a little inspiration here.* She waited for the words to come, the one lonely paragraph mocking her. After a while of staring at the screen she finally gave up, put her laptop away, and headed out the door for dinner.

Rachel pulled into her parents' driveway twenty minutes later, navigating the cracks in the pavement where the tree roots had disrupted the cement before parking behind her mother's ancient Volvo. Returning to the house where she'd grown up never failed to elicit a childhood memory of one kind or another. Today she caught a glimpse of younger versions of her and Daphne hanging on the tire swing in the backyard under the summer sunshine.

When she got out of the car she took a quick look at the house across the street where Daphne's parents still lived. The shades were down, as usual, and the grass was long. She couldn't remember the last time she'd seen them.

She turned back to her parents' house and opened the door, stepping into the living room and inhaling to see if she could guess what was cooking. But all she could smell was the familiar scent of the house.

"Mom?"

"Hi Rach. In here."

Rachel took off her sandals and walked to the kitchen. Her mother, looking haggard, sat at the table where a stack of takeout menus lay in a pile. "Oh, Mom, you poor thing. This must be one rough cold." She kissed her mother's cheek and sat down across from her. The woman looked awful. There were bags beneath her eyes, untouched by makeup, her cheeks sunken and pale. She had always looked at least ten years younger than she really was, but today she looked ten years older. Rachel's heart pounded in her chest. "Mom? You okay?"

Her mother dabbed at her eyes with a crumpled tissue. "I don't have a cold, Rachel. But there is something I have to tell you."

No, no, no. I can't take any more bad news. God, please. Not cancer, God. Not a tumor. Oh please … "What is it, Mom?"

"It's your father. He … he left."

Rachel's heart stopped. "Left? You're not saying … You don't mean …"

Her mother took a deep breath and sighed. "We're separated, Rachel. And we're getting a divorce."

Rachel felt sick. She stared open-mouthed at her mother before she finally spoke. "I don't get it. Did you guys have a fight? Was he cheating on you? Were—Mom, *you* aren't having an affair, are you?"

Her mother let out a humorless laugh. "No, Rachel, I am not. And no, we didn't fight, and no, he wasn't cheating, either. But there is a reason. I didn't think you'd ever need to know, but now it looks like you do." She stood and pulled a glass from the cabinet, then filled it at the sink. "Your father has bipolar disorder. He's always been fairly good at staying on his medication—by the time you came along we had his dosages pretty well figured out, and when he did get unstable, we were usually able to quickly sort out his levels."

She handed her glass to Rachel, who held it without drinking. "But the last few years he's been fighting the medication, insisting he doesn't need it, that sort of thing. In March he got more depressed than ever, and I had to check him into the psych ward at Good Shepherd."

Rachel thought back two months, and remembered going to her parents' house to take in the mail and water the plants. "So … you didn't go to Grandma's? Where did you go when Dad was in the … hospital?"

"I went to Sacramento to see Gayle. She'd been bugging me to visit for ages anyway." Gayle was her mother's best friend. Gayle's daughter Pauline was a year younger than Daphne, and for a number of years Pauline had been Rachel's other best friend, her *Christian* best friend, as opposed to Daphne, her best friend whose soul she needed to bring to the Lord.

"Did Gayle know about Dad?"

Her mother nodded.

"Who else knows?"

"Well, your father's family knows, of course, and my parents, and—"

"Who *doesn't* know?"

Her mother sat back down with her own glass of water. "No one at church knows. Most of our casual friends—the neighbors, the men your father golfs with, those kinds of people—they don't know."

Rachel shook her head, tears blurring her vision. "How could you not tell me?"

"Mental illness is one of those topics you just don't talk about, honey. And he was afraid you'd think differently of him, pity him—be scared of him. He was so stable for so long that there never seemed to be a reason why we had to say anything, so we didn't. And then, when he started to have more trouble, he didn't want to say anything because he didn't know how to admit he'd slipped. We always just kept an eye on you, to make sure we caught any signs that you might have it too. But you haven't shown any, so we don't think you inherited it."

Rachel stood. "I can't believe this. I can't believe any of this. This is nuts." She ran her fingers through her hair, gathering the shoulder-length locks in a wad at her neck and squeezing them tight, then letting her arms fall limp at her sides. "So, what happened? Why did he leave?"

"He's off his meds. Went off them almost a week ago. He's never been manic like this before. He disappeared Saturday night and didn't come back until Sunday afternoon, and when he did he was talking about taking a road trip, going to … I don't know, New York or something." She waved her hand, looking tired of the whole conversation. "He spent all afternoon talking about it, then went out and bought a boatload of food and travel-sized shampoos and toothpastes. Then Monday morning he got up and told me he couldn't be tied down anymore, and he needed to leave to find himself. So he packed a bag and left."

Rachel paced the kitchen for a moment, letting her brain process everything she'd just heard. Then she stopped. "Wait—that doesn't mean he really wants a divorce, right? I mean, he could come back to his senses, realize he was crazy and didn't mean what he said."

Her mother shrugged. "I suppose he could. But he's not the one that wants the divorce. I do."

"*What?*"

"I don't expect you to understand, Rachel." Her mother raised her chin, resolved.

"How could you?

"You can't imagine the stress I've been under, living with him when he's like this. And it hasn't just been the last week, or even the last two months. Over the last five years, things have steadily declined. It's been a nightmare that just keeps getting worse. When he's depressed I have to watch him like a hawk and lock away all the knives and pills so he can't kill himself. I have to come up with one story after another for why he's not at work, why we're not at church, why I have to cancel plans with people." She closed her eyes for a moment. Her lip quivered, but when she spoke again, her voice remained calm. "When he's manic, I have to chase him around, tracking down receipts from shopping sprees, praying like mad that he won't crash the car or do something stupid, worrying when he disappears for hours at a time. He's almost lost his job twice, and I'm pretty sure he won't have one after this week. Our savings isn't going to keep us for long, and we're too young to dip into our retirement without a penalty. If he'd file for disability we'd at least get some assistance, but he won't do it. He's too proud, or embarrassed, or both, or neither—I don't know." She sniffed and pulled a tissue from the box. "Thank God we own the house and the cars outright. I can find some kind of job to pay the bills, at least. But I can't do this anymore with him."

Rachel was stunned. "What about 'in sickness and in health'?"

"It would be a different story if he wanted to get better, sweetheart. But the last few years make it clear he doesn't. And I didn't sign on to be a babysitter." She sat back, shoulders slouched, face lined with fatigue. "If he wants to be on his own, then fine. It's just as well, because I'm done."

CHAPTER 3

Rachel only stayed long enough to try to convince her mother to change her mind. But when it was clear she was resigned to—even pleased with—her choice, Rachel left.

She drove aimlessly for half an hour, eventually reaching a park where a handful of children were playing as a few adults looked on. She parked and leaned forward, her forehead resting against the steering wheel. Her mind was spinning. She couldn't follow a single thought to completion. Driving had given her a focus, but now that she was parked, her emotions got the best of her, and tears began to stream down her cheeks.

She was dumbfounded. It seemed her whole identity was invalidated. Her family, her history—had all of it been a lie? She began to conjure scenes from her childhood, examining them for clues to her father's condition. *Dad's last-minute business trip to Washington—a front for one of the spells? The Christmas when I got twenty presents—the result of a manic-driven shopping spree? What if his enthusiasm for my accomplishments was just the mania? What if he wasn't as crazy about me as I always thought he was?*

She felt as though she'd been punched in the gut. He hadn't even called her to say good-bye.

Her shoulders shook with sobs she couldn't voice. She felt lost, unmoored. Her scattered thoughts finally coalesced into a pointless prayer.

God, how could you let this happen?

When she pulled herself together, Rachel drove to Patrick's house to await his return from the softball game. She needed to see him, to be comforted by him.

She pulled into a visitor space and was grateful to see his car already in its numbered spot. *He must have just gotten home,* she thought. She took a few deep breaths to calm herself and ascended the stairs to his apartment. She knocked, then sank onto one of the two lawn chairs that he kept by the door. The darkening sky with its smattering of pinprick stars was soothing.

The door opened after a minute. "Rachel? What are you doing here? You all right?" He stepped out, closing the door behind him, and sat in the other chair beside her. "You've been crying."

She nodded as tears threatened to come again. "My mom is divorcing my dad."

His eyebrows shot up. "You're kidding."

"Hard to believe, huh?"

"Very."

"There's more."

He sighed. "Oh man. What else?"

Rachel stared at her hands, which were pleating the end of her shirt. "The reason my mom is divorcing my dad is because my dad has bipolar disorder." She hoped he wouldn't jump to any conclusions and worry that she was a carrier. Him worrying about her possibly passing the disorder along to their future children was the last thing she needed.

He frowned. "Like, manic depression?"

"Yeah."

"Wow."

"Yeah."

She told herself not to read into the subtle shift in his body that created another inch of space between them. "When did that happen?"

"Before I was even born, apparently. Everyone knew in my family but me. Can you believe that? How do you not tell your daughter something like that? That's like not telling her that you have diabetes or something. Never mind that she might have it too, or that she could maybe have helped you all these years." Tears began to sting her eyes again. "I'm so angry at them. And hurt. He's off his medication, apparently, and he just left. Told her he needed to go find himself. What kind of crud is that?" She fought to keep her voice from quavering into incomprehensibility. "And how could he just leave without even saying good-bye?"

Patrick squeezed her shoulder. "Sometimes people make mistakes, Rach. We're all broken, you know? We're all fallen. It sounds like something has a hold on him that he can't control. I'm sure he misses you. And of course he loves you. This is all separate from you, though, you know? Don't take it personally."

She sniffed and smudged the tears beneath her eyes. "No offense, sweetheart, but that wasn't helpful."

He shrugged. "I'm not good at this kind of thing—you know that."

Rachel shimmied closer to him and leaned her head against his shoulder. "Eloping has never been that appealing, but I sure wish we could just get hitched right now so I could stay here with you all night."

Patrick laughed.

"Glad my misery is entertaining for you," she said with a quivering lip.

"Oh, Rachel, I didn't mean anything by it." He smoothed her hair and platonically patted her back—not the kind of touch she'd been hoping for. She squirmed beneath his hand and sat up with a sigh, which he echoed as he ran his hand through his hair. "Look, Rachel, I'm sorry. I don't know what to do to help you."

"I know, I know—I don't know what you can do, either. I'm sorry too. I'm just … I don't know. I'm just angry, and sad, and … I just don't understand how God could see all this happening and not step in to fix it. Barb, my dad, my parents' marriage …" She shook her head and shrugged, unable to find the right words.

"C'mon, Rachel—it's not like this is the end of the world. There are other people who have it a lot worse."

"So since other people have it worse than I do, I shouldn't be upset?"

"That's not what I mean. You're just taking it awfully hard, given that, in the grand scheme of things, it's not like these are earth-shattering events. God's not stepping in for actual earth-shattering events … so why would he step in for this?"

Rachel stared at him, mouth gaping. "So God doesn't care what we go through, is that what you're saying? Jesus seemed to say a lot differently in the Sermon on the Mount."

"No, I'm not saying that. I just—" He shook his head. "Look, never mind. Forget I said anything."

They sat in silence, stewing and mulling. Rachel stared at the darkened sky, eyes pulled to the blinking lights of an airplane far in the distance. The sight triggered the conversation she'd had with Daphne. Escaping for a weekend looked a lot better than it had at lunch.

"I'm going to go home." She stood and folded her arms across her chest against the cool breeze that began to blow. "I'll talk to you tomorrow."

Patrick reached out and caught her elbow. "Hey. I'm really sorry, Rachel. I want to help make you feel better—just tell me what I can do."

She shrugged. "I guess there isn't really anything. I'm sorry if I made you feel bad for not knowing what to do, when even I don't know what I need. This is new territory for me. Nothing like this has ever happened to me before."

Patrick pulled her into a hug, his chin resting on the crown of her head. She sank into him. "You still are blessed, Rach. I guess that's what I was trying, poorly, to say earlier. God still has His hand on your life."

"Yeah—I guess." She had offered similar consolations to others over the years, but she had never needed them for herself. She winced at how hollow the words felt.

She drove home with the radio off. The silence gave her space to think, though her mind was stuck on one word: *Why?* Patrick was right, of course—everyone was flawed. No one's life was perfect or free from pain. But when you've lived twenty-six years tragedy-free, you can't help but start to think maybe you've done something right, and that God's smile shines a little brighter when he looks at you.

So what had she done to make him frown?

CHAPTER 4

Rachel awoke Wednesday morning tangled in a stifling quilt of exhaustion and sorrow. Sleep had eluded her for most of the night, though by God's grace she was closing the café instead of opening it, so she was able to hide beneath the sheets for a while.

But soon enough she needed coffee. So when she finally dragged herself from bed, she headed for the kitchen and opened the pantry door. After a short deliberation she pulled the canister of Guatemalan Santiago Atitlan, her go-to for emergencies, from the back of the top shelf and dumped two tablespoons of the grounds into her French press. In the state she was in, she needed something with some hefty body and snap to get her in shape for work.

She took a deep breath, inhaling the rich aroma. With the scent clearing her head as it filled the small galley kitchen, she returned the canister to the pantry and added the boiling water to the press pot. Then she carried a bowl of cereal to the table to wait for the grounds to steep.

Her thoughts swirled like steam as she munched her Special K. She knew she should be praying, but for the first time in her life, she didn't really want to talk to God. Of the three people she typically went to in a crisis, two of them *were* the crisis, and the other had proven himself less than competent at helping her cope. She couldn't really blame him, she realized—he'd had no practice at comforting her since they'd been together because nothing this bad ever happened in her life. Certainly he'd get better with it over time—not that she hoped he'd have more opportunities to work on his skills.

She didn't want to talk to her high school girls about it all—she was there to minister to them, not the other way around, and she didn't feel comfortable being so vulnerable with them. All her other friends were Christians and would come at her with the same clichés Patrick had used and that she had always relied on, but she didn't want to hear them. She didn't want to forgive. She didn't want to trust it would all work out for good for those who love the Lord. She *did* love God and had devoted her life to him. And yet things were most definitely *not* working out for good.

Rachel put the bowl in the sink and finished her coffee preparations, then curled up on the couch with her favorite mug. She took a deep breath and focused her thoughts as she blew gently over the top of the brew. Her mind drifted to Daphne's proposal. Regardless of their differing views, Daphne was the only person left in Rachel's life that she could imagine talking with honestly. There was no pretense or posturing with Daphne. They were practically sisters. Daphne may have taken a path in life that Rachel disagreed with, but that didn't mean she didn't still love her dearly or value her friendship. And for once, Rachel was interested in hearing her friend's suggestions on how to cope. Las Vegas was the last place she felt like visiting, but getting away for a weekend with Daphne could prove to be beneficial.

She took a tentative taste and smiled as the heat moved down her throat. She took sip after sip, savoring the flavor, and let herself contemplate a weekend in Sin City. Considering the week she'd had so far, the word "sin" seemed to fit. Barbara, her mom, her dad—they'd apparently been living in their own versions of Sin City for some time now.

By the time the mug was empty, she felt more prepared to face the day. And she was actually getting excited at the idea of the trip to Vegas. She resolved to shower and dress and give Daphne a call to hash out the details.

What could it hurt?

Rachel was halfway through her walk to *Espress-Oh!* when her cell vibrated in her pocket. "Don't bother coming in," said her boss when she answered. "The kitchen and stock room are flooded."

"Oh no!" She stepped into the shade beneath a storefront's awning and leaned against the brick façade. "What about tomorrow?"

"Plumbers are already here and working. They think they'll have it fixed by seven or eight tonight. I'll need you here tomorrow morning to help clean and get things back in order. Hopefully we'll be open by lunchtime."

"All right then. See you in the morning." After hanging up, she couldn't help but smile. It was a gorgeous day, and she didn't have to work. She tried calling Daphne but got her voice-mail. After leaving a message, she stepped back into the sunshine and crossed the street at the corner, making her way toward the used bookshop where she knew the staff by name. She deserved some serious pampering after the day she'd had yesterday.

She left the overstuffed bookstore with a bag of literary treasures and made one more stop at a corner market for a bottle of water. From there she meandered to a park she always passed on the way to church, where a giant oak stood guard in the center surrounded by benches. She snagged the last empty bench, broke open her water, and pulled Jane Austen's *Emma* from the paper bag.

A few hours later a rumble in her stomach plucked Rachel from the fictional world. She stretched and tossed the book back into the bag before heading home. The beauty of the day, Austen's eloquent English, and the giddy feeling of having started a good new book worked together to buoy her spirits. As she walked home she found herself feeling optimistic and content for the first time in two days.

Patrick's car was in the parking lot when she crossed through from the street. She did a double take, thinking it must simply be the same make and model, but there was the scratch on the fender and the Sports Chalet license plate frame around the familiar numbers and letters.

But it's the middle of the week. Her steps quickened as she smiled—this day was getting even better. *Surprising me for lunch, maybe? How does he know I'm off work?* She thanked God for the small blessing and headed up the stairs. Seeing her fiancé would be icing on today's cake.

When she arrived at her apartment, she was surprised to hear arguing inside. But when she opened the door, the voices suddenly stopped. The ensuing silence was broken by a single surprising epithet from inside Trisha's room, spoken by Patrick and barely loud enough for her to hear.

Rachel stood in the doorway of the apartment feeling like she was in an alternate universe. After she stood silent for a moment, the voices began again to argue, this time in whispers, though they soon evolved into sniffles and consoling murmurs.

Rachel set down her bag of books, walked to Trisha's door, and knocked. "Patrick? Trisha? What's going on?"

The voices stopped again. Then, after a final exchange of harsh whispers, the door opened. Patrick stepped out, and before he shut the door Rachel could see Trisha wipe tears from her cheeks. Patrick took Rachel's hand and led her to the living room. "We need to talk."

A black hole opened in the pit of her stomach.

"I have to confess something." Patrick's gaze hovered somewhere around her chin. "I know I told you that Trisha and I have known each other for a long time. But I never told you that we dated."

"Oh." The hole grew. "When?"

"In college. We broke up but … I've always had feelings for her." He stopped, swallowed, took a deep breath. "I found out recently that she still had feelings for me too."

Rachel felt dizzy. "Patrick—are you breaking up with me?"

"No, I just need to be honest with you … but—"

Trisha emerged from the bedroom. Her face was red, her cheeks still wet. "You are such a coward. Just spit it out already!"

Rachel saw panic slip across Patrick's face. "Just let me do this, Trisha."

"You won't—you can't. You don't have the guts. You didn't back then and you still don't. I thought six years would have changed you, but you're still pathetic."

"Trisha, don't—"

"He's been cheating on you." Trisha stared Rachel down. "With me."

CHAPTER 5

The apartment was silent. The echoes of Rachel's shouts and sobs existed only in her head. She sat on the sofa, black TV screen ahead of her, spinning the diamond ring on her finger.

Patrick hadn't tried to deny it or even soften the accusation. "How long?" had been met with "four months." "Do you love her?" elicited a reluctant "yes"—though the answer had been the same when Rachel asked if he loved her as well. Not that it mattered. There was no forgiving this. The wedding was off, and they were done.

Patrick and Trisha had slunk out together after Rachel refused Patrick's attempts at consolation. And now she was alone.

She'd left the apartment shortly after they had, unwilling to stay where Patrick's betrayal had taken place, but she returned half an hour later when she realized she had nowhere else to go. She'd poured all her relational energy into Patrick over the last year. There were no other friendships in her life with depth or intimacy—except for her relationships with her mother and Barbara. But she couldn't go to Barbara, for obvious reasons, and there was no comfort to be found at her childhood home right now. She had a hard time even considering it home. Just like her childhood, her relationship with Patrick now felt like a lie, which made the apartment not feel like home, either. She'd never felt so isolated.

Daylight faded and night settled in around her. Her body was leaden, her muscles no match for the weight of grief that enveloped her. Her mouth wanted a steaming café mocha with extra whip—she supposed a situation this desperate required not only coffee but chocolate as well—but she didn't have the energy to make one. When her cell phone jangled in her purse, the shock of sound sent an arrow of adrenaline through her gut. *Patrick?* Heart racing, she fumbled for the phone, her hands clumsy from idleness. The caller ID showed Daphne's number.

"I'm so sorry I didn't call you back sooner," Daphne said when Rachel finally flipped open the phone and managed a weak greeting. "It was totally one of those super-sucky days that just would not end! So what's the story—you in for Vegas?"

"Patrick's been cheating on me." The statement renewed the tears, and she began to cry.

"What?" Daphne fell silent as Rachel struggled to get her tears under control, then let out a stream of insults broken up with words of empathy and condolence. "I'm in shock," she said at the end. "And if I'm in shock, I can't imagine what you're feeling."

Rachel sucked in giant gulps of air, trying to get a hold of herself. "I just don't understand," she said between hiccups. "I don't understand why God is doing this to me. I don't understand what I did wrong."

"It's not you, it's not God—it's life. *C'est la vie.* Things are great sometimes, and other times they're awful. It's just … the balance of the universe. A little hell here, a little heaven there, you know? I doubt it's a matter of God doing anything to you—why would he? What did you ever do to deserve it?"

They were the very questions Rachel had been asking herself in the back of her frazzled mind. What happened to "I'll hold you in the palm of My hand?" There was no hand there now, no safety net, and she was in free fall. The God she'd grown up serving didn't do this to the people who loved and obeyed him like she did. At least, she never thought he did.

But if he did—how dare he?

"Listen, Rachel—I'll totally understand if you don't want to come to Vegas, given everything that's going on. But I think it would be good for you to get away from there for a couple days. You need space to breathe and recover. What do you think?"

Think? Rachel couldn't think. Her decision-making ability was shot. "If you think I should …"

"I do."

"All right then." She sniffed. "See you in Vegas."

Rachel dragged herself to bed after hanging up the phone, and tumbled fully clothed onto the mattress. In her despair she forgot to set her alarm before finally falling asleep, and when the phone rang at six-thirty the next morning she was so groggy she almost didn't answer. Her boss's voice on the other line brought her fully awake, however, and after they hung up she scrambled to get dressed and out the door.

Idiot, idiot, idiot. In her haste she'd left her makeup bag on the kitchen table, so she had no way to fix the bags beneath her puffy eyes. Her embarrassment over her appearance compounded the embarrassment over being so late to work. *Good luck getting that time off for Vegas now.*

"Sorry," she said as she jogged into the coffee shop and threw her cardigan into the closet. "Put me to work. What should I do?"

Roy pointed to the stock room. "Help Cora with inventory. We need to figure out what needs to be replaced."

She nodded to her boss but groaned inside. Cora was a fellow Beach Cities Church attendee and the last employee Rachel wanted to work with today. She headed to the stock room and noticed the floor was still slick in some areas, and the bottom three inches of everything was soggy and warped.

"This is so icky," Cora said when Rachel knelt beside her to wrestle a waterlogged box from beneath the counter. Then she got a good look at Rachel's face and frowned. "What's wrong?"

"I look that bad, huh?"

"Sorry, but yes, you do." They unpacked the box of napkins and began inspecting the individually-wrapped packs for damage. "Bad night?"

"Well … yes. But I forgot to set my alarm before I fell asleep. Roy woke me up when he called."

"Oh no. You poor thing. Why the bad night? Did something happen?"

Rachel couldn't stop the bitter snort that escaped her nose. "A few somethings, yeah."

"Do you need to talk about it?"

"No." She sighed. "Actually, yes, I do, but I can't guarantee I won't fall apart."

Cora nodded to the counter full of napkins. "Plenty of tissues here if you need them."

Rachel managed a smile. "True." She took a deep breath and

quickly listed the events of the nightmarish week she'd had so far, eyes focused on the inventory list she was marking. She didn't have to see Cora's face to know what it looked like—the sounds of surprise she made were plenty descriptive. "Rachel, I don't know what to say. I'm so sorry."

Rachel shrugged and began to stack the napkin packs into a dry box. The less she talked the better grip she was able to keep on her emotions.

"Is there anything I can do?"

Rachel gave a mirthless chuckle. "I don't think so, but thanks."

"Can I pray for you? Here—" Cora nudged the stock-room door shut. "Let's pray together."

Rachel gripped the pack in her hand. "You know, normally I'd jump at that, but I'm a little angry at God right now. I'm not really sure I want to talk to him."

Cora was silent for a moment, then said, "I understand. I'd be mad too."

The dangerous thoughts she'd been having for the last few days began to form on her tongue. She knew she should keep her mouth shut, but Cora was as good a sounding board as anyone else, and if she didn't start hashing these thoughts out now, they were going to eat her up inside. "You know, it's not just that I'm mad at God. It's like … why bother praying, even? I just wonder if it's like talking to a wall. Maybe it always has been. I've been pretty disciplined, pretty devout, since I was a little kid. And you'd think all these years of it would add up to some kind of … I don't know … immunity. Maybe one of these things should have happened—no one's life is perfect, right? But all three, in less than a week? What did I do wrong?"

Cora was frozen in the path of Rachel's rant, and when she spoke, Rachel could tell she was searching for just the right words to say. Her caution grated on Rachel a little. "I totally see where you're coming from," Cora said. "But … I don't think it works that way with God."

Rachel threw the napkins into the box harder than she meant to. "Well why not? What kind of God says, 'Hey, thanks for the love. You did really good for the last twenty years, but I'm going to ruin your life anyway'? What kind of father does that, especially one who's supposed to be perfect?"

Cora shook her head slowly. "I—I don't know, Rachel. I know you're hurting—"

"No, this isn't just about hurting. Hurting has just made things start to seem obvious. I mean, honestly—what's the point? If you don't get protection, if you don't get some kind of divine insight that shows you the lessons to be learned or the way this situation can be used for good, then what's the point of all the obedience and the sacrifice and the dying to flesh and all that crap? What does it get me?"

Cora's face was flushed, and for a brief moment, Rachel felt bad for dumping on her. But then Cora said, "But … God is good, Rachel," and Rachel lost all sense of guilt.

"I'm not so sure. In my estimation, He's either an insensitive, promise-breaking jerk, or maybe … maybe He's not there at all, and we've just made him up." Rachel couldn't believe the words that were coming out of her mouth. But somehow, they felt really good to say. "Either way," she continued, "why should I bother? If He's a jerk, then He's not the God we're taught to believe in, which means the whole belief system is suspect. And if it's all just make-believe, then …" She shrugged. "Maybe we should just pack in the whole thing and give it up. Either way, right now He's not doing what He's supposed to be doing, and it's not making me real eager to keep working my butt off to be acceptable to him."

"Wow." Cora was the one avoiding eyes now. She crushed the ruined box with careful steps. "So … that's it, then? You're done with God?"

Rachel ran her hands over her face and sighed as the energy of her anger drained away and left her exhausted. "I don't know, Cora. I don't know what I think. Maybe my anger is clouding my thinking and once I get over it everything will make sense. Or maybe it's making everything clearer and I've struck upon an epiphany. Who knows."

Cora grew silent, and they finished their inventory job without any more peripheral discussion, though Rachel's mind continued to dwell on the things she'd said to Cora. She kept coming back to Cora's question—*You're done with God?*—and running from it, afraid to consider the possibility. Because part of her felt like the answer was yes, and it scared her.

But not as much as she might have thought it would.

Rachel didn't want to spend any more time in her apartment than necessary, so after work she retreated to another coffee shop where she claimed an armchair by the window and sipped her long-awaited mocha. A movie she'd seen during college came to mind as she licked whipped cream from her lips—*The Truman Show*. Jim Carrey's character discovers his entire life is the ultimate reality show—a scripted sham lived out on television for the whole world to see. His hometown is a soundstage, the horizon a backdrop. Nothing he thought to be real actually was.

Rachel could suddenly identify. Nothing was secure. There was nowhere stable to plant her feet. Things she never would have doubted had turned out to be questionable at best, and she was afraid of what would turn on her next.

And what about God? He had promised to be unchanging, but now she couldn't believe it. How could she? All she had was his word, and the last few days had been proof enough that words meant much less than she originally thought. After all, doesn't Scripture say that God is like a father, who provides what his children need? That if they ask for bread, he won't give them a stone? Hard to believe that promise now when all Rachel had done was asked for bread, worked hard for it, and received not just one stone but a whole avalanche of them.

But if she couldn't trust or even believe in God, she stood to lose more than just her faith. Her whole worldview was wrapped up in the doctrines she'd learned in those sixty-six ancient books. She didn't know how to live without that theology as her foundation. She'd always pitied people who did.

The thought of stepping off that platform of faith into the … what? Nothingness? It was beyond unimaginable. Yet there was no point to sticking with something that wasn't real or trustworthy.

Completely unsettled, she left the café to distract her mind with driving and checked her e-mail when she got home, hoping to keep the distractions coming. There in the inbox sat her e-ticket for Las

Vegas. She was more convinced than ever that this trip could be exactly what she needed to get out of her emotional rut.

The Internet provided Rachel with a couple hours of entertainment until her eyes grew heavy. She tumbled into bed and let the cool sheets soothe her. Her thoughts drifted to Daphne, to their childhood, their unlikely friendship. Funny how Rachel had always thought she held the key to Daphne's happiness. Wouldn't it be just the thing if it were the other way around?

CHAPTER 6

"This is the captain speaking. We're about ten minutes outside of Las Vegas, and we'll be landing at gate three at McCarran Airport. We hope your flight has been enjoyable. "

Rachel drained the rest of her soda before she handed the cup to a passing attendant. She stifled a yawn and leaned her head against the window, training her eyes on the ground as it crept closer. A twinge of excitement at the sight of the enormous marquees and casinos in the distance made her smile, something she hadn't done with sincerity in almost a week.

The night before, she and Daphne had made their final arrangements on the phone. "You set the agenda, *mon amie*," Daphne had said. "You're the walking wounded."

"But I don't want to bring you down. You earned this trip, you should get to do what you want."

"I'll get in whatever questionable activity I want to. Don't worry about me. I just want to make sure you leave Sunday night feeling better than you do when you land Friday afternoon."

So Rachel then admitted that she'd much rather hole up in the hotel room and watch movies and eat room service than go out and party. And Daphne, bless her, had agreed. But now that she saw the city up close, Rachel was beginning to think she may have spoken too soon.

A black-suited man in the baggage claim area held a small sign with her name scrawled across it. She wheeled her carry-on to him and pointed at the card. "That's me."

He nodded and tucked the sign under his arm, then reached for her bag. "How many pieces of luggage do you have?"

"Just this."

He nodded again. "Follow me, please."

He led her through the sliding doors to the curbside area where the desert heat hit her like a punch. She followed him down the sidewalk, trailing like a lost puppy, feeling purposeless without her bag to hold on to. When he stopped next to a sleek black stretch limo, she let out a laugh.

Daphne was nestled in the corner with a glass of champagne in one hand and a crustless quarter of a sandwich in the other. "*Bonjour, ma chérie!*"

Rachel slid in beside her and was enveloped in a fierce hug. "Mighty fancy taxi service."

Daphne waved the sandwich-holding hand like a queen greeting her subjects. "Taxi, schmaxy. My Rachel deserves only the best." She opened a small door, revealing a mini-fridge. "Help yourself—it's all stocked."

"I haven't eaten much this week," Rachel admitted before diving into a sandwich. The car slid into the light as they pulled out from under the pick-up canopy, and Rachel settled back in her seat to watch the scenery of Las Vegas roll by as she ate.

Daphne nodded, a look of wisdom on her face. "Ah, yes, the post break-up/splitting-parents/druggie-friend blues often takes away one's appetite." She popped the remainder of her own sandwich into her mouth and finished off her drink. "So, we still doing the girls-night-in thing tonight?"

"I don't know," Rachel said through a mouthful of sandwich. "I didn't think I'd want to do anything, but now I realize I'm in Las Vegas and I'd be crazy not to go out and do *something.*"

Daphne pumped a fist in the air. "Yes! Oh good. I thought it would do you good to cut loose for a little while."

"Cut loose? I was just thinking, you know, shop at Caesars, blow some money on the slots, maybe take in a show. What were you thinking?"

Then Rachel saw the glint in Daphne's eye and knew she wouldn't be in bed before at least one in the morning. "Well, that depends," Daphne said. "Does your luggage contain anything sparkly, satiny, velvety, form-fitting, and/or low-cut?"

Rachel smirked. "Do you really need to ask?"

Daphne grinned. "I didn't think so." She leaned forward and addressed the driver. "Excuse me, is there a mall nearby?"

"Yes ma'am, the Fashion Show."

Rachel laughed. "That's the name of the mall?"

Daphne winked. "This is Vegas, baby," she said. Then, to the driver, "We're going to take a detour."

Shopping with Daphne was always an experience. Never did they wander without purpose between the racks, running their hands along rows of garments and occasionally checking a tag but never trying things on. No, Daphne considered every item, every style, even if it didn't appeal to her at first glance. Her passion for clothes was obvious in her everyday dress, whereas Rachel was the poster child for conservative comfy-casual. But now, facing a fresh start in her life, Rachel was game for taking a few chances on her wardrobe. How lucky that her best friend was a professional personal shopper.

Daphne slurped her blended mocha and eyed Rachel as she modeled the last of the mountain of clothes they'd brought with them into the dressing room. "Bingo, darling. That dress looks like it was made for you. Do I know how to pick them or what?"

"It would appear you do know what you're doing. I will agree."

"Well, why don't you get dressed, and I'll take this all out to the register."

Rachel frowned. "Wait—I'm not getting it all. There's got to be close to two thousand dollars' worth of clothing here."

"Yes, but I get a discount."

Rachel laughed. "Well, unless your discount brings the total down to two *hundred*, I'm going to have to pick and choose here."

Daphne waved her hand. "No, no, it's my treat."

Rachel gasped. "What? Daphne—no way. That's a *lot* of money."

"But it's my pleasure." She gave a warm smile of sisterhood and sympathy. "Think of it as a very belated thank you for all the money your family spent on me when we were kids."

Family. The comment brought back the pain from the past weeks. How could the people who had been so loving back then be the same people who were separated now?

Daphne reached out to give Rachel's hand a squeeze.

"I'm that transparent?" Rachel asked with a small smile.

"Twenty years, my friend. You're like plastic wrap to me now."

Rachel laughed and shimmied out of the dress she was still wearing. "Can't keep a secret from you, I guess."

"From me? Never."

Dressed in a new skirt and blouse, Rachel felt a little more worthy of the limo. They gawked at the extravagant architecture on the strip until the car pulled into the driveway of the Paris Las Vegas Hotel. The driver ushered them from the car, then popped the trunk for the bellhop, who loaded their luggage and shopping bags onto a cart. They followed him into the foyer, where the sight of the lavish décor—gold-accented walls and rich oil paintings, breathtaking chandeliers and imposing pillars—stopped Rachel in her tracks. Daphne moved through the space as though it was nothing of interest and checked them in, then followed the bellhop to the elevator.

Sixteen stories up the bellhop opened their door and unloaded their bags onto one of the queen beds. Daphne pressed a few bills into his hand and closed the door behind him, then let loose with a squeal as she took a running leap onto the empty bed near the window. "Vegas, baby!" She whooped. "Check out this room!"

The blue, gold, and cream theme from the lobby was echoed in the room's pale blue carpet and two-tone striped cream wallpaper. The TV cabinet, desk, and table were of rich dark wood, and the shimmery curtains were striped in blue and gold. A peek into the bathroom revealed cream marble counters and bathtub. Rachel joined Daphne on the bed and they gazed out at the strip below. "This is amazing."

"Better believe it. And now we must vamoose for our beautifying appointment."

Beautifying appointment? Two hours in and already this trip was exactly what she needed.

That evening Rachel and Daphne arrived at the hotel's best restaurant looking like new women. Well, Daphne looked perfect as always. But Rachel hardly recognized herself. Hair and makeup by a professional—and the new wrap dress Daphne had bought her made her look, and feel, like an adult for the first time. Earlier she had stared at her reflection in the hotel mirror, twirled and winked at herself—and had admitted to Daphne that she looked and felt good, even sexy. The only problem was that she also felt self-conscious. Very self-conscious. But, as Daphne admonished her, she'd just have to get over it.

The view from the restaurant window beside their table kept drawing Rachel's eyes away from the menu. The lights, the marquees, the never-ending river of humanity that flowed along the sidewalk, all demanded her attention. She'd never experienced anything like it, and coupled with the feeling of being someone else—a sexier, more sophisticated Rachel—she was starting to think she'd stepped into some alternate reality. The concept was appealing.

"Wine?"

Rachel wrinkled her nose. "I guess."

"Not a fan?"

"Never had it."

"Still?" Daphne shook her head. "How have you avoided it for this long?"

"No one I hang out with drinks."

"What *have* you tried?"

"Um …"

Daphne laughed. "Seriously? Okay then. I'll order for you." When the waiter returned Daphne ordered her a yellow submarine. "It's like fruit punch," she said when it was brought to the table. "But with a kick."

Rachel rolled her eyes. "Fruit punch, huh? If you say so." She took a cautious sip, bracing herself for what she was sure would be disgusting.

But it wasn't. Instead, the sweet drink went down easily. She took another sip, then another. Daphne laughed.

"Wow. That good, eh?"

"You weren't kidding." Rachel fought the urge to down the whole thing in one gulp.

"Easy there," Daphne said with a laugh when Rachel had drained half the glass in just a couple minutes. "Who knows how your system will handle it."

"Right. You're right." Rachel pushed the glass away.

"So, I have a question," Daphne said.

"Shoot."

"How are you *really?*"

Rachel gave her friend a half-smile. "Honestly, I'm not sure. Half the time I'm numb, the other half my mind is moving so fast and my emotions are in such upheaval that I feel like I'm falling off a cliff."

"I noticed when we talked on the phone the other day, and even since you've been here, you haven't mentioned God once. I think that's a record for you, at least in my presence."

Rachel winced. "I could really go overboard with the God talk, couldn't I?"

Daphne smiled. "Sometimes."

Rachel shrugged and folded her arms on the table. "I'm in as much turmoil over my relationship with God as I am over everything else that's happened—precisely because everything *did* happen, you know?" She let her gaze wander back to the window to give herself a moment to quell the rising tears. When she regained control she looked back to Daphne with a shake of her head. "I don't know who I am without my faith. It's my foundation. Everything I've thought and done and ever said has gone through that filter. And now I don't know what to do. Do I throw it all away? Do I soldier through and keep clinging to it even though it doesn't make sense to me anymore?" Rachel shrugged and dropped her eyes to the bread plate in front of her. "I'm at a loss. A total, utter loss."

Daphne was silent. Rachel appreciated that she didn't jump in with a response. When was the last time Rachel had let someone simply sit with their emotions instead of tossing out quips about the Lord's will and all things working together for good? How many of the people she'd "counseled" over the years had mentally rolled their eyes at her while sitting with heads bowed, presenting to be engaged.

After a time, Daphne began to speak in the tone and measure of someone choosing their words carefully. "You know, there are more ways to believe and have faith than just the way you were raised with. If you decided you no longer believed in the God you've grown up learning about, it doesn't mean you're left completely alone and unmoored. Faith can still be a huge part of your life—it can still be a defining characteristic of who you are."

Rachel nodded, though unconvinced. "I suppose," she said. "I hadn't thought of it that way. What about you—have you ever found a religion you believed in?"

Daphne rested her chin in her hand. "I think there's something out there, probably. Some kind of force, like karma plus … I don't know … consciousness, I guess?" She shrugged. "I don't think too much about how that all affects me. I guess I just try to live by the golden rule. I don't like the idea of organized religion, overall, so I just go with what feels right. Served me fine so far."

Rachel considered this. Barring her childhood, over which she had no control, Daphne's life had been pretty good. She had a job she loved and was good at, lived comfortably on her own, and while not completely lucky in love, she had not suffered more than the usual heartbreak—certainly nothing like what Rachel had gone through.

Their meals arrived, and Daphne graciously steered the conversation to less troubled waters. It didn't take long for them to come back to Rachel's life, however, and after finishing her last bite Daphne sat back and crossed her arms. "You know what you need, Rachel?"

"What?"

"A fresh start."

Rachel swirled her fork through a puddle of balsamic vinaigrette on her plate. "I agree."

She looked up to see a slow smile spread across Daphne's face. "You know how you could do it?"

"How, dare I ask? Your face tells me you're scheming."

"You know me so well." Daphne paused, leaned in as though sharing a secret. "Move to Chicago and live with me."

Rachel let out a laugh. "Yeah, right."

"I'm serious!"

"So am I. There's no way."

"Why not? Give me one good reason."

Rachel rolled her eyes. "Because I have a job."

"Quit. Chicago has coffee shops too."

"But my mom—"

"Is an adult and can take care of herself."

"All my friends—"

"Not *all,* seeing as I don't live in California anymore. And seriously, are you going to want to hang out with people who are constantly trying to get you back in the fold?"

Rachel frowned. "You have a point." She didn't know how she'd go back to working with the high school girls, either. She didn't think the church would appreciate her handing down her cynicism to the next generation.

"Plus Patrick and Trisha are still around, and no matter how hard you try to avoid them, you're going to run into things that remind you of them all the time, if you don't actually run into them." Daphne spread her hands. "So what choice do you have?"

Rachel closed her eyes and pressed her palms against them. "My gut says you're right. But it's too much right now." She gave Daphne a small smile. "I can only handle so much upheaval."

"Understandable."

"But I have to admit it sounds fun."

Daphne's eyes sparkled. "*So* much fun. Can you imagine? I totally get that you need some time, but keep it in mind, okay?"

"I will. I promise."

They paid their bill and went on their way to try their hand at the table games. But despite the sights and distractions of the casino, a small part of Rachel's mind couldn't let go of the idea.

CHAPTER 7

The light of late morning was no match for the blackout curtains. The clock read 11:24 when Rachel finally pried her eyes open, and if it weren't for the fact that she was famished she'd have rolled over and gone back to sleep. But dinner had been too long ago, and the snacks they'd scurried out to buy at midnight hadn't done anything to fill her up. Coveting Daphne's ability to sleep twelve hours straight when she wanted to, Rachel hauled herself upright and took a few reviving breaths before stumbling to the bathroom to make herself decent. She needed coffee, stat, and not the complementary bag of instant crystals that sat on the bathroom counter. Hopefully the European bent of the hotel didn't stop with the decor.

Too hungry to waste time on coordinating an outfit, Rachel pulled on one of her new skirts and a shirt of Daphne's that caught her eye. Then she grabbed her key and debit card from her wallet and slipped out into the hall, leaving Daphne still dreaming beneath the rumpled white sheets.

The chaos of the casino jarred her senses when the elevator opened its doors at the main floor. Throngs of people clogged the hall, and smoke from countless smoldering cigarettes watered her eyes as she skirted the slot machines and headed for the hallway that held the stores and cafés. She spotted a small sandwich shop with a hulking espresso machine and knew she'd found the right place to eat. The menu was limited, but they had decent-looking coffee, and that was just as important as food. Dodging knots of tourists, she got herself to the counter and ordered a sandwich and a large cup of the regular, black, which she blew on with impatience while waiting for her meal.

She allowed her focus to be pulled from one sight to another as she ate her ham and cheese baguette, unwilling to think about anything serious until the coffee had kicked in and her stomach had been sated. But once the feeling of hunger had passed and her mind finally felt alert, she settled her thoughts on Daphne's proposition from the night before.

Chicago. She knew next to nothing about it, just whatever tidbits Daphne had mentioned since moving there four years ago. There was a lake and a few beaches—not that she could use them more than a few months out of the year. But it was better than being landlocked. They got snow in the winter, lots of it. That would be a new experience, but nothing she couldn't handle. She may be a California girl, but she wasn't a wimp. Daphne lived near a university, though Rachel couldn't remember which one, but there was one thing almost all college students shared, and that was a love of coffee shops. Surely she'd be able to find a job somewhere. It might mean starting back at the bottom, but since she'd be a full-timer in a sea of part-time student workers, she'd easily work back up to manager, probably in less than a year.

She reached the bottom of the coffee cup, tossed it into a nearby trash can, and started back for the room. A smile tugged at her mouth as she reentered the casino area. It would be fun, plain and simple, to live with Daphne. Especially now, when the pressure to convert her wasn't heavy on Rachel's shoulders. A sliver of her had always been a little jealous of Daphne's freedom—her spontaneity, her non-judgmental fearlessness in the face of the weird and freaky. Daphne's free-form morality might still give Rachel pause, but she didn't feel quite as bothered by it as she once had. To each her own, right?

Rachel's smile grew and a lightness began to bubble up inside her. She would do it. So long California, hello Windy City. She had a past to forget and memories to bury, and more important, a new life to live. Time to get the show on the road.

She made her way back to the elevators, eager to tell Daphne she'd made up her mind. Halfway down the hall to their room she heard yelling, a woman's voice carrying on a one-sided conversation that painted a picture of domestic unrest. She was about to slot her key card when she realized it was Daphne.

She froze, unsure whether or not to enter. She didn't want to interrupt, but she didn't want to just sit and listen without Daphne knowing she had an audience. Biting her lip, she scanned the key and eased open the door.

Daphne stood in the center of the room, pink cell to her ear as she stared out the window. Her voice was sharp with sarcasm. "You take one psychology class and think you know the root of all my problems, is that it?" Rachel cleared her throat and Daphne spun, eyes wide and bright with tears. She paused in her rant, then shook her head and turned back to the window. When she spoke again her voice was considerably quieter, though a bitter edge still barbed each word. "Whatever. Fine. I appreciate your concern." She signed off with a sharp obscenity, then jabbed a finger at the cell's buttons and threw it onto the bed, where it tumbled into the sheets. She huffed and shook her head again as she sank into one of the armchairs against the wall. "That's one of the problems with cell phones. There's just no satisfaction in ending a conversation with the press of a button. That really required a good slamming of a receiver."

Rachel nodded and moved to the other chair. "I agree."

Daphne streaked the tears away with the heel of her hand. "Men."

"You're telling me."

She snorted in agreement and sighed. "I take it back—he's not a man. He's a child. And a coward. Waits till I'm a few thousand miles away before dumping me."

"Marc dumped you? What happened?"

Daphne waved a hand, eyes sliding from Rachel to the view and focusing on something beyond the glass. "He decided to get all judgmental and—know what? Never mind. It doesn't matter." She sniffed and stood, then bent over her suitcase, tossing clothes about and pulling out an item now and then to examine. "It's just as well." She straightened, shaking out a sundress. "I can only put up with younger men for so long."

She stripped off the T-shirt she'd slept in and pulled the dress over her head, then twisted the upper layer of her thick dark hair into a bun and secured it with a rubber band. Approximately fifteen seconds of prep time and she looked like Aphrodite, another thing that had always made Rachel jealous.

"But if hell hath no fury like a woman scorned," she said she tied a silk scarf around her throat, "then two scorned women are a force that can flatten a city. C'mon, sister—it's time to avenge our wounded souls." Her eyes glinted, then she cocked her head, squinting at Rachel. "Is that my shirt? You're smokin', by the way." Without waiting for an answer, she scooped up her shoes and purse and walked barefoot into the hall.

Rachel was afraid to know what two scorned women did to avenge their wounded souls, so she didn't bother to ask as they sliced through the casino and headed out the doors to the Strip. Daphne didn't look upset, though she did look a bit intense—chin up, strides long but with a sway to her hips that made her look like a runway model on the verge of power-walking. Her long legs carried her through the casino at a speed that required Rachel to nearly jog. Once they hit the sidewalk she was forced to slow down by the sheer number of people already there, and Rachel groaned at the heat.

"I'm guessing you already ate?" Daphne asked as they waited for a stoplight to change.

"Yes, but I don't mind eating some more," Rachel said with a grin. "I was so hungry this morning, the first meal pretty much just calmed the fire. I'm ready for another one to actually fill me up."

Daphne laughed, and it dulled the edge she'd had since they'd left the hotel room. *"Pauvre bébé*. I hear there are a ton of places to eat at Caesars. Would that be all right?"

Rachel assured her anything was fine, so long as it was edible. They crossed the street in front of the Bellagio, where the water show was in full swing against the musical backdrop of Sinatra's "Fly Me to the Moon." Swept along with the masses, they ascended to the elevated and blessedly shaded crosswalk that connects the Bellagio with Caesars. A few minutes later they were greeted by an arctic blast of air-conditioning when they entered the casino. They followed the signs to the Augustus Café, the ubiquitous twenty-four-hour Vegas eatery: cheap eats, Denny's-like menu selections, and a mix of families and clusters of hangover-dazed patrons. Daphne ordered a plate of mozzarella sticks to start.

"Well, Daph, I'm really sorry," Rachel said as they sipped their water. "You seem to be doing pretty well, considering."

Daphne shrugged. "We were just killing time, and I knew it. He wasn't long-term material. Still, getting dumped sucks."

Rachel nodded, thinking. "So … explain something for me. You knew you wouldn't be with him long term, so why didn't you break it off sooner? What's the point in staying in a relationship that isn't working?"

"It's not that it wasn't working. It was working just fine, for what it was. I was bored, I was lonely, I wanted someone to be with—enter Marc. I wasn't looking for Mr. Long-Term. I'm not ready to settle down yet."

Rachel pondered this. "Huh."

Daphne grinned. "It's different from the way you think about relationships, I know. But think of it this way: Aren't you going to miss having someone hold you, hold your hand, kiss you? Someone to just hang out with when you're bored? Someone you look forward to seeing, and someone who's looking forward to seeing you? It might be easier to do without if you've never experienced it before, but if you're used to it and then suddenly it's gone …"

"Yeah," Rachel said. "That makes sense."

Daphne leaned in, swirling her straw in her water. "And think about your situation. After being in a relationship like you and Patrick had, that was so committed and had so much expectation, would you really want to jump into another hard-core relationship right away? You might need to detox, give yourself time to get him out of your system … with no pressure about long term, no worrying about whether or not you're ready to commit like that again. So it's a two-fold benefit: You get someone to snuggle and someone to de-Patrick-ize you so you're primed and ready for Mr. Right."

Rachel quirked a half-smile. "It seems logical, but I feel like it shouldn't be."

"That's years of courtship indoctrination talking."

"Ha, you're probably right."

Rachel waved away the conversation. "Anyway, I have big news to share." She mimicked Daphne's secret-sharing posture from the night before. "I think I want to move to Chicago."

Daphne let out a squeal that turned heads at the neighboring tables. "Yes! I knew you'd come around." Her eyes sparkled and she bobbed in her seat like a preschooler hyped up on sugar. "I am *so* excited. When do you think you can come out?"

Rachel couldn't help but be swept up by Daphne's excitement. "I don't know—I haven't thought that far ahead yet." She laughed. "I'm still too caught up with the idea of just … getting away, getting out of the bubble I've been in my whole life."

"It's going to be a heck of a shock, you know."

"Yeah, I know. But you'll help me, right?"

Daphne's eyes gleamed. "Oh baby, you know I will."

They hashed out details as they ate their diner lunches, and by the time they paid the bill, Rachel was fully committed to the move and itching to start packing. She was tired of the routine her life had become, tired of self-sacrifice and getting walked all over. "Do unto others" was a good mantra, but it didn't work as well when all the people around you lived by, "Look out for number one." And she was looking forward to adopting a new motto. She had never put herself first before. It was time to pay herself some well-deserved attention.

After lunch the two women ventured out to the Forum Shops. Daphne was looking for what she called a consolation prize: a purchase that would let her say, "I might not be dating Marc anymore, but at least I have this!" From what Rachel could tell, "this" could apparently be anything—the more expensive the better. Dissatisfied with the merchandise they'd seen so far, they were about to leave when Daphne spotted the Corella Boutique. Rachel followed Daphne as she waltzed in and began looking in earnest at a mannequin clothed in jewelry and not much else. After a moment's deliberation, Daphne looked to the lone saleswoman and asked, "Is this a 34B?"

Rachel spun from the display of earrings she'd been inspecting. Daphne was pointing to the boustier that served as the mannequin's only clothing. It appeared to be made entirely of black crystals. Rachel could easily picture how stunning it would look against Daphne's alabaster skin, but she didn't relish the gawking it would draw when she wore it—and Rachel knew Daphne would definitely wear it. Most likely that night when they went dancing.

Daphne saw Rachel's stare and grinned. "I think Marc would be the consolation prize compared to this, don't you?"

The saleswoman removed the item from the mannequin and led Daphne to the dressing room, holding the sparkly lingerie like a holy relic. "You have the body to pull this off," she said, her tone coated in kiss-up. "Let me get you something to try it on with so you get the full impact of a whole outfit." She enclosed Daphne in the cubicle, then shuffled through a rack of slacks for a moment before choosing a black pair.

Rachel wandered the store while Daphne changed, feigning interest in cruise wear and overpriced accessories while she mulled over Daphne's selection. It was unique, it was gorgeous—and it was shockingly expensive. She might be good at her job, but that didn't mean she was rich. How could she afford to shop the way she did?

Daphne's conversation with Marc came back to her. What had he witnessed to make him think Daphne had a problem—and what kind of problem did he think she had?

Her ruminations were cut short when Daphne swept back the curtain and stepped out into the room like she owned the place. And rightfully so—she *was* gorgeous. The black slacks were slightly flared and rested snugly on her hips, though Rachel didn't even notice them until she'd stared at Daphne's chest for five solid seconds. Rachel had expected her to look like a showgirl on her way to the theater, but she didn't. She looked glamorous, self-possessed, and unabashedly sexy. Rachel could just picture the commotion she would cause when they went out that night—and was embarrassed to realize she was ever-so-slightly jealous.

Before Rachel was willing to shop any more, she insisted on coffee. They stopped at a small café, where a barista took their order, then returned minutes later with a blended latte for Rachel and an Americano for Daphne. For the first time since she began drinking coffee, Rachel found herself wishing she had something else in her hand—like another one of those yellow submarines. Or maybe another Baileys, which Daphne had gotten her in the casino late last night. *But this is definitely better than nothing.* Rachel took a long pull at the frosty drink, then sank back in her seat and sighed. "That hits the spot."

"You're such an addict."

Rachel grinned, though for the first time the label rubbed her the wrong way.

They sipped their drinks in silence for a few minutes until Daphne sat up straight and pointed across the way. "I think I've found your dress."

Cups drained, they went into the boutique, where Daphne hunted down the dress in Rachel's size. She held the midnight blue sheath against Rachel and smiled. *"Sacré bleu,* it's perfect!"

Rachel flicked the price tag around. *"Sacré bleu* is right. That's one month's rent right there. Forget it."

Daphne sighed and returned it to the rack. "You've got to let that go."

"What, frugality? That's not an exclusively religious trait. Besides, I can't afford to let it go, given what I make. You do want me to pay my share of the utilities, right?"

She smiled. "Yeah, I suppose so." She slid hangers along the rack, then pulled out a halter dress. "Ah, we have a contender!" The thin black material was accented with three interweaving lines of crystals that swept down on a wavy diagonal from the neck to the hem. "That is slinky, sexy, and sparkly—the fashion trifecta. Can't go wrong with that." She found the price tag and let out an unsophisticated whoop. "Bingo!"

Rachel conceded with a nod. "And surprisingly, not too over the top. I could actually wear that again. Okay, I'll try it on."

Rachel entered the changing room while Daphne leaned against the wall outside. "Tell me it's okay for me to wear something like this," Rachel called out to Daphne after pulling on the dress.

Daphne chuckled. "It's totally okay for you to wear that."

"I mean, tell me guys aren't going to think I'm begging for … something."

"Well, they might."

Rachel froze. "What?"

"But it doesn't matter what they think. You dress for you, not for other people. You dress for how your clothes make you feel."

Rachel zipped up the back and examined herself in the mirror. She certainly liked how it made her feel—and look. Not that it meant it was okay, regardless of what Daphne said. She opened the door and Daphne let out a hoot. "Hold your horses, cowgirl," Rachel said. "I don't want to get myself in any trouble."

"What do you mean?"

"You just said guys might think this is some kind of invitation."

Daphne waved a hand. "Well, maybe, but your attitude will go a long way in sending that invitation too—or not. Act like a tramp, you'll get treated like a tramp. Act like a lady, you'll get treated like a lady. Most of the time, anyway. And I can't imagine you ever acting any way *but* ladylike, so I wouldn't worry. Plus, you know I'll totally have your back."

"You'd better."

"You know I will." Daphne smiled. "Have I ever steered you wrong?" Rachel admitted she hadn't. *Though there's a first time for everything.*

The evening air as they walked toward the Mirage felt only slightly cooler than it had earlier that afternoon. Despite the time of night, the sidewalk was still bustling and the traffic still bumper to bumper. "This really ought to be labeled the city that never sleeps."

Daphne laughed. "Seriously. What could New York possibly have over Vegas?"

Rachel shied away from yet another person shoving advertisements for escort services in her face. "Class, perhaps."

Catcalls and wolf whistles followed them to the casino, and while each one made Rachel flush again with embarrassment, Daphne seemed to neither care nor even notice. Rachel made a mental note to ask her later how she managed to cultivate such cool confidence. She could use some of that.

They reached the entrance to the JET Nightclub, and Daphne handed over her two VIP tickets. They were directed to the velvet rope and ushered past the long line of those waiting to get in. Rachel followed close behind Daphne as they entered the first of JET's three dance rooms. "Let's stay here," Daphne said over the thumping bass. "Good dance music, and I hear it's a lot more crowded in the main room."

Rachel kept an eye on her, trying to mimic her careless posture and easy confidence. They skirted the dance floor and headed to the bar, where Daphne ordered drinks.

"Cosmopolitans," Daphne explained as Rachel sipped the fruity cocktail. "I'll get some waters later on too—don't want to get dehydrated, and alcohol just makes that worse."

They scoped out the room for a place to park themselves, then Daphne hooked her arm through Rachel's and led her to a place against a far wall. Even after spending a few minutes studying how others were dancing, Rachel still found herself doubting her ability to not stick out like a sore thumb. "Here we go," Daphne said close to her ear, a minute later. "Are you ready to dance?"

"Why don't you start, and I'll jump in when I'm ready."

Daphne swigged the remainder of her drink and set it on a bar table, then headed to the floor. As she undulated in her bra-like top and skinny pants, eyes closed and limbs moving like ribbon in water, Rachel was overcome with a sense of internal chaos. She was so far from her comfort zone she couldn't even spot it with binoculars. She looked down at her dress and smoothed her hair. This was so not her—at least, not the old her. Perhaps she would find this environment inviting after she'd had more time to adjust her thinking. She took a gulp of her cosmo, hoping it would speed up the process.

The music changed, and Rachel found herself drawn to the dance floor. *Might as well give it a shot.* She set her empty glass down and moved toward Daphne, letting her body sway and glide with the beat. She found herself enjoying the experience, despite not knowing what she was doing. She just hoped she didn't look stupid.

Her eyes were half-closed in an attempt to shut out the looks she caught from other people, but when she opened them to check her surroundings, she found she was being closely watched. A man leaned against the wall, hands in the pockets of his khakis, his white T-shirt glowing under the black lights, and the weight of his stare was like a hand pushing gently on her chest.

She looked around for Daphne, but she was in her own little world, oblivious to the people around her. Rachel steeled her nerves and forced herself to meet his gaze. A shaky smile curved her lips, and when he smiled in return, she had to look away to keep from laughing.

The music slowed, but not so much as to drive all the singletons off the floor. Daphne adjusted her moves to the music, and Rachel did the same. She closed her eyes, swaying while fighting the urge to check on the blonde boy, but then she sensed someone in her personal space and opened her eyes. She wasn't surprised when she saw him, though she was surprised when he leaned in, his hand braced on her hip, and said into her ear, "You're gorgeous."

Not even Patrick had ever called her gorgeous.

She flitted her gaze up and away and back again as she flashed a bashful smile and mouthed "thank you." But she couldn't just keep staring back because she felt like an embarrassed idiot, so she closed her eyes again.

She was frantically debating what to do when the city's well-known slogan popped into her head. *What happens in Vegas stays in Vegas....*

Would it kill her to loosen up a little, just this once?

She stood a little straighter and moved herself in a slow circle as she danced. She put a little more sway in her hips, making the skirt of her dress swish around her knees. Her heart was pounding now, not just from exertion or the music, but from a new sense of daring. She hoped, though she wasn't sure, that this was flirting. She'd never really done it before—at least not in a sensual way. But knowing she had a captive audience gave her a boost. She conjured every image she'd ever seen of sexy, powerful women and tried to channel their energy.

Suddenly the stranger kissed her, and she nearly fell over from the electricity. She was acutely aware of his hands, one of which now rested on the small of her back, and of his scent, which was a mix of alcohol and sweet cologne, and of course of his lips, which were soft but strong and were kissing her in a way she'd never been kissed in her life. She beat back memories of all the old "good girls don't" youth-group sermons that flooded her mind because she didn't want it to end.

Then she was aware of all the ways in which her body was not only welcoming this advance but responding to it. She had a whole new appreciation for how easy it was for a girl to get herself "in trouble." With this realization, Rachel's engrained sense of propriety and self-preservation took over, and she gently brought her hands up to his chest and eased herself away.

He didn't take this as a hint to leave, however, and then she didn't know what to say. She scrambled for an excuse and finally blurted, "I'm engaged."

"I'm not surprised."

She laughed. She couldn't help it. "I'm sorry. I—I should, um … go." *Lame*. "But … thanks for the kiss. Made my night."

He didn't appear wounded that she was giving him the brush-off. "My pleasure." He didn't move, though, and she realized she'd have to be the one who left. She removed her hands from his chest, muscular under the T-shirt, and with some kind of extra gravity that made pulling away much harder than it should have been, walked slowly toward the bar, mentally begging Daphne to meet her there.

The mental link developed over twenty years of friendship did its job, and she was beside Rachel in a heartbeat, handing money to the bartender in exchange for two waters. Rachel drained half of hers in one go, steadying herself against the bar, then finally met Daphne's eyes. One look at her and Rachel knew Daphne had seen it all. Daphne put a hand on her arm. "Wow."

Rachel laughed, but her hands were starting to shake and her legs felt like rubber bands. As the heat from the rendezvous slipped away, her veins filled with ice, and a ball of adrenaline sat in her stomach like lead shot. The intimacy of that kiss was more than she'd experienced in fourteen months with Patrick, but for once she didn't see this as yet another shortcoming of that relationship. Instead, she was sickened by what she'd just done.

She took another drink of her water, then caught the man looking at her again from a table where a group of guys stood talking. A little shiver ran up her spine and she turned away, pleased and embarrassed. It was almost a shame that what happened in Vegas stayed in Vegas—she wouldn't mind another one of those kisses.

CHAPTER 8

The plane touched down at LAX, and Rachel's breath was suddenly hard to find. It was so much easier in Las Vegas—easier to relax, easier to forget what had happened back in LA. But the last time she'd landed there she'd been coming back from a missions trip in Brazil, and those memories bobbed to the surface like apples in a barrel: shiny, inviting, promising sweetness and satisfaction if only she bit into one and allowed herself to re-embrace the innocence and faith she'd had back then. What was it about apples and temptation? She smothered the memories with the newer ones of Trisha and Patrick, effectively squelching any desire that might have been stirring for her to go back to the life she'd had before.

She wheeled her carry-on through the terminal, her steps slowing as she reached the exit to ground transportation. There was no one to meet her this time, no one to welcome her back and sling her luggage into the trunk and listen to her stories of the weekend. Instead, she had her choice of a cab or a SuperShuttle, both of which would provide her with a silent trip back to the apartment she used to call home. She and Daphne had settled on early June for Rachel's relocation, and now she didn't know how she'd stand to live in California for one more day, let alone two more weeks.

By the time the shuttle reached her apartment complex, Rachel's stomach was a clenched fist of nerves. Neither Trisha's nor Patrick's car could be seen, so she ran up the stairs to make sure she was safe in her bedroom before they showed up. With the door locked behind her she was able to relax, and after a few minutes of rest she got to work preparing for her move. The sooner she was packed, the sooner she could leave this depressing life behind.

She was in the process of culling her closet when the front door opened and shut. She froze, listening for footsteps. Only one set could be heard—Trisha must be home. She wasn't ready to talk to her—or Patrick—yet. Still, she went over the list of things she needed to say to both of them that Daphne had helped her compose over breakfast that morning. She needed to be prepared for when she finally had to face them both again. Without a script she knew she'd fall apart.

Rachel tried to keep busy until Trisha left again, but as the evening wore on it seemed like she must be in for the night. Rachel's stomach could only wait so long for its next meal, so after bagging up the clothes she'd chosen to donate to Goodwill, she took a deep breath, steeled her courage, and opened the bedroom door.

Trisha's bedroom door was closed, and Rachel let out a sigh of relief as she skittered to the kitchen to throw together a meal. She was just about to celebrate having eluded her roommate when Trisha's door opened and she appeared, empty plate in hand.

The two women froze face-to-face in the living room. Trisha flushed and her eyes darted down after an initial stare of shock. Rachel was about to slip past her and leave the confrontation for another day when a knock at the front door made them both jump.

The door opened to Patrick carrying a stack of flattened moving boxes. His mouth opened and shut, wordless, and his arms gripped the boxes harder as though they could shield him from Rachel's narrow-eyed stare.

They each stood still, tension triangulated. No one wanted to make the first move. Then Rachel recognized her unique position in this situation—she was the one with the power. She could absolve them, guilt them, tear into them—she set the tone. This gave her the confidence she needed to make the opening gambit. "Well, this is ridiculous. Just come in." Patrick pushed the door open and shut it behind him with a light kick. She pointed to the boxes he set down in the living room. "What are those for?"

Trisha licked her lips. "I was, um, going to move out for a bit."

Rachel waved a hand. "Don't bother. I'm moving out."

"You are?" Relief was visible on both their faces. It made her want to scream.

"Yes. To Chicago, actually. The sooner the better. But I'm not going to waste my time trying to find a roommate for you."

"Oh, yeah. Okay. That's fine," Trisha said quickly, nodding like a bobblehead.

Rachel turned her stare to Patrick, and for a brief moment she was overwhelmed with sadness. Those eyes that had gazed so often into hers with what she thought was love, that mouth that had once tenderly kissed hers—how would she ever erase those memories and move on?

She took a deep breath and let the air out slowly, concentrating on not crying. "Do me a favor and don't come here anymore until I move out, all right? It's like being stabbed in the heart again, seeing you here, and I can't bear to have it keep happening over and over." He nodded, gaze cast to the floor, silent. "I don't know what the protocol is supposed to be, but I'm going to keep the engagement ring. Not because I want it, but because I might need the money."

She had nothing else to say, and neither did they, apparently. The silence was deafening. With a sigh, Rachel picked up the boxes and went to her room.

When she went in for her shift the next day, she made it a point to talk privately with Julia, the multipierced, combat-boot wearing agnostic whom she'd been hounding to join her at Bible studies. She found herself identifying a lot more with Julia today. And feeling the need to apologize to her.

"Cute top," Julia said when Rachel emerged from the office to fix herself a drink.

"Thanks—got it in Vegas this weekend."

Julie's eyes bugged. "Rachel went to Vegas?"

"She did."

"What for—some kind of Bible convention or something?"

Rachel laughed. "No—vacation, actually. My life lately has been a nightmare. I needed it."

"Oh no. What happened?"

Rachel tamped a shot of espresso and secured the portafilter to the machine, then launched into an abbreviated version of recent events. After recounting all the sordid details, she put a hand on the barista's arm and said, "And Julia, I am so sorry for … you know, pushing all the church and Bible study stuff on you since you started working here." Rachel shook her head, avoiding Julia's surprised eyes. "I'm so embarrassed now. I was so incredibly misguided; I hope you'll forgive me."

Julia gave her a small smile. "Well, thanks for the apology. But it was sweet that you cared so much. No one had ever shown so much concern for my mortal soul."

Rachel could see now that concern for Julia's soul hadn't been the driving motivation like she thought it had been. In reality, she had craved the praise of her parents, of Barbara and her other Christian friends, when she'd be able to tell them Julia had converted. The realization added to the anger that seemed to sit just below the surface these days.

"So now what?" Julia asked as she mopped up a splash of milk from the counter. "You're not going to keep living with Trisha, are you?"

"Good grief, no. But I'm not just moving—I'm relocating. To Chicago."

Julia giggled and let out an expletive. "No way! You're such a California girl, how will you survive the winters?"

Rachel laughed. "I'm not *that* bad. Besides, there are these great inventions called winter coats. They're apparently quite toasty."

Julia chuckled. "Well, anyway, I'm really excited for you. I can imagine how hard it would be to stay here."

As if on cue, the shop door opened and admitted a knot of women from Beach Cities Church.

Rachel's stomach seized. Undecided on whether to face them or flee, she lost her opportunity to leave and was caught in their sights. "Oh, look—Rachel's working today," said Melanie, director of the women's retreat and summer Bible study. "Good to see you, Rachel. I looked for you Sunday but Patrick said you were out of town. I wanted to see if …"

Hearing Patrick had gone to church Sunday caught her off-guard, and her mind didn't catch the rest of what Melanie said. "I, um … I'm sorry, did you say you saw Patrick on Sunday?"

Melanie nodded. "Yeah. Where did you go? Somewhere fun, I hope."

"Vegas. What else did Patrick say, or was that it? Just that I was out of town?"

All six of them froze, eyes locked on Rachel. She knew well how honed their radars were for juicy news, aka "prayer requests." Melanie chuckled, a look of confusion on her face. "Well … yes, that's all. I mean, I didn't stop him for a big conversation, just asked if you were around. Why?"

Rachel shook her head, stymied. He hadn't said anything the night before about seeking forgiveness, trying to get right with God—was he just moving on, hoping she wouldn't say anything to anyone? How long did he think he could live in that dream world before everyone saw him for the sham he was?

"He's been cheating on me with my roommate. I broke off the engagement."

Six jaws dropped in unison and let out various squeaks of disbelief. Liz, a woman Rachel got along well with but had neglected in favor of Patrick, reached out to grab her hand. "Rachel, that's horrible. I'm so sorry. What can we do for you?"

She snorted. "Honestly? Call him out next time you see him. I can't believe he hasn't come clean."

Apparently it wasn't the kind of request Liz had been expecting.

"I—um, well, I meant, can we take you out to lunch sometime, let you talk through how you're handling things? Or maybe help you find a new place to live—"

"I have a friend with a two-bedroom condo," said Denise, a fellow high school ministry leader. "I could ask her if she'd consider renting out—"

"Thanks, thanks," Rachel said, "but I'm handling it my own way."

"Your own way?" said Liz.

"You're not going to leave for another church, are you?" said Denise.

"No, I'm not going to another church. I'm moving to Chicago."

Six gasps. "By yourself?" said Liz.

"I have a friend who lives there. She's going to let me live with her."

"Oh, well, she'll help you get hooked up at a good church then."

Here we go. "Actually, she's not a Christian."

"Oh." Wary looks ratcheted Rachel's irritation up another notch. Liz continued. "Well, she can still support you, that's great. And I'll bet you could find a bunch of churches on the Internet to try out once you get there. We'll pray that she goes with you."

That they would push church like it was all-important got under Rachel's skin. That they would shy away from confronting Patrick when he was obviously trying to get away with his abominable behavior, and instead try to make things right for Rachel by just offering to take her to lunch made her simmering anger boil over. "Actually, I don't think I'll be going to church when I get out there."

Silence.

"I just need a break," Rachel continued. She knew any explanation she gave would be pointless, but she wanted to give them, the unwitting representatives of the life she was leaving behind, a piece of her mind. "I'm really angry at God right now. My parents are divorcing too—has word of that gotten around yet? And the whole mess with Barb Livingston, too—" She let out a mirthless chuckle. "The last couple weeks have been pure hell. And I'm having trouble just sweeping it all away and pretending like my life isn't completely shattered. I need to take some time away and maybe start my faith over from scratch."

None of the women had a response to that. Rachel shrugged. "So, what can I get you to drink?"

Teas, coffees, and waters dispensed, Rachel flashed one last weary smile before turning her back to them and pulling in a massive breath. Julia squeezed her arm in passing, and Rachel's ears caught snatches of denunciation as the women slinked out the door to spread the word.

At the end of the week, Rachel had a moment of panic.

Half her bedroom was already in boxes, a sizable chunk of her possessions had found a temporary home at Goodwill, and through a serendipitous conversation with a customer, she had a buyer for her car. She'd given her two-week notice to Roy and secured the promise of a glowing reference for whatever jobs she applied for in Chicago. She had a nonrefundable one-way ticket to Chicago and two quotes from relocation companies on the cost of shipping her things. In short, she was almost ready to go.

She'd been walking home from her Friday morning shift when it hit her. This city, this culture, her family, this life—they were all she'd ever known. And she planned to turn her back on it all. Was she out of her mind?

She'd never made such a big decision without spending time in prayer and seeking counsel from her parents, friends, and mentor. And here she was, making the biggest decision she'd ever faced, and doing it entirely alone.

She wanted to believe she was wise enough to make the right move. She wanted to be independent enough to live her life with confidence in her own intelligence and abilities, to not have to feel like every fork in the road required a powwow with five different people. But the truth was, she didn't know if she could trust herself. Not right now, anyway—not with the sadness and anger that still simmered just below the surface. And yet she was forging ahead as though she knew what she was doing. What if she was making a terrible mistake?

As soon as she got home she brewed a cup of the Santiago Atitlan. She'd never had it more than three our four times a year, and dipping into the canister for the second time in less than a month meant life was way too stressful—as if she needed coffee to tell her that.

She'd nearly picked up a four-pack of spiked lemonade on the way home from work. The completely different kind of warmth and relaxation that alcohol provided made for a nice change of pace. She'd sampled a variety of mixes in Vegas, and she couldn't help but laugh at how she gravitated toward beverages for comfort.

But buying alcohol felt like a whole different world from drinking it when someone else gave it to you. She wanted to wait until Chicago when Daphne would be around to educate her some more. She was pretty sure her craving wasn't some precursor to destruction—but she was forcing herself to hold off anyway, just in case.

Steaming mug in hand, she retreated to her bedroom before Trisha appeared and drew up a pros/cons list to help her sort through the wisdom of this move. But even when she saw how the pros outnumbered the cons, she couldn't shake the feeling that she was doomed for failure.

She wanted so badly to pray. Her eyes slid from her list to her Bible, untouched on her nightstand since the night she'd learned of her parents' divorce. Not more than a night or two at a time had gone by in the last ten years where she didn't read Scripture before going to bed, and it had taken a conscious effort for her to avoid it. Her fingers itched to feel the onionskin pages, but she couldn't bring herself to reach for the leather-bound book.

Her thoughts skittered. She couldn't still them long enough to pray. She tried to talk aloud, but for the first time it struck her as ludicrous. Rachel drank her coffee faster than usual, hardly tasting it at all. The panicky feeling was back. She had no one to talk to, no one to turn to—she was alone, truly alone, and she didn't think she could handle it.

Suddenly she was reminded of Daphne. *Daphne!* She'd never thought of Daphne as part of her support system, but now was the time to change that.

She snatched up her cell phone. "I think I'm losing my mind," she blurted when her friend answered.

"What?"

She fought tears as she spoke. "There's no one here for me to talk to about any of this. There's always been *someone,* you know? At least my mom. At least God. But now I'm an island and I feel like I'm going to go crazy having to rely on myself."

Daphne let out a long sigh. "Oh, Rachel. Rachel, Rachel, Rachel." She giggled and began to sing, "You are a rock. You are an iiiiii-land!"

Rachel frowned. "Daphne, I'm serious."

"Me too! Totally, totally serious." Then the line went dead.

Rachel stared at her cell phone in utter confusion as sadness washed over her. She'd been right. She really was alone.

CHAPTER 9

Rachel breathed deep and mounted the steps to the front door, her footfalls slow and heavy as though execution awaited her on the other side. She'd put off this conversation as long as she could, but now, with her flight to Chicago less than twenty-four hours away, she'd run out of excuses and time. She lifted her hand to ring the bell, then stopped. But just walking into her parents' house no longer seemed appropriate, either.

Her mother found her standing at the door, hand half-raised to the doorknob. "I thought that was you I saw pull in—two minutes ago. What's taking you so long?"

"Nothing," Rachel mumbled as she entered the kitchen. She glanced around. Everything looked the same. It didn't seem like it should.

"I'm glad you came over. I really hate it here at night alone. Can I get you some coffee?"

"No, thanks—I can't stay long."

Her mother's face fell. "Oh. I was hoping we could talk."

"Me too. That's why I came."

"I don't think we've ever gone more than three days without talking—this has been a record. How have you been? How was Las Vegas?"

Rachel sat down on a kitchen chair as her mother busied herself preparing tea. "It was—it was fine. It was fun, actually. Exactly what I needed."

"I'll say. You know, honey, I really think you dodged a bullet here with Patrick. There always seemed to me like—"

"I'm moving to Chicago."

Her mother's hand froze above her mug, teabag dangling into its mouth. "You're what?"

"I'm moving in with Daphne."

"You're—to Chicago? Seriously?"

"Yes, seriously. I can't stay here, not with Patrick and Trisha around, and you and Dad splitting up—"

"But—moving? I can see an extended vacation, but leaving home like that …"

"What home? The one where my fiancé was sleeping with my roommate? Or the one where my parents lied to me for my entire life?"

Her mother's chin raised just a fraction. "Rachel, listen: In retrospect I know it wasn't a good idea not to tell you about your father. Really, I know that now. But we only had your best interest in mind."

"Oh, so it's the thought that counts?" Rachel let out a snort.

"Well, what do you want me to say?"

"I don't know. I didn't expect you to apologize. I didn't come here for that." Rachel tugged her hair back from her face and clenched her teeth. "Look, what's done is done. You can't go back and change how you handled things, and I can't just pretend like it's not a big deal. I need more than a vacation. I need to get out of here, out of my sheltered life, and start everything over from scratch."

"You can't run away from your problems, Rachel."

"No? Isn't that what you're doing?"

Her mother slammed the teakettle back onto the stove, making Rachel jump. "Don't you dare judge me. You have absolutely no idea what I've been through."

"You're right, I don't. But that's your own fault, not mine."

Her mother gripped the edge of the counter and closed her eyes. "Oh Jesus, give me patience." A sound of disdain escaped Rachel's throat, and her mother turned to her and glared. "You ought to be praying too, Rachel, for a more respectful attitude."

"If I was going to pray, it would be for something a lot more useful than that."

'What's that supposed to mean?"

"It means, *if* I was willing to talk to God, I'd be asking him for something a little more practical, like an explanation for why all this is happening when I've been so careful with how I've lived my life. I mean, don't you ever wonder why he's repaying all your years of service and obedience with this? A psycho husband and a pending divorce?"

"Your father's illness and our separation has nothing to do with God, Rachel."

"It doesn't? But everything comes back to God and faith—that's what you've always told me."

"But the Bible tells us that in this life we'll have trouble." Her mother's voice cracked with emotion. "What made you think you were exempt?"

"What about how 'he holds us in his hand'? What about 'ask and you will receive'? I don't feel very held, and I certainly haven't gotten what I asked for. Don't throw the verses at me, Mom; I know them all as well as you do, and I'm having a hard time believing them right now."

"Isn't my faithfulness a testament to you? Isn't the fact that God is sustaining me—and has sustained me for twenty years—evidence that he's there? That he loves me, loves us?"

"Maybe you're just too deluded and scared to face reality. All you have left is God. A comforting lie is better than the depressing truth, right?"

Her mother's hand moved so fast Rachel had no time to react. The sting of it against her cheek took a moment to register through the shock. They stared at each other, stunned, tears in both theirs eyes, until Rachel stood on shaking legs and pulled a sticky note from her pocket.

"My new address." She dropped the note to the table. She avoided her mother's eyes as she moved to the front door. "I'll e-mail you when I get there. Say good-bye to Dad next time you talk to him." She let herself out and got in her car before her mother could see her break down. Part of her hoped her mom would come after her, pull her from the car, and wrap Rachel in her arms. But when she didn't, Rachel knew the damage was done.

Her final bridge in flames, she drove home to her empty apartment for one last sleepless night in California.

Rachel had five minutes before the airport shuttle arrived, and she couldn't shake the feeling that she'd forgotten something. Her bags sat by the door, packed to bursting and just a few pounds under the weight limit. The rest of her things had been shipped the day before for an ungodly amount of money, but short of putting them on pack mules, she couldn't have chosen a cheaper option. Her car and her few pieces of furniture had been taken care of, and all the random things she didn't want to bring she was leaving for Trisha to deal with.

As far as she knew, that was everything. So what was she missing?

Dropping her purse by the door, she set out on one last tour of the apartment, eyes peeled for items she might have missed. The frames on the walls—all Trisha's. The knick-knacks on the mantle. Same with the kitchen items. Rachel backtracked and went to the bedroom. Nothing in the closet. Nothing in the bathroom. She knelt to peek under the bed, pulled out the drawers of her dresser one at a time: nothing, nothing, nothing … *oh.*

She set the red velvet box atop the dresser. She didn't have to open it to know what was inside. Unable to determine its fate, Rachel had shuffled it from one resting place to another as she had systematically emptied her room. She almost wished she had forgotten it, left it behind for Julia to find when she came to pick up the dresser on Saturday. That would have been fittingly ironic, actually.

When she had turned thirteen Rachel had been baptized before the BCC congregation. After the service her family went to lunch, and just before dessert her mother had handed her the velvet box. Inside was the cross she had seen her mother wear nearly every day of her life. She'd told Rachel about her own mother, and her mother's mother, and how each of them had worn this cross until the day of their eldest daughter's baptism. "You come from a heritage of faith," she'd said as she'd fastened the delicate chain around Rachel's neck. "I hope this cross reminds you of that. You're never alone."

For the last thirteen years she'd worn that cross as though it was attached to her. Her fingers had worried it during final exams and difficult conversations, had zipped it along the chain with nervous energy, and had spun the clasp to the back of her neck thousands of times. Taking it off at night and putting it on in the morning were as automatic as brushing her teeth and getting dressed. Or at least, it used to be.

She took it off the night before leaving for Las Vegas, and hadn't put it back on since. Occasionally her fingers would search for it, and she'd experience a little stab of panic that she might have lost it. But in the days of packing, when many of the reminders of the faith of her childhood had been chucked in the trash, she'd set this aside to be dealt with later. Over and over she'd run into it, set it aside, put it from her mind, only to find it again—often in places where she hadn't remembered putting it.

She had procrastinated long enough. It was time to make a decision. Had she been thinking, she would have brought it back to her mother when she'd gone to say good-bye. Though, knowing her mom, it would have found its way back to Rachel eventually.

The doorbell rang. Rachel jumped and dropped the box, then scrambled to pick it up again with a shaking hand. As the shuttle driver hauled the first bag down the stairs, Rachel turned the lock on the doorknob and began to move the other pieces outside. She tried to stuff the box in her purse, then in her carry-on, but both were too crammed to fit the bulky cube. The driver returned again and took the second bag, eyeing the remaining carry-on with annoyance.

Rachel pulled the cross from the velvet pillow shoved it in the pocket of her skirt, then dropped the box on the ground and shouldered her bags.

It was an antique, she reasoned. And who knew—she might need the money.

It was raining when Rachel walked out of the terminal at O'Hare Airport and wrestled her baggage cart to the curb. Thunder rumbled off in the distance—or was it a landing jet? Either way, it sounded ominous.

Daphne said she'd pick Rachel up in a taxi. She watched a variety of cabs approach and zoom past for twenty minutes before she started to worry. She tried Daphne's cell but got no answer. She double-checked her location, thinking she'd accidentally parked herself in some special zone, but no. Apparently Daphne was just late.

Forty minutes had passed when a cab swerved to the curb and she saw Daphne's face in the window. She hopped out ahead of the cabbie and grabbed Rachel with a squeal. "Soooo sorry, the traffic sucks because of the weather. It's pouring in the city."

"That's all right; I called you—"

"I figured you would; I left my phone at home, totally forgot it."

That's my Daphne. "No worries, just glad you're okay. Is this—" Rachel waved a hand to the weather—"normal for June?"

They settled into the cab. "Yeah, it can rain pretty much any time of the year here, but we get tons of storms in the summer. This is pretty tame compared to what some of them are like. And of course the tornados keep things interesting too; those pretty much just come in the summer, though."

"I didn't realize you got tornadoes here. I've always imagined them sweeping through little farming communities in Kansas and Iowa."

Daphne just laughed. "Don't worry, they mostly hit in the 'burbs." She grinned. "Rethinking things?"

Rachel chuckled. "Earthquakes can hit anytime; at least there's a tornado *season*. How about you—are you rethinking things?"

"What, about you living with me? No way!" She squeezed Rachel's arm as the cab took a sharp right onto a freeway entrance ramp. "I'm totally psyched. Your room is all scrubbed and ready for you, and I even cleaned the bathroom in your honor."

"Wow, that's some serious sacrifice. I owe you one."

"Nonsense; anything for my little *Raquel*." Her expression sobered. "So how was leaving?"

Rachel sagged into her seat, letting out a deep sigh. "I won't lie—it was hard. Well, part of it was, anyway. Mom and I had a huge fight when I went to say good-bye last night."

"You and Karen fought? That's, what, your first ever?"

Rachel chuckled. "Well, of this magnitude, yes. Though I don't think I've ever called her deluded or accused her of living a lie, either."

"Ouch."

"Yeah. Not my finest moment."

"But kind of true, all the same ..."

"Yeah … I guess. Difficult to say, though."

Daphne wrapped a comforting arm around Rachel's shoulder. "I know. It's hard to admit, especially out loud, that you don't totally believe the things you used to anymore. Trust me, in a year you'll be a new woman. No, wait, correction: You *are* a new woman; in a year you'll be comfortable being a new woman."

That made her laugh. "That sounds about right." Rachel bit her lip, eyes cast out the window as she formulated her next sentence. "Hey, the other night, when I called …"

Daphne frowned. "When did you call?"

"Friday night."

Daphne shook her head. "I don't remember you calling."

"Well, you were sort of … weird on the phone. I was telling you about how I was having a moment of panic, and you—"

"Ohhhh. I remember now." She grasped Rachel's knee, shaking her head. "I'm so sorry. When you called, I was hanging out with a friend from work.…" She gave Rachel a sheepish look. "We were smoking. I was a little—" She whistled and flourished her hand around.

"You were high?"

Daphne laughed. "As the stars in the sky. Anyway, sorry. I feel terrible that I was not in the right frame of mind to be of more help."

Rachel wasn't sure how to respond. "Oh—um, it's all right. So ... how long until we get to the apartment?"

"Another twenty minutes or so. What's the plan for tonight?"

Rachel glanced out the window at the freeway view. "Not a mosey around the neighborhood, I'm guessing. Any suggestions for dinner?"

"I bought fixings for fettuccine Alfredo."

"My favorite," Rachel said, offering Daphne a knowing smile.

"Yeah, dummy, that was the point." Daphne slugged her in the arm with a wink. "I have to work tomorrow, so no late night for me.

But I can help you unpack or draw up a map of the area or help you look for jobs. There's a mini-mart around the corner—we can pick up a paper if you want the classifieds."

They spent the rest of the ride brainstorming the plans for Rachel's first day. By the time they reached the apartment the rain had stopped, though the sidewalk in front of the Victorian house where Daphne rented was more puddle than asphalt. They split the fare at Rachel's insistence, then began the trek down the alleyway beside the house and up the rickety wooden steps which led to the second story.

The apartment was unlike anything Rachel had ever seen in stucco-and-tile-crazed Orange County. Though the front room was small, its high ceilings prevented it from feeling cramped. Molding surrounded all the windows and doorframes, and a beautiful brick fireplace with a tiled hearth was centered in the far wall. To the left a bar separated the front room from the galley kitchen, and a short hallway ended in a white tiled bathroom with bedroom doors facing each other on either side. A giant bay window provided a view of the oak-lined street as well as copious amounts of natural light. "This place is amazing!"

Daphne smiled. "I know. I love it. The University of Chicago is just a couple blocks away, so there are tons of students in the area. Really fun neighborhood. Lots of parties." She continued to talk as she hefted one of the muddy-bottomed suitcases toward the left-hand bedroom. "This is your room. Not super spacious, but quieter because it's in the back. No furniture, sorry—but there are a couple cool consignment and resale places in the area, so you should be able to pick stuff up for cheap."

The room was indeed simple, though being in the corner it had two windows and was well lit even with the cloudy weather. They set the bags in front of the closet, then agreed to change out of their wet clothes and start making dinner.

While they ate at the bar Daphne drew a map of the surrounding area and made a list of places for Rachel to check for furniture. She was in the middle of explaining the bus system when the phone rang. "*Pardonnez moi.*" She glanced at the caller ID, then hopped off the barstool and retreated with the cordless phone into her bedroom. The look on her face as she disappeared and the tone of her voice as it wafted under the door made it clear a boy was on the other end.

Rachel pinned her with an expectant stare when she emerged, and her reward was the whole story spilled without any prompting. "His name is Paul, he's adorable, and I met him at work."

"Oooh, office romance."

"Well, dressing-room romance; personal shoppers don't spend a lot of time in offices." She grinned and swirled her glass of soda. "Has a psycho ex-wife, poor thing, and is in the middle of the divorce. One of those 'we married too young' kinds of things, you know?" She grabbed Rachel's wrist. "I'm so glad you escaped the same fate! Married at twenty-six—you would have been doomed!" She shook her head and took up her fork. "Anyway, he's a doll and so much more mature than Marc, and he knows how to treat a woman." She popped another forkful of pasta in her mouth. "Speaking of which, I need to explain the alert system for when we have guys over."

Rachel looked at Daphne askance. "The what?"

She waved her fork impatiently. “You know, a way of warning when one of us is up here with a guy, so when you come home you don’t, you know, walk in on anything.” She wagged her eyebrows.

Rachel playfully rolled her eyes. “Okay, I’m with you now. What’s the system?”

She motioned with her fork to the bay window. “See the Coke can on the floor under the window? That’s the Make-Out Can. Stick that on the sill if you’re in the front room ‘with’ a guy, if you know what I mean. And when you’re coming home, always make sure to look for it. If you see it, walk heavy on the stairs, as slowly as you can, to give us time to vamoose to the bedroom. My last roommate came up with this. It worked great.” She flashed a wicked grin. “The walls aren’t exactly sound-proofed, either, so you might want to turn up your stereo or something.”

Make-Out Cans and smoking pot. *Well, you wanted a new life.*

“Oh, and if your guy is gonna spend the night, slip a note under my door or something so I know not to walk around in my dainties.” She winked. “Of course I’ll do the same. You’re okay with that, right? With guys spending the night?”

“Oh, um, sure.” Like she’d say no. “How often do you have guys overnight?”

She shrugged and took a sip of her Coke. “Not super-often. Kinda depends. Marc and I were like rabbits the first couple months, so we practically lived at each other’s place. But Paul is a totally different story; it’s a much more adult relationship. Marc was an undergrad at the uni and totally into the party scene. So it was that kind of wild and crazy, sex-on-the-kitchen-floor kind of relationship.” Rachel made a face of surprise and Daphne burst out laughing.

"We only did that once. No, twice! But it was very uncomfortable; I don't recommend it."

"Don't think I would have thought of it."

Daphne laughed. "Of course not. But don't worry—we'll get you set up with all the necessary gear if and when you're ready to take that step."

"Gear?" Rachel raised her eyebrows. "There's gear involved in sex? Look, I may not have experience but I know how it works. I don't remember there being a need for gear."

Daphne gazed at her with pity. "Oh, you sweet, innocent thing, you. So much to learn."

Rachel stared out the bay window at the clouds that illuminated with lightning. Thunder grumbled in the distance, but the sound was just unfamiliar enough to keep her from sleep—along with the fact that her body was still on California time. Daphne had turned in early to catch up on the sleep she'd missed the night before when Paul had stayed over, so Rachel wandered the tiny apartment alone, looking for something to do.

She reread her list of tasks for the morning but could think of nothing else to add. Not that she needed more to do—shopping for furniture, opening a bank account, and job hunting at the local coffee haunts were more than enough to keep her busy. List abandoned, she perused the small bookshelf next to the hearth. The collection there—which included Harlequins and self-help books that centered around sex and relationships—was the polar opposite of the collection her shelves had held at home. She looked at the stack of magazines on the coffee table only to discover it was nothing but back issues of *Cosmo.*

Curiosity got the better of her. She took the top issue off the stack and settled onto the couch to read. She flipped through it, unimpressed with the relatively shallow content. Though she did notice that a few of the outfits Daphne had chosen for her in Las Vegas were apparently very "in" right now, according to the fashion section. She never would have pegged *Cosmo* as Daphne's job research, but she supposed it made sense. Remembering Daphne's comment about sex gear, she lingered in the sexual Q & A section for a few minutes before tossing the magazine back onto the pile. Regardless of how her views about God had altered, her views of sex were still the same, and she didn't anticipate them changing any time soon.

She opened her laptop and saw the icon for her seminary application on the desktop. Anger like she hadn't felt in a week bubbled to the surface. All the time she'd wasted trying to craft that stupid essay, trying to explain how she'd been a Christian her whole life … when she wasn't sure she'd ever felt God's presence or heard his voice. Was it a sham? All of it—her faith, God's goodness? She felt like she was seeing her faith more clearly, and it seemed almost obvious how ridiculous it all was.

Her pride stung. She was an intelligent woman—how had she been so delusional, so suckered for so long?

Stewing, she sank further into the couch. The boudoir red curtains that hung in the bay window were more decorative than functional, and the pulses of silent lightning gave her something to stare at as she let the night settle in around her. She was struck again by her aloneness, despite Daphne being ten feet away on the other side of the wall. Her thoughts rattled around in her head and gave her no peace for reflection, let alone the possibility for prayer, which seemed laughable anyway. Exhaustion eventually overcame the anger, and she fell asleep fighting thoughts of the contentment she so missed.

Yesterday's storm had blown out in the night, leaving a sparkling summer morning sky and humidity so thick you could practically drink the air. Despite a rough night of sleep on the battered couch, Rachel was full of energy and feeling positive about the move for the first time in days. Having a productive morning helped as well—she'd found all the furniture she needed but the bed at the first thrift store she'd visited, and an extra twenty paid to one of the staff got it delivered. She'd found the bed she wanted at a mattress store that provided free shipping, and they put her on the schedule for the next day. It meant one more night on the uncomfortable couch, but it was a small price to pay.

After lunch at the apartment, Rachel set out again in search of the most important part of her new life: a job. She consulted the list of local coffee shops Daphne had given her, and after the third shop she started to lose confidence. With the university so close by, most were not lacking for staff. She'd hoped to find something nearby so as to avoid the cost and inconvenience of public transportation, but unless one of the last few places on her list was hiring, she'd have to branch out.

She stopped by the fourth shop on the list and ruled it out almost immediately. It was a chain—not one she'd heard of in California, but a chain nonetheless—she could tell from the generic-hip decor and the plethora of commercially-printed materials. It had a "help wanted" sign in the window, and if she couldn't find anything else, she'd come back, but she wasn't about to settle for a big company when she still had more options to investigate.

The fifth shop was independent but not hiring. She left it with a heavy heart. Only one left on the list and she'd call it a day. She was exhausted from all the walking and eager to get back to organizing her bedroom. She parked herself on a chair outside the café and consulted the map Daphne had given her. She brightened when she saw how close the final shop was to the apartment. *Please let there be a job for me there, God!*

She was back on her feet and moving down the sidewalk before she realized what she'd done. It was the first prayer she'd uttered in weeks, blurted purely from habit. And she knew now that's all it had been, really—habit. He'd never spoken back that she could tell. And if he really was there, he'd already proven he couldn't be trusted with big things like keeping her family and relationships together, so what was the likelihood of him caring about her commute?

If he's even really there.

The idea slowed her steps. She'd allowed herself the occasional thought that God might not exist, but being mad at him and walking away from faith had been a big enough step to deal with. Taking the leap to full-on atheism had been a bit too much to take on. But other than an occasional ache for the comfort of her old life, there hadn't seemed to be much fallout yet from her inching away from God. If God were really there, wouldn't he have made it clear to her when she'd started to leave him?

She thought about all the evidence she'd heard over the years, all the philosophical arguments, the books she'd read about Christianity. They were always presented and written by Christians. But what about all the scientists and philosophers and college professors who claimed Christianity wasn't true? If the evidence were that clear, then wouldn't they acknowledge that?

Her eyes caught the profile of a woman ahead of her. A colorful scarf was draped over her head and shoulders in Muslim style. She considered what little she knew about Islam. It had all sounded ridiculous to her, but then again, it had been told to her by Christians, and of course they would accentuate the absurd. But there were millions of people who believed Allah to be the one true God—could millions of people really be completely wrong? Wouldn't word get out that it was a sham if it was that easy to disprove?

Though she could say the same about Christianity.

Rachel rubbed her forehead. She felt a headache coming on. She needed coffee. Or maybe something stronger.

She forced the thought away, focusing instead on the thought of an iced mocha as she quickened her pace. She was parched by the time she reached All Together Now Café, but not so desperate for a drink that she didn't notice what a great little shop it was. Truly an independent, its funky vibe made her smile as she drank a cup of water while waiting for her coffee. A Beatles theme was integrated into every aspect of the decor and menu, from a psychedelic mural and framed album covers on the wall to the "Come Together Cappuccino," "John's Java Special," and the "Across the Universe" list of international blends.

Rachel took her drink to a seat in the corner and let her eyes roam the room. Mostly students made up the current clientele—lots of U of C garb and laptops surrounded by thick textbooks and notebooks with bent spirals. The shop was small, but clean and well lit, and the staff seemed to keep busy even when there were no manager types around. The music—she knew it was the Beatles playing, though she wasn't too familiar with their music—wasn't loud, and the menu was simple but not sparse: sandwiches, soups of the day, and a few bakery items were listed on the chalkboard menus along with the coffees and noncoffee drinks. She smiled. She could see herself here.

After finishing her mocha, she sent a prayerlike wish to whoever might be listening and stood to approach the register. The barista chose that moment to disappear into the back, leaving the counter unmanned. She was about to sit down when a new barista entered from the back, tying on his apron and singing along with the music. He looked at her and smiled—then smiled wider. Rachel's heart almost stopped in her chest.

It was her Kiss from Las Vegas.

CHAPTER 10

He shook his finger at Rachel, eyes glinting. "Weren't you supposed to stay in Vegas?"

She laughed, completely shocked. "I could say the same to you."

He came out from behind the counter, hand extended. "I suppose I ought to properly introduce myself. Jack Hanson."

"Rachel Westing."

He rubbed a hand on the back of his neck, looking sheepish. "So, um … is it just me or is this a little awkward?"

"Maybe just a little." She tried to control the nervous grin that threatened to split her mouth. She was completely embarrassed. She looked nothing like she had that night. Certainly he was asking himself what on earth he'd been thinking. "So … were you in Vegas for long?"

"Just the weekend. My brother's bachelor party. He got married at the end of May. How about you?"

"Just the weekend too. A getaway with a girlfriend."

The bell on the door chimed the arrival of a group of students. "Uh oh." Jack made a dash for the counter, then gave Rachel an apologetic smile. "Duty calls."

"Of course. No problem." She took her seat and sipped her mocha, trying to regroup. Her job-hunt mojo had gone out the window the minute she'd recognized his face. *Focus, focus! You need to ask him for a manager....*

He finished with the group and came back around to her table. "So how is it that I've never seen you before?"

"I just moved here yesterday."

"You're kidding! Well there's kismet for you. Where from?"

"California. I actually came in because I'm looking for a job. I know there's no sign out front, but I figured—"

"Oh, you'll want to talk to Ruby Jean then." He leaned in, smiling. "We just lost a couple people, so you're in luck." He disappeared into the back for a moment, then returned with a tall red-headed woman that reminded Rachel of Rosie O'Donnell. "Hey there. How can I help you?"

Rachel forced herself not to be distracted by Jack and turned on the professional aura. "I know you don't have a sign in the window, but I really like your shop, and I'm looking for a job. I don't suppose you're hiring?"

The woman paused for just a beat, then nodded. "I am, actually. You caught me in the middle of writing up the classified. Got a minute to talk? Come on back."

Kismet is right. Rachel followed her to the back office, which was also Beatles themed, sitting opposite her in the only other available desk chair. "I'm Ruby Jean Cronin, by the way. Or Ruby, or R. J., or whatever comes to mind when you need me. I own and manage. What's your name?"

"I'm Rachel Westing." She offered her warmest smile.

"I haven't seen you in here before."

"Well, I just moved from California, arrived yesterday."

"Oh—welcome to Chicago then. Coming to the university, I assume?"

"No, actually. I have a friend who lives a few blocks down, and I moved in with her. Just … needed a change."

Ruby Jean chuckled. "I'll bet this is a change from California. Maybe not now, but in six months—whooee!" She grinned, and Rachel felt the positive vibe growing. "So do you have coffee-shop experience?"

"I do, yes." Rachel handed Ruby Jean a resumé. "I worked at an independent café called *Espress-Oh!*, first as a barista, and then as a manager. Five years total."

Ruby Jean took the resume and cocked a brow. "Really?"

Rachel nodded. "And I noticed you operate a portafilter machine—that's what we used as well. I know those aren't as common anymore, but I prefer them to the automatic machines. I'm glad to see you have one."

Ruby Jean smiled. "Why do I get the sense you really know your coffee?"

Rachel matched Ruby Jean's smile with her own. "I'll be honest. I'm a bit of an addict. You don't just get an employee if you hire me. You get an expert."

Ruby Jean leaned back in her chair as her expression took on the look of a challenge. "I prefer African and Central American coffees over those from South America. Know much about them?"

Rachel took a deep breath, savoring the feeling of familiarity that came with a discussion about one of her favorite obsessions. "Let's see. Well, Guatemalan coffee comes from one of three growing regions and is usually medium- to full-bodied. It usually has a spicy or chocolatey flavor, and the taste is usually described as rich or complex. Costa Rican coffee is considered to have perfect balance between body and acidity. Ethiopian coffees come from one of three growing regions and are usually named for them—"

Ruby Jean let out a laugh and held up her hands. "Okay, okay, you win. I'm impressed, I really am. I'm used to these college kids who just need a job for beer money; I never thought I'd find someone who actually knew their stuff without me trying to drill it into them. What turned you on to coffee like that?"

"Mission trip to Brazil when I was in college. I'd never had it before that, but the host family my team stayed with gave us each a giant thermos full of it when we left in the morning. After drinking it on and off all day for a week, I was hooked." She didn't bother with the rest of the story—how everything about that trip had intensified and solidified her faith and how, for the months following, the taste of coffee had brought back those emotions of being so close to God, so alive in her spirituality. Upon arriving home she'd begun to brew a cup every morning as a symbol of her devotion, and only after getting the job at *Espress-Oh!* had she begun to branch out into other roasts and regions and start experimenting with flavors. Somewhere along the line the connotation had been lost, though she hadn't noticed it happening. She wondered what had made her stop thinking of God when she drank it.

Ruby Jean's eyes sparkled. "A mission trip? With a church, you mean? What religion are you, if I may ask? And just so you know, it has no bearing on the job—if your references check out you've totally got it."

Rachel's jaw dropped. "I do? Thank you! Oh—and I was with a Protestant church."

"So you're a Christian."

Rachel squirmed, embarrassed now that she'd shared so much. "Um, well—I was, yes."

"Ah." Ruby Jean nodded. "Well. I'm going to call your previous boss after we're done here, and assuming his report is as glowing as I expect it to be, you're hired. I'll start you at barista just to get you used to the place, but I foresee you moving to manager in a few months, provided all goes well. How does that sound?"

Rachel couldn't stop the smile that stretched her face. "That sounds fantastic!"

"Great! Well, why don't we go to the front and you can show me your skills on the machine. Not that I doubt you, but I suppose I should be thorough, eh?" She led Rachel to the front where she made the next three coffee orders that Jack rang up. Ruby Jean promised to call Rachel that evening with her schedule for the rest of the week. She left for home with "Twist and Shout" stuck in her head, Jack's face etched in her mind, and a nagging reminder that she'd gotten exactly what she'd prayed for.

CHAPTER 11

Rachel nearly pounced on Daphne when she walked in from work that evening. "You are never, ever going to guess what happened to me today."

"You got a job."

Rachel laughed. "Yes …"

Daphne let out a whoop and wrapped Rachel in a bear hug. "Congratulations! Where?"

"All Together Now Café. It's just down the street."

"Oh, I've been there before. Cute little place. My bus passes it every morning—I don't remember seeing a job sign there, though, or I would have told you about it."

"They didn't have one out yet. The manager was writing one when I got there."

Daphne gave Rachel a high five. "Time to celebrate!"

"I already ordered pizza. It should be here in five."

"Perfect. I'll get some drinks for us to toast with."

"Okay, but there's more to this story. Remember the night we went dancing in Vegas?" Rachel followed Daphne to the kitchen and hopped onto a barstool as Daphne pulled a bottle of wine from the fridge.

Daphne laughed. "Are you kidding? Of course I do. It's not often I go out looking like Madonna—or see you actually dancing."

Rachel rolled her eyes. "Yes, yes, I know. Okay, so—remember the guy who danced with me?"

"Oh yes, absolutely."

"Well … guess where he works."

Daphne's jaw dropped. "You are making this up."

"Scout's honor, I am not."

Daphne howled. "Did he recognize you?"

"Surprisingly, yes. Even without the hair and makeup."

"Tell me everything!"

Rachel described their exchange as Daphne poured two glasses of wine. "It was so embarrassing," she said when she reached the end of the story. "But at least he seemed as embarrassed as me."

Daphne handed her a glass of wine. "A toast!" Daphne raised her glass. "To Rachel, on whom the goddesses of love and fortune have chosen to pour their blessings. May some of it rub off on me."

They laughed and clinked glasses before Rachel took an eager taste. Her lips puckered against the taste despite her attempt to keep her face neutral, but it wasn't enough to stop her from a second—and third—sip. "So, I do have one problem," she said when she put down her glass. "I'm supposed to start at eight tomorrow morning, but my bed is supposed to arrive between ten and noon."

"No problem, *ma chérie*," Daphne said. "I don't have any appointments tomorrow morning, so I'll just go in once it arrives."

"Saving my butt once again." Rachel bowed in gratitude.

"Happy to do it! So tell me about the job. That's a neat little joint; I've been there before."

The doorbell rang and Rachel answered, wallet in hand, to pay the delivery boy. Daphne brought their drinks to the living room, and they sat on the couch as they ate and Rachel recounted the details of her interview. “Anyway, I like the feel of the place, and being told I practically have a promotion already is exciting.”

“Seriously!”

Rachel took another few sips of the wine. The taste was growing on her. “I feel so good right now. Everything is falling into place. This was such a good decision.”

“Well, it was long overdue. Maybe the universe has just been waiting for you to step up and take control of your life. I can’t wait to see what else is in store for you.”

They made sundaes for dessert and popped in a movie to round out the evening’s celebration. The opening credits had barely ended when the phone rang, and hearing the sexy tone in Daphne’s voice was enough to tell Rachel she’d be preoccupied for a while. Rachel turned off the television and wandered into her room to admire her new furniture. Though mismatched, each piece had character and potential and required only a new paint job. She began contemplating a color scheme, then noticed a change in Daphne’s voice as her muffled words floated under the doors.

Rachel turned on her radio, determined not to eavesdrop, but Daphne emerged moments later and poked her head in the door. “Sorry about that. Man trouble.” She rolled her eyes. “Still up for the movie?”

“Oh—yeah, sure. Everything all right?”

“Yeah, yeah, it’s fine. Paul’s just giving me grief about tomorrow.”

“About coming in late? Look, I can call the mattress place and tell them to wait until the weekend—”

“No, no, you need a bed, the couch is totally awful to sleep on, I know. Don't worry about it." She flashed a smile that Rachel could see right through, but she resisted the urge to push the subject, choosing instead to follow Daphne back to the living room and lose herself in the sappy romance they'd selected.

The light bulb in Rachel's head went off an hour into the movie. She grabbed the remote, hit pause, and blurted, "Paul's your boss, isn't he!" Daphne's cheeks reddened. "Daphne, you can't date your boss."

"Well, he's not exactly my boss. I mean, I report to him, but it's not like he's a whole level above me or anything. He's a personal shopper, too, but sort of, like, the head one, you know? Honestly, it's not a big deal."

Rachel opened her mouth to protest, then promptly shut it again. After a moment she raised her hands in surrender. "Okay, I'll trust you, but it just doesn't sound kosher to me."

Daphne just smiled. "Kosher is overrated."

Rachel walked into All Together Now with five minutes to spare before the start of her first shift. She felt bouncy with nervous energy despite the kink in her neck. She couldn't wait to sleep on her new bed.

Jack flashed her a smile as he finished creating a latte. "Hope you're ready to dance," he said with a wink, nodding to the line that snaked from the register nearly to the door.

She felt her cheeks flush. "I hope so too, for your sake." She made her way to the office and poked her head into the open door. "It's busy out there."

Ruby Jean nodded and pointed to a paper-clipped stack of forms in the center of the other desk. "It is—let's get this paperwork filled out so you can begin working." When Rachel was done with the forms, Ruby Jean tossed them into an inbox and handed her an apron. "Here you go. I'll get a name tag made up for you in a bit. Ready to start?" Rachel tied on the black apron with the café's logo on the front and nodded, butterflies fluttering. She followed her new boss to the front counter, where Jack was tag-teaming with another employee—the male version of Julia from *Espress-Oh!*, it seemed—whose name tag said "Cole, manager." Ruby Jean pointed to a flat, silver surface with a handle in the center. "Sandwich fixings are in here." She pulled it up to reveal a row of condiments, lettuce, sprouts, and tomato slices, as well as three loaves of sliced bread and three canisters of deli meat. "Turkey, roast beef, and ham," she said as she pointed to the canisters, "and white, wheat, and rye. Refills of everything are in the fridge in the back room." She continued to point out various supplies and explain procedures until the door opened and a gaggle of backpack-toting twentysomethings poured in. "Ready to jump in?"

Rachel took a deep breath. "I think so."

"Great. Why don't you fill drink orders while Jack takes them; he'll take three or four, then help you catch up. We'll train you on the register when it's slower." She gave Rachel a pat on the back. "Glad you're here, Rachel."

"Thanks, Ruby Jean. So am I."

Jack greeted the next customer at the till and marked her order along the side of a cardboard cup, then handed it to Rachel. She gave the machine a quick looking-over before diving in and mixing an Act

Naturally Vanilla Latte. With the unfamiliar layout of the supplies on the counter and an espresso machine that sported a few differences from the one she was used to, it took a couple orders before the rhythm Rachel was used to fell into place. But by the end of her first hour she was back in the groove and keeping pace with Jack, who only had to mix a few drinks to keep up with the customer flow.

The morning rush began to dwindle, and after placing the lid on the last standing order and handing it off to the customer, Jack held his hand up to her for a high five. "You're fast. You've done this for a while, haven't you?"

Rachel slapped his hand and straightened a listing tower of cups as Jack wiped down the counter in front of the espresso machine. "Five years, full time for three."

He laughed. "Guess that counts as 'a while.' No wonder. It'll be nice working with someone who knows what she's doing. The guys who quit were clueless, even after two months."

"You know what you're doing too. How long have you worked here?"

"Here—nine months or so. Was at Starbucks during my undergrad in Indiana for two years, though."

"Are you at the university here now, or do you just live here?"

He made a face she couldn't decipher. "Just living here, for now. You a student?"

"Nope."

He pulled a can of Coke from the glass display case and popped the top. "So what made you come out here—that fiancé of yours?"

Rachel frowned, puzzled. "How did you know I'd been engaged?"

"In Vegas you, ah—"

"Oh, right, I told you after we, um ..."

He gave her a sheepish smile. "Yeah … I should apologize for that, by the way. I don't usually go around kissing strangers. I think I'd had one beer too many before we got to the club."

Rachel felt her face warming. "Oh, it's all right."

"So … you said you'd *been* engaged. Meaning you're not now?"

"Right."

"I'm sorry. It's not because I kissed you, is it?"

She laughed. "No. It's not."

"Okay, good." He grinned, then frowned. "But that still sucks. I'm sorry."

She waved a hand, then busied herself with straightening a display on the counter that didn't really need straightening. "Dodged a bullet, actually. So no worries."

"Well, I hope Chicago treats you better."

She couldn't help smiling. "It has so far."

Another customer rush brought their conversation to an end, and for the next half hour they danced around each other behind the counter, taking orders and making drinks. Rachel was steaming milk when her phone vibrated in her pocket; Daphne's name showed on the screen when she took a peek. The rush had died down, and Jack waved her toward the door when he saw her glancing at her phone. "Ruby's cool with personal calls, so long as you're not neglecting customers. Go ahead; I'll be fine."

The voice-mail icon popped up just as she reached the sidewalk. "Hey girl." Daphne's voice was heavy. "The mattress people haven't come yet, but Paul's giving me grief about coming in late, so I need to go. I'm so sorry. I hope you get this in time to come home or call them to reschedule or something. Please don't hate me! See you tonight. Bye."

Rachel groaned. She could call the store and reschedule—but another night on that couch would be awful. Her neck twinged just about every time she raised her left arm. She went to the office. "Ruby Jean, I'm so sorry, but I need to go home, just for a bit. The people delivering my bed are supposed to be coming before noon, and my roommate was supposed to be there but now she won't be, and the couch is a nightmare—"

Ruby Jean held up a hand. "Breathe, Rachel." Rachel shut her mouth, embarrassed. "We'll call it an early lunch. Just come back as soon as possible, okay? We really need all hands on deck when the lunch rush starts."

Rachel had her apron off and was halfway out the door by the time Ruby Jean finished talking. She threw a "Thank you so much!" over her shoulder before the door closed behind her, then broke into a run.

She felt like an idiot. Dodging pedestrians, she panted her way down the sidewalk, willing the mattress people not to arrive before she got there. Daphne had called around 10:10; by the time she got home it would be about 10:25. The delivery window had been ten to noon. What were the odds they'd arrive in the fifteen-minute block that no one was home?

She had her answer as she caught her breath at a red light with the house within view. A truck sat in front of it, and while Rachel couldn't see the side to read the name, she knew in her gut it was them.

Come on, stupid traffic light! Unable to stomach the wait, she scanned the intersection for oncoming cars, then made a mad dash against the signal.

She was halfway through the intersection when the truck roared to life. "No!" she shouted, pouring on what little energy she had left. The truck pulled away from the curb, and she waved her hands like a madwoman as she stared at the driver. As they passed her she saw the driver was on his cell and the passenger was studying a map. Neither of them saw her as they blew past, and she stood gasping on the parkway.

It's just a bed. It's just a bed. She chanted to herself as she limped the rest of the distance to the house and hauled herself up the stairs. Yanking the "Sorry we missed you!" notice off the door, she let herself in and collapsed on the couch that would be her bed for at least one more night.

Daphne couldn't help it. She had to go to work. It's just a bed. How could she know how close they were? She sat for a few minutes before pushing herself to her feet and going to the kitchen for some water.

She made herself a sandwich, and shortly after eating it, she felt ready to make the trek back to work.

"You look like you just ran a marathon," Jack said as she took her place behind the counter.

"Close." Rachel told him what happened.

Jack shook his head. "That sucks. I'm sorry. You know, I have a pickup. If you're not busy after we get off I could drive you over there and pick it up for you."

Her heart swelled. "Are you serious?"

"Sure. We could get dinner, too, if you want—you work until five, right?"

"Right."

"So we'll need to eat anyway. Will the mattress store still be open?"

"Until eight, I think."

"Great—works for me if it works for you."

"It definitely works for me. You're a lifesaver. My neck and back thank you."

They fell back into their routine, and as she made sandwiches and drinks she found herself developing a real crush on Jack. Her thoughts returned to Daphne's theory of rebound dating, and she found herself beginning to see the draw of it.

The lunch rush was half over when they were joined by a member of the next shift and Rachel met her competition for Jack.

"Nice to meet you! I'm Leah." She looked exotic. She oozed friendly. And judging by the ichthus necklace, she was a Christian.

Rachel took a deep breath and fixed a smile on her face. "Nice to meet you, too." She turned back to the drink she was making and tried to send out an alpha female vibe.

Either the vibe didn't work or Leah simply didn't care. She grabbed a cup and began to make a Maggie Mae Mocha. "I'm so glad R. J. found someone. It's been tough here with the staff being so slim. I've been part-part-time because of my class schedule and other stuff, but I've been trying to put in extra hours whenever I can to help out. But I haven't been here in a week. How you doing, Jack?"

Jack had finished ringing up customers and was setting himself up at the sandwich counter. "Hey, Leah, I'm good. You?"

"Good!"

"So how has your first day gone, Rachel?"

"Fine, thanks. I managed a place like this back in California, so I haven't had too much trouble." Rachel tried not to sound like she was bragging while still asserting confidence.

"Oh wow, that's great! Maybe you'll be able to help take some of the managerial pressure off Ruby Jean, then. Did she talk to you about being a manager?"

Leah didn't seem as intimidated as Rachel had hoped. "She mentioned something about it. After I've been here a few months."

"Awesome!" She gave Rachel another perky smile, then keyed her code in to the register and began ringing up more customers. Rachel moved beside her and held out her hand for the cup she was marking, intent on showing her she could keep up with the orders.

Rachel's mind did not stay on the espresso machine, however. It was on The Moment of Truth, the time when Leah would ask The Question, try to initiate The Conversation, and Rachel would be forced to admit that she not only knew a lot about Christianity, but she had been a devout one until recently. Rachel knew how the game was played. She'd done it with new employees, new neighbors, customers she'd known for a long time. Leah's wheels were likely already turning. Rachel would never be just another coworker, or just her manager, or just her friend. She'd be that Lost Soul Who Needs Jesus. Like Julia had been to her, Rachel would be Leah's project. Rachel could just imagine Leah's prayers before bed that night as she journaled in her cloth-covered notebook—she was definitely the cloth-covered notebook type. *Thank you for the opportunity to work with Rachel, Father! Please give me an opportunity to tell her about you.* She'd never think to pray for them to just be friends. Which was just as well, since Rachel wasn't about to repopulate her social circle with the kinds of people she'd left California to avoid.

She handed off another drink and picked up the next cup. As she tamped the grounds into the portafilter, she shot a glance at Jack, who was putting together a turkey sandwich. Now *he* was the kind of person Rachel wanted to get to know. Friendly, chivalrous, attractive—and a great kisser. She wondered if Leah had tried working her conversion charm on him yet.

Leah finished ringing up customers and began to clean up the mess Rachel made at the base of the espresso machine as Rachel put the finishing touches on a chai latte. Her conscience cringed as she watched Leah from the corner of her eye. She was aware of the fact that she was doing the very thing she'd just condemned in her head—not liking Leah for who she was—but without the religious motivation. Old habits really were hard to break.

She handed the drink to the waiting customer, then took a deep breath and summoned her inner Daphne. *Live and let live. Tolerance to all. So what if she's a religious freak? It's a free country. I'll show her I can be just as nice and friendly as she is, without a hidden agenda.* She grabbed a stack of cups from the side counter and restocked the supply next to the machine. "Thanks for clearing my station, Leah; I appreciate it."

"Oh, not a problem. Man, you're fast with the drinks. I'm impressed!"

"Oh, thanks. Just had a lot of practice, that's all." The three of them dodged around each other as they refilled coffee pots and cleaned countertops between customers, chatting and joking all the while. Not wanting to be stuck on drink duty forever, Rachel excused herself after a bit to ask Ruby Jean if someone could train her on the register before the next rush. Ruby Jean roped Jack into the task, and for a while Rachel's mind was too preoccupied to wander.

Late in the afternoon a cluster of five collegiate-looking types walked in and called to Leah as she cleaned the sandwich station. "Hey guys," she said, then leaned over the counter to kiss one of the preppy boys in the front. Rachel found herself breathing a sigh of relief.

Leah chatted with the group as she started marking cups with everyone's orders. Rachel wasn't eavesdropping, but her ears still picked up "worship service" and "Bible study" from the conversation they were murmuring at the register. She glanced at Jack, who caught her eye, looked to the group, then back at Rachel with a roll of his eyes. Rachel smirked. She shouldn't have been so concerned about Leah stealing Jack—girls like her would never date a non-Christian. Oh well. Leah's loss.

After Jack and Rachel punched out together he led her to his F-250 in the back parking lot. "Thanks again," she said as they pulled out to the street. "You're saving my back from a week's worth of chiropractic appointments—which is good, since I don't even have a chiropractor yet."

"Glad I could help. It's not often I get to play the knight in shining armor."

"So, I'm starving. What did you have in mind for dinner?"

He laughed. "A woman after my own heart." He sped through a

yellow light and swerved into the right lane for the next turn. "Have you had any proper Chicago-style pizza yet?"

Rachel nodded. "Back in California. There are a few restaurants that do deep-dish pizza. That's what you mean, right?"

"Well … I don't think I'd trust Californians to know what they're doing when it comes to authentic Chicago deep-dish."

She smiled. "I didn't know it was such a specific recipe."

"Oh yes. There are two distinct styles—stuffed and deep dish—and about four different chains out here that insist they're doing it the true Chicago way. We'll have to make sure you try them all so you can make an informed opinion."

"Well, I would hate to be accused of ignorance when it came to pizza. Where shall we start?"

The restaurant was called Edwardo's, home of Jack's favorite, the spinach-stuffed pizza. By the time they entered the foyer after lugging all the various parts of Rachel's bed up to the apartment, she thought she'd faint from the heavenly smell. Their waitress set down a basket of what looked like thin pizza dough baked and broken into pieces when she brought their sodas. "This is croccante," Jack said as he grabbed a handful. "It's really addicting, so don't ruin your appetite."

"Not a chance—I'm running on fumes right now. I might even have room for dessert, I'm that hungry."

He shook his head. "You won't want dessert, trust me. The pizza will take every spare inch of room you have."

Their conversation followed the typical style of first-date Q and A, but with a weird undertone of intimacy Rachel could only assume stemmed from the fact that they'd already kissed. He had a sister and lived on the other side of the university from Rachel and Daphne. He'd gone to Indiana University and graduated with a degree in athletic training. "Do you play any sports, or just want to treat people who do?" Rachel asked.

He made a face. "Well, I used to. I pitched baseball in high school and for three years in college, but then I tore my flexor mass muscle and ulnar collateral ligament." He traced a finger along the inside of his elbow and Rachel winced.

"Oh no, that's awful."

He nodded. "Yeah, it was. Threw me for a loop, because I'd been hoping to go pro eventually. There were a couple scouts showing interest my junior year, but once I had the surgery I just couldn't perform anymore. A psychological thing, I think." He shrugged and popped some more croccante in his mouth. Rachel caught a vibe that told her the subject was closed, which was confirmed when he said, "So how about you? Did you go to college in California?"

"Yep."

"And? Where?"

She waved her hand. "A little college you probably wouldn't have heard of. It's private."

"The information or the school?"

She laughed. "The school. And, I suppose, the information. For now, anyway."

He grinned. "You women … always with your mystery."

She wagged her eyebrows but said nothing. He laughed. "Can you tell me what you majored in, or is that classified as well?"

Rachel grinned. "Secondary education, minored in history."

"High school teacher? That's brave. What made you decide to sling coffee instead?"

"Just couldn't find a job. Then I got promoted to manager and … here I am."

"Lucky us."

Rachel felt her cheeks redden and steered the conversation to a less personal topic. But by the time Jack drove her home, with a new favorite pizza and the promise of a second date, she'd begun to think she was the lucky one.

Things were finally looking up.

"I saw your bed!" Daphne said when Rachel walked in. "I'm so glad you made it back here in time! I'm so sorry; Paul totally pulled rank on me." Daphne tacked on a couple choice names for him to show just how mad she was as she pulled Rachel into an apologetic hug.

"Well, actually, I didn't make it back in time. But it's okay because I got a date out of it."

Daphne let out a squeal and pulled Rachel to the couch with a command to divulge every detail. Apparently kissing and telling was a standard in Daphne's world. Rachel told her everything, from his sweet apology for kissing her in Vegas to meeting Leah, which had Daphne fascinated.

"It's like you're a double agent or something. You know all her tactics! How does it feel?"

"Weird, honestly. I mean, you're right, it's like I know what the motivation will be behind certain conversations or questions. But really it just makes me sad to think that I was like that for so long, that I saw everyone as a target and not just as a person."

"It sucks, doesn't it?"

Her words hit home. "Daphne, I'm so sorry I was like that with you. I mean, I think it was a little different with us, because we'd known each other for so long and really were friends. But I know that I was pushy with you over religion. Thanks for not dumping me."

Daphne laughed and wrapped Rachel in another hug. "It's okay, really. You and your family were there for me more than anyone else my whole life, and it was kind of sweet, in a way, to know you cared so much about my immortal soul." Her eyes twinkled. "But it's fun knowing you're on my side now." She stood and made a grand gesture toward the kitchen. "And so we shall toast! To your first date as a new woman with a new life and a new attitude." She made a dash for the pantry, then rummaged for a moment before extracting a bottle of vodka.

Rachel was excited at the prospect of a drink. "What are we having this time?"

"Vodka and Coke. Vodka is my personal fave for mixed drinks." A generous amount of vodka was poured into one glass, and then a modest splash into the other. "We'll start you off slow." She topped both with Coke and handed a tumbler to Rachel and raised hers with a flourish. "To Rachel and her day of firsts—first day of work, first encounter with a Christian, and her first date. Oh, and her first vodka! May all the rest of your firsts go as smoothly."

They clinked their glasses, and Rachel tried not to look too eager as she took her first sip. "This tastes good."

"What did I tell you?" Daphne finished off her tumbler and took out another Coke. "Here, finish yours and I'll give you a stronger one."

Rachel swallowed the rest and Daphne concocted another one, this time adding about as much vodka into it as she did into hers.

"You don't have to have another one, Daph."

"Of course I do! I'm not gonna let you drink alone!" She gave Rachel a crinkly-nosed grin and handed her the tumbler. "Try that."

She took a sip and was hit quickly with the taste of alcohol. "Whoa."

"Too strong?"

"Well ..." She took another sip, slightly longer than the first. Warmth spread through her stomach and her throat twinged. "Not *too* strong, but I definitely can't drink this as quickly as I did the first one."

"No reason to pound it down anyway. What shall we do now?" She tapped a finger to her chin in classic Daphne style. "Oh! Let's go put the sheets on your bed and admire your room all put together. You'll need somewhere to crash if the alkie does you in."

Rachel laughed. "What, don't think I'll be able to handle it?"

"Well ... I didn't say that. I'll bet you have a stomach of steel after all those years of milk and coffee."

They tossed more verbal jabs as they unpacked the sheets from Rachel's suitcase. Her tumbler was drained in three minutes, and not long after Rachel noticed she had started to feel strange.

"Hey." She turned her head from left to right. "When I do this, it's like the world isn't keeping up with my eyes." She turned again and her vision blurred along for a second before snapping into place.

Daphne giggled. "You look like you're watching a tennis match in slow-motion."

"I … hey now." Her mouth was working in slow motion too, it seemed. "You gave me a lot of vvvodka."

"Wow." Daphne's tone was one of wonder. "It's really getting to you. Your stomach isn't made of steel at all. Do you feel sick?"

"Sick? No. Not sick. Just … slow."

"Well, that's good." She gave Rachel's knee a pat. "You'll build up a tolerance—don't worry."

Rachel let out an accidental snort, which sent her into a fit of giggles, which sent Daphne into a similar state.

Still laughing, Daphne said, "Now. I still need dinner, so—"

"Wait—you had two drinks on an empty stomach?"

"Yeah. So?"

"Wow. *You* have a stomach of steel."

"And buns, too, but not for the same reason."

It took Rachel a minute to process the joke, but when she did her laughter shook the bed.

"I'm going to make a sandwich. Want anything?"

"No. You wouldn't believe how much pizza I ate tonight."

Daphne left for the kitchen. Rachel stared at the ceiling as it seemed to slowly rotate, and after a while her stomach felt like it was rotating too. Fifteen minutes later she was, as Daphne put it, making her first sacrifice to the porcelain gods.

"Don't worry—it gets easier," Daphne assured her as she trudged back to her bed. Her words weren't the comfort she probably meant them to be.

CHAPTER 12

July brought Rachel to the end of her first month in Chicago. The oppressive heat drove customers into All Together Now in record numbers, even with the majority of the university population missing for the summer. Her paychecks were hard-earned, and her time off—what little of it she got—was too sweet to be squandered in her stuffy apartment that lacked air-conditioning. She poked around Chicago's tourist attractions (when they offered climate control) and visited the other independent coffee shops in the city. In a fit of creativity she painted all her consignment store furniture a deep plum and splurged on a new bedspread to replace her old one. She even played around with the idea of tutoring in an attempt to put her degree to use.

But most of her free time was spent with Jack, who took it upon himself to educate her in the city's pizza tradition and make sure she was never without entertainment on the afternoons and evenings they were both off work. One of their first outings was to the Billy Goat Tavern, where Jack had to explain both the Chicago Cubs' "Curse of the Billy Goat" and the *Saturday Night Live* skit that was inspired by the tavern's cheeseburger-hawking cooks. "I can't believe you've never seen *SNL,"* he said while they finished off their chips.

"I don't watch a lot of television. And it's on at eleven-thirty in California; I was never up that late."

"Not a night owl, hm?"

"Not unless something has me really engaged, no. And I'm a wreck the next day if I don't get eight hours."

"I'll have to remember that." He wrote with his finger in an invisible notebook and muttered, "No late-night dates on work nights."

Another date took them to a Second City improv show. "To continue your introduction to Chicago's contribution to popular culture," Jack said. "Jim Belushi, Bill Murray, Mike Myers—they all got their start there. You *do* know who they are, right?"

Rachel socked him on the arm. "I'm not that uncultured."

"Oh good." He wiped his brow in relief. "So you've seen *Blues Brothers*, right? And *Wayne's World*?"

She bit her lip and gave him a sheepish look.

Jack groaned. "You *are* that uncultured. That's our next date. You bring the popcorn, I'll bring the movies."

She did, and it was her first time visiting his apartment, which he shared with two grad students named Stefan and Dale. "Dude, I didn't know you had a girlfriend," Stefan said when he happened on them in the kitchen salting the popcorn.

"Oh, I'm not his girlfriend," Rachel said, then froze. She wasn't, right? She glanced at Jack. He winked.

"What does that mean?" she asked Daphne about the awkward interaction later that evening.

Daphne laughed as she mixed Rachel's first Harvey Wallbanger. "You didn't ask him?"

"I was embarrassed. I didn't know what to ask."

"How about, 'So, what exactly *are* we, anyway?'"

"That would have been good. I didn't think of that." She tasted the drink and wrinkled her nose.

"Too strong?"

"No, I'm just not a huge fan of orange juice."

Daphne laughed. "So tell me—do you want to be Jack's girlfriend? You sure spend a lot of time with him."

Rachel took another sip and shrugged. "I don't know. I like him, obviously. I think I'm just nervous about jumping into another relationship."

"Do you like him enough to want to date him for years and years? Because if you don't, then he's perfect for your rebound relationship."

"But we're together at work nearly every day. How ugly will it be when we break up?"

Daphne waved her hand dismissively. "Totally depends on why you break up. If he dumps you—well, then I'll kill him, and you won't have to worry about it." She grinned, and Rachel rolled her eyes. "Look, breakups don't have to be bad. If it's mutual it won't be a big deal. And if he does dump you, you can be adult about it and show him you're not going to pine after him—which may very well bring him crawling back. Guys are suckers for a woman who so obviously doesn't care when she gets dumped. And if you want to dump him—well, yes, that might be tricky, but if you do it right then there should be no hard feelings."

She put the cap back on the Galliano and put the juice back in the fridge as she talked. "The key is not to overanalyze, especially when you're in a rebound relationship. If you keep it light, then he'll keep it light." She raised her glass. "Here's to living in the moment!"

Living in the moment. Rachel couldn't remember a time when she didn't extrapolate out the consequences of her actions. It was difficult to live in the moment when you were so busy analyzing the effects. And why? Because she had been so concerned about how her behavior would reflect on her family, her church, her faith. It wasn't her own reputation she'd been worried about, it was everyone else's. But now?

No one was watching her here but Daphne. There were no fellow congregants to run into at the mall or the movie theater who might disapprove of what they saw her buying or watching, who might think less of Karen and Owen's parenting. Her coworkers weren't judging her God by the way she interacted with them and snarky customers. To everyone here she was just Rachel, the new girl from California.

"Earth to Rachel," Daphne said in a sing-song voice. "What's going on in that head?"

Rachel sat up straighter. "I think it's finally sinking in that I'm totally starting over here. I can be whoever I want and no one will know any different—except for you."

"Who do you want to be?"

Rachel let out a laugh. "Honestly, I don't know. I've been 'the Christian' for so long, I can't even think of what else to be."

"Then just pick something you've always wanted to try. Get your Illinois teaching credential. Or go with the coffee thing. Or pick nothing, just see what life brings your way."

Rachel nodded. "You're right. You're absolutely right." She bit her lip. "But what if I totally flop at whatever it is I try to become?"

"Then you can be someone else. Identities aren't concrete."

That took a minute to sink in. The idea that God had made her for a specific reason and with a specific role in the kingdom had been the foundation of her identity for as long as she could remember. Who she was hadn't been up to her; it had been created for her and handed down from on high. To be in charge of her destiny had its appeal, but it was scary, too. And what was the point, the end goal, if everyone was just doing their own thing for their own gain? What was the purpose of a life lived for itself?

It was one of the few aspects of her new life she didn't like, and as she finished her drink and mixed another, she found herself longing for someone to just tell her who she was.

Because she was really starting to wonder.

Rachel was pulled from sleep by the persistent ring of her cell phone. She groped for it on her nightstand as she struggled to sit up. "Hello?"

"Rachel?"

Her eyes opened as the unexpected voice of her mother brought her fully awake. "Mom. Hi."

"I woke you—I'm sorry."

"No. I mean, yes, but it's all right." *Why didn't I look before I answered?*

"I went as long as I could without calling. We don't have to talk long, I just … needed to know you were still okay."

"Yeah, um, I'm fine. Daphne's got a nice place, I work at a coffee place down the street … it's all good."

"I'm glad, honey. Really, I am. Just knowing you're okay makes me feel so much better."

Guilt bubbled up. *Why didn't I just call her once to let her know I was all right? Of course she was worried.* "I'm sorry, Mom." She thought back to the fight they'd had before she'd left. "About everything."

"Water under the bridge, sweetheart."

Rachel didn't really want to talk, but she couldn't bring herself to cut the conversation short, either. "So … how are things?"

"They're all right, although …"

"What?"

"Well, your father." Rachel's stomach clenched. "He's in Nebraska, at a hospital there. He crashed badly—not a car accident crash, I mean mentally. Emotionally."

This was more than Rachel wanted to know. "You know, I think I liked it better when I had no idea any of this was going on."

"I know, honey. I'm sorry."

She felt her temper rising the more she dwelled on it. "I mean, what am I supposed to do about it? What do I do with that information? Am I supposed to go visit him or something? Send him a card?"

"No, Rachel—there are no expectations on you when it comes to all of this."

"Then why tell me anything? Now I get to sit and worry that my dad might be some mental patient wacko and that I might be next."

"Wait—first you're mad at us for not telling you about all this, and now you're mad when I finally do? You need to make up your mind." Her mother's tone belied her exasperation.

"At this point, unless there's something I can actually do to fix the situation, I don't want to know the details. What good does it do me?"

"All right then, I won't tell you anything else." The line was silent for a moment before her mother added, "So tell me about Chicago."

Rachel shrugged. She didn't really feel like letting her mother into her life right now. She was enjoying the autonomy. "It's … I don't know. It's a city, it's big, it's hot. We're near the University of Chicago, so there are a lot of younger people in the neighborhood. Everyone's friendly. Daphne and I are having fun as roommates. The job is good, I like my boss and the people I work with. Yeah … everything's fine."

"That's good, that's good. Glad to hear it."

Rachel opened her mouth to end the conversation, but missed her opportunity as her mom spoke again. "Well, the legal separation is in place, and as soon as your father is, um, back in town, I'll start moving on with the divorce. Claire came over the other day and helped me box up his things. Grandma and Grandpa Westing are coming to get it all on Monday. I already feel so much better—"

"Stop." Anger had built with every word her mother had spoken. "I don't want to hear about it. I don't want to hear about how my family is falling apart, all right?"

There was a beat of silence. "I—I just thought you should know where things stand."

"Fine, then tell me you're separated, don't tell me how thrilled you are about it."

"All right. Okay. I'm used to telling you about my life, but I can understand that you might not want to hear about it right now." Her mother's voice held a note of wounded pride, and Rachel couldn't help feeling badly about it.

"It's not that I don't want to—oh, never mind. Look, I should go, I have to work soon."

"All right then. Oh—I'm going to put a check in the mail for you—for winter clothes."

"It's July, Mom. The high yesterday was ninety-two."

"I know, I know, but you know how far ahead of the season they bring things out these days."

"Thanks, Mom. But … I know you probably have lots of expenses right now. And I'm okay. I have a job, remember?"

"I know, but you also have a whole new wardrobe to build."

Rachel finally recognized the olive branch being extended and felt bad giving her mother a hard time about it. "Okay, Mom. Thanks. Send the check." Her alarm clock began to buzz, making her jump. "Okay, Mom. I gotta go."

"Take care of yourself, Rachel. Don't forget I'm still here for you, if you need anything at all, okay?"

"Okay, okay." She sighed. "Thanks."

"You're welcome. I love you."

"Love you too." She winced at the words as she hung up, hating how false they felt in her mouth. Not that she didn't love her mother, but her mother wasn't who she used to be anymore. Did she love the woman who was kicking her husband to the curb and gushing about how good it felt?

Her heart ached the more she thought about the conversation. Truthfully she missed her mom, the woman to whom she'd spent her life telling every secret and triumph and fear. Now so much was new in her life that she could have filled an hour with description. But she didn't feel right telling this newly unfamiliar person all the intimate details.

Rachel dragged herself to the shower, depressed. *What a way to start the day.* But knowing she'd be seeing Jack soon started to lift the fog.

I didn't even tell her I'm seeing someone.

She sighed. Nope, she was still depressed.

On the afternoon of July 3, Rachel and Jack went to the Taste of Chicago, the city's annual food and music festival in Grant Park. Shuffling along through the crowd of thousands, they traded food likes and dislikes and discovered they'd both rather stick to the safer Italian and American cuisines and skip the more adventurous foreign fare.

"See, I would have expected you to be all into sushi and Mediterranean and … I don't know … weird stuff."

Rachel laughed. "Why?"

"Because you're from California. I thought all Californians ate weird food. I mean, look at their pizza."

"I can see why folks might think that. But isn't that like thinking all Chicagoans are in the mob and can trace their family roots to the Capones?"

"Who said we couldn't?" He wagged his eyebrows. "Remind me to call Machine-Gun Jack after we're done so I can have him check the shipment of moonshine."

Jack steered Rachel to the classic Chicago vendors—Vienna Beef hot dogs, Lou Malnati's for another take on Chicago-style pizza, potato chips from Harry Caray's, and Eli's Cheesecake for dessert. They ate as they walked from one booth to another, dodging the knots of fellow eaters and eventually making their way to the Petrillo Music Shell to listen to the orchestra while they waited for the fireworks to begin.

They found a spot on the grass and sat. Jack set down his beer on a level patch of ground and leaned back on his elbows. Rachel remained upright and held her iced coffee to protect herself. She was oddly nervous. Of all the times they'd been out together, this one most felt like a real date. And she still didn't know if she could call him her boyfriend.

They sat in silence for a while, people-watching and listening to the music. After a while, Jack drew a deep breath and Rachel steeled herself for what she suspected might be coming.

"So I get this sneaking suspicion you're not comfortable with me."

It wasn't what she expected. "What? Why?"

He grinned, which set her a bit at ease. At least he wasn't mad. "Well, we've gone out about ten times, and not once have you let me kiss you."

An anxious giggle bubbled from her stomach. "*Let* you kiss me? You didn't wait for permission the first time."

She melted a bit when she saw the embarrassment in his face. "*Touché*," he said. "But that was different. And I've already admitted it wasn't the most chivalrous thing to do. The thing is, a guy doesn't have to make a move to be able to tell if a girl is going to let him. And what's more, you haven't tried to kiss me, either. Now, I'm guessing that we wouldn't have had a second date, much less a tenth one, if you didn't think there was a spark. And since we *have* already kissed, kissing again shouldn't really be that big a deal. So that leads me to believe that you're interested, but not entirely comfortable. Am I right?"

Rachel hung her head, then nodded. "But it's not you," she said as she forced herself to look him in the eyes.

Jack looked at his watch. "Fireworks don't start for an hour. That's plenty of time for you to tell me what has you so spooked."

Rachel bit her lip. Embarrassment made the words stick in her throat. She took a sip of her coffee and heaved a deep breath. "Okay. Well, for starters … remember how I told you I'd been engaged back in California?"

Jack snapped his fingers. "I knew it. Your fiancé screwed you over, didn't he?"

Rachel laughed. "An interesting metaphor, given the situation. He cheated on me, with my roommate. Not just once, either—for a few months."

"Unbelievable. I'm sorry, Rachel." Jack shook his head. "So that's why you moved?"

"Well … one of the reasons, yes."

"There's more? What else did he do?"

"It wasn't all about him." Rachel took another drink from her coffee and debated whether or not to explain it all. Sharing all this personal information didn't feel like the right thing to do if she was going to "keep things light" like Daphne had suggested. Though what good was any relationship if you didn't know a person well?

Wasn't being known by someone the whole point of relationships in the first place? Even casual ones?

Rachel rubbed her forehead and frowned. "Okay, here goes … my parents are getting a divorce because my dad is bipolar and went off the deep end. And a good friend of mine ended up in rehab for a drug problem that she hid from everyone for over a year. So that, plus what happened with Patrick, is why I moved. Everyone close to me, except for Daphne, turned out to be someone else, in one way or another. I felt completely betrayed. And the whole foundation of my life was rocked—I couldn't get over it and move on with all of them right there, you know? So Daphne offered for me to come live with her." She shrugged and gave him a small smile. "So there's the long reason for why I'm gun-shy. It's not you. It's what I'm still processing and trying to get past."

Jack drained his beer and crushed the plastic cup. "That's messed up. Not you," he said quickly. "Your whole situation. I don't blame you for leaving the state. And I definitely don't blame you for wanting to go slow."

Relief flooded her. "I'm so glad you understand." She leaned back, bracing herself on an outstretched arm and chuckling. "You have no idea how—"

Her words were muffled by a kiss that first stopped her heart and then sent it beating double-time. It was brief, and low on the intensity scale compared to their first, but it did the trick. When it stopped, she sat up straight and stared at him in shock.

"Yeah, I know you said you wanted to go slow, and we will," he said, looking chagrined. "But I figured if there was anyone who needed a good kiss, it was you."

She opened her mouth to speak, but the words in her head weren't queuing up into anything intelligible. She sipped her coffee and tried again. "Um, wow. Thank you?"

He laughed. "I think that's what you said the first time. Anyway, you're welcome. There's more where that came from, but I promise not to spring any of them on you again. You take all the time you need."

"Okay." She let out a nervous chuckle, flustered and unsure what to say or do next. "I'm going to go … um … find a bathroom. I'll be right back." She jumped up and forced herself to walk at a casual pace. *What now?* She found a cluster of portable bathrooms and got in the longest line to buy herself more time. She needed to think.

But when she tried to think, she realized her mind felt made up already. There was no denying his kisses were electric—or that she liked them. More than liked them. She wanted more of them, and not just because of how intense they were—but because it gave her hope that decent men could like her. She wasn't destined to be alone forever. She didn't only attract losers. She had a shot at a normal relationship.

By the time she returned to their patch of grass, the sky was nearly black. Jack overacted a gesture of relief. "You're back! I was worried I'd scared you off. Honestly, I promise not to do it again."

Rachel sat beside him, leaving little room between them. "In general, I would appreciate that you keep your promises. But that one …" She gave him a slow smile that she hoped conveyed permission. "That one I'll be happy to see you break."

Rachel had gone to the Taste of Chicago as a single woman, but she returned home as a girlfriend. She couldn't wipe the silly grin from her face, despite how her cheeks ached. She had little recollection of the fireworks—her memory was too concerned with the various kisses she had given and received beneath the light show. The confidence and relief she felt knowing that a good guy like Jack was interested in her did much to soothe the raw wounds on her heart. She'd floated to bed where she stared at the ceiling for far too long, reliving the evening and fantasizing about the future.

Daphne was a squealing mess over breakfast the next morning when Rachel told her the news. "So romantic!"

Rachel laughed. "Not really."

"Well, the kiss itself might not have been romantic, but the gesture, the sentiment … I love it. I'm so happy for you."

Rachel poured the Venezuelan Mérida into her mug and debated her next statement before making it. "I have a question for you. And don't read too much into it—I'm just curious and nosy." It wasn't entirely true, but she knew Daphne wouldn't mind.

Daphne raised her eyebrows. "My life is an open book for you, *mon amie*."

"When did you first have sex?"

"Hm." She smirked slightly. "Prom, senior year."

Rachel choked back her mouthful of coffee. "High school? And you never told me?"

"I was afraid of what you'd think."

"Oh. Yeah." Guilt rose in her stomach. "So, let's see, you went with Rob Panner, right?"

"Yeah, well …" She took a sip and waved her hand in a vague way. "I went to the dance with Rob. But I actually slept with Justin Fellows."

"What? Who was his date?"

"Tracie Gardner."

"Did she ever find out?"

"No, she was so blitzed she passed out in their room, like, half-way through the dance."

Rachel shook her head. "I can't believe I didn't know this." She rubbed her forehead and took another sip of her coffee. "Okay, well, that's all ancient history, doesn't apply to this conversation anyway." She sat up a little straighter. "Okay, so the next question is: Were you glad you did it?"

This time the answer didn't come so quickly. Daphne thought for a moment, swirling her spoon through her cereal, then said, "Well, I was glad I'd gotten it over with and knew what all the fuss was about, you know? I wasn't glad I'd let Justin be the first one, because he really didn't know what he was doing, and it wasn't all that great. But at least the mystique was gone. I knew the mechanics, I knew what to expect, so the next time I did it I knew what to do differently to make it better. So … yeah, I wish I'd picked someone a little more experienced so my memory of my first time wasn't quite so 'blah,' but it's not like it ruined the act for me forever."

At least the mystique was gone? Rachel thought that was supposed to be one of the great things about sex—the mystery, the intimacy, the secret two people shared of each other's most vulnerable spaces.

"So you're considering it with Jack, is that it?"

"Good grief, no." Rachel squirmed in her seat. "Well … honestly, I don't know."

"Well, don't do it if you don't want to, but if you're all wrapped up in the hang-ups from your upbringing then it might do you good to break out of them."

"I don't know … it seems like an awfully extreme way to 'break out of them.' From a purely health-conscious standpoint—"

"Oh, of course, you have to be safe about it. Condoms, tests, all that."

"How do you know if the guy is telling the truth about being clean? What can you do—ask to see the blood-test results?"

Daphne shrugged as she took another swig. "Not much you can do. That's why you have to be vigilant about your own health. I can take you to the clinic I go to; you would just go in every once in a while to make sure you're clean."

Rachel felt a headache coming on. "Yeah. I'm just gonna wait."

Daphne stood and slid her bowl into the sink. "Well, just in case you ever find yourself needing one—there's a box of condoms in my top dresser drawer. Feel free to take a couple for your purse or something. You never know when you might find yourself more than willing to change your mind."

Later that week Rachel used the Make-Out Can for the first time. She felt even more embarrassed putting it in the window than she had on the evenings she'd come home and seen it placed there by Daphne. But

Jack didn't give her long to ponder the appropriateness of it. They ate the dinner they'd prepared after their shift and then put in a movie that they didn't watch. To feel someone's arms around her again, someone's mouth on hers—and with a lot more interest and passion than Patrick had even shown—gave her ego a much-needed boost.

They came up for air when Daphne's footsteps could be heard on the stairs outside. "I should go anyway," Jack said as they broke apart. "I'm working the morning shift tomorrow."

Rachel sighed. "If you insist. I'll—"

Daphne opened the door, and the look on her face told Rachel all was not well. She took Jack's hand and led him to the door, offering Daphne a sympathetic look. Daphne just walked by them in silence and disappeared into her bedroom.

"I'm second shift tomorrow, so I'll see you then." They exchanged one more kiss, then Rachel closed the door and took the can out of the window before checking in on her friend.

She tapped a timid knock on the door and heard a faint, "Come in." Daphne was face down on the bed with a box of tissues beside her. Rachel sat next to her and waited for Daphne to speak.

"I hate men."

"I'm sorry."

"Really hate them."

"What happened?"

A few sniffles later, Daphne hauled herself upright. "He broke up with me."

"Oh, Daphne. I'm so sorry. What happened? I thought it was going so well."

Daphne blew her nose and rearranged herself against the mound of pillows at the head of the bed. "So did I. And it was! But I told Courtney, one of my friends—heh, 'friends'—at work about us, thinking I could trust her, and she blabbed to someone who blabbed to Paul's superior. So she called him on it today and he said that no, we weren't dating, that we'd gone out a couple times but nothing ever came of it." She dabbed the tissue to her cheek. "So I was all relieved and touched, thinking that he'd lied to protect us, right? But then after work he told me it wasn't worth the risk. His job is more important to him than me." Her face screwed up as the tears began to flow again. She leaned her face against her knees and sobbed.

Rachel had never seen Daphne lose it, especially over a guy. Not knowing what to say, she gave Daphne a pat on the back and said, "Don't move. I'll be right back." She slid off the bed and went to the kitchen, then pulled two glasses off the shelf and dumped in some ice. Rachel didn't know many drinks, but she knew at least one. Unsure of the measurements, since Daphne tended to simply slosh in rough approximations, she poured half a glass of Coke into each glass and then added her estimate of a shot's worth of vodka.

"Drown your sorrows, *ma chéri*e," Rachel said as she handed a glass to Daphne.

Daphne gave her a small smile and took a sip. "Not bad. Well done." She took another long sip, then settled back against the pillows again. "What really sucks," she said, staring into the ice cubes, "is that I thought this might be it."

"I didn't realize how into him you were. I thought it was just a 'for the fun of it' relationship."

"I know. I played it off like that because I didn't want to jinx it. And we hadn't been together that long. But I really thought we clicked. He was mature, he had a real job—he was a *man*, you know? Not a guy, a man." Tears welled in her eyes again. "I … I actually thought he might love me."

Rachel set down her drink and wrapped her arms around Daphne's slumped shoulders. "You know I understand, Daph. And it's awful. I'm so sorry."

After a few more minutes of crying, she sat up and began mopping her face again. "I'm such an idiot. It's my own fault."

Rachel wasn't about to agree aloud, even though she'd tried to warn her about dating her boss. "No, don't let him off the hook like that. If he felt that way then he shouldn't have waited until he got caught before he ended it. He used you and misled you with his affection. It's not your fault."

Daphne nodded as she crumpled and unraveled her tissue. "You're right. You're absolutely right. He is a cretin. I am the victim here." She downed the rest of her vodka and Coke and made a face. "You may have to keep reminding me of that, though."

Rachel smiled and gave her another hug. "I will gladly be your broken record."

Daphne gasped. "And I have to go to work tomorrow! I have to see him! And everyone knows!"

Rachel pulled a tissue from the box and handed it to Daphne as her tears began again. She was at a loss. Daphne was the one who was supposed to have the answers for situations like this.

"I know!" Rachel hopped off the bed and made a dash for the door, accidentally knocking a stack of papers from Daphne's desk as she did so. "Oh shoot, I'm sorry."

"That's all right—just throw them back up there. I'll organize them later."

Rachel hastily gathered the papers and tried to shuffle them into a neater pile. She was about to set them down when the top sheet caught her eye.

"Do me a favor and grab me some Tylenol from the bathroom on your way back? I'm getting a crying headache."

"No problem." Rachel tore her eyes from the paper and stopped into the bathroom before going to her own room. She untethered her laptop from its power cord and returned to Daphne's side. "Let's see what the online bible says."

"Um … I thought you—"

"No, not that Bible." Rachel typed for a few seconds, then showed her the screen where the *Cosmopolitan* website was loading. "This bible."

That elicited the laugh she was hoping for. They created a fake profile, then surfed to the Breaking Up message board. A quick scan of the subject lines revealed Daphne was not alone in her relationship-with-a-coworker-gone-wrong dilemma. They spent the next hour reading about other women's misery and criticizing them for their stupidity—they were, on the whole, so much more brainless than Daphne had been.

Rachel finally bowed out in the wee hours of the morning, leaving her laptop with Daphne so she could continue to peruse the message boards for comfort and commiseration. But once she was in bed, sleep eluded her. It wasn't just Daphne's boy troubles that kept her awake, or the memorable kisses she had given and received that day. What also bothered her was the credit card statement with a red "second notice" stamp on it that had fallen from Daphne's desk.

CHAPTER 13

Summer rounded into Rachel's first Midwestern fall, and she fell in love with autumn for the first time. She invested in a form-fitting sweater that both Daphne and Jack called "sexy," along with some skinny jeans. She kicked herself for discouraging that check from her mother— dressing fashionably was a lot more expensive than her old approach to clothing had been.

Her step had a runway bounce to it when she walked to All Together Now, her feet crunching through colorful leaves that settled in drifts along the sidewalk. The sound reminded her of potato chips—she almost always had a craving by the time she got to work. Daphne said the sound made her think of hot chocolate and scarves.

Daphne had quit her job at Nordstrom's two weeks after the breakup debacle and took a temp position doing data entry. She didn't have to describe the job much for Rachel to know it was not at all enjoyable or rewarding, but there was no drama and, more important, no cute boys to get involved with.

Rachel could tell that Daphne was depressed, though, because she spent most of her free time holed up in her room, or "just out." Rachel felt a little guilty because she was so wrapped up with Jack, but Daphne didn't seem to mind her frequent absence, and when they both happened to be home they always made a small party out of it—cocktails, eclectic dinners thrown together from whatever they found in the fridge, and either a movie afterward or music pumped up to a level just north of respectable so they could dance in the living room. Sometimes they'd go out to a club, where Daphne typically hooked up with someone and spent most of the time lip-locked in a corner. Rachel hated being left alone but wasn't about to hook up with someone when she was already dating Jack—though she did enjoy flirting and being flirted with, and that was almost as rewarding.

Twice Rachel received phone calls on her cell from her father, neither of which she answered. She asked Daphne to listen to the voice-mails because she was just too afraid of what he had to say.

"Afraid—why?" Daphne had asked. "Like, afraid it'll be abusive or mean?"

"No, afraid it'll make me feel bad for him. I don't want to pity him. I don't want to feel sympathy for him. I'm angry at him. I don't want anything to do with him. And I like it that way."

Daphne raised her eyebrows. "Now those are words I never thought I'd hear Rachel Westing say."

"Well, Rachel Westing never thought she'd utter them, either."

"Holding on to hate isn't healthy, you know."

Rachel rolled her eyes. "I won't hate him forever—don't worry. There's even a small possibility I'll grow up and accept reality someday. I just don't want to right now. I need to stay angry, because letting down my guard means opening myself up to all the doubts and worries that coming out here was a mistake."

Daphne looked hurt. "You regret moving in with me?"

"No! No, not at all. I just mean—everything. Leaving California to go anywhere, not just coming here. Daring to live by my own devices and not by faith. I can't explain how radical it is for me. I have to fight doubt all the time."

Daphne let out a snort. "Oh please. Your life is golden right now, Rachel. Awesome job, awesome boyfriend, money in the bank, roof over your head, and a friend who supports you through everything. I'd kill to be you. How could you possibly doubt this was the right decision?"

Rachel was surprised at Daphne's tone. She hadn't guessed her to be the tough-love type, but Rachel had to admit she had a point. "You're right, you're totally right, as usual. Sorry if I sounded ungrateful."

Daphne gave an impatient wave. "No, no, you didn't sound ungrateful. You just need to let go of the past and move on, that's all." She held up the phone. "Still want me to listen?"

Rachel bit her lip, then took the phone back. "No, I have a better idea." She flipped it open and dialed her voice-mail, then erased the message before it had a chance to begin. "How's that for letting go and moving on?"

"Good. Dinner?"

"Yes. Do we have any potato chips?"

Rachel had been working at the café for almost three months, but so far Ruby Jean still hadn't mentioned the manager position. Rachel looked forward to the extra money and benefits, but a part of her was glad it hadn't happened yet. Once it did, she knew things with Jack would get dicey. They'd work it out somehow—they were both mature adults, neither of them had the tendency toward drama that Daphne did—surely they could navigate a romantic relationship without problems. But Rachel couldn't help worrying that it might all blow up in her face.

She was pondering this issue while stacking supplies in the stock room when Jack came in to get more cups. "Penny for your thoughts."

She grinned. "You know, you'd think inflation would have that up to at least a buck by now."

"Haha—don't change the subject."

She waved a hand. "Nothing important."

He pulled a box from the storage shelf. "So hey, Wednesday is your birthday, isn't it?"

Rachel smiled. "Yes, the big—oh wait, a lady never reveals her age, what was I thinking?"

Jack laughed. "Don't worry, your secret's safe with me. Anyway, you don't have plans, right?"

Rachel thought as she capped her pen and motioned toward the front of the store. "Like, with Daphne? No."

"Good. Keep it that way. We're going out."

She laughed, pulling a cup from the stack Jack set up and pouring herself coffee. "Gee, that'll be a big change from the usual."

Jack's eyes gleamed. "Oh no, I'm talking high-class going out."

"Oh really?" She wagged her eyebrows. "Shall I dust off my dancing shoes?"

He laughed. "No, but heels would be appropriate."

"Sounds like a fun night," Leah said, chiming in from the sandwich station.

"Doesn't it though?" Rachel flashed a girly smile at her. She was still wary of Leah, but thought it prudent to be friendly since she'd eventually be her boss.

Though if she were honest, Rachel would have to admit Leah hadn't been who she'd expected her to be. She had anticipated the full-blown assault, but nearly every remark about church or God had been fitting for the conversation, rather than a pointed attempt to engage Rachel on the topic. The one conversation she'd steered that way had been natural, and Jack had actually seemed interested in what Leah had to say, which freaked Rachel out a little. The last thing she wanted was for him to convert.

"Rachel?" Ruby Jean peeked her head out from around the corner. "Would you be able to stick around tonight after your shift?"

"Sure, R. J." Ruby Jean nodded and disappeared back into the office.

"What's that about, you think?" Jack asked quietly as Leah moved away to serve a customer.

Rachel shrugged, though her heart began to beat a little faster. "I don't know—but I know what I hope it's about."

The afternoon was slow, and Rachel was antsy. She tried not to let herself get too excited, in case the promotion was not the reason for Ruby Jean's request. But if that wasn't it, then what was it? They hadn't interacted a ton, but nothing they'd discussed in the past gave Rachel the impression that she might be in trouble.

In fact, if anything, she felt like she and Ruby Jean were on the same wavelength. Be it her experience with the business side of running a coffee shop or simply a matter of like personalities, Rachel felt a connection with the quick-witted, extroverted woman. She reminded

Rachel a little bit of Barbara: wise, easy to talk to, outgoing and friendly with everyone. The way she'd reacted to Rachel's comment about her mission trip to Brazil had made her nervous—she'd expected to discover she was a Christian too. But she'd never said anything else to indicate she was, and Rachel hadn't noticed any telltale signs—no Jesus fish on her car bumper, no cross around her neck.

By the end of her shift Rachel had decided that, depending on how things went at the meeting and with her promotion—whenever it came—she was going to work at connecting more with Ruby Jean. With Barbara and her mother both out of her life, at least for now, she could see the wisdom in having an older woman to go to for advice. She loved Daphne dearly, but even with religious differences no longer an issue, she knew Daphne wasn't always the wisest person.

Rachel removed her apron when her shift was over and gave Jack a little wink before going back to the office.

Ruby Jean waved Rachel in, then glanced at the clock above the door. "Do you have dinner plans tonight?"

"No, why?"

"I've been in this office all day and I need to get out. Let's go next door; my treat."

Rachel followed Ruby Jean out to the front, where she told Cole to come get her if disaster struck. They entered the sandwich shop just east of All Together Now and laughed after they both inhaled and sighed in unison at the scent of fresh bread. "Next best thing to coffee," Ruby Jean said.

"You've got that right."

They ordered their sandwiches and sat at a corner table. Rachel felt like she was on a first date and almost wished she could calm her nerves with a drink. Instead, she gave herself a quick pep talk to help herself remember how much she deserved the promotion.

"I'm glad we could get together tonight," Ruby Jean said. "I've been wanting to hear how you're settling in to your new home, how things are going for you, that sort of thing. I'm sorry it's taken me so long to check in." She chuckled. "Part of the reason why I need another manager. I have no time to catch up on things like that."

Rachel opened her bag of chips and smiled, trying not to show that she noticed Ruby Jean's hint. "Things are going pretty well. I love the weather right now—the cool air, the leaves all so beautiful. I mean, it's not like I haven't seen a tree's leaves change color before, but those kinds of trees are sparse in Southern California. And it gets cool there, too, but …" She felt her cheeks reddening when she realized she was rambling. "Anyway, it's very different here, despite how alike they sound."

Ruby Jean chuckled. "Always wanted to go to California. Maybe once I have some solid leadership at the café I'll be able to take a vacation. I haven't done that since I started the place."

"When was that?"

"Six years ago now. One of those things I'd always wanted to do but was too afraid to try. I spent ten years managing someone else's place and dreaming about how I'd do my own, and then one day I realized I was forty and tired of letting someone else be in charge of my career. So I turned in my two-week notice, drafted a business plan, and here I am."

"Wow. That's fantastic." They talked about the café's inception and Ruby Jean's obsession with the Beatles as they ate until Ruby

Jean changed the direction of the conversation. “So what else do you do besides make coffee and make out with Jack?”

Rachel nearly choked. She swallowed down a chunk of sandwich and took a long pull on her soda. “So I guess you know we’re dating.”

“I may be single, but I’m not ignorant of relationships. All it takes is five minutes in the same room with you two—you don’t even have to talk to each other.”

Rachel pressed a hand to her forehead, distressed. “Is it all right? I mean, I didn’t think—”

“It’s fine, it’s fine. Don’t panic.” Ruby Jean’s smile was kind. “What was I getting at is, what do you like to do outside of work?”

“Not much, actually. I had a lot on my plate back in California, but I haven’t gotten involved with anything here yet.” She grinned. “Means I have a lot of time to devote to, say, my job, if it were to suddenly get more complex.”

Ruby Jean let out a laugh. “Is that right?” She set down her sandwich and sat straighter in her seat. Suddenly nervous, Rachel did the same.

“Well, now that you’ve mentioned it … I’ve been impressed with your performance, Rachel. You’re professional, your customer service is excellent, and I don’t think I’ve ever seen someone churn out so many orders in such a short amount of time. You’re a machine.”

“Thank you.”

“So tell me your thoughts on the shop, the staff—whatever. Anything and everything.”

“Sure. Well, I love the shop. I love the vibe, how relaxed it is, the loyal clientele—I like how the people who come back every day or week or whatever feel like they have a relationship with us, and us with them. I know people's names, and if they work or are a student or both. I enjoy being connected with them like that. And I think I get along well with the staff, for the most part. Not everyone is the kind of person I'd hang out with as a friend, but I feel like we work well together."

Ruby Jean nodded. "That's what I've observed as well. Everyone knows I want another manager, and I think they all know you're up for the job, whether you've talked about it or not. None of them either want it or are qualified, but they know you've got a lot of experience, and I have a feeling they've been viewing you as a possible superior since you started. How do you think you and Cole do together?"

"I think we do well. I haven't worked with him as much since he does so much office and back room stuff, but I think our communication is good, and from what I've observed, our managerial styles are similar."

"I'm glad to hear that." Ruby Jean finished her drink and sat back from the table. "Well, Rachel, if you're ready, I'd like to promote you to manager, starting next week. Are you up for it?"

Rachel tried not to smile like an idiot. "Absolutely."

"Great. There's one thing we need to discuss first, however."

Her stomach sank. "Jack?"

"Yes. But here's the thing: Some people know how to set aside their personal lives and maintain professionalism, and some don't. I don't like to make blanket rules unless I have to, and so far I have never had a problem with any of my employees dating each other. However, I've never had a manager date a subordinate, either. So, point being, I'm not going to make you choose between Jack and the job. I am, however, going to ask you to convince me that you can be objective while in the café, and not let your romantic life interfere with how you interact with Jack at work."

Anxiety and relief roiled like oil and water in her head. "Convince you? Like, right now?"

Ruby Jean chuckled. "No, I mean over the next, say, month or so. Show me he's just another employee when the two of you are both on the clock. You can go make out at home once you're done for the day for all I care, but when you're working I need to be able to trust you to manage him the same way you would any other staff member."

Rachel nodded along with Ruby Jean's words, desperate to show her willingness to comply. "I will. Absolutely. Thank you so much."

"You're welcome, Rachel. Let's finish up here and go back to the office to get the paperwork straightened out and figure out your new schedule."

Jack caught Rachel's eyes when they came back into the café, and she gave him a quick thumbs-up. He had a celebratory mocha awaiting her when she came out on her way home. "Congrats, babe!" he said before planting a kiss on her cheek. "Oh wait—am I going to get fired for kissing you now?"

She smacked his arm. "We'll discuss that later. You're on second shift tomorrow, right?"

"Yeah."

"Me too. Let's do breakfast in the morning and we can talk about it." They set a time and place and said good-bye. Then Rachel headed home, a large envelope of benefits package information clutched to her chest, eager to tell Daphne the news.

Daphne wasn't home when she got there, however, and she didn't stumble in until nearly one. The door slammed and Rachel awoke, confused by the noise. She got up and saw Daphne weaving through the living room on unsteady feet. "You're just getting in now? Wow, what have you been up to?"

Daphne stopped, one hand on the wall. "Courtney called. We went out."

"Courtney—the one who snitched on you and Paul?"

"What else was I supposed to do, wait around for you?"

"I'm sorry, Daph," she said, surprised at the snappy tone in her friend's voice. "Ruby Jean asked me to stay so we could talk. I got the promotion."

Daphne snorted. "Well, whoopee." She stumbled past Rachel into her room and slammed the door, alcohol fumes eddying behind her.

Rachel stared at the door, shocked and hurt. She reached out to knock, but then lowered her hand and retreated to her own room. She had breakfast with Jack in the morning—she needed to get her sleep. Though the smell of Daphne's drink gave Rachel an idea. Back in the kitchen, she poured herself a small glass of Baileys. A nightcap was the perfect way to celebrate.

"A toast to my girlfriend the manager," Jack said, holding his orange juice aloft.

"Here, here." Rachel clinked her coffee cup to his glass and took a sip. "Though I'm still just a plain old barista until Monday."

"Oh, a 'plain old barista,' eh? Is that all we are to you management types?"

Rachel smirked and kicked him lightly under the table. “Watch it there, mister, or I’ll write you up for insubordination.”

“Yeah, yeah, whatever. So—tell me everything. You got a raise, right? You’re gonna have to start treating me to dinner now, instead of the other way around.”

“Ha, that’s a great way to a girl’s heart.”

”I’m just saying. You’re the one with the big important job. I’m just a plain old barista.”

Rachel rolled her eyes. “Yes, I got a small raise. My schedule’s going to change too.” She listed her shifts, knowing he’d be as disappointed as she was with the arrangement.

Jack frowned. “Looks like we only have two nights free together.”

“At least we work together almost every day. It’s not like we’ll never see each other.”

“True. Maybe you can work a little magic on the schedule and coordinate our time off.” He wagged his eyebrows and wiggled his fingers as though trying to put a hex on the syrup pitcher.

Rachel chuckled, though unease began to creep into her chest. “Ruby Jean did tell me she was concerned about something, though. I’m sort of in a probationary period for the next month. She wants to make sure I don’t show you any preferential treatment.”

Jack gave a slow nod. “Ah.” He sat back, the fun gone from his face. “So you told her.”

“No—she said it was obvious.”

He gave her a small smile. “Well, I guess I can see why.”

She smiled back and shrugged. “At least she’s not making me choose between you or the job.”

“Which one would you have picked?”

Rachel froze.

"No, never mind—that was an unfair question." Jack waved away the words, then brushed invisible crumbs from the tabletop. "You told her she had nothing to worry about, right? That you wouldn't treat me any differently?"

"Of course. Because I wouldn't. Not that I wouldn't want to—"

"Of course, but it wouldn't be fair."

"Right."

"Right."

Jack nodded, but the look on his face made Rachel uncertain. "We can make this work, right?"

"Absolutely."

"So what are you thinking that's making you look like you're mad at me?"

"I—what? No, I'm not mad." He wiped a hand down his face and sighed. "Would you totally hate me if I admitted I'm a little jealous?"

"Hate you? Of course not! But jealous of what, the job? I thought you didn't want to be a manager."

"I don't. But I don't want to be a plain old barista for the next ten years, either. I'm closer to thirty than I am to twenty and I'm not totally thrilled that my lot in life is coffee, you know? It's one thing if you're moving up, like you are, and you've got actual responsibilities and a job description that's longer than one sentence. Plus you really love coffee—so it suits you. But me …" He shook his head and sipped his juice, then sighed. "I'm sorry, Rach. We're supposed to be celebrating you. Sorry for dumping my junk like that."

Their food came and Rachel was rescued from having to respond. The conversation turned to their meals and then meandered through a myriad of topics, never returning to the coffee shop or Rachel's new position. When they finished they walked together to the café for their shift. Jack gave her a kiss before they were in sight of the café, then said, "I really am happy for you, Rach. Good for you. And I promise not to cause you any trouble."

She kissed him back and thanked him, then spent the rest of the day wondering what Jack really wanted to do with his life. And if she wanted to be a part of it.

Daphne was there when Rachel came home that night. Daphne gave her a sheepish smile when she walked in. "Hey."

"Hey."

"How are you?"

Rachel chuckled. "I'm okay. How are you?"

"Sober—which I wasn't last night. But I wasn't blitzed enough to forget how I acted. I'm sorry."

Rachel relaxed. "Thanks. I forgive you."

"And congratulations on the promotion. That's really awesome. Although, you know you're crazy, right?"

Rachel laughed. "What? Why?"

Daphne rolled her eyes. "Have you learned nothing from my woes?"

"Oh. Well … I guess this just seems different to me."

"Yeah, right."

"No, really!" Rachel sat down in the armchair and ticked the reasons off on her fingers. "First of all, my boss already knows about it. Second of all, Jack and I talked it over, so we're both cool with it. We know the boundaries we have to have. And third, *I* am the superior, so I'm the one with the power. Do you really see me misusing it?"

Daphne shook her head. "You're playing with fire, *mon amie.*"

Rachel was annoyed. Why did Daphne have to be such a wet blanket? She tried to keep her tone casual when she said, "You're just being overprotective because you got burned. And I appreciate it, truly. I'm thankful I have a friend who has my back. But I honestly do not think there's going to be a problem."

Daphne raised her hands in surrender. "You're a big girl—you know what you're doing. I promise not to say anything else about it."

Rachel brightened. "So Jack's taking me out Wednesday for my birthday. He won't tell me where we're going, but he said to get dressed up and that 'heels would be appropriate.'"

Daphne wagged her eyebrows. "Sounds fancy."

"Yeah. What do you think, the wrap dress from Vegas?"

"Sure. Use my silver shoes, though. Those will snazz it up a bit."

"Oh cool, thanks."

"Do you guys have plans on Saturday?"

"My new schedule starts next week, so I'm opening, but I'll be home by one. "

"I was thinking we could go out for your birthday. I have an idea for a gift that I think you'll really like. But it might take some getting used to."

Rachel laughed. "Well, that's intriguing. But really, you don't have to give me anything. You've given me so much already, I know money's tight for you—"

"Oh, it's totally nothing, don't worry about it. And money is fine. Really."

Rachel wondered if she should admit she'd seen Daphne's credit card statement. She didn't want to embarrass her, but she also didn't want her spending more money on Rachel when she couldn't afford to. *She's an adult. Maybe she's already paid it off—who knows?*

"Okay, well … thanks. So, what's the gift?"

"Promise you won't write it off as soon as I say it. Think about it, okay?"

Rachel rolled her eyes. "Okay, okay. Tell me already!"

Daphne scrunched up her face in excitement, then whispered, "A tattoo!"

Rachel burst out laughing. "What? You've got to be kidding!"

"No, I'm totally not! I'm gonna get one, too. We'll do them together."

Rachel sat back in her seat. "Hm," she said. "So what are you going to get?"

Daphne rubbed her hands together. "Okay, so, I'm thinking either some kind of flower or a laurel wreath—to go with my name, from the Greek myth."

Rachel nodded thoughtfully. "That's cool."

"What about you?"

"I don't know. I've never even considered getting a tattoo."

"Never?"

"Nope."

"Wow. Well, let's see. You could get … a Bible with a big X through it."

She couldn't help laughing. "Um, no, I think not."

"Okay, fair enough. Um … how about a cup of coffee?" They both laughed at that. "Or … what does Rachel mean, do you know?"

Rachel rolled her eyes. "It's Hebrew, and it means 'lamb.'"

Daphne giggled. "Okay, so … a cute little sheep, maybe."

"Yeah, I'm going to get a sheep permanently inked on my … Where are you getting yours?"

"Lower back, I think."

Rachel shuddered. "Honestly, the thought of it makes me queasy."

Daphne patted Rachel's knees. "Well, it's totally up to you. But there's no need to over think it. Cute, dainty women like yourself get them done all the time—if they can do it, so can you."

"Well, I'll definitely come support you when you do yours. I just have to ponder it for a while. Is that cool?"

"Yes, of course." Daphne clapped her hands. "A toast! To tattoos and promotions."

Rachel smiled. "Thanks, Daph."

"Well, I'm happy for you. But I still think you're crazy."

Rachel raced home Wednesday evening to be ready in time for her night out with Jack. She was combing out her hair when Daphne poked her head into her room. "Need any help getting even more gorgeous than you already are?"

Rachel chuckled. "You know me. I'll take any help I can get."

"Silly girl, you should have told me sooner. Hold on." She disappeared for a moment, then came in with her makeup bag. "Take a seat and let me beautify."

Rachel did as she was told. "I wonder where we're going."

"He hasn't given you any hints at all?"

"Nope."

She sighed. "I have to admit I am so jealous."

"I'm sorry. I hope I'm not rubbing it in your face."

"Not at all. And I'm happy to help make you look like a million bucks." Daphne gave Rachel's cheek a final dab of foundation. "I just wish I had a reason to do the same to myself."

She worked in silence for a few minutes, then stood back. "Okay, check it out."

Rachel stood to look in the mirror. "Wow. You're really good at this. You should get a job at one of those makeup counters at Macy's."

Daphne wrinkled her nose. "Nah. It's more fun doing it with friends." She rummaged in her makeup bag and pulled out a small gold jar. "Okay, this may sound a little out there, but it's awesome."

"What is it?"

"Body glitter."

Rachel laughed. "I'll look like a disco ball!"

"You'll look swanky and glam, I promise."

"I don't have time for another shower if I don't."

"Trust me, *ma petite chou.*"

Rachel sighed. "If Jack thinks it looks stupid I'm totally blaming you."

Daphne unscrewed the lid with a smile. "Men are simple creatures. When something is shiny their attention is completely captivated."

When Jack arrived, Rachel noted with pleasure that Daphne once again knew what she was talking about. "Whoa" was the first thing out of his mouth. "You look amazing, babe."

"Doesn't she though?" Daphne sidled out of her room, and Rachel's jaw dropped. In the less than ten spare minutes they'd had before Jack was to arrive, Daphne had given herself a turbo makeover and dressed as though she were heading to the clubs.

"Hey, Daphne." Jack said with a smile. Rachel couldn't help noticing his eyes lingering a little longer than necessary on Daphne's svelte frame. "You going out tonight too?"

Daphne sniffed and gave her shoulders a little shrug as though shaking off a chill. "I'm meeting some friends for drinks in a little while."

"You are?" Rachel raised a brow. "You didn't mention that before."

"I didn't think you'd be interested."

The silence in the room lasted a beat too long. Rachel finally broke it. "Well, have fun then. Shall we go, Jack?"

"Sure." He gave Daphne a final nod and smile, then held the door open for Rachel. "This way, gorgeous. Have fun, Daphne."

"You too, love."

Rachel fumed all the way to the car. Once safely inside, she let out a huff of anger. "I cannot believe her."

"What?"

"She was coming on to you!"

Jack chuckled. "I doubt it."

"I don't. 'Love'? Give me a break."

"But I'm dating you; why would she do that?"

"Because she's jealous."

Jack tipped his head, conceding. "I understand that. I am a rather desirable bachelor...." He winked and she couldn't help smiling.

"But you have nothing to worry about because I don't believe in two-timing on my girlfriends."

Rachel laughed. "Thanks. I'm very glad to hear it, believe me."

"Ah, right." He gave her a squeeze. "Had your fill of that kind of thing, eh?"

"Oh yes."

"I'll make a note of her interest in the event that we break up, though."

Rachel smacked him on the arm. "Enough of this, before *I* start getting jealous."

Jack laughed. "A compliment I don't take lightly. Thank you."

He navigated through the Chicago rush-hour traffic with his usual driving gusto, and by the time they pulled into the parking lot Rachel's hand was cramped from clutching the door handle. He led her through the parking lot to Ballo, a brick-façade restaurant that screamed "hip" before you even saw the interior. Funky 70s hits streamed out onto the sidewalk when the door opened. Rachel quickly saw Ballo was a couple steps up from the average Italian eatery. The partylike atmosphere coupled with the décor and music gave it a nightclub feel. It was by far the nicest restaurant she'd ever been in. Jack scored yet another handful of points in her mind—the best Patrick had ever done was The Cheesecake Factory for their one-year anniversary. He scored some more when they sat down. "We're doing the whole shebang, okay? Appetizers, desserts, wine, everything. So go crazy."

They did just that. The food kept coming, huge portions and all delicious. Rachel deferred to Jack on what wine to order, and he deferred to the waiter, who brought a chardonnay to accompany their main courses. Jack had tipped off the waiter about Rachel's birthday when she was in the washroom, and her dessert came with candles. By the time they left, Rachel felt overfed and tipsy, but was charged by the music and atmosphere and the fact that she'd been treated to such a wonderful evening.

They wandered back to the car, Rachel hanging on to Jack's arm to keep her balance in the potholed lot and letting her thoughts swim in her mind. She felt daring, a little reckless, uninhibited by the almost three glasses of wine she'd imbibed. When they reached the car she let herself pin him to the door with a kiss. "This was the best birthday present ever."

"Glad I could wow you," Jack said, his arms encircling her waist. "You deserve it. It's a little sad that a nice dinner out is the best present you've ever gotten, though. What kind of loser was your fiancé, anyway?"

Rachel laughed, though she was embarrassed. She'd settled with Patrick, but she hadn't even realized it. Why not? Had she really been that blinded by his charm? She felt foolish when she realized how much better Jack treated her when they weren't even engaged.

"Uh-oh—I shouldn't have brought him up. I can see it in your eyes. Why did I bring up bad thoughts on such a good night?"

"No, no, it's okay." Rachel leaned her face against Jack's chest and inhaled the scent of his aftershave. It brought back the memory of Vegas. "I just feel dumb for having stayed with him for so long. I didn't realize at the time how lame he was."

He shrugged and rested his chin on her head. "Well, it could have ended a lot worse. You could have figured that out five years into your marriage."

She shuddered. "I can't believe I could have been married to him by now!" She stood back, swaying slightly. "What a colossal mistake that would have been. Whew! And a lucky thing for you, too," she added, her eyes twinkling. "To think you could have missed out on me."

Jack laughed. "Thinking pretty highly of yourself now, aren't you?"

"Well, you know ..." He laughed, and she fell against him and kissed him again, and a rush of desire made her whole body tingle. Jack's response told her he was experiencing the same thing. She broke away just enough to ask, "So … what now?"

"Your place or mine?"

"Mine." She wanted to be home, where she felt safe, if things started getting serious. She had a feeling Jack wouldn't just drop her off with a quick kiss on the landing. In fact, she hoped he wouldn't.

Their conversation was sparse on the drive back, but the sexual tension was palpable. Rachel's palms were damp with anticipation. She thought of all the times she and Patrick had made out and then broken apart, breathless and flushed, one of them saying, "No, we need to wait." She was tired of waiting. She was tired of closing off a part of her mind and body to something that was so natural. And frankly, she was starting to think waiting wasn't the big deal everyone made it out to be. How unromantic would it be on your honeymoon to be fumbling around, completely clueless, embarrassed at being seen naked for the first time? Didn't it make more sense to get a little practice in first, so The Big Night was memorable for something other than awkwardness?

The closer to home they got, the surer she was that tonight would be the night. Jack would certainly be game, and chances were he had some experience, so at least one of them knew what to do. Better to get the first time over and done with than to hold on to it as though it made her a better person.

Jack parked on the street and opened her door. She slid out of the seat and wrapped her arm through his, allowing him to lead her to the stairs. Once they were inside, she closed the door, dropped her purse to the floor, and wrapped her arms around his neck, more than ready to get things going.

When she began to tug at his shirt, his hands grabbed hers and he broke the kiss. "Whoa, whoa—what are you doing?"

She tried unsuccessfully to suppress a giggle. "I thought it would be obvious without me spelling it out." She leaned in to kiss him again, but he edged back and she nearly fell over.

"Rachel, no."

Her breath caught in her chest. "What?"

"I'm pretty sure you're drunk. And we've only been together a few months—"

"You're shooting me down?" Her voice squeaked. Embarrassment squeezed her chest.

"I'm not rejecting you, I'm just … I don't think we should tonight, that's all."

She let out an ungracious snort, ire rising to defend her pride against searing humiliation. "What are you, a teenage girl? Don't tell me you're a virgin or something."

"What if I am?"

Her jaw dropped. "You are?"

His chin raised a fraction of an inch. "I didn't think you were the type to mock me for it."

"I—I'm not. I'm just surprised."

His eyes narrowed. "You thought I was some player or something?"

"No, I—I mean, you were so forward in Vegas—"

"Kissing is one thing. But not every guy lives for sex, you know."

"I know, I just didn't think you, um …"

"I what?"

She rubbed a hand over her forehead, flustered. "Jack, I'm sorry, I swear I wasn't trying to suggest—"

"Look, Rachel." The firm set of his mouth told her she wasn't being let off the hook. "Don't think I don't know that you're a virgin too. And I don't appreciate being taken advantage of. If you're with me just so you can sow your wild oats or something, then we need to end this. I'm not just looking for a good time, okay?"

She sniffed and blinked back the tears of shame that stung her eyes. "That's not my intent."

"Good." He took a deep breath. "I'm gonna go. I open tomorrow, so I need to get to bed."

"Okay."

He kissed her forehead. "See you at lunch."

"Okay."

He let himself out and she was left alone in the living room, stomach roiling, soul aching, and hating herself for the first time in her life.

CHAPTER 14

Fortified with her strongest brew—which had been further fortified with a shot of Baileys—Rachel entered the café the next afternoon determined not to avoid Jack out of the embarrassment she still felt. He greeted her as though nothing had happened, but that didn't make her feel any better. She'd rather have it all out than dance around it or pretend nothing had happened.

She'd wondered a few times what she'd do in this situation, but she'd always assumed she'd be the one standing up for her virtue. She hadn't expected to be the offending party. All of her "what if" musings had ended with her graciously extending forgiveness—not hoping it would be extended to her. She grew itchy with anticipation as the first hour of her shift ticked away without them having enough time to talk one on one.

Finally a lull in business and a chance meeting in the supply room gave her an opportunity. "I'm so sorry," she blurted before he had a chance to say anything. "I'm so embarrassed and I really hope you don't think any less of me. I didn't mean—"

"Rach, calm down, seriously." Jack hugged her and kissed the top of her head. "It's all right. Forgiven and forgotten." He pulled back and studied her. "But I did mean what I said. I'm not in this just to waste some time and have some mindless fun. I'm serious about you. I enjoy being with you, and I really care about you. If the feeling isn't mutual—"

"It is," she said quickly, unwilling to give herself any time to think about the words she was saying. When she was sure no one was watching, she gave him a quick but solid kiss to back up her statement. "And thank you for not holding it against me."

She saw relief written in his features. "I'm glad to hear we're on the same page. And you're welcome." The sound of the front door chimes distracted them both, and Jack pulled away. "Customers call. If we don't have another chance to really talk today, have a good shift, all right? Call me when you get home."

"You too, and I will." She watched him duck back into the front room and take a cup from Leah to start a drink before she went back to hunting for the box of plastic utensils she'd been looking for while her mind churned.

She felt unstable in her friendship with Daphne and her relationship with Jack, and the insecurity colored every minute of her day. Daphne was like Jekyll and Hyde lately. One minute she was snarky and bordering on cruel. The next she was sympathetic and sisterly. Rather than laugh or tease her when Rachel told her about Jack shooting her down, Daphne had been consoling and encouraging, albeit a little distracted. "He doesn't know what he's missing, poor guy. I doubt he'll hold out for much longer."

Rachel had waited for a biting comment, but it never came. She was even more surprised when Daphne apologized to her. "I know I've been a jerk lately, and I'm sorry."

"Oh—that's all right."

"No, no, it's not. I just want you to know that I know it's

been weird. I'm dealing with some of my own junk right now, and I've been taking it out on you. You're safe, you know? I know you'll always love me and want to be my friend even if I suck."

"Of course I will," she had said with a hug. Then, puzzled, she'd pulled away. "So what junk is this?"

"Oh, just … stuff." She'd waved a hand and wandered into the kitchen, changing the subject to something else entirely. Rachel had been unable to steer things back before having to go to bed and had fallen asleep wondering why Daphne was being so secretive.

And Jack—If only he hadn't put her on the spot like that, asking about her intentions in their relationship. How was she supposed to be honest when the truth would have required a serious discussion? He should know better than to ask heavy questions like that in passing. But now he believed she was in this relationship all the way, even when her intentions had never been more than to just ease back into the dating game.

She found the box she needed but procrastinated bringing it out to the front. She needed to think for a minute. *Would it really be so bad to devote myself to this relationship and try to make it work long term? Jack's a wonderful guy. Why wouldn't I want to be with him for … years? Or even decades?* It wasn't Jack that made her gun-shy, she realized. It was commitment. She wasn't ready to take that chance again. But what was she going to do about Jack, then?

She felt a headache coming on. She hauled the box up front and poured herself a cup of the day's special blend and gave Jack her warmest smile when they made eye contact. *It'll all work out*, she assured herself as she refilled the utensil holders on the counter. And if it didn't, well, it couldn't possibly be worse than the mess she'd left behind in California.

Rachel had just finished balancing the register when Ruby Jean came out. "Looks like you're about done," Ruby Jean said as she glanced at the clock.

Rachel was embarrassed at how long past her shift her closing duties were taking her. "Just about, yeah. Leah already left. I'm just slow tonight."

"Something on your mind?"

She laughed. "How did you know?"

"Just a lucky guess. Want to talk about it?"

Rachel shut the register drawer. "I don't even know where to start."

"Want to go for a drink, vent a bit? I know when I'm hashing something out in my head it helps to get it out—sort of releases it all from the confines of my skull and gives it all a fresh perspective."

"Absolutely, I'm up for it. Where to?"

Ruby Jean led her down the street to a small pub where the artistic bottles behind the bar made Rachel's head buzz with anticipation. They took their seats at a booth next to the window, and Ruby Jean bought the first round. Rachel savored her first taste of Skyy Blue, then chased it with two more sips before posing a question to Ruby Jean. "Are you at all religious, R. J.?"

"Oh, absolutely." Ruby Jean set her beer on a coaster and settled into her seat. "I believe we're all spiritual beings, not just physical.

And the way people explore and express their spirituality fascinates me. My mom was a sociologist, and she studied a lot of religions in her work. I think I picked up a lot of my interest from her. My dad was a philosopher, not a big believer in organized religion, and he always seemed to me like he was fighting something—always arguing with my mom about metaphysics and all sorts of other things I never really understood." She shrugged and took a sip of her drink. "It always seemed to me that he was fighting the idea of spirituality, and I think that's why he never seemed calm." Her gaze locked onto Rachel's. "How about you? You mentioned a mission trip at your interview—I take it you're a Christian?"

Rachel sighed. "I think that's part of my problem right now. I always was, from as far back as I can remember. But now … I don't know where I stand with God, or even on the concept. Honestly, I can't even wrap my head around a world where there's no God or Jesus. It makes no sense to me. But I left behind a lot of crap in California that really made me question him for the first time."

"I'm sorry to hear that." Ruby Jean's expression was one of sympathy, and Rachel was encouraged to have found someone to talk to. Daphne had no interest in spirituality, and Jack was neither here nor there on the idea. She needed input from someone who could relate to her connection to the spiritual world. "I wasn't raised with any one belief system," Ruby Jean continued, "but I can imagine it must be very difficult to have that rug pulled out from under you."

"Yes, exactly. Though I can't imagine what it's like to grow up without any kind of spiritual guidance, the way you did. It formed the foundation of my whole world. Some of my earliest memories are of church activities."

"Oh, I wasn't raised without spiritual guidance—just without a focus on one specific religion." Ruby Jean spun a coaster on the table as she talked. "My mom was a great believer in the spiritual world, even though my father wasn't. She taught me about all the religions she studied, and our house's decor was a mishmash of religious stuff—Chinese Buddhist prayer rugs on the walls, statues of Hindu gods on the mantel, and Egyptian goddess statues on the bookshelf, prayer wheels and crosses and altars, you name it."

"So did any of it actually affect your everyday life? Or was it just a bunch of stuff around your house?"

"Oh, no, it definitely sank in. I grew up celebrating all sorts of holidays and trying to connect to the spiritual world through all kinds of rituals—meditation, yoga, chanting, praying the rosary."

"The rosary? Seriously?"

"Oh sure. It's very calming, very soothing. You know how sometimes you need to relax, but you're too keyed up to just let everything go and quiet your mind? Praying the rosary was great for that. The repetition was relaxing, almost hypnotizing, and the words gave my mind something to focus on, and the beads gave my hands something to do. Great all around, and a lot healthier than, say, lighting up a cigarette."

"But did you believe any of the words? I don't know much about the rosary, but I know that Mary and Jesus and the Lord's Prayer all figure into it. Did you—*do* you—believe in Jesus and Mary and the words of the Lord's Prayer?"

"Well, yes and no. I believe Jesus existed, and he certainly must have had a mother if he did. And given the kind of man Jesus was, his mother must have been pretty amazing, too. You could do a lot worse than to look to them for inspiration."

"But the Lord's Prayer—'Our Father, who is in heaven' and all that—those are specifically Christian beliefs. How could you pray those words and also pray to Buddha and Zeus or whoever?"

Ruby Jean laughed. "Well, Buddha wasn't a god, so people don't pray to him. But I know what you're saying." She thought a minute. "I guess I just see it all as different manifestations of the same entity, or life force, or whatever. Christians call it the Trinity, Muslims call it Allah, Native Americans call it the Great Spirit, and so on. They're all just synonyms, really. And depending on my mood, or the situation at hand, one spiritual tradition feels more 'right' and makes more sense to turn to than the others."

Rachel opened her mouth to ask another question and found she had nothing to say. She knew the responses she would normally give—she was well armed with Christian apologetics. But now, without solid faith in Christianity, she had no basis from which to evaluate Ruby Jean's beliefs. She filled the gap with another long sip from her drink. "I'm stumped, honestly," she said finally.

Ruby Jean chuckled. "It's a very different approach than what you were raised with; I'm not surprised it doesn't make sense to you. But, for the most part, it's worked for me for forty years. I just feel people get very insular and exclusionary when they start making absolute assertions about their beliefs. It makes more sense to me to acknowledge that we're all looking for the divine and have our own way of connecting with it." She cocked her head, staring Rachel down. "So, if I may ask—since moving to Chicago, what has your spiritual life been like?"

It didn't take long for Rachel to come up with an answer. "I haven't had one. I haven't prayed, I haven't gone to church, I haven't read my Bible. Not a day went by in California when I didn't do at least one of those things, if not all three. But since I've been here …" She shrugged. "Nothing."

"And have you noticed the absence of those things?"

The answer that came to her was a surprise. "You know, I think I have. I just haven't let myself think about it much. It's all too confusing. I mean, if those things were … I don't know … vital? True? Right? I don't know what word to use for them. But whatever it is, if they were that, then I guess I feel like things would have turned out differently. I wouldn't have been completely screwed over by the most important people in my life."

Ruby Jean rubbed her thumbs through the condensation on her glass. "In the Baha'i faith, suffering is believed to be either the consequence of your own actions or a test sent by God to perfect you. If you take the position of the victim, rather than the position of a student being challenged, then you can miss the lesson that suffering can teach you. Buddhism teaches that suffering is the result of desire, and that eradicating desire will eradicate suffering. Both Hinduism and Buddhism include doctrines of karma—the belief that 'what goes around comes around,' essentially."

Rachel frowned. "I'm confused. If you were me, which one would you look to in order to make sense of what had happened?"

Ruby Jean shrugged. "Depends on what had happened and what I felt needed to happen in order to make up for it or help me feel better."

"So … you don't have some hard-and-fast rule saying that you'll go to Buddhist beliefs when X happens, or Catholic beliefs when Y happens—you just go wherever you think feels right?"

Ruby Jean beamed at her, as though she'd just deciphered the spiritual Rosetta stone. "Exactly."

Rachel ruminated on this for a moment, trying to make herself think the same way Ruby Jean did. But all she kept coming back to was how illogical it all sounded. She didn't want to come off like some religious snob, but at the same time she couldn't shake the belief that the tenets of a religion should make logical sense. And to say all religions were true when so many of them directly contradicted each other just didn't fit that belief. "I guess it's hard for me to make sense of that. Hope that doesn't offend you…."

"No offense taken." Ruby Jean took another sip, then said, "I don't expect you to think my approach to spirituality makes sense. It goes completely against your upbringing. I get that, so you don't have to worry. But let me ask you this: You say you've missed all those things you used to do—praying, reading your Bible, going to church. But is your life—your everyday existence—any different without it? You may miss the ritual of it, but is there a gaping hole in your life where those things should be? Or has it been business as usual, minus the trappings of Christianity?"

Rachel knew the fact that she didn't want to answer the question spoke volumes. "I think," she said slowly, eyes focused on the amber bottle in Ruby Jean's hand, "I think it's just been business as usual." The truth of it became clear once she admitted it aloud. And it scared her.

But Ruby Jean seemed pleased. "Honesty with yourself is the first step in looking honestly at the world."

Rachel knew she meant it to be comforting. But in reality, it made her feel lost.

Rachel had no sooner walked in the door on Saturday afternoon when Daphne hustled her back out again to go to the north side for their tattoo date. "Let's go, baby, let's go!"

"Someone's excited."

"I know! Aren't you?"

"I'm nervous!"

"*Pauvre bébé*," Daphne cooed. "No fear now, it's just pain—and pain always ends eventually."

"Gee, that's comforting."

Rachel cast a sidelong glance at Daphne as she skittered along the sidewalk to the L station. "Have you been dipping into my coffee stash?"

Daphne laughed. "No, why?"

"You look like you're hopped up on some serious caffeine."

"Nope, just excited." She flashed a toothy grin at Rachel, then linked her arm through hers. "So what are you going to get—did you decide? I'm going for the laurel wreath."

Rachel shrugged. "All I came up with is a Celtic knot, but I'm not sold on it."

Daphne grabbed her arm. "I had an idea for you.... Wanna hear it?"

"Definitely."

"Something that symbolizes freedom. Like—the freedom you

have now to live your own life—freedom from the constraints you were living with, freedom from a totally crap relationship with Patrick, freedom to make your own decisions, your own way."

The idea resonated with Rachel, though not for the reasons Daphne apparently thought it would. "I like that. Though it would be more like 'freedom, please' than 'freedom, yes I have it.'" She smiled. "It's a great idea. What symbol could I use?"

Daphne bobbed her head from side to side as she thought. "I don't know."

Rachel laughed. "You're a lot of help."

"Oh! I know! We'll find a bookstore and see if we can find a Chinese dictionary, and you can get the Chinese calligraphy symbol for it!"

Rachel mulled this over as they waited for a stoplight to change. She liked the idea of the Chinese symbol—no one could look at it and know right away what it meant. It would be her little secret. Though, that meant constantly being asked what it meant—and did she want to have to explain it all the time?

But she definitely liked the idea of some kind of symbol, rather than just a random image like the Celtic knot idea had been. If she was going to get something permanently inked on her body, she at least wanted it to mean something. And freedom—well, wasn't that why she'd moved in the first place, just like Daphne had said?

Rachel nodded as they crossed the street. "I think a Chinese symbol could totally work. I'll do that." Daphne clapped. "Where should I get it?"

"Your wrist or your ankle—those would be my suggestions."

Her wrist seemed too exposed, but she liked the idea of having a constant reminder for the days when she was starting to doubt the wisdom of all this freedom. She'd been having a lot of those since her discussion with Ruby Jean. Plus, she could hide it with sleeves or a watch if she really wanted to. "Wrist it is."

They hopped the L and found seats in the back. Rachel tried not to think too much about the process that was awaiting her at DragonLady Tattoos, the parlor one of Daphne's friends had recommended. *It's just pain—it won't last forever,* she chanted to herself as the train slid along the rails. A mantra with all sorts of application these days, though she had a hard time imagining a day when the memories of her dad and Patrick and Barbara wouldn't hurt. *We'll just see if time really heals all wounds.* She turned to Daphne. "So tell me what—" Rachel frowned. Daphne's mouth was clenched shut and her jaw sliding back and forth as she stared out the window. "Oh my gosh, how can you do that? It makes my skin crawl."

Daphne clapped a hand over her mouth. "Sorry. Bad habit."

"I've never seen you do that."

"Yeah, I think it started when I quit my job."

Rachel nodded. "Nerves, maybe."

"Yeah, that's probably it."

"How is the job these days?"

Daphne sagged against the blue upholstery of the seat. "It sucks."

"I'm so sorry."

"I mean, it's a job, and it's better than being unemployed, but I swear I lose more brain cells every day I'm there."

"Have you been looking for anything else?"

"Not really. I should, I know."

"I'll help you if you want."

Daphne snorted. "Yeah, in all your free time."

Rachel frowned. "I'm sorry. I know I'm not around a lot. I really do feel bad about that—we finally get to live together, and I'm hardly ever home."

"It's all right." Daphne shrugged, fingernails raking up and down her arm, and turned her gaze to the window. "You've got a life. You shouldn't feel bad about that. I'm sorry I get so jealous sometimes." She smiled a quirky, lopsided grin. "I didn't think I'd ever be jealous of you for anything but your family."

"Ha, well, not much to be jealous of there anymore."

"They still love you, though."

Rachel's heart hurt. "Yeah, you're right."

"But seriously—I always felt so bad for you. All that church, all that clean living." Her eyes sparkled with the mischievous look Rachel had so often seen. "I always figured once I converted you to the dark side I'd be your mentor, and now here you are with the hot boyfriend and the totally cool job and no need for a best girlfriend anymore."

The snarky undertone that edged Daphne's words took Rachel by surprise. "What? Are you nuts? Of course I need you. You're my best friend—you always have been. Guys have never gotten between us before. Why would they now?"

"It's not just guys." Daphne's voice hinted at irritation. "You've taken to your new life so well. You didn't need help from me like I thought you would. And then, just when it seemed like we were finally on equal footing, my life blows up in my face, and I'm back to needing you again like I did when we were kids. I'm tired of being the needy one. I wanted you to need me for once."

"Oh, Daph." Rachel's heart ached. "I'm sorry if I've ever made you feel like I was better than you. I never thought that, and I never will. And believe me, I do need you. You're the only person in my life who knows me inside and out. And any success I've had since moving out here has only been because of your support. Who else would I go to for advice about Jack? I have no idea what I'm doing in that relationship, seriously!" She laughed and was happy to see Daphne's mouth pull into a small smile. "I'd be sunk without you, sister. Really."

Daphne leaned into Rachel for a brief moment, then sat up straight and rolled her head on her shoulders. "Okay, okay, okay, enough of this. Where are we, anyway? We need to change trains soon, I think."

The rest of their ride was uneventful, though Daphne's mood continued to sink. By the time they found a bookstore she looked downright depressed. "You okay?" Rachel asked as they entered the chain store's double doors.

"Yeah, yeah. Gonna go to the bathroom, though. I'll meet you at the Chinese dictionaries, okay?" She disappeared between the tall shelves, and Rachel was left to navigate the labyrinth alone.

Her thoughts were distracted as she hunted for the right section. The fact that Daphne felt the way she did gnawed at her. But other than trying to reassure her and being careful to spend more time at home, she didn't know what else to do. She remembered the statement she'd seen on Daphne's desk and wondered if part of Daphne's life "blowing up" in her face had to do with financial strain. She didn't want to bring it up, but she wanted to be able to help if she could.

She found the dictionaries, and then the symbol she wanted, before Daphne got back. She borrowed paper and a pen from a student hunkered down in the café and sketched out the calligraphy to bring to the parlor, then made her way to the bathroom just as Daphne was coming out.

"Sorry, long line." She nodded to the paper in Rachel's hand. "Found it?"

"Yeah, what do you think?"

"Love it, love it!" Daphne's mood seemed to have improved. "Okay, DragonLady, here we come."

They entered the shop and approached the counter near the front. A woman with more ink than Rachel had ever seen on one person was carefully drawing on tracing paper but stopped and looked up as they stepped closer.

"Hey ladies. You both getting tats today?"

"Yes," they answered together and traded smiles.

"Got pictures or you need sketches made?" Rachel put her paper on the glass counter and Daphne pulled a photocopied picture from her pocket. The woman asked them about sizing and where the images would be placed, then stood up straight and pulled down two more sheets of tracing paper. "Give me a minute to prep these, okay?"

They nodded and retreated to a bench in the waiting area, neither of them speaking, though Daphne's knee bounced rapidly as her eyes locked onto another customer sitting at one of the stations whose arm was being decorated with a twining vine. Rachel was glad to know that Daphne was more nervous than she was admitting. Rachel stared too until the sight of the needle made her ill and she had to look away. The drone of the tattoo in progress was harder to ignore.

Ten long minutes passed before the woman finished her job. "Okay, ladies. These are done." She looked over to the main part of the shop and hollered, "Mikey, you up?"

"Yeah, hold on." A young, skinny man with a shaved head appeared from behind a beaded curtain at the far end of the shop. The woman pointed to the station where he sat down. "One of you can go to Mikey's station; the other can go to mine. I'll be right over, just wanna finish this other sketch."

Rachel's nerves zinged as she wiped sweaty palms on her skirt and followed Daphne deeper into the shop. *No turning back now.* Daphne perched herself on the edge of the chair at Mikey's station and introduced herself when he reached out to shake her hand. In typical Daphne style she had him engaged in conversation before Rachel had even gotten herself comfortable on the chair at the woman's station. She watched with fascination as he began to prep Daphne's back, but ripped her gaze away when the woman approached.

"I'm Shaundra, by the way."

"Hi—I'm Rachel."

"Nice to meet you, Rachel." She sat on a wheelie stool and pulled herself over to a tray that contained a number of frightening looking objects. "This is your first tat?"

"Yeah."

Shaundra gave her a kind smile. "I kinda thought so." She set the tracing paper on the tray and pulled on a pair of rubber gloves. "So where we putting this?"

"My wrist."

"All righty, just rest your arm here. then." Rachel put her arm up on the armrest and took a deep breath.

"Nervous?"

"Yeah, just a little."

Shaundra chuckled as she shaved Rachel's wrist smooth, then rubbed a deodorant stick over the area. "This will make the transfer darker so I can see it better." She carefully laid the transfer paper against her skin and pressed it down, then peeled it away. "How does that look?"

"Hm, nice—maybe we can just leave it at that."

She laughed. "Having second thoughts?"

Rachel took another deep breath. "No, it's all good. Go for it."

Shaundra began to prep her instruments. "This is a small one; it really should take less than twenty minutes. Trust me, you'll be fine."

Her tone wasn't mocking or patronizing, and Rachel appreciated her understanding. "Thanks."

She shuffled various implements on the little table beside the chair, then said, "Okay, last piece of prep before we start. This is just petroleum jelly; I'm going to smear a little on the design so the needle moves more smoothly."

Rachel tried not to shudder from the cold of the jelly—or from the thought of the needle—as Shaundra's fingers gently applied the ointment. She closed her eyes and began to breathe slowly and deeply. *You can do this. You can so do this. Women give birth without pain meds all the time; you can withstand twenty minutes of a needle. Just keep breathing.*

"Okay, gonna start in a second here. It'll feel sort of like scratching on your skin, but a bit hot. Something like that, anyway. Just keep breathing. Holding your breath will just make it worse." The needle whirred to life, and Rachel clenched her teeth. "Okay, here we go."

A hot scratch. *Sure. Times twenty.* Rachel forced the air in and out through her nose and pushed her mind to concentrate on absolutely anything else but what was happening. She ran through lyrics of songs, even allowing herself to mentally sing through Christian tunes from CDs she'd chucked back in California—anything to keep her mind occupied.

"You're doing great—halfway done!" Shaundra's voice jarred Rachel from her concentration, and she realized the needle didn't hurt as much as it had in the beginning. Now it was just the idea of it that made her queasy. She turned her thoughts to herself dancing with Jack back in Vegas, then conjured the memory of her make-out session with him at the Taste of Chicago. She walked through each kiss, each fireworks explosion they'd managed to see, until suddenly the whirring stopped. "All right. You're done."

Rachel opened her eyes and let out a deep breath. The ink was dark and edged in an angry red. "Oh wow," she said, then let out a laugh. "I can't believe *I* just got a tattoo."

"Like it?"

"Yeah! Although it looks pretty nasty."

Shaundra nodded. "Yeah, it'll take a day or two to calm down. I'll bandage it up before you go and give you a list of aftercare instructions." She stood and walked to the back room, and Rachel gazed at her wrist with a dazed smile on her face. *Jack is going to love this.*

Beside her, Daphne called out, "You done?"

"Yeah, look." She went over to Daphne, who was leaning over the back of a chair while Mikey drew the laurel wreath on her back. The fingers of Daphne's hand were drumming on the chair. Rachel flashed her wrist in front of Daphne's slitted eyes. "Sweet."

“You hanging in there?”

“Yeah.” Her voice sounded strained, and Rachel had to go sit down at the thought of a needle on her own back—which seemed somehow worse than on her wrist. Shaundra came back and smeared ointment over Rachel’s tattoo and laid a bandage over it. “There you go,” she said, pulling off her gloves. “All done. Cash or charge?”

“Oh—I’m not sure. Daphne’s paying. Hold on.” Rachel went back over to Daphne. “You paying with cash or charge?”

“Charge. Go ahead and get my Visa out and have her run it.”

Rachel rifled through Daphne’s crammed wallet until she unearthed the silver card, then brought it up to the front counter. Shaundra ran it and Rachel went to sit in the waiting area. The thought of what she’d just done was making her knees a little weak.

After a few minutes Shaundra said, “Sorry, this card won’t go through. Got another one?”

Oh no. “Yeah, hold on a second.” She walked back to Daphne, but slowly, trying to decide if she should just pay it herself or ask Daphne for another card. She stopped halfway to Mikey’s station, then turned back and dug out her debit card from her own wallet. “Here, just put it on this. And Daphne’s too.” Shaundra ran the card and handed Rachel a pen. She signed the receipt, feeling sick.

Though the more she thought about it, the more confused she became. When was the last time she saw Daphne in a new outfit? Or saw her bring home anything other than groceries when she went out shopping?

It took another twenty minutes for Daphne’s design to be completed. They were halfway back to the L station when she slapped her forehead. “I never signed the credit card receipt!”

Rachel swallowed hard. "Oh—I'm … sure it's fine."

"How do you figure?" She gave Rachel a look, then frowned. "What aren't you telling me?" Daphne looked into Rachel's eyes, then punched her arm playfully. Rachel could tell she was trying to keep her tone light. "You idiot, did you pay? For your own birthday present? Did you pay mine, too?"

"Um … yeah."

"Why?"

"Well … your card wouldn't go through."

Daphne was silent for a minute, then unleashed a flurry of excuses. "My payment must have gotten lost in the mail. Or something. I wonder if this is because I just used it yesterday. You know how sometimes when you use a card a bunch they get all worried it's been stolen? I wonder if—"

"Daph, listen." Rachel decided it was time to clear the air. "I saw the statement on your desk last week. The one with 'final notice' stamped on it."

Daphne's eyes went dark. "Why were you snooping on my desk?"

"I—what? I wasn't. I was in your room, we were talking, it was sitting right there—"

"Well, it's not what you think, so don't get all excited."

"Excited? Look, you don't have to be embar—"

"I'm not, Rachel, I'm not. I'm fine; that statement was wrong." She stopped in the middle of the sidewalk and pulled her wallet out of her purse. When she opened it, Rachel was stunned to see how much money was stuffed into its folds. Daphne yanked some of it out and shoved it into Rachel's chest. "Here. Happy birthday." She swore under her breath and shook her head. "Some friend."

Rachel was rooted to the sidewalk. *What did I do?* "Daphne, you're totally overreacting."

"Whatever." She began walking faster, muttering under her breath, and Rachel decided not to try to keep up. She didn't know what else to say, and Daphne obviously wasn't in the mood to talk. She watched her friend disappear up the steps of the L, and fished out her own train token from her pocket. *Hope I remember how to get back home, because it looks like I'm on my own.*

CHAPTER 15

A week after Rachel got her tattoo, something else got under her skin.

She walked in from her shift to find her apartment in complete disarray. The sofa and armchair cushions were on the floor, the sofa itself pulled away from the wall. Kitchen cabinets and drawers stood open, an empty laundry basket lay upside down beside a scattered collection of clothes, and the sounds of general mess-making could be heard coming from elsewhere in the apartment.

"Daphne?"

The sounds stopped. Daphne appeared from Rachel's room, eyes narrowed. "I'm missing a hundred dollars."

"That sucks, but why would it be in my room?" Rachel brushed past Daphne and gasped. She had tossed Rachel's room as well. "Daphne! What are you doing?"

"You must have taken it—there's no other explanation."

Am I going crazy, or did my best friend just accuse me of theft? "You don't seriously think I'd take anything from you, do you?"

"How else did it disappear?"

"I don't know. But—I can't believe you'd blame me. What reason would I even have? I don't need your money. This is insane." She began heaving the mattress up onto the box spring, incredulous. "I can't believe this, Daphne. Unreal."

"That's what I was thinking. Why would my 'best friend' steal from me?"

Rachel slammed her hand onto the mattress. "I didn't! Stop saying that!"

"So what are you implying?"

"I'm *implying* that you obviously lost it. Don't blame me for your mistake, Daphne. It certainly wouldn't be the first time your messiness led to something getting lost."

"How dare you." Daphne's tone was menacing.

"How dare I what? Seriously, you're debating that you're messy? Your room looks like this on a good day. Why don't you clean instead of ripping the place apart? That would be more productive than trying to pin your problem on me."

Daphne shouted obscenities as she stormed out of the room and slammed her own bedroom door behind her. Rachel sniffed back tears as she went about setting her room to right, emotions tangled.

Who was Daphne anymore? Certainly not the person Rachel grew up with. Not even the person she went to Vegas with. How can someone change so much in less than six months? And why? Rachel had no answers, but one thing was clear: Home was becoming less and less friendly. This is not what she had in mind when she decided to move. But where on earth would she go if she wanted to leave?

It took her half an hour to return everything to its rightful place. Satisfied with her cleaning, she went to the kitchen for dinner, defenses up in case Daphne was still on the warpath.

The living room and kitchen were still a mess. Empty bottles were scattered everywhere. Why Daphne thought she'd find money in the recycling bin was beyond Rachel, but it did make Rachel notice how many bottles of vodka they'd gone through recently. For this, she couldn't entirely blame Daphne. Rachel really liked vodka Cokes.

Daphne's door was still closed. Too overwhelmed to tackle the living room, she tidied the kitchen instead, then began to pull dinner together. Normally she'd make dinner for both of them, but not tonight—Daphne would probably accuse her of poisoning it or something.

The ludicrous thought made her smile, and she doubled the spaghetti she'd pulled from the box, deciding she'd rather attempt a truce than propagate more wall building. Daphne didn't have to eat it if she didn't want to.

The pasta was just about ready when Daphne's bedroom door opened. Rachel steeled herself for another onslaught, but Daphne acted like nothing had happened. She simply walked into the living room and piled the cushions back into place.

Rachel stirred the sauce. "I made some spaghetti, if you're hungry," she said. "Would you like something to drink?"

Daphne said nothing.

Rachel felt her blood beginning to simmer. "All right," she said, trying to keep the edge from her voice. "I'll leave some here for you if you change your mind." She brought her own plate to the bar and sat down, though she no longer had an appetite.

She swirled pasta around on her plate for a minute, trying in vain to actually want a bite, then set down her fork. "Look, Daphne, I'm sorry if I hurt your feelings earlier when I made those comments about your room. I shouldn't have been so critical." *I shouldn't be apologizing, either, but if it cuts the tension and gets us past this, then fine.* She waited for Daphne to reciprocate, but she was met with more silence as Daphne continued to re-shelve books. Rachel didn't know whether to yell or cry. "Daphne, this is ridiculous," she finally said, voice cracking as tears stung her eyes. "Not just today, but the last three weeks—"

"Don't judge me!" Daphne yelled. "For the last twenty years that's all I've gotten from you. I'm sick of it. I don't know why I thought you'd change."

She stared open-mouthed as Daphne shoved books back onto the rickety bookshelf and continued to rant. "I can't believe what a mistake it was letting you come here. What was I thinking?"

Rachel finally found her voice, and she didn't restrain it. "Fine, then! If you're so miserable with me here, I'll leave. God knows I don't want to live with someone who can't stand to have me around." She left her uneaten dinner on the bar and retreated to her room, shocked at the words that had come out of her own mouth. It was an empty threat, but what if Daphne took her up on it and booted her out?

A few silent minutes passed before a knock came on the door. Rachel tensed. "What do you want?"

The door opened slowly. A concerned-looking Daphne walked in. "You wouldn't really leave, would you?"

Rachel felt cautiously optimistic. "I don't know. You're not giving me much of a reason to stay."

"Don't leave."

"Well, I—"

"Seriously, don't. I promise not to go through your stuff again."

“Thanks. That wasn’t my only concern, though.”

“Just promise me you won’t go.”

Rachel was confused. “Okay, okay. I won’t go.”

Daphne nodded silently and left. Rachel stared at the door. *No apology. No remorse, even. What is going on?* Rachel didn’t appreciate her one last longtime friend freaking out on her. She’d moved to Chicago to get away from insanity—she didn’t want to deal with it again.

She tiptoed to the door and peeked out. The coast was clear. She snuck out, into the kitchen, and grabbed a can of Coke and the vodka bottle from the pantry, then scooped a glass through the ice container in the freezer and made a mad dash back to the bedroom. These days coffee couldn’t hold a candle to the calming power of alcohol. And after an evening like this, calm was just the beginning of what Rachel was looking for.

Rachel didn’t see Daphne at all the next day. She left for work before Daphne was up, and the apartment was empty when she came home. Just as well—she didn’t know how to act around her anymore. She was relieved to be alone.

Jack came by after his shift to take her out for dinner. He frowned when he kissed her. “Have you been drinking?”

“I needed to unwind; I had a rough afternoon.” She told him what had happened with Daphne and how this was yet another odd event that had her questioning Daphne’s sanity. “It’s weird. I mean, all of it, not just ransacking my room and calling me a liar and a thief. The last few weeks she's been so different, and I don't know what to do."

Jack shook his head. "Seriously, Rach, I'd make good on that threat and move out. You seriously want to keep putting up with this?"

She remembered what Daphne had said to her the night Jack had turned down Rachel's advances. *You're safe.... I know you'll always love me and want to be my friend, even if I suck.* "We've been through so much together," Rachel said. "I would feel so bad if I left and then found out later that I could have helped her with … whatever it is that's going on."

"That's noble—but it's also borderline codependent." He wagged a finger at her. "You need boundaries."

She laughed. "What are you, an armchair psychologist?"

"My mom was a therapist before she started having kids. I have just enough knowledge to be mildly helpful to friends in need."

He brought her home just before midnight and didn't pout too much when she gently refused to let him come up with her. "I haven't slept well the last few nights," she said. "I really need to just get to bed."

"Okay, okay, I understand." He opened the door for her and kissed her good-night. "I hope it's a better night for you. See you tomorrow."

She climbed the stairs and waved good-bye as he flashed his brights in parting and drove away. Anxiety clenched her insides as she prepared herself for yet another confrontation.

She let herself in and felt the tension ease away when she saw Daphne asleep on the couch. She walked softly to the bar, draped her coat over one of the stools, and was about to make for her bedroom when she spotted something on the floor in front of the sofa.

The bottle of vodka she'd mixed drinks with the night before lay empty on frayed area rug.

Rachel frowned. A niggling fear made her tiptoe over and pick it up. *When I put that bottle back, it was half full.*

"Daphne?" She dropped to her knees and grabbed Daphne's shoulder. "Daphne, come on, wake up." She shook her, then again, harder. Her hands begin to tremble. "Daphne, come on!"

Not a sound, not a movement.

Rachel scrambled to her feet and grabbed for the landline mounted on the wall beside the bar. "My roommate," she gasped when the dispatcher asked what was wrong. "She drank half a bottle of vodka, and I can't wake her up." She answered the dispatcher's questions as she fumbled with shaking hands through her purse, looking for her cell phone. She hit the speed dial for Jack, trying to keep calm like the dispatcher told her to, and when he answered said, "It's Rachel, come back over quick," and hung up.

He arrived as she was pulling the coffee table away from the sofa to make room for the paramedics. She pulled him in the room while answering another question for the dispatcher, then pointed to Daphne's unconscious form. He let out a curse and dove to the floor in front of her, checking her pulse and listening for her breath like an emergency pro. Rachel sank into the armchair, relieved someone else could take over her attempts to rouse Daphne, and continued to talk with a quaking voice to the dispatcher who kept her on the line until the EMTs were tramping up the wooden steps.

Jack wrapped his arms around Rachel as the paramedics started an IV and strapped Daphne to a body board. She numbly answered the questions a police officer asked her, repeating much of what she'd told the dispatcher.

"We'll take her to the University of Chicago hospital," one of the EMTs said as they prepared to take her down the stairs. "You can meet us there if you want."

Jack took her hand and they followed the police down to the sidewalk. She climbed into Jack's truck and burst into tears. "Hey, hey." He squeezed her knee as he pulled away from the curb. "She'll be okay. She was still breathing, that's good. It'll be okay."

"I can't believe this is happening." Rachel struggled to get her tears under control. "I don't know what's going on. I can't believe she …" Rachel couldn't bring herself to admit Daphne may have tried to commit suicide. *She must have just gotten carried away.*

They ran from the parking lot into the ER, and Jack explained what was going on to the front desk nurse. "I'm sorry, family only," she said. Jack looked to Rachel for what to say next. "She doesn't have family here," she said. "They're all in California. I'm her roommate, and her best friend. I've known her since I was six."

"Do you have her parents' phone number?"

She shrugged, feeling helpless. "If their number is the same as it was five years ago, yes." She gave it to the nurse, who told them to go sit in the waiting room. Jack led her to a chair and then left to go get her coffee.

An hour passed. Rachel felt invisible. The phone number she'd given the nurse now went to a donut shop, so there was no one to tell the nurse that Rachel was as close to a sister as Daphne had ever had. Eventually she fell asleep, her head on Jack's shoulder.

She woke up when a nurse came and told them to go home. "What, and just leave her here?" Rachel gasped. "Does that mean she's doing all right?" The nurse gave her a look that told Rachel she wasn't going to fall for it. She tried another approach. "Look, put yourself in my shoes. She's my best friend. We've known each other since we were little kids—we're practically sisters. I moved all the way out here from California to live with her. You can't honestly expect me to just dump her off here and then leave."

The nurse huffed a deep sigh, then finally caved. "Okay, fine. Bottom line is, she'll live. She'll be here for a day or two, probably, then she can recover at home. When she's out of sedation we'll ask her if she wants you to come, and if she does, we'll call you. Okay?"

It wasn't okay—Rachel wanted details, wanted to know what was happening to Daphne right now. But Rachel could tell the nurse had given her all she was willing to. "Okay. Thank you."

She gave Rachel a sympathetic smile. "You're welcome."

Jack wrapped an arm around her shoulder and walked her out to the car. They drove home in silence, Rachel's eyes barely open when they reached the apartment. "What do you want me to do?" Jack asked gently as she stared unmoving out the window. "I can come up, I can leave, I can stay … it's up to you."

Rachel felt small and scared. The thought of being in the apartment alone freaked her out. "You'd stay?"

"Of course."

It was all she could do not to cry again. He held her hand as they trudged up the stairs, then headed straight for the kitchen once they were inside. “Go get ready for bed,” he said. “I’ll make us a couple of nightcaps.”

When she finally had her hands on the tumbler, it was all Rachel could do to keep from chugging it. She paced herself so as not to concern Jack, then snuck two more tumblers’ worth while he was in the bathroom with the toothbrush Rachel had given him from Daphne’s “overnight guest supplies” stash in the tiny linen closet.

Jack tucked her in and kissed her forehead. “I’m right on the couch if you need me.”

She stared at the ceiling, exhausted but unable to sleep as her thoughts skittered like frightened mice through her head. In light of Daphne’s recent behavior, Rachel had a hard time thinking this had been a temporary slip in judgment. Obviously her finances were in bad shape—but *that* bad? Why not ask Rachel for help, or get a second job? There had to be something else going on. But what?

She watched the moonlight shift across her room, thoughts chasing each other, until sleep finally won out.

Rachel awoke to sunlight streaming onto the bed. For a brief second she was free of the memory of the night before, but then it all came back and hit her like a truck. Her stomach roiled, though from hunger or stress she couldn’t tell—either way, she needed to get up and get moving before the weight of reality pushed her back under the covers.

She was about to leave the bedroom when she remembered Jack had spent the night on the couch. She ran a brush through her hair before venturing out to the living room, but found it empty once she got there. A note sat on the bar, written in hasty block script.

MORNING SHIFT FOR ME. I'LL LET R. J. KNOW WHAT HAPPENED. HOPEFULLY YOU CAN SLEEP IN AND SHE WON'T CARE IF YOU'RE A LITTLE LATE. SEE YOU WHEN YOU GET THERE.

A little smiley face closed the note, which brought a smile to her own face. She poured some cereal and a strong cup of espresso-strength roast, and after breakfast she showered and dressed in slow motion. It was almost noon by the time she left the apartment. *Just in time to help with the lunch rush.* The thought of the mad scramble behind the counter that accompanied the noon hour overwhelmed her. Her brain wasn't firing on all cylinders.

She strolled to the café, but ducked into the sandwich shop next door instead of going in to work. The cereal had barely made a dent in her hunger, and there was no way she'd survive without some more food. She ordered a sandwich and took a seat at a corner table, away from the window in case any fellow employees happened by.

Three thoughts tumbled through her mind as she ate: why Daphne had drunk all the vodka, the future of their friendship, and the steps she ought to take, if any, to separate herself from Daphne and move out.

The first thought was scary. Daphne was a champion drinker. She knew her own limit. She knew how to pace herself. So to think that she'd accidentally finished off half a bottle of vodka was highly unlikely. Which meant she'd done it on purpose. Which meant she'd been trying to harm herself, or even, God forbid, kill herself.

Yet another uncharacteristic move for the woman Rachel had known for twenty years.

Daphne was changing, and Rachel had no reason to assume she'd suddenly go back to how she used to be. How long could she, or should she, put up with it?

The last few weeks of tension and arguments had been bad enough, especially for someone like Rachel who avoided confrontation at all costs. What if that was the blueprint for the rest of their friendship? It would be one thing if she was living somewhere else and only saw Daphne now and then. Their friendship had been like that for the last five years and had survived just fine. Maybe that was the better way to go. Sharing living space wasn't shaping up to be the most comfortable arrangement, and if things continued in this vein, Rachel knew she would have no choice but to move out.

To where?

One obvious possibility stared her in the face, but she pushed the thought away as she finished her soda and brought her tray to the trash. She wasn't going to go there. Not yet.

It was a quarter to one, and Rachel knew she had to get in to work. She was two hours late already, and even if she wasn't up to the bustle of the café, it was better than sitting alone mulling over the depressing reality of a friendship that was evolving into something she didn't want.

She had one more stop before she went to work, however.

Rachel jogged across the street, then walked down a block

to a small liquor store she'd noticed a week ago. She went in and purchased a small bottle of vodka and a chilled Coke, along with a water bottle and a box of Altoids. Her mouth watered as she walked with an ever-quickening pace back to the café. Standing at the back entrance, she emptied the water bottle and some of the Coke onto the pavement, capped the bottle and returned it to the paper bag, then took a deep breath and let herself in.

"There you are." Ruby Jean was just coming out of her office. "I'm so sorry to hear what happened, Rachel. How are you?"

"I'm doing okay, thanks. Tired, though."

"I'll bet. I was just headed to the bank, I'll be back in a bit. I've got inventory all set up and ready to go, so if you could tackle that first, that would be great."

"Sure thing."

Ruby Jean left, and Rachel headed for the office. With the door shut and locked, she sat down and quickly opened the empty water bottle and the vodka. She took one quick sip from the vodka before dumping the rest of its contents into the water bottle and Coke can. Then she popped a breath mint, set the water bottle on the desk, and threw out the bag with the vodka bottle in it before unlocking the office door and sitting down to start work.

The alcohol swam through her veins and calmed the anxiety that had been building all morning. She felt like she could finally think.

After the inventory was finished, she ventured out into the café to check on operations and get some coffee. Jack gave her a warm smile when she appeared. "Hey, how did you sleep?"

"All right, actually. Thanks for staying."

"Of course."

"Was it a miserable night for you? I know how awful that couch is."

He chuckled as he mixed a Sgt. Pepper Mint Hot Chocolate. "Now I know why you were so desperate to get that bed. But I was pretty wiped out; I would have had a half-decent night anywhere. I was just glad I could be there for you."

She gave him a brief, platonic-looking hug. "Thanks."

She left him to work and poured herself the largest cup of coffee they had. "Jack told me what happened," Leah said as she came by to make a sandwich for a customer. "I'm so sorry. What a nightmare."

Thanks a lot, Jack. "Yeah, it is."

"I've been there and done that, so if you need someone to talk to let me know. I'd be happy to commiserate."

This took Rachel by surprise. "Your roommate nearly drank herself to death?"

"Well, not exactly. It was my brother."

Her cynicism toward Leah instantly decreased. "Oh wow. I'm sorry."

"It was a couple years ago, and he's fine now—well, he's not dead, anyway—so I'm over it." She layered lettuce and tomato over turkey and slathered mayo on the bread as she spoke. "But it can be hard to process, as can the circumstances that caused the person to do it in the first place. So, point being, feel free to let me know if you wanted to talk or vent or whatever." She took the sandwich to the counter, leaving Rachel to process the completely unexpected sliver of Leah's story.

As the afternoon passed, Rachel found it harder and harder to concentrate. She kept alternately checking her cell phone to see if she'd missed a call from the hospital and taking sips from her inconspicuous bottle. Her thoughts kept going to what she'd say to Daphne when she finally saw her, to what life would be like at their apartment now and into the future. Jack's shift ended and he went home, promising to come back for Rachel when hers was over so he could drive her home, or to the hospital, or to his place if she preferred. Rachel wished she could leave, too, since she wasn't being very productive. But with two hours left of her shift, she had plenty that needed doing, regardless of whether or not she felt like doing it.

"I'm off—but not exactly," Leah told Rachel when her shift ended. "I'm going to hang here and work on some stuff for school."

"Oh—okay." Rachel bit her lip, debating whether or not to satisfy her curiosity, then checked the clock to figure her break time. *Close enough.* "Would you mind if we talked for a few minutes first?"

"Of course not." Rachel followed her to a table in the corner where Leah dumped her well-worn backpack.

"I don't think I've ever asked you—what's your major?"

Leah unzipped the bag and pulled out a binder and textbook. "Biblical studies."

Rachel's eyebrows arched as her defenses began to creep back up. "Oh, I thought you were a U of Chicago student."

"Nope—Lakeshore Seminary." She dropped the backpack to the floor and settled back in her seat. "So do you know when your roommate is being released?"

Rachel shook her head. "They won't tell me anything because I'm not family, which is stupid because I'm the closest thing she has to family. She's an only child, and her parents checked out on her years ago, back when we were kids. She spent more time at my house growing up than she did her own."

"That's awful. Talk about baggage."

"You've got that right." Rachel searched for a suitable segue but could think of nothing that wasn't blunt. "So," she finally said, "what happened with your brother?"

Leah sighed. "The short version is that he drank two cases of beer pretty much on his own."

Rachel wrinkled her nose. "I can't imagine drinking that much beer. It's so nasty."

"Yeah, I agree." Leah chuckled. "But he wasn't trying to kill himself—at least he says he wasn't. And it makes sense, since other drinks would have done the job a lot faster if it had been a premeditated decision. He had some friends over, they were drinking in the basement, and he just … kept going. His friends left after a couple of hours and he stayed down there alone, watching movies and polishing off bottle after bottle. I couldn't sleep, so I went to the kitchen for a snack and heard the TV on, so I went downstairs to see if Aaron had insomnia too. He was passed out on the couch, and I couldn't wake him."

A shudder passed through Rachel at the description that hit so close to home. "Then what happened?"

"Called 911, got my parents, went to the hospital with them. He was in for just a day before he came home."

"So …" Rachel didn't know how to phrase her next question without coming off as completely nosy. "I'm guessing there was more to it than he just got carried away and didn't realize how much he was drinking, right?"

Leah nodded, the look in her eyes telling Rachel she knew what she was getting at. "This is the thing," she said, resting her arms on the table, "my dad is … forceful, you might say, about the paths he wants his children to take in life. He's a strong leader, has a very strong personality—everything about him is powerful and dominating."

"You must take after your mother, then."

Leah laughed. "I do; you're right. But my brother takes after my dad. So they've been butting heads since Aaron was about two." She sobered a bit. "The other thing is that my dad is sort of well-known in Chicago. He's the pastor of one of the biggest churches in the city, and when we were growing up, there was a lot of pressure to put on a good face, be a good reflection of the ministry, that sort of thing." She began to roll the corner of a sheet of notebook paper, a nervous habit Rachel could identify with. "Aaron always fought against it, but I, being the responsible firstborn, toed the line and did whatever was expected of me." A half-smile quirked one corner of her mouth. "Although lately I've been pulling away from all that, so for once Aaron and I have been on the same page."

"Pulling away—as in, leaving the church?" For a brief moment Rachel thought she might have found a kindred spirit.

But Leah quickly shook her head. "No, no—just pulling away from *that* church. I haven't been comfortable there for a really long time, and when I started going to Lakeshore I met some people who felt the same way I did about things, and we've been toying with the idea of starting a "house church."

The phrase "house church" triggered the memory of Macy. Rachel cringed as she remembered her condescending treatment of the concept when she'd ambushed the poor girl that one night. "Yeah, I know about house churches."

Leah's expression brightened. "You do?"

Rachel chuckled. "Yeah. I actually know quite a bit about Christian culture and … stuff like that." She waved a hand. "Anyway, what were you saying about house churches?"

"Oh, well—just that we're thinking of starting one. There are about five of us at the seminary, and then a few friends that are disillusioned with the institution of church."

Rachel smirked. "Your father must be thrilled."

Leah rolled her eyes. "Yeah, it hasn't gone over well. Plus he's been paying for school, but now he's threatening to stop if I don't come back to his church and take the job he offered me there."

"He offered you a job? Doing what?"

"Leading all the young-adult ministries." Her tone told Rachel exactly what she thought of that idea.

"So what are you going to do?"

"Honestly, I don't know. I've got an apartment with three other girls, and my dad pays my share of the rent, as well as my tuition. If he sticks to his word, then I'm going to be on my own come new year. I might be able to get loans for school, but I can't afford the rent with what I make here. As it is I'm just barely scraping by with books and food and utilities." She sat up straighter and pinned Rachel with her green eyes. "So how is it you know so much about Christianity?"

Rachel's stomach leapt. "Look at the time," she said with a wry smile as she examined the imaginary watch on her wrist. "I think my break is over." She stood as Leah began to laugh.

"I'm not letting you off the hook."

"I know. I'm just not ready to talk about it yet. Sorry."

Leah's mirth was instantly gone. "Totally okay."

"But … maybe we'll talk about it some other time." Rachel said the words before she had too much time to think about them.

"Fair enough." Leah opened her notebook. "I'll be praying for you, Rachel."

Rachel nearly asked her not to, but shut her mouth and nodded instead. "Thanks." She never thought she'd be willing to talk so much with Leah—and be so close to actually opening up to her. It seemed that all her relationships were completely upside down.

Jack pulled the truck to the curb. "Walk you up?"

"Thanks."

"So what do you think it means that the hospital hasn't called you yet?"

She sighed as she searched her purse for her keys. "I don't know. I think I'll call there this evening, see if I can get through to her room." She unlocked the door. "And if not, then I guess tomorrow—"

Daphne sat on the couch, legs curled beneath her, staring at the TV that wasn't on. "You're home!" Feeling awkward, she turned to Jack. "I guess I'll—"

"Talk to you tomorrow." He gave her a kiss and slipped out the door, shutting it behind him and leaving Rachel to figure out how to navigate the situation alone.

"So, when did you get back?" she asked as she set down her things.

"Six."

"The hospital never called me. I thought they were going to tell me when you were discharged. I could have picked you up."

"No big deal." Daphne spoke without taking her eyes off the television. Rachel wondered if she'd had a mental snap.

"Um … have you eaten? Want me to fix you something?"

"No."

No to which question? Rachel was getting concerned. "You doing okay?"

"I'm fine." She finally tore her gaze away from the blank screen. Her eyes looked dull. "I'm just tired."

Rachel nodded. "Yeah, that makes sense." She sat down on the armchair and kicked off her shoes. "Is there … anything you want to talk about? I'm dying to know what happened. You really had me scared." Daphne shrugged as her eyes drifted down to the coffee table, where the *Cosmo* back issues were in disarray. "I'm still your friend, Daphne. I'm still here for you. I want to help you if there's anything I can do. And even if there isn't, maybe whatever it is that's bothering you wouldn't be so bad if you got it off your chest."

"Thanks, but no." Daphne unfolded slowly and stood. "I'm going to bed. 'Night."

Rachel watched her walk away, scrambling for something to say that might bring her back or at least snap her out of the fog she seemed to be in. But her bedroom door was shut before she came up with anything.

Concern was replaced with frustration, then fear. There was nothing she could do if Daphne didn't want to cooperate. And Rachel had no recourse, no way to sneak in the back door of Daphne's struggle. Without appealing to God—or to whatever nebulous "higher power" might be out there—to move in someone's life, their only strength came from within themselves. And if they had no desire to change, or they had the desire but didn't have the strength, then what else could you do?

Maybe Jack was right. Maybe I just need to leave. If Daphne didn't want her help, and Rachel was going to keep bearing the brunt of her "junk," then there wasn't much point in staying. And yet again, maybe just being there, just being *around*, was enough help for Daphne. What if that was all she needed but Rachel bailed? Honestly Rachel wasn't sure she was willing to stick it out either way.

But where would I go? How would I find a roommate? She longed to hash things out with her mom, or Barbara. *What about Ruby Jean?*

For some reason she was reluctant to go to Ruby Jean for more advice. Her wisdom seemed to be based on such shaky ground. No matter how much she tried to get on board with it, her stubborn belief in absolute truth—which she was trying, albeit unsuccessfully, to shake—made that difficult. Rachel didn't trust it. Though she wasn't ready to think yet about where that truth was rooted. She had enough on her mind without trying to tackle that.

Then who can *I trust?*

She squeezed her eyes shut in frustration. That was a good question.

CHAPTER 16

Halloween was drippy and cold. Rachel felt bad for the trick-or-treaters already roaming the neighborhood when she left for her afternoon shift. It was the kind of day that made her glad she worked in a coffee shop, the kind of day that begged for hot chocolate and an overstuffed chair from which to watch the costumes that paraded down the sidewalk.

Ruby Jean had a tradition of throwing a Halloween party for her staff every year. They closed the shop early, and dinner was catered from a local Italian place. She bought soda and wine and an obscene amount of candy and told everyone to invite a friend of two if they wanted. Rachel invited Daphne, but she turned her down in favor of a party one of her friends was throwing. Rachel almost hoped Daphne would invite her along, because she didn't know if Daphne had told anyone about her hospitalization and feared no one would stop her if she started knocking back drinks. *There's that codependency Jack warned you about.*

But Daphne didn't invite her, and Rachel spent the evening trying to keep up with the conversations around her while her thoughts were somewhere else. She didn't feel like being there, either, which made it even more difficult to loosen up and have a good time. She'd been in a perpetual bad mood ever since Daphne's overdose. She felt like a cartoon character with a black cloud above her head; she couldn't seem to escape the shadow that hovered behind her all the time. But she knew it would look bad if she didn't show, so here she was, helping Ruby Jean set up the bar.

"So why Halloween?" she asked Ruby Jean. "Why not the traditional Christmas party?"

Ruby Jean opened a stack of plastic cups. "There are already a million Christmas parties," she said. "Everyone's already busy and overbooked, and I didn't want to put one more obligation on my staff, especially since so many of them are students who are crunching for finals or leaving to go home for the holidays. So when else was I going to do it? Thanksgiving? Not much of a party holiday. Same with Easter. But Halloween already has a party vibe. Plus, it's one of our slowest nights of the year." She ripped into a bag of mini candy bars and began to fill a row of mismatched candy dishes she'd lined along the counter. "It's also the Wiccan new year, so why not join the festivities?"

"Wicca—do you pull any practices from that religion?"

"One of the few I haven't, no. I like some of the tenets, though—their respect and reverence for the earth, the idea that there is a balance in the natural world between male and female, for example, the idea that there's both a god and a goddess. It's one of the few religions where women tend to rank higher than men, too, which I appreciate." She popped a chocolate in her mouth and pocketed the wrapper. "I've known a few witches, too, and they were sweet women."

"So … just like all the other religions we talked about, you think Wicca is just another manifestation of people trying to connect to the divine?"

Ruby Jean smiled. “Bingo.”

Rachel though for a minute. “What about the idea of black magic? Do you believe it exists?”

Ruby Jean shrugged. “Sure. But I don’t think witches practicing black magic is any different than any other religion doing harm in the name of their god. The Inquisition, jihad, bombing abortion clinics—they all think they’re doing what their god wants them to do.”

Their conversation was cut short when the caterer arrived. Rachel pondered Ruby Jean’s thoughts while she balled up the foil that had covered the pans of lasagna and fettuccine Alfredo and set up the cutlery and paper plates. By the time folks were sitting down to eat, Rachel had come up with more questions. “Okay, so, do you think God exists, R. J.?”

She thought a moment, then nodded. “I do, yes. I don’t know what form he or she takes, or if it’s more of a force than a sentient being—but yes, I believe there is some kind of higher power.”

“I guess I’m just wondering how it all works in your opinion. I mean, doesn’t it seem like God, whoever he or she or is, reveals Himself in contradictory ways? To these people over here he says, ‘Love your enemies,’ but to those people over there he says, ‘Wipe out the infidel.’ Or ‘I am the one true God’ versus the Hindu pantheon versus Buddhism that says there’s no God at all. I guess I don’t know how to find peace in affirming the validity of so many different beliefs. And …” she said, emphasizing her point with her plastic knife, “what comes when you die? Which one of those religions has the right idea about the afterlife? How do you know what you’re going to get in the end?”

Ruby Jean listened to Rachel’s interrogation with patience, then set down her plastic ware and folded her arms on the table. "Well," she said slowly, eyes focused on the basket of garlic bread in the center of the table, "I'll be honest with you. I *don't* know what I'm going to get in the end. I think that's one of the reasons I approach it all buffet-style—I figure I'm bound to hit on the right thing now and then, and I guess I'm just banking on God—whoever that is—to recognize that I always tried to do the right thing." She looked to Rachel and gave her a small smile. "I have doubts too. I think everyone does at some point, regardless of how devoted they are. Sure I wonder if I'm missing something, if there's something else I should be doing. But I don't think we can know for sure who is right, and I don't want to waste my energy worrying about something I have no control over."

She twirled fettuccine onto her fork. "Do I have peace? Eh, maybe 85 percent of the time, which is a lot more than some people, so I'm grateful for that." She took a bite, leaving Rachel to ruminate on her response.

Rachel felt the dark cloud above her grow heavier. For some reason, it felt like one of the most depressing confessions of faith she had ever heard. To live with no anchor for truth beyond your own thoughts and devices, to have no certainty about what came next—to just strike blindly into every tradition in the hopes of hitting the bull's-eye …

But where was Rachel these days? How was her stance any less depressing? At least Ruby Jean was making an effort to find truth. What had Rachel done lately to sort out her beliefs?

Rachel pushed away her plate of pasta and drained her cup of wine. Suddenly she didn't have much of an appetite.

Later in the evening Jack pulled Rachel onto one of the purple-upholstered wing chairs and offered her a Hershey's kiss. "It sounded like you and Ruby Jean were having quite the discussion at dinner," he said.

"Yeah, we were. I'm interested in her views on spirituality." She munched the chocolate, then said, "You and I haven't talked much about religion. Were you raised with any specific beliefs?"

"No, actually, I wasn't. My mom was raised Catholic, but didn't practice. Though we did go to Christmas and Easter Mass most years. My dad was a lapsed something-or-other; I don't remember what."

"I know you don't have any religious beliefs, but have you given spirituality any thought at all?"

He rolled the candy foil in his fingers as he spoke. "Eh, dabbled a little bit with the thought of a generic higher power in college, but never really settled on any one idea or belief system. Sometimes I wish I had been raised with something, though—I think it's a lot easier to work toward goals when you've got something driving you. Like, you pursue a particular career because you believe God has destined you to be 'that,' whatever 'that' is, and because you want to go to paradise, or heaven, or whatever you want to call it, you really devote yourself to pursuing that calling. When your life is comfortable and you don't have anything egging you on like that, it's easy to let yourself get lazy."

Rachel gave him a sideways glance. "You sound like you've thought about this."

He flashed a sheepish smile. "Well—I have, actually. Remember when you got the promotion and I told you I was a little jealous?"

She nodded. "It made me start thinking more about my own life, my own goals—or lack thereof. I've coasted since college. My sights were set on baseball, and when that got taken away, I just started to drift. I never pursued accreditation after getting my sports medicine degree. I've been thinking lately that I want to get back to that, start building a career instead of just having a job."

Rachel squeezed an arm around his shoulder. "That's really great. I'm happy for you."

Jack ducked his head, looking embarrassed. "Yeah, well … anyway, I started thinking I might start looking into religion, too."

Rachel sat up. "Why?"

He shrugged. "A man reaches a certain age, he starts thinking about what the next life holds."

Rachel laughed. "Jack, you're not even thirty!"

He grinned. "I'm kidding. Not about the religion part, though—that I'm actually serious about." She gave him a questioning look. "I know, I know, I don't look like the churchy type. But still, part of me feels like I might be missing something important."

This was too much for Rachel to think about. "I'm going to get another drink. Can I get you something?"

"Maybe. What are you having?"

"Wine, probably." Jack gave her a look she couldn't decipher. "What?"

"I don't know … maybe I'm just imagining it, but it seems like you're drinking a lot lately."

Her defenses rose. "Not 'a lot.' Not more than you."

"It's just weird, that's all I'm saying. It doesn't seem like something you'd do."

She pushed herself from his lap. "If you had two beers it wouldn't be a big deal at all. I have two glasses of wine and suddenly I'm some lush, is that what you're saying?"

Jack ran his hand through his hair, frustration written on his face. "No, that's not what I'm saying." He waved her away. "Fine, go, get a drink, forget I ever said anything."

She gritted her teeth against the words fighting to be voiced as she poured herself another glass. He obviously had no idea how much it helped her or he wouldn't have brought it up. She swallowed down half her cup, topped it off, then poured one for Jack. She knew he was just being hypocritical—he was way more of a drinker than she was. Heck, most of the staff were already completely tanked—this was only her second glass. At least she knew when to stop.

Rachel and Leah were the official clean-up crew. Almost everyone else was gone, having left behind the typical party detritus. "It's surprising how much trash such a small group of people can generate," Leah said. She was going from table to table with a garbage bag, cleaning up the plates and empty cups. "There were, what, twenty people here? You'd think it had been three times that."

Rachel was moving slowly with the broom, frustrated with her body's lack of coordination. *I really need to get home and into bed. I'm exhausted.* "Yeah, yeah, it's nuts," she said, trying not to let on that she wasn't really listening.

Things with Jack had been tense the rest of the night. He had the morning shift the next day, so he'd left early in the evening, and Rachel had been almost glad to see him go. She wished she could have gone as well; all she really wanted was to sleep. It was all she ever wanted to do these days. And yet she had the hardest time doing so when she finally crawled into bed.

"Penny for your thoughts?" Leah asked.

Rachel shook her head. "Sorry?"

"Are you all right? You're really quiet tonight."

"Oh." Rachel made an effort to stand up straighter and look more awake. "Just had a rough few nights, that's all."

"Ah. Understandable."

They cleaned in silence for a while more, until Rachel said, "So I have a deep question for you, if you're up for it."

"Sure."

"Who do you think God is?"

Leah stopped what she was doing and laughed. "That's out of nowhere."

"It's my question *du jour*."

"Gotcha." She smiled and resumed her cleaning, then said, "Well, I was raised to think of God as sort of a Big Brother. Not the mentoring kind, the Orwellian kind. But the more I study the less I agree with that view. I don't think He's that punitive, or that … I don't know … that sneaky, trying to always 'catch' us, you know?" She gathered a paper tablecloth in her hands and scrunched it to a ball. "I've never been happy with my relationship with him, and I think my false view of him is to blame. I mean, on the one hand, I was taught he loves us, but then in the next breath I was told to watch out that I didn't disobey him, as though that love he had for us was based on what we did. But now I don't think that. I think he loves us, unconditionally, and we're sort of like a bunch of toddlers who keep making stupid mistakes. You don't tell a two-year-old you love them, but they'd better watch out. Right?"

Rachel shrugged. "Makes sense."

"I think my faith has been characterized by a lot of working—working to earn God's favor, his love, his guidance. Go to church, read the Bible, pray, do this, don't do that."

Rachel frowned as Leah described the life she herself had led for years. "But isn't that what the Bible tells us to do?"

Leah looked at Rachel with curiosity. "Us?"

"You, us, whatever." *Way to blow your cover.*

Leah shrugged and went back to work. "Well, not really, no. It says to love God with all your heart and soul and mind and strength. It doesn't say, 'Here's a checklist; get to work.' I think those things come because we're motivated to connect with God and learn more about him. They shouldn't be conditions that we try to meet in order to earn his favor, and if we skip a Sunday or go to bed without praying, God's going to withdraw his love until we're back on the right track." She shook her head. "A friend of mine reminded me the other day that God loves us, first and foremost, and that in any healthy relationship *both* parties work toward deeper intimacy. It's not just up to one of us—like, it's not just up to me to make our relationship deeper and closer. God's working at it, too, meeting me halfway—more than halfway, sometimes, when I'm really struggling. It's a way different view than the one I was raised with, where I thought God was sitting on his throne aiming lightning bolts at my feet and telling me to dance."

Rachel had stopped sweeping as Leah's personal revelation became more and more enlightening. To hear the idea that a relationship with God was a two-way street was eye-opening. *Although what does that say about the way he abandoned me? Where was that mutual effort when the crap hit the fan?*

She was about to ask another question when a rap on the door made them both jump. Then Leah let out a laugh and ran to unlock it. "Declan, good grief, what are you doing here so late?"

Declan polished the rain from his John Lennon glasses. "What, the party's already done then? It's not even half ten." His accent—some kind of British that she couldn't place—drew Rachel's attention, as did the way his eyes locked with hers. "Oh, hi there."

"Hi."

"Rachel, this is Declan. I invited him to come tonight—"

"Which I did."

"Well, yes, but four hours past when I told you to!"

He grinned. "Sorry, I was studying with the boys and lost track of time." He reached out a hand to Rachel. "Nice to meet you."

"You too." She shook his hand—strong and warm, and lingered slightly longer than necessary—then gestured toward his outfit that was beaded with rain. "Still pouring out there, I guess?"

"Aye, but just a wee sprinkle, really."

Ah, Scottish then.

"I'll drive you home when we're done," Leah said to him, then turned to Rachel. "You, too—you usually walk, don't you?"

"After day shifts, yes. But I take the bus at night."

"Definitely give her a ride then," Declan said. "No need for you to be standing at the stop in the rain."

"True." Leah motioned to a chair. "Make yourself comfortable. I was just telling Rachel what you and I were talking about the other day, about a relationship with God being dependent on both parties and not just us."

Rachel groaned inside. *He's probably one of her seminary friends. Never mind then.*

The thought took her by surprise. Why would she even think about him that way, given she was going on four months with Jack? What if Declan *had* been a "possibility"—would she have just dumped Jack like their relationship was nothing? *But I'm* not *serious about Jack, right? He* is *just a transitional guy, and unless I want to deal with a really messy breakup, I need to start making that clearer—*

"Right, Rachel?"

Rachel jumped. "What? I—I'm sorry, I got caught up in my own thoughts. I didn't realize you were talking to me." She felt her cheeks warming with embarrassment.

Leah spoke again. "I was just telling Declan that I'd told you about our house church the other day, and that you'd said you were familiar with the concept."

"Oh—right, right."

"If you're interested, we'd love to have you join us," Declan said. His brown eyes drew Rachel in like tractor beams. "Not that we're doing anything formal right now—though I suppose that's the whole point, aye?"

Rachel swept the small pile of debris she'd made into the dust trap. "Oh, thanks, but no. I'm not, um—I'm not really a Christian anymore."

Leah's eyes widened. "Anymore?"

Rachel concentrated her eyes on her broom, not wanting to make eye contact with either of them. "It's a long story. I don't really like to talk about it."

"I'm sorry to hear that," Declan said, his voice sincere.

"It's okay," she said, offering a small smile that was probably more flirtatious than she had intended. She suddenly realized how tired she was, which she blamed for her apparent inability to control her facial expressions. She needed to be home, in bed, with this night behind her and Declan out of her space before she said something stupid.

And yet, once she was home and in bed, she stared at the ceiling, unable, as usual, to sleep. Thoughts of Jack's comments about making a career rather than just having a job were buzzing around in her head. Was coffee destined to be her career? Surely youth ministry hadn't been her only other option.

And was that all life was—finding a job you could tolerate for thirty years, then retiring and playing bunko and knitting until you died? She thought about heaven and the beliefs she'd had about death. Without some kind of afterlife to aim for, what was the point of life? And without God, what was life's value?

It was past midnight when she finally rolled out of bed and shuffled to the kitchen for a drink. As much as she'd always loved coffee, sleep had always been the one thing it couldn't deliver. She was glad she'd finally found something that could give her a hand in that department.

She drained the shot of vodka and cringed at the heat on her throat. As it dissipated, however, she felt more at peace, knowing in a few minutes her mind would stop racing in circles and she'd finally be able to sleep.

Rachel nearly dropped the espresso she was making when Declan stepped through the door. He saw her and waved. She waved back, then quickly bent her head to her work and willed him to wait to order his drink until she'd gotten back to the office. She wanted to grab another Altoid before they spoke, and she'd left the container on the desk.

"Hey, Rachel," he said as he approached the counter. "Feeling better today? You looked pretty shattered last night."

"Yes, thanks, got some good sleep," she lied as she slid the drink down the counter and then called out the customer's name. "What can I get you?"

"Just a large coffee, thanks."

She smiled. "Easy customer." She poured the coffee and handed it to him, then took the money he handed her. "Looks heavy," she said, nodding toward the backpack that hung off his shoulder.

"The thing's a beast. I'll likely be paralyzed by the time I graduate."

She handed him his change with a smile she couldn't help. She loved his accent, for one thing. "There you go—enjoy. You sticking around?"

"For a while, aye. Just to get a change of scenery while I study. You working long?"

"Another four hours."

"Well, if you get a break, come chat with me. I'd love the excuse to procrastinate."

She smiled, though inside she felt guilty at the warmth that came at his invitation. "Maybe, yeah. Thanks."

He nodded and smiled before leaving to claim a table. She checked the clock and decided to do two more office tasks before taking a break to chat with him. Though she wasn't sure why—she wasn't in the mood to talk. But something about him made her want to just sit next to him. He didn't even have to talk to her. Maybe just stare at her with those eyes—

Stop it!

She served customers until Brian was back on shift, then ducked into the back to tweak the following month's schedule and place an order. Once she had those done, she took one last drink from her water bottle and ate another Altoid, then went out for her hard-earned break.

"Perfect timing," Declan said when she appeared beside him. "I was just getting to Tertullian, and he bores me to tears." He grinned and pushed out a chair for her. "I'd buy you a drink but you probably get them free, yes?"

She smiled her first genuine smile in days. "I do. But thanks for the sort-of offer."

"Do you drink a lot of coffee then?"

"Oh yes. You?"

"Well, more than I did back in Scotland, but only because I can't find a decent hard cider here to save my life." He shut his book and pushed his glasses back up on his nose. "So tell me more about how you aren't a Christian anymore."

Had she been drinking something she'd have choked a little. "That was subtle." But the look his eyes was like truth serum. She wanted to tell him everything.

"Yeah, diplomacy isn't my strong suit. I find out someone has a story to tell about God, I want to hear it, good or bad. I don't do a lot of beating around the bush. Life is short, no point in wasting it on small talk."

She meant to only give him the bare minimum, but his questions kept her talking until Jack materialized beside her. "Hey, babe."

She jumped, hand on her heart. "You startled me." She looked at the clock and realized she'd been talking with Declan for half an hour. Jack was just coming on shift. She stood as she made the introductions. "Declan, this is Jack. My boyfriend. And Jack, this is Declan. He's a friend of Leah's from school."

They shook hands as Rachel pushed her chair in. "It was good talking to you, Declan. Sorry I have to run, I lost track of the time."

"No worries, Rachel. It was a pleasure. We'll have to talk some more again sometime."

She walked with Jack back to the stock room where she saw for the first time the disappointment in his eyes. "Why didn't you ever tell me you were so religious back in California?"

"Oh." She cringed. "You heard that, huh?"

"We were actually talking about religion at the party and you still didn't bring it up."

"Because it's not that big a deal."

"The way you were talking with Declan, it sure sounded like a big deal. 'Eating me up inside' were the words I think you used."

She let out a huff of frustration and pressed her palm to her forehead. "Well … he's a Christian, so he understands where I'm coming from. That's all."

Jack shook his head. "I just can't believe you'd talk with a virtual stranger about that and not your boyfriend. It certainly would have explained a lot."

"What do you mean?"

"Your mood lately—you've been so subdued. Knowing that something has been weighing on you like that would explain it."

She leaned into him, wrapping her arms around him and resting her head on his chest. She noticed it took him a few moments to reciprocate. "I'm sorry, Jack. Honestly."

"It's all right," he said after a long moment. "Just promise me you won't keep any more secrets, okay?"

She promised, knowing it was a lie—she certainly wouldn't divulge the way Declan made her feel any time soon, or the doubts about being with Jack long term. They broke apart and went back to work, though Rachel couldn't concentrate on anything long enough to finish it. Rachel needed Daphne's help to sort through this. She felt so guilty for enjoying Declan's company so much, and awful for making Jack feel bad. Something wasn't right with their relationship. She didn't know what it was, but she didn't think she'd be lying so much to him if things were as they should have been. She finished the remaining contents of her water bottle. *This is when I need Daphne to be the friend she used to be.*

She had three hours left of work. It was going to be a long afternoon.

Rachel's phone rang as she sorted laundry in the living room. She crawled over the pile of clothes to her purse, which hung from the barstool. Her chest tightened when she saw her mother's number on the display.

The mess of laundry was the result of three weeks without a visit to the laundromat. Lately she'd been too tired or preoccupied to deal with it, but she had to do at least one load if she wanted to wear clean clothes tomorrow. The last thing she felt like doing was talking to her mother—to anyone, really, even Jack—but she and her mother hadn't talked since July. She deserved to know Rachel was at least alive and relatively well.

"Hey, Mom."

"Hi, sweetheart! I thought for a minute there I'd be getting your voice-mail again."

"Yeah, sorry about that." She sank into the couch. "How are you?'

"I'm doing well. How are you?"

She'd never lied to her mother before, but she wasn't about to tell her the truth. "Fine, fine. It's getting chilly here these days, I'm looking forward to the first snow."

"Did you get yourself some nice new things for winter?"

"Yeah, got some sweaters, a new coat."

"Oh good. Wish I could see them."

She knew her mother didn't say it to guilt her, but the words stung anyway. "How about you? It must feel empty, being in the house alone now."

"Yes, well … about that. That's one of the reasons I called, actually. Your dad and I are working on reconciliation."

"What?"

"I mean we're not getting a divorce."

"Oh." Rachel wasn't sure what to think. "Um ... that's great. What happened?"

"Well, he came back in mid-August, and he was his old self. He told me he'd started drinking in March, which is why his medication stopped working and he became so unstable. He'd gone from the hospital in Omaha to a rehab facility, and when he came back he was off the alcohol and back on his meds and stable again. He told me he understood if I still wanted the split, but God really hammered home to me while he was gone that I had promised for better or for worse, sickness and health, and I just didn't think I could go through with it anymore."

It took Rachel a moment to absorb all the new information. "So … how do you know he's not going to just start drinking again?"

"Well, the drinking was precipitated by some issues he was having at work, which I didn't know about. Part of why he left home was because he got laid off, but when he came back Ross Reynolds from church hired him to do the books for his construction company. It's a much more laid-back place than the firm was, so I think the change will be good for him. Plus, I think the fact that I took the steps I did for the separation scared him into realizing he'd nearly lost his marriage. I don't think he'd take that chance again."

Rachel felt genuine gladness, which was, sadly, a foreign feeling for her these days. "That's really great, Mom. I'm happy for you guys."

"Thank you. I'm happy for us, too." After a pause, her mother continued. "I don't suppose you'd consider coming home now?"

"Like, for a visit?"

"No, for good. Moving back."

"What—just because you and Dad are getting back together?"

"Well, wasn't that why you left?"

"One of the reasons, yes. But not the only one." Irritation pinched her voice. "I really am glad that you guys aren't splitting up, but you have to understand that I still don't think of you—either of you—as the people I grew up with. The people I thought you were never would have hidden such an enormous secret from me, or even *talked* about divorce, much less actually get separated. That doesn't all get deleted just because you changed your mind and think everything is back to normal."

"Oh." A long silence deflated some of Rachel's anger. "I guess I hadn't thought of it from that perspective." Her mother's voice held a hint of embarrassment, and Rachel groaned inside.

"I'm sorry if I hurt your feelings, Mom. I didn't mean to."

"No, no, my feelings aren't hurt, exactly." Rachel heard her mother take a deep breath and sigh. "So anyway … what else ..."

Now's my chance. Rachel was scrambling for a good way to end the conversation when her mother asked the question Rachel had been hoping to avoid. "Did you ever decide to look for a church?"

Oh no, here we go. "Actually, no, I didn't. I was really mad with God when I came out here, and I really haven't thought much about him since." *Until lately, anyway.* Not that she was going to go there right now. "But I've met some great people—some Christians, even—and life is really good." She searched for examples that would prove her life didn't suck now that she didn't have God in her corner. "Oh, and I got promoted. I'm a manager now. And I'm dating this great guy, Jack. He's a total gentleman, you'll be happy to know. A nice change from Patrick, that's for sure."

"Hm. Well, congratulations." Her tone suggested that the congratulations wasn't all that heartfelt. "That's wonderful about the job. And this boyfriend, is it serious?"

"Um, well, I don't know. We're just, you know, taking it slow."

"Well if it turns into a serious relationship I hope the two of you will come out. I'd like to meet him."

"I'll keep that in mind, but I don't think it will get serious." It was the first time she'd admitted that aloud. A sense of relief washed over her.

They both fell silent, and Rachel wasn't about to lose another chance to hang up. "Well, I should get going."

"Oh, yes, okay. Oh—I'll send you another check this week. Just, you know, in case you find yourself needing some extra cash. Put it in your savings if you don't want to spend it; I don't care."

Rachel frowned. "'Another' check? You never sent the first one, right?"

"Sure I did, the day after we spoke, back in July. Then another in August and September."

"You sent three?"

Her mother tsked. "Hold on, let me look at my check register." The line was silent for a moment, and Rachel racked her brain as she waited. "No, here it is," her mother said. "I have it ticked off so it must have been cashed. Same with the ones in August and September."

"Are you sure you have my address right?" Her mother read off the address of the apartment, and it was indeed correct. "That's really weird, Mom. I know I didn't get them. I just assumed you decided not to send the first one since I told you I didn't need it."

"Well that's a disturbing mystery. I'll call the bank tomorrow and see if I can get it straightened out. And regardless, I'll send you another one tomorrow."

Rachel sighed, unwilling to argue about it this time. "Okay, thanks. Nice talking to you."

"You too, sweetheart. Love you."

"Love you too."

Rachel set down the phone, suddenly exhausted, and looked back to the mountain of laundry. What small motivation she'd had to tackle it had disappeared, and the job was once again too overwhelming for her to deal with. She stepped over the mess and went to her room to take a nap before her shift.

As it turned out, the nap didn't help. She woke up late and barely made it to work in time. Then, once she was there, she couldn't seem to keep her focus. It wasn't that she was thinking of other things. It's that she could barely think at all.

All she wanted to do was hide in the office. Unfortunately, Leah had called in sick, so Rachel had no choice but to work the front. In her first hour she'd messed up two drink orders and forgotten to wipe down the steamer wand after frothing milk for a latte, a rookie mistake resulting in a backup of drink orders while she scrubbed off the caked-on milk residue. The next two hours after that were no better, and by the time her meal break was over, she was ready to go home.

Then, as if things weren't bad enough, Declan came back.

"Rachel, hey," he said as he approached the counter. "I thought Leah was working today. No?"

"Hi, Declan. Sorry—she's home sick. Stomach bug, I think."

"Ah, pity. I thought she looked a bit poorly when I saw her in class this morning." He cocked his head. "You're looking a bit poorly yourself. Are you not well?"

Why did the question make her want to cry? "I'm just preoccupied, that's all. What can I get you?"

"How about a hot chocolate. It's one of those days out there."

She pulled a hot drink cup from the stack and the entire stack fell to the floor. She cursed under her breath and cleaned them up with fumbling hands. "Sorry, just give me a minute."

"No worries."

She carried the now-sullied cups to the back room and dumped them in a trash can, then grabbed a new stack to bring to the front. "My reflexes aren't the fastest today," she said as she carefully pulled the top cup from the stack and went to work on his drink. "Thanks for your patience."

"Of course, it's not a problem, really. I'm sorry you're having a bad day."

Try a bad month. "It happens," she said, trying to blow it off as she mixed the hot chocolate powder with the steamed milk. But when she tried to push the lid onto the cup, she spilled the entire thing on the counter. Gaping like an idiot at her mistake, she grabbed a towel and threw it over the spill. "I feel like a total idiot. What did I just do?"

Declan smiled, his eyes kind. "I've done that before. Those lids can be tricky."

"You'd think doing hundreds of them a week would make me an expert." She kept her eyes down to hide the tears that were forming.

"Everyone misses now and then, right? Being a pro doesn't make you perfect."

His sympathy just made it worse. She grabbed another cup and made the drink again, positioning herself behind the espresso machine while she blinked away the tears and sniffed. With exaggerated caution she snapped on its lid and slid it across the counter to Declan. "Here you go."

"Thank you, Rachel." He handed her his cash. "I don't suppose you're going on break soon?"

"No, but if it stays slow I might."

"No offense, but you look like you need it."

"Heh. Seriously." She handed him his change and watched him walk to his table as she considered his question. *Was that an invitation? Or just friendly concern since I look like crap?*

She served a few more customers, then went to the back to do some office work when Brian came on shift. But she couldn't think straight, couldn't shake the fog that hampered her common sense, and finally just gave up.

She told herself it wasn't specifically Declan that she wanted to talk with, but just that she was frustrated and wanted to vent to *someone*. She told herself that, if Jack were on shift, she'd want to talk to him instead. *How worried should I be that I'm lying to myself now?*

She wandered back out to the front, saw that Brian was serving the only customer currently at the register, and decided that taking a break would not be a bad idea.

"Your timing is impeccable," Declan said with a smile.

"Tertullian again?"

"No, Kierkegaard. Different class." He stood and pulled out a chair for her. "Can you sit a while?"

"A few minutes, sure." She sat down and glanced at his textbook. "So what class is it?"

"Philosophy 301. I'm not doing very well."

"I won't keep you from studying for too long, then."

"I'd much rather talk than read. I'm far more relational than I am academic."

"Well, I'm not the most relational person these days, so don't get your hopes up too much."

He shoved his books aside and folded his arms on the table, bringing himself close enough that she could smell the cologne he wore. "And why is that?"

She batted away the answer with a half-hearted wave of her hand. "You don't want to hear a virtual stranger venting her issues."

"Sure I do! I'm relational, remember? Talking with people and helping them process their problems is one of my favorite things to do."

"Well, processing is not my strong suit these days, so I suppose I'd be an idiot to turn down an offer." She took a deep breath, rubbed a hand nervously against her arm as though cold. "I feel like my life is falling apart." *Way to be blunt.* "Every single important relationship in my life is broken in one way or another. Some of it is my fault, some of it isn't, some of it is just … mutual dysfunction, I suppose. But the whole reason I came out here from California is because all my important relationships out there fell apart too. I'm starting to feel cursed. Or maybe I'm just the common denominator." Her embarrassment at baring her soul to someone she barely knew was overshadowed by her need to unburden herself and be heard by someone outside of all her problems. "I can't shake this feeling that something bad is going to happen, like I'm on the edge of a cliff but can't see over the edge to tell how far down it is. There's a constant shadow over me." Her voice began to quaver, and she swiped away tears that formed on her lashes. *Oh please do* not *start crying in front of him.* "I don't know who to go to for advice anymore. Everyone's way of thinking is so different from how I was raised to think. But I don't know anymore what I think about the way I used to think." She chuckled and used the levity as an opportunity to compose herself. "Am I making any sense at all?"

"Aye, I follow you."

She kept talking, spilling her fears about Daphne, her trepidation about her relationship with Jack, her disappointment with her parents. She even told him about how God seemed to disappear when she needed him most. It wasn't until the door opened and a stream of customers entered that she realized how long she'd rambled on—yet again. Mortified, she dragged a napkin down her cheeks to dry them and dashed back behind the counter. When the crowd dissipated, she debated hiding in the back room until Declan left, but had a feeling he wouldn't until they'd spoken again. Humiliated by her self-absorbed tirade, she slunk back to the table to apologize.

"Nonsense," he said, giving her the warm smile that made her tingle. But the smile faded quickly. "I'm sorry to hear you're so distressed. I'd like to pray for you, if I could."

"You did hear me say that I'm not really sure I believe in God right now, right?"

He grinned with a twinkle in his eye. "I did. But *I* still believe in him. May I?"

She shrugged, both uncomfortable with the idea and secretly thrilled that he cared enough to want to. "I guess so. Knock yourself out."

He closed his eyes. "Father God—"

"Wait a minute—you're going to pray aloud, right now?"

He opened his eyes. "Did I not just say that?"

"I thought you were going to do it in your head. You know, another time." Rachel had prayed aloud for countless of her youth group students, but she felt awkward being on the receiving end.

He tipped his head, considering. "I suppose I could. Might not do you as much good."

She frowned. "What—you think God grants prayers better when they're prayed out loud?"

He chuckled. "No, of course not. But hearing what someone prays for you can be a powerful thing. Sometimes just knowing what someone is praying for you can be an encouragement, even if God doesn't choose to answer the prayer the way you'd hoped."

She glanced around. Brian was engaged in cleaning the sandwich station. The shop wasn't very full; the nearest customer was at least ten feet away. "Well … okay, fine. Just keep it down."

"Yes, ma'am." He smirked as he closed his eyes. She kept hers open, on the lookout. She listened as Declan prayed, asking God for peace and comfort, wisdom and grace, an end to the depression she was suffering from and healing in her relationships. The words weren't fancy, the prayer was mercifully brief, and she had no confidence at all that God would hear and even care. But she grudgingly admitted in her heart that Declan had been right—hearing him pray on her behalf softened her mood a little. Not much, but enough to let hope get the smallest of toeholds.

He finished with "amen," then opened his eyes and smiled. "Did you survive?"

She chuckled. "Yes, thank you."

"Pleasure. I'm honored you felt comfortable enough with me to tell me all that you did. And you needn't worry; I may not be a pastor, but I still won't go blabbing your personal struggles to anyone."

Her phone vibrated in her pocket. It was a text from Jack, which reminded her again that she'd spent too much time talking with Declan and needed to start working on her end-of-the-day duties. "I need to get going. Thanks again, Declan. I really do appreciate you letting me just talk."

"You're welcome, Rachel. Anytime—and I mean that."

She knew he did, and she knew it wasn't a good sign that she was so pleased to hear it.

She went back to the office and read the text from Jack. *Go out 2nite? Can pick u up from work.* She tapped out an answer, feeling guilty as she did. *Bad day. Just want 2 sleep. Thx tho. CU 2moro. XOX.* She knew that if tonight was anything like her nights had been for the last month, she wouldn't actually do a lot of sleeping. But still, she looked forward to crawling into bed because for once she was just going to let herself do what she'd wanted to do for a while now: daydream about Declan. She was too tired to fight it, and if it brought her some comfort, then it would be worth it. She wouldn't even let herself feel guilty about it.

At least, she hoped she wouldn't.

When Declan walked into the café the next afternoon, Rachel had to work to convince herself he wasn't there to see her. *He likes the coffee. It's a great place to study. Who knows, maybe he's just a really big Beatles fan.*

She wasn't working the counter when he came in, just restocking the to-go selections in the deli case. She knew Jack would be coming in any minute for his shift, and she didn't want him to see her talking with Declan because she knew he would take it the wrong way and get jealous. Though technically he would be taking it the right way. Rachel knew that, in truth, he did have a reason to be jealous.

She tried to look preoccupied in her work, but there was only so much brain power necessary to stock sandwiches and yogurt. Declan took a seat at the table closest to her. "Feeling any better this morning?"

"I did sleep a little better," she said. "Thanks." She smiled and found it didn't feel as forced as it usually did these days.

"Glad to hear that," he said. He sounded genuine, and she almost wished he'd stop being so caring. "I'm still praying for you, just so you know. Not out loud," he said, eyes twinkling, "but praying nonetheless."

"Thanks. I appreciate it." She saw Jack emerge from the back and picked up her work pace, trying to offer subtle hints to Declan that she wasn't available to talk. "Good luck studying today."

He chuckled. "Thanks. I need all the help I can get." He gently grabbed her wrist as she began to walk away. "And hey, I wanted to say something about this last night, but I didn't."

Her breath caught in her throat, anticipating the confession of attraction that would complicate her life even more but would make her so happy.

"I guess I just wanted to say that depression isn't something to just grin and bear through. Regardless of whether or not God chooses to heal you, maybe you could find a therapist, or at least talk to a doctor. I've seen depression get pretty rough for people—it'll steal your life away before you know it."

Just as she was about to respond, Jack was right there and she knew he had heard what Declan had said. To Rachel's further embarrassment, he looked plainly annoyed that she and Declan had been talking. "Hey, babe," he said slowly. He looked to Declan. "It's Declan, right?"

"Aye, nice to see you again—Jack, right?"

"Right." He looked to Rachel. "Just wanted to come say hi," he said quietly. "But I'll leave you two to talk."

"Oh, we were done," she said quickly. "Enjoy your coffee, Declan." She allowed herself a brief smile in his direction before retreating to the back room. Jack was needed at the counter, so she was safe in the office. She popped the sports top on her water bottle and took a few sips, then at an Altoid. She then ate an Altoid as she settled in to get some work done. Ruby Jean wanted to revamp the All Together Now website and had asked Rachel to take a stab at the content. She'd been tackling it on and off all day since coming in for her shift, and she still had only one paragraph to show for her time. She typed a sentence, deleted it, typed another one, then stared unseeing at the computer screen for untold minutes as she mentally flogged herself for thinking Declan might like her. When a knock sounded on the door she nearly jumped out of her chair. "Come in."

The door opened and Jack leaned in. "Got a minute?"

"Yeah, of course."

He closed the door and sat on the other office chair. "You're depressed?"

Embarrassment burned in her cheeks. "I … I don't know. I think maybe Declan overreacted to what I told him—"

"What did you tell him?"

She couldn't bring herself to look him in the eye. Her gaze settled on Ruby Jean's small Asian tapestry that hung behind him on the wall. "I don't remember, exactly," she said, which was mostly true. Jack's sigh told her everything she had been afraid he'd think. "Look, it's not what you're thinking," she said, forcing herself to meet his stare so he wouldn't think she was lying. "Nothing is going on with him. He's just a nice guy who likes to chat, that's it. There's no reason to be jealous."

Jack slowly shook his head. "He may just be some nice guy, but it's clear you've been more open with him than you have been with me. So don't tell me I have no reason to be jealous."

"Look, Jack—"

"I don't want to get into this here—it's not right, we're both on the clock." He stood and went to the door. "Tell me one thing, though," he said as he opened it. "You've never said a thing to me about being sad, much less depressed. Why? Why did you tell some guy you barely know and not your boyfriend?"

She had an answer, but there was no way she could give it, not at work when she had no time to try to soften the blow. "I don't know," she said. The words sounded as hollow as her heart felt. She hoped he didn't hear them that way.

His shoulders dropped, along with his eyes. "I think you do." He shut the door behind him.

CHAPTER 17

It had been a long four days. Rachel and Jack danced around each other at work, interacting when necessary but never getting personal beyond the polite, "How are you today?" When she wasn't at the café she was in her room trying (usually unsuccessfully) to get lost in a book, or watching mindless TV to try to drown out the noise in her head. She avoided Daphne as much as possible, and Daphne was apparently doing the same. She was going through the motions of work, sleep, and eat, while slowly sinking deeper into an inescapable pit of despair.

She came home Thursday night with a headache, wanting nothing more than to make the fastest, easiest dinner possible and then go to bed. As she headed up the stairs, she noticed the motion-activated porch light wasn't working. She waved her hand in front of it to no avail, then let herself into the apartment.

All the lights were out. She flicked the switch next to the door, waiting for the ceiling light to come on, but nothing happened. She looked around the living room and kitchen for signs that the power was on but found none. The digital clock on the microwave was out, as was the little red light on the DVD player. She switched on the lamp beside the sofa. No luck.

"What on earth?" she said aloud, moving into her bedroom. Her clock glowed, but there was a backup battery in it. She turned on her computer to check the battery, then took a peek in Daphne's room, which yielded nothing different.

She sat in front of her computer as it booted up, then realized she couldn't get online—the modem had no power. Groaning, she called the electric company's outage line, which provided troubleshooting tips after stating there was no known outage in her area. "Blown fuse" was the only possibility that made sense.

She went back to the kitchen and rummaged through the junk drawer until she found a flashlight, then set about finding the fuse box. She finally located it in the closet with the water heater, but when she opened it up, nothing looked amiss. Tossing the flashlight on the couch, she steeled herself for her first visit to the marijuana-dealing neighbors downstairs.

She was halfway down when she caught a glimpse in the neighbors' window—and saw a lit lamp. She frowned, descended a few more steps to get a better look. Yes, the bottom floor was well lit, as was every other house around them. Their flat was the only one that was dark.

She ascended the stairs again, frustration growing. There was only one reason this would be happening. The bill hadn't been paid.

Where is Daphne!?

She opened the fridge and moved as many items into the freezer as possible to help keep things cold, then made a peanut butter and jelly sandwich and tried to call Daphne's cell. It went straight to voice-mail. Her frustration morphed to anger as she ate, then did her dishes, then fixed a drink, and then another. By ten-thirty she was exhausted, irate, and ready to make good on her threat to move out.

She heard Daphne's feet on the stairs at nearly eleven. She barely let her get the door closed before she started in on her. "When did you pay the power bill?"

"Why are you sitting in the dark?" Daphne flipped the switch, then flipped it again.

"Take a wild guess."

"I don't know why —" Daphne's indignation was just a second too slow in coming.

"I checked my checkbook," Rachel said. "I wrote out my half of the bill two weeks ago. Why didn't you pay it?"

"I did pay it."

"Then why did they shut off our power?"

"It must be something else. Like the circuit breaker."

"Checked it already."

"Maybe the folks downstairs—"

"They're just fine, Daphne, and you know it."

"I'm sure it's just a mistake."

Rachel laughed. "A mistake? Like, someone accidentally elbowed the switch that keeps us on? Tripped on the plug, ripped it out of the generator? Right, Daphne, it's just a big mistake." Rachel slammed her glass on the counter. "Get me our account number. I'll take care of it."

"What?"

"I'll take care of it."

"No—I'll do it."

"Forget it."

"Why not?"

"Because I don't trust you anymore."

Daphne fell silent, then finally spoke after a long glare at Rachel. "Fine."

Rachel called the payment line and keyed in their account number. The account history listed payments of half the amount owed being deposited late for the last four months. The outstanding balance was nearly three hundred dollars. She groaned as she entered her credit card number. *How long until our power is back on?*

She went to Daphne's bedroom and opened the door without knocking, then threw the bill inside. "Three hundred bucks, Daphne." She slammed the door and retreated to her bedroom, where she locked her own door and went straight to bed.

It was like a warped sense of déjà-vu. Rachel stood in the shower, waiting for the hot water to start running. No matter how far she turned the lever, nothing but cold water came out.

Do I have "sucker" written on my forehead? Or has Daphne seriously lost her mind?

She put on her robe and rapped twice on Daphne's door to announce herself, then entered uninvited. "Really, Daphne? The gas, too?" Daphne rolled over and clamped a pillow to her head. "Unbelievable, Daph. What is going on with you?" Rachel began rummaging through the clutter on Daphne's desk.

"Hey, what are you doing?" Daphne rolled off the bed and moved to the desk.

"I'm looking for the gas bill. One of us has to pay for it."

Daphne hip-checked Rachel out of the way then yanked open a drawer of files. Rachel was surprised to see an oasis of organization in the drawer, but she was too angry at Daphne to pay her a compliment. She saw the file marked with the name of the gas company and pulled it out, then went to her room to call and see how much this bill was going to cost her. Her savings account had been diminished by more than half when she'd paid off the electric bill. Hopefully that check from her mother would arrive soon.

This time not even Rachel's payments had been received. The bill was just under a hundred dollars.

After Rachel paid the bill, she steeled herself for conflict and headed back to Daphne's room to try and get to the bottom of what was going on with her. Where had all her money gone, and why was she acting so irresponsibly? But when Rachel opened the door, Daphne was gone.

During a rare moment when they were alone together at work, Jack asked Rachel if she'd go out with him after their shift. "Maybe we can get some dinner or something," he said, eyes cast down like he was nervous to talk to her. She hated that he felt that way. She was sure her lack of enthusiasm was becoming more apparent to him. Given the fact that she'd turned down all his invitations over the last two weeks, he had a good reason to be nervous.

"Yeah, that would be great." The surprise on his face made her hate herself.

She spent the rest of the day dreading the evening and even briefly considered just breaking up with him when they went out. They weren't much of a couple these days anyway, and she wasn't planning on staying with him forever, so why keep dragging it out? But she changed her mind when she realized it would mean losing yet another person in her life. At this point he was the only one she trusted at all.

They drove in relative silence to a Chinese place they'd gone to once over the summer, and after their food was ordered, Jack seemed to draw himself up taller and square his shoulders. Rachel had a bad feeling. What was he gearing up for?

"So, I wanted to talk to you." *Oh boy.* "Rachel, I'm really worried about you."

Huh? "Worried? Why?"

"Two reasons. First, the fact that you're obviously struggling emotionally and haven't said anything. I'm your boyfriend. Why wouldn't you share that?"

She squirmed in her seat. *Tell him the truth or keep band-aiding until I can figure out how to get out?* "I'm sorry, Jack. I guess … I don't know … I didn't want to burden anyone. I don't think I'm really depressed, just … struggling. Like you said. And I guess I was hoping it would just go away if I didn't pay it too much attention."

He shook his head. "It's not a burden, Rach. I'm the person who's supposed to help you with stuff like that. Man, your fiancé must have been one heck of an idiot for you to have such a warped idea of how to have a healthy relationship."

His words gave Rachel something to think about. "I never thought of that."

"Well, the idea must have come from somewhere." He picked up a pair of chopsticks and began to click them together. "The fact that you've been *struggling* helps me understand some other things, though."

"Like what?"

"Like your drinking."

"What do you mean?"

He rolled his eyes. "Drop the act, Rachel. I've lost track of the number of times I've smelled alcohol on your breath—even at work. For someone who was so excited about that promotion you sure have been taking chances with it. And don't give me that whole 'it's just a couple drinks—it's like you having two beers' crap, because I won't buy it."

Indignation burned in her cheeks and her chest. "Why is alcohol any different from drinking a Coke, or an energy drink? I like the taste, it helps me relax—you make it sound like I'm gulping down gallons every day, and I'm just not. Daphne's the one who got alcohol poisoning, not me. And if I was that bad, don't you think I'd have come into work totally drunk by now? Just because you smell it on my breath doesn't mean you know how many I've had, and who are you to say how many is too many for me?"

Jack stared at her, silent, for far longer than Rachel was comfortable with. Finally she returned it with an exaggerated stare of her own. "Why aren't you talking?"

"Because I'm trying to figure out if I trust you or not."

"I lied about feeling a little depressed so I must be lying now, is that what you're thinking?" She shrugged. "Fine, think whatever you want." She slouched back in her seat, sullen, silently daring him to push the issue.

He sighed and sat back, running a hand through his hair. "Look,

I don't want this to turn into a fight, all right? I'm not out to get you. You're my girlfriend and I'm worried about you. That's all."

The disappointment in his voice tugged on her conscience. "I'm sorry," she finally offered. "I appreciate your concern. Just … don't be concerned, okay?"

She could tell he wasn't convinced, but he dropped it anyway—not that the next topic was any better.

"And I know you said this Declan guy is just a friend—"

"Yes. Barely even that. He was in the right place at the right time, that's about it. I happened to be on the verge of a mental meltdown, and he happened to be there and ask just the right question to get me going." Again doubt was evident in his eyes. "Look—he's a Christian, and a serious one at that. Not only would I not want to get involved with a Christian, a Christian wouldn't want to get involved with me. I left the faith when I moved out here. I don't trust it anymore, I don't know if I believe in God anymore, and someone who *did* wouldn't want to get involved with someone who didn't." She spread her hands, surrendering. "End of story."

"So … I don't have to worry about getting some Dear John letter and then finding out you two have run off together?"

She rolled her eyes, hoping to look convincing. "No."

His eyes narrowed for a moment, then he nodded. "All right then." He reached across the table, his expression softening. "Truce?"

She took his hands and squeezed. "Truce."

"No more awkwardness?"

"No more awkwardness."

He nodded again, then leaned across the table to kiss her. She indulged the gesture, but all she really wanted to do was leave.

She could hear music thumping in the apartment the moment she stepped out of Jack's car. Rachel looked up to the windows and saw only the accents of mood lighting, though no Make-Out Can sat in the window. Not that Daphne would hear Rachel coming up, anyway. She waved to Jack and ascended the steps, bracing herself for Daphne's attitude. She wasn't likely to take it well when Rachel asked her to turn it down so she could try to sleep.

She opened the door and quickly shut it without going in. Daphne was dancing in the middle of the living room in her underwear.

"Good thing Jack didn't come up," she muttered as she opened the door again. This time Daphne saw her. She made brief eye contact before turning away. She didn't stop dancing.

Maybe this was a good sign. She certainly wouldn't be in a lousy mood if she was dancing like that. Maybe she and Rachel could actually talk, something they hadn't done in months. If she stopped dancing, of course. She didn't look like she was going to.

Rachel went to the kitchen and pulled out her vodka. "Want some?" she shouted over the music. Daphne whirled to face her, then gave her a thumbs-up. Encouraged by the possibility of a true conversation, Rachel mixed up the drinks—making a particularly weak one for Daphne—and perched herself on the edge of a barstool. Daphne kept dancing until the song began to fade, then she sauntered over with a smile on her face. "Thanks."

Rachel didn't mention Daphne's lack of clothing; she didn't want to say anything that might break the spell of this rare moment of camaraderie. "You're in a good mood," she said with her warmest smile.

"Sometimes a girl's just gotta dance."

"Well, think you'd be able to give me some advice while you take a breather?"

"Of course, *ma chéri*e, I'm all ears."

It was like they'd never fought, like Rachel hadn't bailed her out of four hundred dollars of debt—like Rachel had just gotten here and things were still as fun as she'd always thought they'd be living with Daphne. "Well, here's the thing: I met another guy."

Daphne's eyes grew round. "Ooooohhh—"

"Now, it's not what you think. He wouldn't—doesn't—want anything to do with me, romantically. He's a really nice guy, we've talked a few times, but there's no chance there because he's a Christian. But—it's made me realize that I'm not really content with Jack. He's great, he's sweet—"

"He's hot, he's perfect, but you still don't want him?" Daphne swore. "How picky *are* you?"

Rachel's heart sunk, but she soldiered on, hoping things would recover. "It's not that I don't want him. It's just that I don't think he's the person I want to be with long term. I don't know—I really like him, I mean *really*, but love—not so much. And I don't know why, I mean, like you said, he's perfect."

Daphne slammed back the remainder of her drink and shook her head. "I told you so. I told you to learn from my mistake and not date a coworker."

"Yes, I know, but this isn't so much about Jack's and my relationship, it's more about me and—"

"Of course it's about you! It's *all* about you, Rachel. All the freaking time."

Rachel tightened her grip on her drink. "What are you talking about?"

Daphne's voice took on a whine. "Wahh, my fiancé cheated on me. Wahh, my perfect family has problems. Wahh, my pretty little God hates me—"

"What are you talking about? Daphne, what is *wrong* with you?"

"With me? *You're* the one who can't keep a relationship alive. And I thought I was the dysfunctional one!"

Tears threatened. "How could you?" Rachel said, voice choked by the lump in her throat. "*Why* would you? What have I ever done to you?"

Daphne didn't answer, and instead stalked to the stereo and turned it back on.

Rachel had had enough. "Fine!" she yelled over the music. "Fine. Start looking for a new roommate, Daphne." She went to her bedroom and slammed the door just as the music cut out. A sudden pounding on the door made her jump.

"No! Don't move out," Daphne said from behind the door. "Please. I'm sorry, Rachel, I'm sorry, I won't do it again, I promise."

Rachel turned up her own stereo to drown out Daphne's begging, then changed into her pajamas and pulled a bottle of vodka from the bottom drawer of her dresser. She uncapped it and took a swig, then another, then crawled into bed and waited for it to take effect. Eventually Daphne stopped pleading with her, and a few minutes later Rachel heard the front door slam. She closed her eyes in relief and waited for sleep to come.

An hour later she was still wide awake, and annoyed because the vodka still hadn't kicked in. She took another couple swigs from the bottle, then a few more minutes later, just to be on the safe side. She *really* needed to sleep tonight. When her muscles finally began to unknot she was filled with relief. *Does vodka go bad? Maybe I'll get another bottle tomorrow, just in case.* This one didn't seem to be doing the trick.

The next day Rachel was working on inventory when her cell vibrated in her pocket. She saw her mom's number come up and reluctantly answered it. "Hey, mom."

"Hi, honey. Is this a good time?"

"Well, I'm at work, but if we're quick it's not a big deal."

Her mother sighed. "I'll make it fast, and you can call me back later if you want to."

"All right, what's up?"

"Are you sitting down?"

Rachel laughed. "Um, no. Do I need to be?"

"Well, this came as an awful big surprise to me. Just want to make sure you're prepared."

Rachel's knees felt weak. She went to the office and sat. "Okay, I'm sitting. What's wrong? Are you and Dad okay?"

"Yes, yes, we're fine sweetheart. But … I finally heard back from the bank, about those checks."

"Oh. And?"

"They were cashed by Daphne."

“I’m stunned. Seriously, I’m so in shock I don’t even know what to think.” Rachel leaned her head back against the headrest. “And on top of what happened last night … seriously, Jack, I’m worried she’s losing her mind.”

Jack reached over and gave her hand a squeeze. “She’s falling apart.” He pulled the car into a parking spot in front of Subway and came around to open Rachel’s door. “Are you sure Subway is all you want to eat?”

“I don’t have much of an appetite.” She hadn’t for a week now. All the winter clothes she’d bought hung loose.

Rachel sank into her seat with her sandwich. “I don’t know what to do anymore. I get sick to my stomach when I go home at night, wondering what’s going to happen this time. I can’t keep doing this.”

“No, you can’t. Honestly, Rach, I think this whole mess with Daphne is the root of your depression and all the stress that you’re drinking to alleviate. She’s sucking you dry, emotionally and mentally and physically—even financially. She’s all take and no give, and while, yes, she’s an old friend, and yes, we should, in theory, stick by our friends when they go through hard times, she is so dysfunctional that you need to start considering your own health. This isn’t the same as, ‘My roommate drinks the orange juice straight from the carton and borrows my clothes without asking.’ This is serious. The utilities that you paid for? The emotional abuse? The flat-out stealing of those checks? It’s time to cut bait and run.”

Rachel groaned. "But run to where? I don't want to move in with some stranger I found on the Internet. And I don't make enough to get my own place."

"Well, I've been thinking about this for you."

She sighed and picked at her sandwich bread. "Thanks. Come up with any solutions?"

"Yes. Move in with me."

She almost dropped her drink. "Are you serious?"

"Yes. I told you, I've been thinking about it."

She chose her words with care. "That's a really big step."

He smiled. "Yeah, it is. But here's the thing: I haven't dated a ton of women, but I've dated enough to know that you're different, in a good way, and I want to do whatever I can to make our relationship last. We're good together, when you're not being ravaged by a psycho roommate, and I'd like for us to take the next step, with all that it entails."

It was the straw that broke the camel's back. Tears began to stream down her face faster than she could blink them back. His hopeful face crumbled. "Rachel, I'm sorry—"

"No, no. Happy tears," she lied. "It's just … I wasn't expecting it." *Get a grip, get a grip, get a grip.* She sucked in a few deep breaths and mopped up her cheeks. "I didn't see that coming at all. And given what a crappy girlfriend I've been, it's a total shock to think you would want to go deeper."

He looked cautiously relieved. "Okay, good. For a second there you had me worried."

Rachel bought some more time with a long sip of her soda. "I don't know what to say, Jack. I mean, this is a huge step. I didn't even move in with my fiancé when I was engaged. And I don't want to do it for the wrong reasons. So … can I think about it?"

"Oh, yeah, of course." She could tell he was disappointed, but she was grateful for his understanding. "You're totally right, it's not something that should be a snap decision. I've been thinking about it for a while, but you should have time to think about it too. I'm just relieved you didn't just say no." He grinned, and put up his hands in a gesture of retreat. "I promise not to push you on this. Take whatever time you need. I won't bring it up again, okay?"

She sniffed and gave him a small smile. "Thanks."

"So anyway, changing subjects …" He began to tell her about the refresher course he was taking to prepare for his sports therapy certification, and, while she was excited for him, she was also slightly tuned out. She felt a bit panicky. All she could think was that she wanted out—out of her apartment, out of her relationship with Jack, out of the colossal emotional mess that was consuming her.

The first thing she did once she finally got home was to go straight to her bedroom and drink a couple giant swallows of her vodka. Then she sat at her desk and began looking at rental websites, just to see what all was out there. Not much, it turned out, at least not in her price range without a roommate. And where would she find one of those? She rubbed a hand across her forehead and slapped the laptop shut, then laid down on the bed with a book in hand.

Why isn't it kicking in?

She took another swallow, then opened the book and tried to read. But she couldn't track with the plot; her thoughts kept wandering.

Frustrated, she shut the book and turned on the radio, then closed her eyes and took a few deep breaths. *Just relax. It's been five minutes. Just give it a little more time, then it'll hit and you'll be able to think more calmly.* But ten minutes later she felt no different.

Drink it all.

The idea popped into her head. She tried to shove it away.

It shoved back. *All of it, just chug it down. There's more there than Daphne drank, and it's not like she's going to come looking for you until it's too late.*

Rachel sat up and gave her head a shake. Where had that come from? Even after finding Patrick and Trisha she hadn't felt that desperate. Maybe Jack had been right—maybe she was depressed. *It's been the year from hell. Who would blame me?* Then she thought of her father and wondered if this was a sign of things to come. How had it started for him? With a flash of mania, energy zinging through him as though his veins were high tension wires? Or with a depression that snuck up on him, enveloping him in a haze that put a damper on his emotions and sucked the enjoyment from his life?

Because that would be just my luck, adding mental illness to the mix of crap I'm facing.

No, she wasn't going to go there. She was blowing all of this out of proportion. *Just focus on right now. Right now, I need to calm down.* Which is what she'd been trying to do for ten minutes, if the stupid vodka would ever start working.

She took another swallow, then another. For a brief moment she considered praying. But then she remembered what happened the last time—the silence, the way things didn't get better—and realized her situation was bad enough without adding to it with even more expectations that didn't get met.

She changed into her pajamas and slid beneath the covers. She didn't want to think about anything else tonight.

Rachel didn't know when she fell asleep, but when she woke up the next morning, her head was pounding. Feeling hung over, she staggered into the bathroom to get some aspirin, then to the kitchen to make a screwball. She remembered Daphne once telling her that fruit juice helped get rid of hangovers, and that a little alcohol would dull the pain. She took two tumblers of the concoction, then idly flipped through a magazine on the couch.

An hour passed before she felt any better, but after that she continued to improve, and by the time she was showered and dressed she felt almost normal. Still, her issues loomed large, and now that the pain in her head was receding, the rattle of her thoughts was getting louder. Her day had barely started and she was already wishing she could just go back to bed. She wanted to call in sick, but she was supposed to go over some new inventory software with Ruby, who was finally going on vacation.

She made a pot of coffee, hoping the caffeine would perk her up, and spiked her first two cups. Still, her mind wouldn't stop churning. Her third cup, which she downed ten minutes before leaving for the café, was almost equal parts coffee and alcohol. If only the stuff would just work a little better she wouldn't need so much.

She walked slowly to work, feeling exhausted. She was barely walking a straight line, and her vision seemed to take half a second to catch up when she moved her head. She was not looking forward to a day spent like this.

"Hey, Rachel," Leah said when she walked in, then gave her a funny look. "You feel all right? You look like you're sick."

"You know," she said, the words coming slowly from a mouth that didn't feel like it was working right, "I thought it was just that I didn't sleep well last night, but yeah, I think I might be getting sick."

"I saw Cole here; maybe you should just go home and have him take over for you today?"

Rachel shook her head, then swayed on her feet as the movement wreaked havoc on her balance. "No, I can't—he's here so R. J. can show us some new iven—invet—in-ven-tor-y soft-ware." She formed the words carefully to get them through her malfunctioning mouth. What on earth was wrong with her this morning?

Ruby Jean came out of the office and motioned her in. "I thought I heard you out here. Come on in and we'll get started with this."

"Right." Rachel turned and nearly walked into the doorframe, catching herself at just the last second but nearly falling over in the process.

"Whoa, you all right there?" Ruby Jean put a hand on her arm to help steady her, then frowned. "You getting sick?

"I don't know. Maybe."

Ruby Jean made a face. "Hold on a minute." She led Rachel into the office, then said to Cole, "Could you give us a few minutes?"

"Sure thing." Cole hopped up from his seat and disappeared out the door. Rachel sat down, relieved to be off her feet.

Ruby Jean shut the door, then turned to Rachel with a frown. "Rachel, did you have any alcohol this morning?"

Rachel sighed. "Yes, I did. Just some Irish coffee this morning to soothe some frayed nerves. Why?"

"I think you're drunk."

Rachel's mouth gaped like a fish. "I—wha—no, not drunk. No."

"Yes, I think you are. How much did you have?"

"Three cups of coffee."

"But how much alcohol?"

Rachel's mind tried to scramble for an answer but failed. "I don't remember."

Ruby Jean sighed and sat down. "Rachel, I'm worried about you."

Rachel rolled her eyes. "That seems to be the trend."

"Well, doesn't that tell you something?"

"What, that my friends are all nosy?"

Ruby Jean smirked. "No—that you're having trouble and need some help." Rachel opened her mouth to protest, but Ruby Jean held up a silencing hand. "Listen. I know you're experiencing a crisis of faith. And I know that can wreak havoc on a soul. And if I have read the signals properly, you and Jack have been on the rocks as well. All that on top of what happened over the summer that drove you to move out here—that's a lot for one person to deal with. It makes sense that you'd be struggling. But alcohol isn't going to solve anything." She glanced at the calendar. "I leave tomorrow afternoon, so I'm going to train Cole on the software today, and then have him train you tomorrow. I know tomorrow's your day off, but just come in for a couple hours so he can get you up to speed. Today, I want you to go home and meditate. You need to wipe the slate clean and start over. Light a candle, draw the curtains, put on some white noise if it helps, and then work on emptying your mind. Practice some deep breathing; focus on peace and tranquility. Your mind needs a reboot, and I think this will help."

Rachel was dumbfounded. This wasn't the consequence she'd expected. "Okay," she said slowly. "Thank you, Ruby Jean. And I'm sorry. I'm so, so sorry. I promise it'll never happen again."

Ruby Jean gave her a reassuring smile. "We all make mistakes, and we all struggle with something, and eventually we all make a bad decision in how to deal with it. It's not the end of the world. Do you need a ride home?"

"No, no, I can walk, it's not far."

Ruby Jean nodded. "All right then. I'll tell Cole you'll be in tomorrow."

Rachel nodded and stood, steadying herself for a moment before leaving. Her thoughts alternated between self-hate and trying to come up with a plan of attack for when she got home. She did like what Ruby Jean had said about a reset for her brain. Maybe it'd help calm the swirl of confusing thoughts she couldn't untangle.

Once she was sitting on her floor, however, in the lotus position that she always associated with meditation and a sugar cookie-scented candle burning on her desk, she was stymied. How was she supposed to clear her mind? She tried to focus on peace and tranquility like Ruby Jean had suggested, but she needed something concrete, an actual image for her mind's eye to look at. She tried thinking of the beach back in California, the waves lapping the sand, the call of the gulls, but it just made her think of all the other things in California that she missed, which then led her to remember all the things she'd run away from, and there went the peace and tranquility she'd been seeking.

She gave up on that and started deep breathing instead. *In for a count of four, out for a count of eight.* She'd read that somewhere but had never tried it; she found now that it was actually quite relaxing.

The phone rang, startling her awake. A quick glance at the clock radio revealed she'd been out for almost half an hour. She saw Jack's number on the screen and groaned inside.

"R. J. said you went home sick. You all right?"

Bless you, Ruby Jean. "Yeah, yeah, just had a really bad night and felt really awful this morning."

"Sounds like I woke you up. I'm sorry."

"It's all right. Thanks for checking up on me."

"'Course, baby. I'll give you a call at the end of my shift; if you're feeling up for it, I'll bring some dinner over."

"Okay. Thanks, Jack."

"Go back to sleep."

She sat back down and tried once again to meditate. After a few unsuccessful minutes, she stood up from the floor and blew out the candle. "This is ridiculous."

Meditation wasn't going to do her any good if she couldn't figure out how to do it without falling asleep. Ruby Jean was partially right, at least—Rachel was in crisis. Whether it was a crisis of faith or something else was irrelevant. But it was clear that being here with Daphne the mental roommate was not at all helping. Maybe all she really needed was to be in an environment where she didn't fear a giant confrontation every time she came home. If she could shake the depression—or whatever it was—then chances were she'd feel better about a lot of things, like her relationship with Jack, and maybe even the whole God thing.

She squared her shoulders beneath the ever-growing weight of anxiety, then spoke to the silence to kick herself into gear. "All right. I'm moving out."

Saying it aloud made it feel real, and it felt good. This must be the right decision. But to where would she move?

There was only one place that made sense. She picked up her phone and sent a text to Jack. *Bring boxes when u come over and help me pack, roomie.*

CHAPTER 18

Jack showed up on Rachel's porch with three giant plastic tote boxes and sub sandwiches for dinner. When she let him in, he scooped her up in a hug and kissed her. "I'm so psyched you said yes."

She smiled. "Yeah, I know. It'll be fun."

"Are you feeling any better?"

"Sort of. Slept most of the day." It was nice to be able to tell the truth every now and then. Though, she had also spent time writing a list of what she was going to do to improve her life. Being more forthcoming was at the top. So was being a better girlfriend.

"Eat first or pack?"

"Eat." They set up their meals on the bar and Rachel poured sodas for both of them.

Jack raised his eyebrows. "A soda without anything added?"

Also on the list had been not drinking around people who might give her grief about it. "Trying to cut back."

He nodded. "That's good. I was actually going to mention tonight that depression can be made worse by alcohol. Another tidbit I picked up from my mom. You might want to just cut it out altogether until you're emotionally back to normal."

The thought of giving up the one thing that relaxed her made

Rachel crave a drink even more. "That's interesting," she said trying to sound interested. "Good to know."

Jack looked relieved. "Awesome. I really think it'll help you. And if it doesn't, I'm sure my mom can recommend a doctor."

"A doctor? Not necessary, Jack."

"Why not?"

"Because I don't want to be put on some stupid pill that's going to give me all sorts of crappy side effects."

"Could they be any worse than being depressed?"

He had a point there.

After they finished dinner they brought the boxes into the bedroom and started packing. It didn't take long to fill the three bins, and Rachel secretly hoped he'd leave since there was nothing left to do. Unfortunately he'd thought ahead.

"So I was thinking we could just bring these over and unpack them, then bring them back."

"Oh—so you're ready for me to start moving in? Who moved out, Dale or Stefan?"

Jack looked confused. "No, they're both still there. But they're both fine with you moving in. Makes everyone's rent cheaper."

"But then where am I going to sleep?"

Jack chuckled. "Where do you think?"

"Wait—with *you*? But I thought you didn't want to, um … you know, do that yet."

He laughed, wrapping his arms around her waist. "I told you I was ready to take the next step, remember? With *all* that it entails."

Her mind scrambled. "But—but your bed, you just have a twin—"

"And so do you. We'll put them together and buy bigger sheets. And I'll move my dresser into the corner to make room for yours, and I was thinking we could put your desk under the window. It'll be a tight squeeze for everything, but we'll make it work." The light in his eyes faded. "You're having second thoughts."

"I—no—I just—maybe because of feeling down lately—I'm not, you know, all that … *interested* in being, um … intimate."

Understanding dawned. "Oh, babe, I got it. Don't worry. No pressure, okay? When we're both ready, it'll be great." He gave her a gentle kiss and squeezed her in his arms. "Listen, I'll take this stuff over tonight when I go home and then bring the bins to work tomorrow. We can move stuff in phases until you get things squared away with Daphne. Have you told her yet?"

"No. She hasn't been home all day."

"All right then. Why don't we go watch a movie or something? Unless you have some boxes stashed somewhere."

"No, I don't have anything. A movie sounds good." It was a lie, but she was determined to make it truth. Fake it 'til you make it—wasn't that what people said? She was moving in with this guy, she needed to work harder at being fully present in their relationship. What choice did she have?

Rachel tried to get through the night without a drink. But by one in the morning her self-control had waned. Later, she awoke feeling fragile and anxious, and was not at all looking forward to going in to work, even if it was for just a couple hours.

In the meantime she searched for something to fill the role vodka had been filling. She knew she was technically hungry, but she had no appetite. She tried reading one of her favorite books, but her focus was so shot she couldn't track with it, even though she knew the story backward and forward. She found a yoga DVD on Daphne's movie shelf and gave it a try, but walking to and from the café was the only real exercise she'd done in ages, and the poses were awkward and her body too stiff and uncoordinated.

She was desperate for something to fill her mind besides the chant of *I want a drink* when the phone rang. It was Cole. "So two people have bailed for last shift today and I'm desperate. Can you come in?"

Despite dreading work for the last three hours and having no energy or concentration, she jumped at the chance to have her mind and hands occupied. "Sure. I'll come in for the software stuff in a little bit and stay for the shift."

"You're awesome, Rachel. Thanks."

She finally stopped stalling and began preparing her room for the move to fill the last half hour before she had to leave. *Though I suppose I can't move until I talk to Daphne, and she's been awful scarce lately. Maybe I'll manage to not run into her for a few more weeks and can put off the move.*

When she left the house, the bracing November chill didn't clear her head like she'd hoped it might. She walked to the coffee shop with her head bent against the cold and her hands tucked deep into her pockets. By the time she reached the café she was nearly running to escape the frigid air. She burst in the back door and shut it quickly. "Out for a run?" Cole asked when he saw her bright-cheeked and panting.

"Of a sort," she said between gasps.

"Can I get you a drink?"

Yes! Vodka, please! "The strongest stuff we have, straight." She smiled wide to convey a lightness she didn't feel.

"Coming right up," he said as he left the office, then returned shortly with an espresso.

"Perfect. Thanks."

After two hours of training with Cole she was able to teach back the basics of the program to him. "Great. Let's call it a day." He shut down the program, then nodded toward the front. "You're sure you're okay taking the shift?"

"Yeah, at least it's just drinks and nonmanagerial stuff."

He chuckled. "Yeah, I know the feeling. Making the drinks is nice and mindless after a while."

Not too mindless, hopefully. She pulled on her apron and went out to the counter, entering the fray with the only other person working the front. Her old speed was gone, replaced by methodical movement and careful attention to every step of the process.

By the time they closed, Rachel was exhausted. She wondered if she'd even be able to fall asleep unaided tonight. She and Cole closed together, and she was getting ready to leave when Declan's face appeared at the locked door. "He's a friend of Leah," she told Cole when he asked who it was. She unlocked the door. "Hey there. Leah isn't here."

"What? I missed her again, eh? That girl is terrible about calling." He smiled. "Well then … how are you?"

She hunched her shoulders to an exaggerated effect. "I'm five minutes from falling asleep standing up."

He chuckled. "Well, don't let me stop you from getting on with your duties, then. Do you have a ride home?"

"Just the bus."

"Alone? That's not safe at all. Let me go with you."

She shook her head. "No, really, that's not necessary—"

"Aye, but my mother raised me to be chivalrous, and I'd hate to disappoint her."

Rachel rolled her eyes. "Okay, you win. Give me five minutes to finish up."

She tried to concentrate on what she still had left to do, but all she could think was, *Remember your boyfriend. Remember Christians aren't supposed to date unbelievers. You have nothing to offer him. You're a project to him, nothing more. Don't be fooled.*

Except he was really good at not making her feel like a project.

She pulled on her coat and wrapped her scarf around her neck, then followed Declan out to the bus stop. "Shouldn't be long, probably just five minutes or so," she told him as they walked to the stop down the block. "So what were you and Leah going to work on so late at night?"

"A, uh—a project for class."

"What class?"

Declan chuckled and ducked his head. "All right, you win. I'm bluffing. I actually stopped by to see you."

Her chest squeezed. "Oh?"

"I wanted to see how you were. I've been praying for you, just thought I'd follow up."

Her hopes—which she knew she shouldn't bother raising in the first place—were dashed yet again. *I* knew *I was just a project.*

"Yeah, I'm doing great. I'm moving in with Jack in the next few days. Stopped drinking to see if it helps my mood. Life is peachy."

He was silent for a moment, then spoke with a voice tinged with a quality she couldn't identify. "Moving in with Jack—that's quite a step."

"Well, you know, commitment and all that. Plus Daphne's gone off the deep end, and I can't take living with her anymore. I have to get out of there, and where else was I going to go? Seemed like a reasonable decision."

"That doesn't seem like the kind of step you should take out of desperation. I'll bet you could find a, um, more neutral place to live if you tried."

She snorted. "Yeah, like I'm in the frame of mind to move in with a stranger."

"Leah's got a room open."

"She does?"

"Aye, one of her roommates just moved out."

No. It's too late. What would you tell Jack? "That's nice, but I wouldn't want to live with Leah—and I doubt she'd want me to live with her."

"Do you love him?"

The question made her heart jump. "Jack? Sure, of course." But to her own ears she knew how false the words sounded, and she knew they wouldn't sound any better to him. *Forthcoming, remember?* "Well … okay, I don't know that I love him. But he's a really good guy—a lot better than my 'Christian' fiancé—and he cares about me. I'm lucky to have him. And given how cursed I seem to be when it comes to relationships, I'm not going to leave one that seems to be working without a really, really good reason."

Blinding headlights bounced into view as the city bus turned a corner at the end of the block. Relief flooded through her. "Here's the bus. Thanks for waiting with me."

"I'll come with so I can see you home."

"Declan, you don't—"

"I will whether you want me to or not." He grinned, though it was brittle, and she saw sadness in his eyes.

They rode in silence for the short drive. When they stepped off at her stop he folded her arm through his as he walked her to the house. She hated herself for letting him do it, but wasn't willing to stop him, either.

She stopped in front of the Victorian. "This is it, up the stairs there." She gently pulled her arm from his. "Thanks for walking me home. That was really sweet."

"You're not home yet." He ushered her up the steps and she hoped Daphne wouldn't be there to further complicate things.

She unlocked the door and flicked on the lamp near the door. The apartment was blessedly silent. "I am now. Thanks again."

"You're welcome, Rachel." He dropped his eyes, focusing on the space between them. "Listen, I won't bother you anymore, since it seems that things with Jack are, um … serious. But I want you to know that he's not your only choice." He glanced up and gave her a small smile. "I hope you'll let me know if things don't work out."

"Oh." She was stunned. "Declan … I didn't know."

"Does it change anything?"

"Actually, yes, it does," she said, deciding to tell the truth. She gave way to a genuine smile, and realized he was the only person who made her truly happy these days. "It changes everything."

Declan pulled her close and kissed her. She returned the kiss without reservation, pulling him into the apartment and shutting the door. She felt as though her mind and body were detached from each other, that her hands were moving on their own and her mind was floating somewhere outside of her, blissful and abandoned to whatever the next minutes might bring. Until suddenly Declan stumbled back and raised his hands in defense.

"Oh, God—what am I doing? Rachel, I'm so sorry. I—God forgive me, I'm so sorry."

"Declan, it's okay—"

"No, it's not, Rachel. I can't believe I let myself—I mean, you're with Jack, I can't just—"

"Yes, you can."

"No, I can't, Rachel. I meant no disrespect." He inhaled deeply, shaking his head. "I'm sorry, Rachel. I—I won't come 'round again." And before she could summon the words to convince him to stay, he was gone.

CHAPTER 19

Something snapped.

Maybe it was the whiplash between finally feeling happy and then having it ripped away, or the tremendous guilt she felt when she realized how easy it had been to kiss Declan. Maybe it was seeing yet another relationship turn to ash, or realizing she would have to break Jack's heart in order to soothe her own. Whatever it was, something inside her finally broke, and she knew of only one thing that could fix it.

She didn't wait to see if three—or four, or five—swallows of Vodka were enough to do the trick. She merely drank from the bottle as if it were prescribed medicine.

When she woke in the morning to the buzz of her cell phone, the pain in her head was almost too much to bear. Unable to stand the sunlight, she groped the nightstand with her eyes closed until she finally found the phone.

"Rachel, you're an hour late. You all right?"

When she answered, her voice was thick. "I … um … my alarm didn't go—"

"Rachel." Ruby Jean's tone told her not to bother trying to lie. "You're hung over."

She barely managed a whisper when she answered yes.

"I'll give you another hour to get here. If you don't work today, we may need to discuss a demotion. I need to be able to count on you."

Rachel nodded. "Okay." She pushed herself upright and the whole room swayed, making her stomach lurch. She pushed through the nausea and the pain in her head to change shirts and pull her hair back into a ponytail. She swallowed a couple aspirin and forced herself to drink a glass of juice as well. It was a long trek to the front door. She had trouble tying her shoes.

Despite the clouds that obscured most of the sky, she donned sunglasses to shield her eyes from what felt like a blinding summer sun, then took slow steps down the staircase to the sidewalk.

How would she make it through the day?

How could she have been so stupid?

And if Jack found out …

When she arrived at the café, she slunk in the employee entrance and realized she'd forgotten her apron. *I am totally going to lose this job.* She took a few deep breaths and stood as straight as possible, then went into the office to get another apron.

Ruby Jean was there. She put down her pen when Rachel walked in. "I'm sorry," Rachel began before Ruby Jean had a chance to start in on her. "I screwed up again—I know it. But I'm going to be fine today, and it won't happen again, I promise."

Ruby Jean nodded slowly. "I'm glad to hear it, although that's what you said the last time."

Rachel's head bowed. She couldn't look Ruby Jean in the eyes.

"Rachel, listen." Ruby Jean's voice was kind, which somehow made Rachel feel even worse. "I'm your friend. And I'm willing to keep you on staff, okay? You're going through a lot, and I understand that. I want to work with you, help you get things sorted out, and I'm not going to write you off just because you make a mistake or two. Three, however, and we may have to renegotiate your job description."

Rachel looked up, confused. "I thought you said if I didn't work today—"

"Yes, I know—that was maybe a bit hasty. I apologize. I should have thought longer before making that statement. Your job is still safe, for now. I'm having a hard time giving up on you because you've got so much potential, and not just as a coffee shop manager." She gave Rachel a smile, then nodded to the door. "Check and see what it's like out there. If they don't need you, then come back here and start the reviews."

Rachel nodded and left, shutting the door behind her and sagging against it in relief. The aspirin had begun to take effect, and while her stomach was still a mess, her head wasn't pounding as hard as it had been. *I can do this.*

The second Rachel was able to take her first break, she went outside. The shift had been painful—the most menial tasks took far too much effort and she felt clumsier than ever. She hoped the cold air would help somehow, but a light rain had begun to fall, and the small overhang above the door wasn't enough to protect her. She was about to go in when Jack pulled into the parking lot.

Oh no.

There was no point running inside now; he'd just come looking for her. Might as well face him with no one else around.

"Hey, babe," he said. His smile faded as he saw her face. "What's the matter? You look sick."

Her hope was renewed. *Maybe he won't find out.* She opened the door and they escaped the rain. "Yeah—I'm not feeling well."

"Why are you here then?"

"I had to come in. I didn't have a choice."

"That sucks. I'm so sorry." He rubbed her arm, then stepped back, anger seeping into his expression. "I smell alcohol."

"What? You do?"

He shook his head. "Don't lie to me."

What could she say? There were no words to cover for her actions, no way to make up for how her body had betrayed her. So she said nothing and waited for the ax to fall.

But Jack didn't say anything. He just took off his coat and hung it on the coat rack, then walked past her toward the front to start his shift.

She stood, waiting to see if he would come back, then went back into the office. No point sitting around awaiting the inevitable. Might as well try to get some work done.

Somehow she made it through the day. The last four hours she'd managed to actually work, though she still had not accomplished nearly as much as she should have. She snuck three folders of work she wasn't able to get done on the clock under her sweater, tucking them into the waist of her jeans, then quickly put her coat on and buttoned it to conceal them. "I'm going now, Ruby Jean. Thanks again for extending me some grace."

"You're welcome, Rachel. See you tomorrow."

Bracing herself for the rain, she snuck out the back door without saying goodbye to anyone.

The rain was falling hard now. She pulled her baseball cap low on her head and turned up the collar of her coat, then stepped out from under the awning and began the walk home.

She was almost down the block when a car honked. She looked up and saw Jack pulled over on the other side of the street. He motioned for her to come to the truck. She froze on the sidewalk, unsure if she understood his gestures correctly. Finally he rolled down the window and shouted, "Let me drive you home."

The folders jabbed her when she slid into the cab. "Thanks," she said, avoiding eye contact.

"You're welcome." His voice was grim. He pulled away from the curb and they drove in awkward silence. She knew she should apologize, but the words were so inadequate she was afraid he'd be insulted. She searched for the right thing to say but had found nothing suitable by the time they reached the apartment. Jack pulled over, then said "wait" when she unlocked her door.

"I've been trying to figure out all day what to do. I'm so worried about you, babe. You couldn't even make it forty-eight hours without a drink?"

"It's not that easy," she said, her voice weak.

"It should be for someone who drinks just because she 'likes the taste.'" He made a noise of disgust. "Admit it, Rachel—you've got an addiction."

"I've barely been drinking for six months—"

"Obviously that was plenty of time for you to get hooked."

She said nothing. He sighed and continued. "Look. I don't want to see you ruin your life, but I also don't want my life ruined in the process. I think, out of self-preservation, I need to back out of this relationship. Maybe once you get yourself straightened out we can give it another shot. But until then, I just don't think I can keep doing this."

A lump formed in her throat, but not because he was breaking up with her. She just felt bad for having hurt him. She nodded, eyes down, so he knew she heard and understood, then opened the door and slid out without saying good-bye.

As she went carefully up the stairs, trying not to slip on their slick surfaces, she felt at least one of her burdens take flight and leave. She didn't have to move in with Jack. She didn't have to worry anymore about how they'd break up, or about staying with him when she knew their relationship was doomed. Despite the circumstances, she was smiling.

Her smile didn't last long, however. She walked in to the apartment just as a man she'd never seen came out of Daphne's room, zipping his fly. He saw Rachel and froze for a second, then gave her a brief nod as he grabbed a jacket from the back of the sofa and pulled it on as he walked out the door.

"Daphne?" she said. She went to her room, afraid of what she might find, but was met with a scantily clad Daphne lighting a cigarette. "Who was that? Are you all right?"

"That was Shane, and I'm fine."

"New boyfriend?"

"Not my boyfriend, and none of your business."

"Come on, Daph—"

"Drop it, Rachel." Daphne waved a finger toward the door.

"I can't just drop it. I'm worried about you. I never thought you were that kind of person."

"What kind of person? The kind that isn't afraid to grab some fun when she finds it?"

"There's fun and there's seriously risky behavior. Sleeping with some guy you're not even dating doesn't qualify as fun."

"Maybe not in your world. And if you're going to pull some maternal lecture thing here, I'd rather not have you in *my* world." Daphne blew smoke in Rachel's face. "Get out."

Coughing, Rachel backed out of the cloud and into the hallway. "Geez, Daphne, what are you, in junior high?"

Daphne said nothing and shut the door before Rachel recovered.

Oh no you don't. Rachel let herself back in, wedging her foot against the door so Daphne couldn't muscle it closed. "Hey, quick question. Why have you been stealing my mom's checks?"

"Whatever." But the look in her eyes told Rachel Daphne knew she'd been caught.

"I can't believe you'd stoop that low. Stealing from a friend—"

"You are no friend of mine." Daphne yanked the door fully open and shoved her way out of the room past Rachel. Rachel followed her into the living room, not ready to give up.

"No friend of yours? Where did that come from?"

Daphne seemed possessed. She kept scraping her nails up her arm, leaving angry red tracks on her pale skin. She was sucking on her cigarette like it was oxygen underwater. She was pacing around the room like a caged animal. Rachel's concern ratcheted up to serious worry.

"You've been a bad-luck charm ever since you moved in here. You're sucking my life dry! Paul broke up with me, I lost my job—"

"You *quit* your job—didn't you?"

"—you stole my money—"

"I did not!"

Daphne flung open the door as she ranted and grabbed a handful of Rachel's jacket in her hand. Shoving her outside, she continued to hurl accusations. "You jinxed me. Your own life sucked so bad you had to curse mine."

"Daphne, let go!" Being taken by surprise left Rachel at a disadvantage. She stumbled back under Daphne's manic strength and fell back against the railing of the porch. Pain radiated from the spot where the wooden railing's edge had caught her back.

Daphne grabbed fistfuls of Rachel's jacket and yanked her forward. "Get out of my life!" She tried to throw Rachel down the stairs, but Rachel grabbed the railing with one hand to steady herself and then instinctively struck out with her other fist.

It was a weak punch, but she caught Daphne in the stomach with enough force to take her by surprise. Daphne let go of Rachel's coat, and Rachel shoved her aside and headed back into the house.

But the push sent Daphne off-balance. She staggered back against the end corner of the hand rail that was mounted to the side of the house, then shrieked in pain as she twisted away, her feet slipping on the wet steps and sliding out from under her. Rachel lunged to grab her, but the thin camisole that was her entire outfit was plastered to her body. There was nothing for Rachel to grab. She screamed as Daphne tumbled down the stairs and finally lay still on the sidewalk.

Déjà vu.

Rachel sat in a hard plastic chair in the University of Chicago Hospital ER, waiting for someone to bring her some news. The parts of her not covered by her coat were soaked from standing in the rain waiting for the EMTs and police, and the parts of her under the coat—including the folders which were still beneath her sweater—were damp with sweat and fear. Every once in a while her body would give a violent shudder. She wanted a drink so badly she could taste it.

A nurse walked by, and Rachel jumped to her feet. "Excuse me!" The nurse turned and a thin ray of hope lit in Rachel's chest as she recognized her. "Can you please help me? I'm here with my friend—I was here with her a month ago when she had alcohol poisoning." Rachel lowered her voice. "You told me what was going on with her even though I wasn't family, because she basically doesn't have any family. Do you remember?"

The nurse stared at her a moment, then nodded. "She's back in? Alcohol again?"

Rachel shook her head. "No. She fell down the stairs."

She looked Rachel up and down. "You want some coffee? You're gonna catch pneumonia, dripping like that."

"Sure, thanks. But I really just want to know what's going on with Daphne."

The nurse gave Rachel the same look she'd given her the last time she'd had to plead with her for information. "Take a seat. I'll see what I can do."

"Thank you so much." She went back to her seat, marked with a giant puddle, and tried to be patient.

The nurse returned with some coffee and shrugged. "I talked to the doc handling her case and told him the situation. He said he'd be out in a minute."

A small measure of relief allowed Rachel to finally relax. She sipped the coffee, hands wrapped around the paper cup to soak in the warmth. "In a minute" turned into half an hour, and by the time the doctor showed up the coffee was gone and anxiety had begun to thrash her stomach.

"You're Daphne's friend?"

"Yes, Rachel Westing."

He nodded. "Rachel, could you come with me?"

She jumped up and followed him, sneaking a peek into every room they passed, looking for Daphne. He ushered her into a private ER room and shut the door, then pulled a stool out from a counter and motioned for her to sit. His gaze hovered just beneath her eyes. "Daphne had bleeding in her brain. We're unsure if it was caused by her fall or by the crystal meth we found in her system. If it was from the meth, the bleeding may have caused a stroke, which in turn may have caused the fall." He rubbed a hand over the stubble on his chin. "Regardless, too much damage had already been done. I'm sorry—she's gone."

Rachel was speechless. Her mouth hung open, on the verge of speaking, but her mind was on tilt. She started to shake. The nurse who had brought her the coffee appeared and walked her back to the waiting area, then asked if there was anyone she wanted to call to get a ride home.

She shook her head, feeling numb. "No," she said. "There's no one."

CHAPTER 20

Daphne is gone.

Daphne is gone.

Daphne is gone.

The broken record in her head kept her from sleeping. She stared at the wall, helpless, bereft, and slowly suffocating under the cloud that had descended once more to blacken her thoughts. The vodka she'd drunk when she'd gotten home hadn't touched the pain in her heart, and she'd finally given up trying to make it go away. Instead she stared it in the face, drew the razors of memories over her mind, over and over and over, bleeding out loneliness and fear and hopelessness.

Although the past six months had revealed Daphne's ugliest sides—and some of Rachel's—she couldn't help but think about the things she loved about her friend. Daphne had always been one of the people Rachel had most admired. Rather than let her upbringing hold her back, she had broken free of it and forged a new life for herself. She had pursued her passions, however frivolous they might be. She had tried to make every day memorable.

And she did, right up until the very end. I'll never forget this day, no matter how hard I try.

It wasn't just the shock of the day's events that kept Rachel awake. It was knowing how helpless Daphne had been in the face of her problems. Even though she'd had friends, they hadn't been enough. Including Rachel. She felt the sting of guilt for the hundredth time that night. She hadn't been the friend Daphne needed, and there was no going back.

But what if people—friends—were never enough? What if there was nothing Rachel could have done? Where could Daphne had gone then?

Bits of the conversations she'd had with Ruby Jean came to her as she watched the minutes tick by on the clock. Ruby Jean was grasping just as Daphne had been; she was just grasping at something else. But she had no confidence in the rituals and objects and traditions that she turned to—just hope, hope that they would be the right thing at the right time. When one didn't work, she grasped another one, and another, until she felt some peace. What happened when she ran out of things to try?

Where—Who—are we supposed to go to in this life if not God?

The answer was surprisingly clear to her—it was the only thing that wasn't surrounded with cottony confusion in her mind. It *was* God. But how could she try *that* again when it had failed her so thoroughly?

It's only clear because it's been hammered into me since birth. Was the God she grew up on any different than the gods Ruby Jean turned to or the crystal meth Daphne used? Weren't they all crutches, all just a way to numb the pain and get through the day?

Let go of it all, said a voice in her head. It was eerie, but it soothed her. *Your life is a shambles, it will never be better, there's no use in trying anymore. Why bother? Let go, just let go....*

Rachel was vaguely aware of someone in her apartment. She didn't call out from bed, didn't open her eyes—mostly because she couldn't seem to move anymore. But even if she could have moved she would have stayed just as she was.

Someone was talking to her. The voice, distinctly different from the voice she had heard earlier, was muffled, distant, though the hands that held hers were much closer. She couldn't make out what the person was saying, other than one word: Jesus. Over and over. "Jesus." Not cursed, not hurled like an epithet, but pleading.

The name made Rachel want to smile. It made her think of warm summer days. The image of a strong hand reaching out to her floated through her consciousness, and she imagined reaching for it, feeling its sure, steady grasp. She let herself slip back into sleep, the hand still clutched in hers.

Rachel awoke once again aware of someone in the apartment. Two someones actually—they talked in garbled voices and then faded away. Slowly more sounds came to her—beeping, a voice calling for Dr. Stein, someone crying—growing louder and more confusing until she realized these were not the sounds of her apartment. Nor were the smells: pine-scented disinfectant and her own stale sweat. She felt like she was rising up through a lake of honey, moving in slow motion, immobilized by its sticky, viscous grip. Sounds grew more distinct, sensations grew stronger—scratchy material on her body, something poking the top of her hand—and smells grew sharper until she was finally able to open her eyes.

On either side of her were green curtains hanging from tracks on the ceiling. Before her was the bustle of the ER. An IV snaked from the back of her hand to a bag on a pole, dripping a clear liquid into her veins. She felt scrambled inside, physically and mentally. Emotionally, she just felt dead.

She stared silently at her surroundings until a nurse happened by. “Oh, you’re awake. I’ll let Dr. Thoms know.”

She didn’t know how much time passed, but she didn’t mind the wait. Still, the patch of sunlight that had first fallen on the foot of her bed moved a significant amount before Dr. Thoms—a middle-aged woman with red hair—finally showed up. She introduced herself, then pulled a rolling stool beside the bed and sat down. “How are you feeling?”

“Like I’ve been beat up.”

“I’m sorry to hear that. You were severely dehydrated, and your blood sugar levels were extremely low. What have you been doing for the past three days?”

Rachel raised her eyebrows. “Three days? I didn’t know it had been that long.”

“How long did you think it had been?”

She shrugged. “I don’t know. Just … not that long.”

“So … you didn’t answer my question. What were you doing?”

“Nothing. Literally.”

“Why is that?”

A little voice told me to. Not that she’d admit it. “I was depressed.”

Dr. Thoms nodded, her features revealing nothing of what she thought about Rachel’s approach to problem management. “There was alcohol in your system, too. Not a lot, but given the size of the bottle your friend found beside the bed, I assume you weren't just having a nightcap."

"My friend? Who brought me in?"

Dr. Thoms checked her chart. "Ruby Jean Cronin."

Rachel frowned. "Really?"

"Yes, why?"

Rachel could remember hearing Jesus' name being said aloud—had Ruby Jean been praying for her? Why wasn't she on her vacation? "Just not who I was expecting you to say."

Dr. Thoms closed the chart. "So, about the alcohol. Do you drink a lot?"

"'A lot' is relative.'"

"True. How much do you drink in a day?"

"Depends on the day."

"Has anyone ever expressed concern at how much you drink?"

Rachel dropped her gaze to the patch of sunlight near her toes. "Um … yeah."

"Have you ever thought you ought to cut down on how much you drink?"

She remembered the day she went into work drunk without even realizing it. "Yeah ..."

"Have you ever had a drink first thing in the morning?"

"Yes." Dr. Thoms nodded and opened the chart again. "So, what—I'm an alcoholic?"

"Well, you're not engaging with alcohol in a healthy fashion, let's just put it that way." Dr. Thoms glanced up at her. "You don't seem particularly upset about that."

"I don't really feel anything."

The doctor nodded slowly. "I'd like to have you speak with one of our social workers. Would you be willing to do that?"

Rachel shrugged. "Whatever."

Dr. Thoms hung the chart on the foot of the bed and walked away, leaving Rachel to entertain herself. She closed her eyes, bored with the traumas around her. She wanted to sleep, but a nagging question kept popping up in her mind.

What was I doing for three days?

"Rachel?"

Rachel opened her eyes. A young woman, maybe only a few years older than her, stood at the end of the bed. "My name is Amelia. Dr. Thoms asked me to come down and talk with you. Are you up for it right now?"

Rachel pushed herself up a bit on the bed. "Sure. Nothing else to do."

Amelia sat on the stool Dr. Thoms had left beside the bed. "The doctor told me a little bit of what happened, and that you seem to be struggling with alcohol and depression."

"I never thought I was struggling with alcohol, but with depression, yeah."

"Do you think there's a specific reason behind your depression?"

Rachel almost smiled. "One specific reason? No. More like six or seven."

"Would you mind telling me about them?"

"How much time do you have?"

Amelia chuckled. "All the time you need."

Rachel took a deep breath. "All right, then. Back in May …" She chronicled her life over the last six months, sharing every tragedy and struggle in a dispassionate voice as though reading the dictionary. When she finished, she waved a hand weakly. "And there you go. The end."

Amelia raised her eyebrows. "Wow. I'm not surprised you used alcohol to get a little peace." She made a note on the clipboard she held, then said, "I have one more question for you. After Daphne died, what did you do when you went home?"

Rachel shrugged. "I don't remember. I think I was just … done."

"Done—with what?"

"I don't know. Life, I guess."

"Dr. Thoms said alcohol was found in your system, so obviously you were drinking over the last few days. Did you drink with any particular purpose in mind?"

A memory suddenly came to her—taking swallow after swallow as a voice in her head recounted how much it had taken Daphne to pass out from drinking. "I—I might have been drinking to try to escape," she said slowly. She wasn't sure how honest she wanted to get about this.

"Escape from what?"

"Um … life?"

"You sound unsure."

"That's because I am. Like I told you, I don't remember much."

Amelia nodded. "Rachel, I'd like to recommend you for our inpatient program. It will help you dry out from the alcohol, learn how to handle the addiction to it, and address the depression you've been experiencing. Would you be willing to enter that program voluntarily?"

Rachel sighed and closed her eyes. "Sounds like you think I should, huh?"

"In my professional opinion, yes."

Rachel pictured hours spent weaving lanyards and watching game shows on a community television. She had no idea if this was an accurate assessment of inpatient programs, but even if it wasn't, it had to be better than the half-human feeling she had right now and the inescapable feeling of impending doom that shadowed her every day.

"All right then. I'll go."

The next five days were surreal. The withdrawal hadn't been too bad, given she hadn't been drinking for very long, but the mental addiction was far worse than the physical. Luckily they kept her busy, with minimal downtime for her to dwell on how soothing a drink would be.

Through the various forms of therapy used in the program, she came to admit, albeit grudgingly, that she had been abusing alcohol. By her last day she'd accumulated a list of tools to help her cope with life, though she had a feeling she'd be returning to her coffee habit to help as well. Thankfully Ruby Jean, who had come to visit her, had assured her that her job was still there if she wanted it.

On the advice of her psychiatrist she began journaling on her second day there, and by the time she left she had twelve pages front and back filled with stream-of-consciousness chatter. When she was feeling particularly fragile, she wrote about shallow, inconsequential things, like the kinds of coffee she was going to buy when she got out. But when she felt brave, she drilled deeper, asking herself "why" over and over to every statement she wrote.

Why had she fallen apart in Chicago and not California? Why hadn't she wanted to stay with Jack for the long haul? Why wasn't she able to embrace Ruby Jean's approach to spirituality—and why did she still care so much about spirituality in the first place?

That question came up more than once. She still was unable to answer it.

Jack picked her up when she was discharged. She'd been reluctant to accept the offer, but he'd read her mind and assured her she had no reason to feel weird. Nevertheless, embarrassment burned in her cheeks when she walked out of the psych ward with her duffel into the circle drive where he waited in his truck.

"Come here often?" she quipped when she got in, hoping to break the ice.

"A lot more than you'd think." He grinned, then leaned over and gave her a friendly hug. "How are you feeling?"

"Not a hundred percent, but not too terrible. Mostly I'm just tired. It's been a long week."

"That's the understatement of the year."

The closer they got to the apartment, the worse Rachel's anxiety got. She mentally checked off the tools on her list—visualization, calming breaths, positive self-talk—and a block before home admitted, "I'm a little freaked out about going home knowing that Daphne is … you know."

Jack squeezed her hand briefly. "Want me to stay for a bit? I can if you want."

"Maybe just for a little bit. If you don't mind."

"Not at all." He gave her a smile and changed the subject to idle gossip about his roommates, and Rachel was grateful for the distraction. When they pulled up to the curb in front of the house, he helped her from the cab and gave her hand a squeeze. "You can close your eyes, and I'll lead you up if you'd rather not look."

This made her laugh. "Thanks. I think I'll make it. But keep an eye on me just in case."

Once in the house she thought she'd feel better, but after a few minutes she realized it would take a lot longer than that to feel comfortable.

"We could go out, get something to eat," Jack offered when she admitted her discomfort.

"No, running away won't solve anything." She gave him a self-deprecating grin. "Therapy 101. My insurance dollars at work."

He smiled, but spoke seriously. "Listen, I know this—" he waved a hand between them, "might be awkward, given we're not together anymore. But I want to help you, if there's anything I can do."

"Thank you, Jack."

"And don't feel like you have to put on a brave face for me, either. You've had a horrible week. Don't try to be Little Miss Sunshine, okay?"

She nodded. "I know. I think I'm a little afraid to be honest with myself about how I feel. I'm afraid I'm going to fall off the wagon. Being here alone …" She shook her head. "It's just eerie. But—" she held up a hand, "I don't want you to even think about offering to stay over. I know you would because you're such a gentleman. But I don't want things to get … confusing."

He gave her a brief hug. "I understand."

They separated and took seats opposite each other in the living room. "So, by the way," he said, "Leah told me to tell you that she wants to come over tonight and bring you dinner."

"Really?"

"Yeah. She said for one of us to let her know if that would be okay. She's off at three, so we can still catch her at the café."

The thought of talking to Leah comforted her. Rachel pulled her cell from her pocket and dialed, then asked for Leah. "Hey, it's Rachel."

"Rachel, hi! Are you home now?"

"Yeah—and Jack said something about you wanting to bring dinner over."

"Only if you're up to it. And I understand if you aren't."

Rachel shrugged. "I don't mind, as long as you're not expecting engaging conversation."

Leah chuckled. "There's no pressure on you, believe me. I won't stay long, either, though I do want to run something by you. Anything in particular I can bring you?"

"After five days of hospital food, everything sounds like gourmet."

"Ha, I'll bet. I'll bring pizza."

Jack stayed while Rachel unpacked, and later, as he was preparing to leave, he suddenly blurted, "I feel awful, Rachel, for everything, but especially this."

"For 'this'? What do you mean?"

"The whole … psych-ward thing."

She almost laughed. "Jack, that is not your fault."

"Are you sure? I thought maybe it was because I, you know, broke up with you—"

"No, no, this is not because you broke up with me." She took a deep breath and sighed. "Honestly, I was actually glad you did. I really didn't want to move in together, but I didn't think I had any other choice. That *was* feeding into my anxiety and depression. But it still wasn't your fault. It was just one of many things that I couldn't figure out how to handle, and they all built up until Daphne's death put me over."

His relief was clear on his face. "I'm glad to hear that. I've been feeling pretty guilty."

She gave him a hug. "Hey, thanks for staying."

"Of course." He stepped back, his look intent. "Listen, Rachel … I meant what I said that night, about giving it another shot when you're feeling better. I know it might be a while, but I don't mind waiting."

The admission was an arrow in her heart. "That's … that's really sweet, Jack. I'm flattered, and grateful. But …" She scrunched up her face, gathering courage to be truthful. "But I don't think we're meant to be together. I don't know, maybe I'm wrong, and I'll change so much from this experience that we'll work better together, but … there was something missing for me, or maybe *in* me, I don't know. And without it—whatever it is—I don't think we'd last for much longer than we did the first time. I'm really, really sorry. You don't know how much I wish we *did* work better together. You're—it sounds cliché, I know—but you're a great guy, and I'm sure it's not you, it's totally me. Please don't hate me."

He laughed, though his eyes belied his disappointment. "I don't hate you, Rachel. And I understand what you're saying. I'm bummed, but I understand."

"Will we be cool at work?"

"Completely professional, I promise. When do you think you'll come back?"

"I don't know—I have to talk to R. J. and see what she says. I don't know if I even have a job anymore, honestly."

"Oh, you know R. J.—she's all mush inside. I'm sure she'll let you stay on." He gave her one more hug. "I should be going."

"Okay. Thanks again for everything."

"Of course." He gave her a quick kiss on the cheek, then let himself out.

Rachel surveyed the room as though Daphne's ghost might suddenly materialize. "What to do, what to do?" she said aloud, then turned on the television to keep her company. Soap operas dominated the lineup, however, and the last thing she wanted was more drama.

My journal. She found the notebook in her bedroom and brought it out to the bar, then set herself up with a glass of water. She flipped through the pages until she found her most recent entry and reread what she'd written to get back into the line of thinking she'd been following. It was yet another musing about what she'd been trying to run from when she'd lost those three days after Daphne's death. She still barely remembered anything, and that scared her.

She set her pen to the paper and let it scratch out a word.

God.

She wrote the word in capitals and stared at it. Yes, that was it. She'd wanted to run away from God. She'd known it for a while now but hadn't been ready to analyze it yet. But now, alone and away from prying nurses and creepy fellow patients, her pen began to fly across the page. *But didn't I already do that? Isn't that what moving to Chicago was? And giving up on church, and not reading my Bible or journaling anymore, and dating someone who wasn't a Christian? How much more running do I need to do to feel like I've finally gotten away?*

Running myself to death, apparently.

Maybe the therapists at the hospital weren't the people she'd needed to talk to after all. Maybe she needed to talk to someone who understood where she was coming from, spiritually speaking. Like a pastor. Not that she wanted to hash out her troubles to yet another stranger. *I wish there was someone who knew me already, knew what I'd been going through, but also understood the way I was raised—in the church, believing in God, having such a specifically formed worldview.*

Her pen stopped. She *did* know someone like that. Two someones, actually. But she knew only one would be wise for her to talk to right now.

She shut the notebook and began writing out a shopping list for her empty kitchen, biding her time until Leah arrived.

Rachel took a bite of her slice of deep-dish and smiled. "I can't tell you how good this tastes. Thanks again."

"Of course! I had hospital food once, and it was horrible. I can't imagine five days of it. Gross."

"Yes, exactly." They ate in silence for a few minutes until Rachel found the courage to talk about what was really on her mind. "So,

I had a few insights while I was in the hospital, and I realized today that I needed to talk to … well, to a Christian, actually. Think I could sort of vent to you for a bit? You don't even have to have any answers—I think I'm just looking for someone who can relate to where I'm coming from."

Leah smiled. "I'm all ears."

Rachel sipped her cherry Coke and mulled over where to begin. "Well," she finally said, "once upon a time, when I lived in California …"

As Rachel told her story, Leah was sympathetic and angry for her in all the right places, and when Rachel was done she spread her hands in surrender. "So there you go. That's me in a nutshell, up until I walked into All Together Now. Everything that's happened since then—my off-kilter relationship with Jack, the alcohol, the never-ending bad mood—has all been rooted, I think, in what happened back in California. And today when I was journaling, I realized that all my issues since moving here have to do with the fact that I'm trying to run away from God. I *want* to run away from God, but at the same time I don't know where else to go. But I don't want to go back to him, that's for sure. So I'm stuck. And I don't want to slip back into how I was, so I'm trying to figure out what to do." She gave Leah a small grin. "Any insights or advice would be welcomed, but I don't expect you to be able to fix everything—or any of it, really. So if you don't have anything to say, that's okay."

Leah smiled, head nodding. "No, I definitely want to respond. Just give me a minute to mull, okay?"

"Take all the time you want." Rachel finished her pizza, now nearly cold, and helped herself to another slice while basking in how good it felt to share her story to someone who knew where she was coming from. Despite what she'd said, she really did hope Leah had some kind of advice. Something had to change, she just didn't know what it was.

Leah finished her own pizza, then sat back with her drink. "Okay, so, here's what I'm thinking. First of all, I understand why you might feel betrayed by God and are so angry with him." She thought for another long moment while Rachel waited, feeling awkward. "But I'm wondering ..." Leah flourished her soda can in a thoughtful way. "What if the God you're angry at doesn't really exist?"

Rachel sighed. "Yeah, I've tried that—the whole 'God is a myth' thing, but I—"

"No, no, that's not what I mean. I mean, what if God as you designed him in your head does not exist? What if the character you thought God possessed was actually the result of confused theology? What if your view of him was so skewed that, in reality, you were trying to have a relationship with someone who wasn't there at all?"

Rachel's thoughts began to skitter in her head. "Um … concrete example, please."

"Okay. For example, you thought God required this checklist of activities—pray at meals, read your Bible, go to church every Sunday—and that fulfilling that checklist was the way to his heart, the way into a relationship with him."

"That's what Christianity is … yeah."

Leah smiled wide. "See … I don't think so."

"But … that's how you get close to God."

"Well … okay, kind of. But I think the problem comes when you view those things as part of some sort of bargain, like you put in X amount of time and you receive Y amount of whatever from God. Thinking of disciplines like that turns them into homework, required tasks—it robs them of their meaning. It's a world of difference in terms of motivation and mind-set."

Rachel cradled her chin in her palm. "Wow. That's, um … interesting."

"It's huge—that's what it is. Your view of God, and correct me if I'm wrong, was that you did everything by the book, so God should have had your back. You did everything right, and therefore your obedience deserved to be rewarded."

Rachel's eyes went wide. "Exactly."

"Well, what if God really *was* there when everything went down, but his reaction wasn't what you expected, so you thought that meant he wasn't there—or that, if he *was* there, he didn't care."

Rachel frowned, thinking. "Well, okay, but … that doesn't seem any better. To say that he was there but just didn't respond …"

"I never said he didn't respond. I just said it was possible that he *did* respond, but not in the way you thought he should."

Rachel sat back, her eyes rolling heavenward. "That *still* isn't any better. How else should you respond when someone is going through a crisis? It seems to me that stepping in and helping would be the best reaction, so what does it say about God that he didn't?"

Leah chewed her lip for a second, her brow furrowed. Her words came slowly as she responded. "I think we tend to assume God is silent, or absent somehow, when he doesn't respond the way we think he should … when in reality, he's working in the background, orchestrating and preparing and doing who knows what else to take care of us. But we don't see that—we don't know what he's doing—and so we think he's not doing anything at all." She shifted in her seat. "It's like—think of a child, and how a child doesn't always understand why his parents discipline him the way they do. The child doesn't necessarily see past the reality of, say, something sharp being taken away—all he knows is that he wants it and his parents won't let him have it. He doesn't recognize that getting what he wants might hurt him." She spoke more quickly, engaged in her explanation. "Or if they discipline him for being rude—he can't reason the way they can and understand that, by not allowing him to act a certain way, they're training his character and helping him grow into a respectable adult." She nodded, looking pleased with her analogy. "I think God is more concerned with our sanctification than in our earthly comfort, and sanctification is hard to come by when life is easy. Hence the need for the 'refiner's fire,' as they say."

"So … so he let everything happen because he thought it would make me grow?"

Leah smiled. "I can't speak for God, but I think it's a reasonable possibility."

Rachel let out a snort. "How is a cheating fiancé, alcohol abuse, and a stint in the mental ward growth?"

"Well, it's brought you to a place where you're analyzing your relationship with him, right? To a place where you're realizing that what you had before wasn't a relationship of intimacy and faith, but of checklists and obligations?" Leah quirked a brow. "Sounds like growth to me."

Rachel opened her mouth to retort, but none came. She thought about her faith before May, about her relationship with God and what it had been like for the last twenty years. She'd been devoted, yes, but to a system. She'd loved God, but in the same distanced and dispassionate way that she loved other concepts, like freedom of speech. Save for that mission trip to Brazil, she'd never felt his presence or felt any kind of real connection, and the connection she *did* feel in Brazil faded once she got back to her Orange County life. Her amazement over God's love had been stirred by heart-tugging worship songs, but when simply thinking about his love, she'd end up wondering what exactly that felt like. She'd always wished she would sense him more, and often prayed God would draw her to him—was that what he had been trying to do when everything fell apart?

"Okay, so, assuming you're right that He didn't abandon me, then what does that mean? I wasn't supposed to be mad about what happened in California? I was just supposed to grin and bear it?"

Leah quickly shook her head. "Oh, no, I don't think God wants us to stuff our emotions. What happened was awful, and I'm sure he thought so too." Her mouth twitched to the side as she thought. "I can't think of the references right now, but I know that we're told a couple times in the New Testament to praise God for all things, give thanks in every circumstance, that sort of thing."

A song lyric bubbled to the surface of Rachel's mind. "Sort of like, 'I will praise you in the storm'?"

"Right." Leah snapped her fingers. "Oh! One's in Ephesians: 'Always giving thanks to God the Father in everything.'"

Thank God all this happened? Patrick's betrayal, Barbara's admission, her parent's divorce, Daphne's death, her addiction … she cataloged all that had happened and tried unsuccessfully to imagine being thankful for it. "Thanking God feels a bit masochistic."

Leah chuckled. "I don't think he means it that way. I think it's more like, 'Thank you for the fact that, when life sucks, I still have you to turn to,' and 'Thank you for the chance this gives you to grow me and show your power.'"

"So … maybe this was one of those 'God works good from evil' kinds of situations?"

"Could be. Like it says in Romans, in everything God works for the good of those who love him."

Leah sat back and sipped her soda, giving Rachel the time she needed to process. Finally, Rachel ventured a response. "So … if it's true that he wasn't up there stonewalling me, and he didn't actually leave me … then running to him now wouldn't be like running back to someone who hurt me." She felt a jolt of pleasant surprise. "Maybe I still have a shot at the relationship I thought I had."

"No, not the relationship you thought you had. A *better* one. A real one. A relationship, period. All you had before was what *you* thought was a mutual arrangement—you scratch my back, I'll scratch yours. I'll obey you and do all these things I think I'm supposed to do, and in return you'll help me out when I need it." Leah shook her head. "That's not a relationship at all."

Rachel was silent. She had no idea what to say. But the longer she sat with the ideas, letting them steep in her mind, the more she thought Leah might actually be on to something.

Leah was getting ready to leave when she got an almost shy look on her face. "So, hey, I have something to ask you."

"Okay, shoot."

"Well, you know how I'm doing this house church with Declan, right?"

Hearing his name made Rachel's insides flip. "Um, yes."

"Well, we've been praying for you ever since Jack told us what happened. And we all feel like God is prompting us to help you."

"Help me?" Rachel didn't like the sound of that.

"Nothing weird," Leah said quickly. "Just … with whatever you need to do in regards to your roommate's belongings, finding a new roommate, and— "

Rachel sat down hard on the sofa she'd just stood up from. "Oh my gosh. I never thought of that. All her stuff—do her parents even know? I can't believe this—they might not know." She hung her head into her hands and groaned. "And I don't think the management company even knows I live here. I never signed a lease. I just gave Daphne my share of the rent every month."

Rachel felt Leah's hand on her shoulder. "This is what I'm talking about. Let us help you. No strings attached. Please?"

What choice did she have? She was still so worn out, so mentally and emotionally shaky, she had a hard time concentrating on little things like what to eat. The tasks before her felt monumental. "Okay."

"Cool." Leah squeezed her shoulder. "So how do you feel about the rest of your night? Are you all right being alone tonight?"

"I've been trying not to think too much about it."

"If you want company, I'd be happy to sleep over."

Rachel eyed Leah. "It's the world's most uncomfortable couch."

Leah grinned. "I have an excellent chiropractor."

"You'd really do that?"

"Absolutely."

Rachel hung her head again with a sigh. "This is so embarrassing."

"Hey, don't be embarrassed, seriously. Knowing that Daphne … just right out there … heck, I'd be afraid to sleep alone here and I didn't even see it happen."

Rachel gave Leah a small smile. "Thank you."

"You've got it. And look, you're not playing hostess or anything, okay? Do your own thing, even if that means locking yourself in your room from now until morning. I don't care, seriously. I'll go home in a bit and get my stuff and just set myself up here in the living room."

Rachel rubbed a hand over her face. "When do you work tomorrow?"

"I have the afternoon shift, so if you want to start tackling things in the morning, we can do that together. And I'll call the others and let them know what's going on. They can come over or not, it's up to you—whatever you're comfortable with. They're all eager to help in whatever way they can."

"And why is that, exactly? I don't know any of them, other than Declan."

Leah shrugged and smiled. "Because that's what the body of Christ does."

CHAPTER 21

Rachel thought it might be difficult to sleep that night, but once her head hit her own pillow, she was out. When she woke in the morning, she stayed in her bed for far longer than necessary, enjoying the feel of the clean, soft sheets and the absence of a roommate and intrusive nurses.

The sounds of conversation occasionally floated in from the living room where Leah had spent the night. Rachel heard the front door open and shut twice; she recognized Declan's voice and but not the other two. The thought of Declan in her apartment made her curl up under the covers even longer. She was still embarrassed by her actions the night they had kissed, and despite the fact that she was now single and available to take him up on his offer, she knew this would not be a good time for her to attempt another relationship.

She got bored of the bed after an hour of lounging and knew she should go out and meet the people who were so willing to help her. She pulled some clothes from her dresser and snuck out to the bathroom without anyone seeing her. She luxuriated in a long hot shower that was uninterrupted by a nurse calling that her time was up, and took her time getting dressed before going out for the breakfast she could smell through the door. She was guessing pancakes, though whatever it was would definitely be better than what she'd had the last few mornings.

"Hey, Rachel," Leah said when she finally emerged. "How are you feeling this morning?"

"Not bad. It's a lot easier to sleep in my own bed."

Leah pointed out the other two people standing in the kitchen. "This is Mark and Jasmine. Jasmine is one of my roommates."

Rachel couldn't help but notice how Declan, who was leaning against the far wall, avoided making eye contact. "Hi, Mark, Jasmine. Thanks for coming over."

"You're welcome," Mark said. "Jasmine made a serious breakfast over here, if you're hungry."

Rachel nodded. "Yes, please. Just a small plate, though."

"No problem," Jasmine said. "Anyone else want more?"

Leah and Declan called out requests as Rachel took a seat beside Leah at the bar. Declan left the wall and pulled a container of orange juice from the fridge. "Can I get you some?" he asked her, finally meeting her eyes.

"That'd be great. Thanks."

He poured her a glass and slid it across the formica, but the taste of it triggered a craving that made her stomach clench. She made a face as she set it aside.

"Has it gone off?" he asked.

"No, no, it's fine—I just can't drink it yet. Long story. Got any coffee?"

"You got it," Declan said.

Jasmine set a plate of pancakes, quiche, and bacon in front of Rachel, and she found her appetite growing just from the look of it.

"Jasmine, I can't believe you made all this," Rachel said. "It smells delicious."

Her smile was warm. "It was no trouble. I love to cook."

"She has a gift," Leah said. "And we make sure she gets plenty of opportunity to use it."

Rachel ate while the others regaled her with stories of the meals Jasmine had made for their frequent "community" dinners, and the camaraderie she sensed among them made her heart twinge with jealousy. It was enough to make her almost hope they'd invite her to join them sometime.

"Listen, Rachel," Mark said after helping Jasmine clean up the dishes. "We're all happy to stay, but we don't want to overwhelm you, either. Let us know what you want us to do, okay? We're at your service entirely, and if that means taking off for a while, that's cool."

"Everything is a little overwhelming right now, to be honest." She blinked back her emotion and focused on the pancake left on her plate. "I know there's so much to do, but I don't know where to start."

Leah pulled the notepad from beneath the landline phone. "Last night you said you weren't sure Daphne's parents knew about what's happened." She made a note on the paper. "And you weren't sure about staying here, since your name's not on the lease." She made another note. "And Daphne's belongings need to be boxed up."

"So you'll need some boxes. I can get those," Mark said. "A guy in my hermaneutics class just moved. I'll give him a call and see if I can take his boxes off his hands."

"Rachel, do you know her parents' names?"

Rachel nodded to Jasmine. "Yeah. And their address—or at least, what used to be their address. The phone number they had when we were growing up isn't theirs anymore, though. I can call my mom and ask if they've moved." Rachel slapped a hand over her eyes. "Oh man. My parents don't know about what happened, either. To Daphne or me."

Leah made two more notes on the paper. "Deep breath, Rachel. It'll be okay." She smiled, then glanced at Jasmine. "So, quick question—do you *want* to stay here if the management company is okay with it? Or would you prefer to move?"

Rachel shook her head. "No. I want to move, definitely." She sighed. "Add 'apartment hunting' to the list, I guess."

"Well, Jasmine and I talked last night with our other roommate, and we both agreed we'd love to have you come live with us."

"What? Are you sure? Jasmine, you don't even know me."

Jasmine folded her arms and leaned on the bar. "No, but Leah vouches for your character. The three of us have been praying for a new roommate since our other one left, and we all feel like the four of us would do really well together."

Rachel clutched her coffee mug tighter. "But what if I don't want to join the house church?"

Leah shook her head. "This has nothing to do with the house church, Rachel. Our other roommate, Anne, isn't a member. Of course you're welcome to join us, but even if you didn't, we'd still love to have you come live with us."

"Though we do have a tendency to congregate at their place," Declan said. "So if you *really* want to get away from us …" The others laughed, but Rachel could see the concern in his eyes.

"Think about it," Leah said. "We can talk about the specifics later if you want. But for now let's start tackling this list—if you feel up to it, that is."

"Write down Daphne's parents' info, whatever you've got, and I'll get on the Internet," Jasmine said.

"If you have the name of the management company I'll give them a call and figure out what needs to happen with the lease here," Declan said.

Rachel sighed. "I guess I'll call my parents, at least find out if they know where Daphne's parents went." She squeezed her eyes shut and sighed. "I don't suppose any of you want to tell them where I've been for the last week?"

Leah wrapped an arm around Rachel's shoulders. "I think that job falls to you. But we'll pray for you."

"Thanks."

Mark looked at his watch. "I have class in an hour, so I'm going to get going, see if I can track that guy down beforehand." He looked to Leah. "Someone give me a call this afternoon and let me know what the plan is for tonight."

"Will do." Everyone waved as Mark headed for the door. "Jasmine, what's your day like?"

"I'm going to go to a meeting at noon, and I work tonight."

"Cool. Declan? Don't you usually have something Monday mornings?"

"Aye, philosophy—but I skipped it."

Leah laughed, but Rachel frowned. "What? Why?"

His look was sheepish. "This felt more important in the long run."

Rachel felt a catch in her chest and looked away.

"You're sweet, Declan," Leah said. "Rachel, what would you like to do now?"

Rachel finished her coffee and shrugged. "I guess I should call my parents."

"Would you like us to stay, or do you want to be alone?"

"Um … alone, I think."

Leah nodded. "All right then. Should Declan and I bring back some lunch? Maybe around noon?"

"Sure, that would be great."

"All right then." They all got up and pulled on their coats, then Leah picked up the notebook again. "Here's my cell number, Rachel. Give me a call if you think of anything you need."

Rachel watched them leave, receiving one more loaded look from Declan before he shut the door behind them. Then she poured herself more coffee and sat for a while, somewhat enjoying the stillness and quiet and gearing up for what would certainly be a stressful call to her mother. An idea dawned, and while most of her knew it was a bad idea, the rest of her had little control over the impulse. She walked over to the liquor cabinet.

Empty.

She cursed aloud. Someone had removed its contents. Ruby Jean?

My room! She hurried to her bedroom and dropped to her knees to peer under the bed where she'd always kept her vodka. Excitement raced through her when she saw it was still there, along with her cell phone, but when she pulled it out she gasped. It was empty.

"I drank it all?" She stared at the bottle, fighting once again to remember the days before Ruby Jean found her. Had she really drank that much?

She sank against the bed, bottle in hand. Her liquid courage might be gone, but she had coped without it for twenty-plus years; certainly she could recapture that confidence and inner strength.

I can do all things through Christ who strengthens me.

The verse came unbidden, and she glanced to the ceiling as though expecting to see the words written there. *Well, I might as well give it a shot.* She fished the cell phone from beneath the bed and clutched it in her hand. She took a deep, calming breath, then looked again to the ceiling. "Help me?"

No bolt of courage, no voice of encouragement. But regardless, she opened the phone and began to dial.

Leah and Declan had already returned when Rachel came out of the bedroom after calling her mother and taking a brief nap. "We got sub sandwiches," Leah said, pointing to the stack of wrapped sandwiches on the bar. "I took a guess for yours, but I'm sure any of us would trade with you if you didn't like it."

"I'm not picky. I'm sure whatever you got me is fine. Thanks."

Declan got a stack of plates from the cupboard. "Did the chat with your mother go all right?"

Rachel gave him a small smile. "It went about as well as it could have. Unfortunately stints in mental wards are not uncommon in my family, so it wasn't the shock it could have been. Oh, and she said Daphne's parents moved last month, but she three-wayed the realtor whose name is on the sale sign, and we talked to her. She's passing my contact info to Daphne's dad's sister; apparently she's handling the sale of the house."

"That's good."

"We heard from Mark," Leah said. "He talked to his friend about the boxes, and he said we could have whatever we could haul away. Jasmine has a car, so we'll coordinate something with her and Mark's friend and get some boxes tonight."

"That's amazing. Thank you."

Declan waved a hand to the living room and kitchen. "So how much of this is yours?"

Rachel's eyes scanned the space. "Nothing. Furniture, books, TV, dishes … it's all Daphne's. When I moved out I didn't even have a bed, just a bunch of boxes, and it's all pretty much stayed in my room." She rubbed a hand over her eyes. "Maybe I should put all the furniture up for sale on the Internet or something—"

"I think we can take care of that."

Rachel looked at Declan. "Oh good grief, no. I'm not going to make you guys deal with all that. You've done so much already."

"You wouldn't be making us do anything. You'd be letting us help you."

"Although," said Leah as she poured soda into a glass, "it means you'll be left with nothing out here. You'll need to figure out where you're going to move before we start packing up the kitchen and selling off the furniture."

Rachel sighed. "Ah yes. Moving." She glanced to Leah. "Are you sure you and Jasmine aren't just making your offer out of pity?"

"Positive. And look, you don't have to stay forever, or even a year. Stay until you're in a better position to analyze your next move, be it back to California or to a different part of the city, or to somewhere completely different. It'll take one more decision off your plate in the meantime, one more bag of stress from your shoulders, and you'll be freed up to just concentrate on rebuilding your life."

She grinned. "I'd be a fool to turn you down, wouldn't I?"

Leah chuckled. "Well, I hate to pass that kind of judgment … but yes."

Rachel laughed. "All right," she said with a smile. "Let's do it." Her smile grew wider as Leah and Declan let out a cheer. "So when should we make the big move?"

"We can start sorting through things while the others are gone this afternoon," Declan said. "Then once Jasmine and Mark come back with the boxes, we can all pitch in to get you packed. I'll bet we can get you out of here in less than twenty-four hours if you want."

Maybe it wouldn't be so awkward being alone with Declan if we have a task to complete. "Okay, that sounds good."

Declan offered to pray before lunch, and without thinking Rachel bent her head and closed her eyes. She felt a warmth in her chest as Declan spoke that made her aware of the cold that had been there without her knowing. When they raised their heads he caught her eye and smiled. She quickly focused on her sandwich.

So we're going to be alone, eh? It was going to be an interesting afternoon.

Declan surveyed the living room, hands in his pockets. "So, how should we start?"

Rachel looked around. "Why don't you start by throwing out the magazines in here and Daphne's room. Heaven knows I have no need for *Cosmo* and *InStyle*. I'll go around and make sure all my stuff is moved into my room so it doesn't get mixed up with Daphne's things."

Declan nodded and began to gather the scattered back issues while Rachel took a slow tour of the room, looking carefully at every object to make sure it wasn't hers.

She thought of a question she'd meant to ask earlier but had forgotten. "So what meeting was Jasmine talking about, do you know?"

"Oh, she goes to AA."

Rachel stopped. "AA, like, Alcoholics Anonymous, that AA?"

"Yeah."

"She's an alcoholic?"

"You wouldn't know it, looking at her, you're right." He placed a stack of magazines on the bar. "She's very open about it, though—you should talk to her sometime. She really likes the meetings. I'm sure she'd be happy to bring you if you thought it would be helpful."

"Oh, I don't know …"

"I know she says those meetings are what kept her sober for the last few years. If nothing else you might find some people who can relate to what you've gone through."

She nodded, then asked the question she'd be wondering about ever since that morning. "So … you didn't tell anyone what happened, did you?"

"You mean how I completely took advantage of your emotional vulnerability?" His tone told her how disgusted he still was with himself. "Yes, actually, I did."

She froze. "Seriously?"

"Yeah. I wasn't going to share it with anyone, but when Leah told us what had happened and that she thought we should help, I realized I'd be making a mistake not to let them know what I'd done. If I hadn't, then this—with you, right now—would be a lot more … difficult."

He held her gaze with his earnest stare. "I want you to know too, that regardless of how I may feel, I won't bring it up to you again. And if you feel uncomfortable around me, I won't come 'round when you move in with the girls."

"But—but you can't just stop coming over. They're your community."

He ran his hand through his hair and shrugged. "Aye, but you're part of that community too, even if you're not an 'official' member. And it would be selfish of me to ignore your discomfort just so I could keep getting that fabulous cooking of Jasmine's." He smiled, but it didn't reach his eyes.

Rachel shook her head. "I wouldn't ask you to do that, even if I was uncomfortable. Which … well, I'm not as uncomfortable as I thought I'd be." She pulled at the hem of her sweater. "I just wish the timing was different."

He chuckled. "So do I."

"So … how *do* you feel?"

"About—about you?"

"Yeah."

He was silent for a moment as he studied her, and she cringed inside. She should have known better.

But then his features softened and she thought she'd melt from the look he gave her. "I feel like if we were talking two months from now, I would probably stop talking and just kiss you again."

Her breath caught in her lungs. "Oh."

"Aye." He gave her another smile, then went into Daphne's room. Rachel resumed her tour, though her thoughts were somewhere else altogether. After a few moments she said, "I looked for the alcohol."

"As I recall, Jasmine was the one who thought to take those out this morning."

She sighed, feeling defeated. Maybe Declan was right. Maybe she'd talk to Jasmine about AA this evening.

Like father, like daughter—in more ways than I like to admit.

CHAPTER 22

It was Thanksgiving Eve when Rachel finally got up the courage to join Jasmine at AA. She'd been out of the hospital for over a week, and when she woke up that morning she noticed the clouds in her head had begun to disappear. She didn't feel as fuzzy, as *down* has she had been. She was able to get out of bed without five minutes of psyching herself up.

She fixed herself some cereal and plunked down in the recliner that sat in the corner of the living room. From that spot she could see the doors that led to the other bedrooms. Leah's was open; she was working first shift that morning and had left a couple hours ago. Anne's was open as well; she had an early morning class on Wednesdays and Fridays. Jasmine's was still closed, though Rachel thought she detected quiet music playing behind it. Besides being a talented cook, Jasmine was also an accomplished violinist, and the music she listened to most often tended to be classical pieces featuring her favorite instrument.

Two days ago Rachel had started back at All Together Now. Ruby Jean had gone easy on her, setting her up with busywork that didn't require a lot of concentration. By the end of the day she'd accomplished much of what she'd been given, but had been exhausted in every possible way. Yesterday she'd had no choice but to work the front because two employees called in with the flu, so she and Jack had worked the lunch shift together. It was awkward at first, but thankfully the rush of customers had been so heavy they'd had no time to socialize until nearly two hours had passed. By then the ice had broken and they were able to chat amiably, albeit guardedly, until his shift ended. When she'd come home that evening she'd again been exhausted, though not as emotionally drained as she'd been the day before.

She spent the rest of her morning transcribing the notes she'd written in the hospital. She'd started them just after moving in with Leah and the others, and found that typing was therapeutic. She wasn't sure what she'd do with them once she was finished, but she found that the more she typed, the more ideas came to her for stories and characters. Creative writing had been a favorite pastime during high school and college, but she'd stopped when life had gotten busy after graduation. Now she was writing down the ideas as they came, which slowed down the transcribing but also motivated her to keep with it. *Maybe coffee isn't my only option in life.*

She heard Jasmine in the kitchen around lunch time and decided to join her. Jasmine gave her a bright smile when she entered. "I'm making egg salad. Want some?"

"Absolutely. I'll eat anything you make. Declan was right, you're an amazing cook."

Jasmine batted her eyes and smiled. "I just like to play around."

"Uh huh," Rachel said sarcastically.

Jasmine gave Rachel a sidelong look. "You seem just a smidge more … chipper today."

"I *feel* a smidge more chipper."

"Hey, that's great!"

"Yeah, it is. It really is."

"Work's been all right for you the last couple days?"

"Better than it had been, yes. And today I am almost looking forward to work, if you can believe it."

"Now that is a major improvement. Amen."

Rachel smiled. "Thanks."

Jasmine squirted mayonnaise and dijon into the bowl of mashed egg, then sliced off a ring of red onion and began to dice it. "So, you're still coming to AA with me after lunch, right?"

Rachel bit her lip and nodded. "Yeah. Not sure how I feel about it, though."

"Just remember you're not committing to coming forever."

Rachel poured them each a glass of water. "What was your mind-set when you went the first time? Did you anticipate going regularly or were you just checking it out?"

Jasmine smirked. "I didn't have a choice, actually. My parents basically drove me there and walked me to the door. If I hadn't agreed to go, they'd have stopped paying for college."

"Ah, gotcha."

"I was twenty and stupid and thought they were overreacting. I would go to the meetings and sit in the back listening to music on my phone. I didn't participate or pay any attention at all, but they didn't know that, so I figured we were all happy." She rolled her eyes, dumping the diced onion into the bowl and then adding a dash of paprika. "I was still drinking—they just didn't know it. But then I nearly got myself killed while driving drunk. Off I went to rehab, and then AA again, but this time I was listening. My mentor is the one who led me to Christ."

"Wow. Heck of a story." Questions filled her mind, but she didn't want to intrude on Jasmine's privacy. "So … how long have you been sober?"

"Um …" She stopped mixing and counted on her fingers for a moment. "Four years, three months, and seventeen days."

Rachel laughed. "Wow, down to the day, huh?"

"It's a big accomplishment for me. I started drinking when I was twelve."

"Twelve?!"

"Alcohol was imbibed very freely in my family. It was easy to find and no one minded if I took a sip of their wine or beer or whatever, just to try it out. But no one else has an actual addiction. They can all take it or leave it—in fact, ever since I went into rehab, they've all stopped drinking when I'm home, and my mom told me she barely drinks at all anymore; it just doesn't appeal to her." She crumbled a strip of bacon into the mix and followed it with a spoonful of sour cream. "I, on the other hand, can't even keep wine in the house to cook with, which makes some recipes a bit difficult. I've occasionally had Leah run down to a neighbor to beg off whatever amount I need for a dish. It's that hard for me."

"Even after four years?"

"Four years is less than half the time I spent drinking before going to rehab. I still get a pretty decent-sized craving once a week or so."

"So what do you do then?" Rachel had had a pretty decent-sized craving, albeit only a mental one, nearly every day since coming home. The only thing that had stopped her from running for the liquor store had been the omnipresence of the house church gang. Once she'd started back at the café, it had been her fear of letting Ruby Jean down and losing her job. But she worried that she'd break one of these days.

"It depends. If I'm home, I try to go for a run, or pop in an exercise video, or play my violin for a while. Keeping myself busy helps get my mind off it. If I'm in class and I can't stop thinking about it, I just start praying like a madwoman. Sometimes I'll text my mentor, or call her if I can. She's really good at talking me down."

She pulled two rolls from the fridge and ripped them open, then placed them in the toaster oven. "The first meeting I went to after rehab, when I was actually in the right frame of mind about it all, I was so scared. I was afraid I would never stay sober, that no one would ever understand how hard it was for me, or that I'd never find a mentor because they'd all think I was a hopeless cause. But Nell—that's my mentor—came up to me right away and took me under her wing. She told me later she recognized the fear on my face because she'd felt the same way when she'd first gone. She was ten years sober then and helping to run the meetings."

"Will she be there today?"

Jasmine shook her head. "No—I moved out here last year from New York. She's back in Floral Park, leading a women's-only group."

"Women's only—is that what today's meeting will be?"

"No, there isn't one that meets at this time, but it's not a big deal. My parents were more concerned about it being women's only when I was younger. But everyone's really friendly—either that or they just keep to themselves. You'll see."

They left after lunch, catching a bus and riding for ten minutes before disembarking at a Presbyterian church. Rachel followed Jasmine's lead and served herself coffee before taking a seat in the circle of chairs and was relieved by how friendly most of the other attendees were. Many knew Jasmine by name and encouraged Rachel to start coming more often.

The meeting was not what she had expected. No smoke-filled room, no silly rituals. Just people talking about where they were on their journey, admitting when they'd fallen and offering support to each other.

The one element that really gripped her came during a testimonial. A woman not much older than Rachel had been sharing her story when she'd made a comment that flipped a switch in her mind. "I know not everyone here relies on the God I rely on as their higher power. I didn't rely on him, either, for the first two years of my attempts at sobriety. But I kept falling off the wagon, or taking giant, willful leaps off the back of it, and I blamed the program because I thought it should work better than it did. But when I stopped praying to some nameless higher power and started praying to the one true God, that's when things really began to change. That was three years, nine months, and twenty-eight days ago."

The remark felt like yet another attempt by God to get her attention. She'd been mostly ignoring the spiritual discussions Leah and the others got into, trying not to think too hard about the conversation she and Leah had the day she'd come home from the hospital and generally shoving aside any thoughts about God. But it felt like each instance was another rock hurled at her fragile defenses. She wasn't sure how much longer she could hold out.

The group had closed with the Serenity Prayer, recited on their feet with their heads bowed. Rachel didn't know the words well enough to recite them, but she took a chance and took them to heart. "God grant me the serenity to accept the things I cannot change"—*I can't change what happened, or the things I've gone through, or the fact that I'm apparently an alcoholic, so I'm going to stop whining about them*—"courage to change the things I can"—*I think I want to give it another shot with you, God. I'm not 100 percent sure, and I might go home and totally change my mind on this, but right now, anyway, I think I want to try*—"and wisdom to know the difference"—*There are things I can't fix, so you're going to have to help me let them go and give them to you, because I've really gotten used to trying to do it on my own, despite the lousy job I was doing of it.*

When she'd pulled on her coat, her eye caught the edge of her tattoo peeking out from beneath her sweater sleeve. *Freedom.*

Maybe. She'd followed Jasmine from the church, her heart feeling lighter than it had in a long time. *Maybe.*

"So how was AA?" Leah tossed Rachel the bag of marshmallows and leaned her skewer toward the fireplace. "If you want to talk about it, that is. If you don't, that's cool."

Rachel pushed a marshmallow onto her own skewer and dropped the bag beside her. "It was … interesting. I'm really glad I went."

"That's good. Think you'll go back?"

Rachel knew from looking at the materials Jasmine had picked up for her that they recommended attending ninety meetings in ninety days. "I might. To do it like they say you should is a big commitment."

"It's a big addiction."

"True." Rachel slowly turned her skewer over the fire. "I didn't know they talked so much about God there. It took me by surprise. I feel like, since I've been back from the hospital, God's been following me like a lost puppy, nipping on my heels and trying to get me to pick him up."

Leah laughed. "That's an interesting metaphor."

"Well, it's true." Rachel grinned. "Today was another example. This woman got up and talked about how she didn't start to really improve until she stopped relying on a 'higher power' and started relying on God. I nearly wanted to just stand up and say, 'Okay, point taken. Leave me alone now.'"

"He's a persistent fellow when he wants to be."

"Yeah, he is."

"So, what are you going to do about it?"

Rachel sighed, watching the shell of the marshmallow brown and bubble. "I don't think I can *not* believe in him. Which means I have to figure out if I'm going to admit he's there and just ignore him, or else give in and start trying to figure out how to follow him again. And given how he keeps popping up everywhere, I have a feeling ignoring him is going to be difficult."

Leah chuckled. "Crazy puppy."

"Seriously!" Rachel laughed, but sobered quickly. "Part of me feels … I don't know, intruded upon. Like he wants me back so he thinks he can just bug me until I relent. How rude is that? But then I remember this is *God* I'm talking about, and if he is who the Bible says he is, then he pretty much has that right. And then I feel sort of flattered—like, God's pestering me because he … he *loves* me?" She pulled off the marshmallow and thought as she chewed. She thought back to the last time she was in a worship service in California. She was amazed by God's love then, too. But she couldn't believe how differently she had viewed him. Somehow—thanks in part to Leah and, she hated to admit it, thanks in part to recent events—her perspective was taking a new shape. God's love had once seemed to Rachel like a report card for a job well done. But she could no longer rest on her laurels, and yet now, God's love seemed even bigger. Still, questions lingered.

"I still sometimes get frustrated and think, 'Well, if he loved me, why didn't he make it clear to me earlier that I wasn't on the right page?'" She shook her head. "It's a never-ending cycle of questions that I can't seem to break out of."

Leah blew out the flame that had engulfed her marshmallow and pulled the charred mess from the skewer. "It's not an easy question to answer. But I honestly believe that if you trust him—just *go* for it—he'll sort it out for you. It might take time, it might be a frustrating experience, but I'd bet that he's using every minute of it for growth and good, you know?"

Rachel raised her eyebrows. "Just go for it—that's what I pretty much decided to do this afternoon at the meeting. You read my mind."

Leah wiggled her fingers. "Spooky."

They finished their roasting and said good-night, disappearing into their own rooms. Rachel was restless, tired but not yet willing to go to sleep. She sat for a moment on the bed, contemplating what to do, when her eyes fell on the small box of items she still had not unpacked from her move. She sat on the floor and pulled open the box, knowing it contained knickknacks she hadn't known what to do with when she'd first arrived. Now having seen how the other three women placed personal items on the bookshelves and mantel, she thought she might do the same.

When she opened the box, the first thing she saw was a skirt she'd found beneath her bed while packing. She pulled it out and felt something hard in the pocket beneath her fingers.

Tears sprung to her eyes as she pulled out the cross and chain she'd stuffed in there the day she'd moved. She felt her defenses crumble a little more as she opened the chain and wrapped it around her neck. Was she ready to wear it again?

She connected the chain and sat still, feeling the familiar weight of the pendant on her chest. *All right, then. Have it your way.*

Epilogue

FEBRUARY

Rachel stared out the window at the snow on the mountains below. It was beautiful, but blinding; after a moment she lowered the shade and pulled her laptop from her carry-on, wondering if she'd be able to get anything done when her mind was so scrambled with nerves. She opened the document titled "Lost Days" and reread the last few paragraphs to refresh her memory. It wasn't bad, what little she had written so far. She still didn't know what she'd do with it when she was done, but she was having a good time writing again. She opened another document containing a plot outline and checked for her next scene, then began to type.

"Wow, your fingers really fly." The young woman beside her smiled, looking impressed. "Do you do a lot of typing for your job?"

"Not my job, just my hobby. I'm trying to write a book."

"Oh cool! I love to read. What's it about?"

Rachel faltered. "It's, um … well, it's about a woman who—"

The plane dipped and shook as it hit a pocket of turbulence. The woman cursed through clenched teeth, her face turning white. When the aircraft stabilized the woman blew out a deep breath, looking suddenly haggard. "I hate flying."

Rachel slowly released her grip on the armrest and relaxed her hold on her laptop. "I didn't until just now."

The woman pushed the attendant call button. "I need a drink or I'm never going to make it to California."

Rachel sucked in a breath. *Oh no.*

The attendant came by and the woman asked for a Bloody Mary, then turned to Rachel. "Want something? My treat."

God, give me strength. "Just—just another Coke. Thanks."

The attendant brought the drinks and Rachel shot one prayer after another to heaven, begging God to remove her craving. The woman gulped down half her drink, then sighed. "That hit the spot. Usually I try to grab a couple drinks before I get on the plane, but my stupid taxi was late to the house, and I barely made it to the gate on time."

Rachel searched for a way to change the subject. "You fly a lot, by the sounds of it."

"No, only a couple times a year. But that's plenty for me." The woman took another sip, then glanced down at Rachel's laptop. "So, before we nearly died you were telling me about your book."

"Oh, right. Well, it's about a woman who loses everything and goes on a spiritual journey, looking for peace. I'm not trying to get published or anything—at least, not yet. This is just practice."

"That's awesome. I wish I could write. I read an article about one of my favorite authors once, and she talked about writing what you know. That totally wouldn't work for me—my life is so dead boring."

Rachel chuckled. "Yeah, I had that problem for a while, too."

"For a while? Then what happened?"

She smiled. "I lost everything and went on a spiritual journey."

A voice on the intercom announced they were approaching LAX. Rachel handed her empty cup to the attendant, then stashed her laptop back in her bag. Her stomach began to churn with nerves as she thought about seeing her parents for the first time in so long. She'd never been away from them for more than a few weeks, and now she felt like they were all—them and her—completely different people. Her parents' recommitment ceremony was tomorrow, Valentine's Day, and she was reading a poem her mother had chosen as a surprise for her father. She was worried she wouldn't be able to get through it without crying. At least there wouldn't be any booze at the party to tempt her afterward—with both she and her father in AA, that decision had been easy for her parents to make.

As they began their decent, Rachel's craving grew stronger. To occupy her mind she pulled out Jasmine's copy of the *Twelve Steps and Twelve Traditions* and opened to her bookmark. She was working on step number nine—making amends to people she had wronged. A Post-it note on the page listed the people she'd been writing letters to. Some of the names were crossed out already—Ruby Jean, Jack, and Daphne, whose letter she had dropped into the mail without an address. Her parents' names were the last ones on the list; she'd be presenting a formal apology later that evening over dinner.

The plane landed, and Rachel turned her phone on and sent a new text to Declan. *Just landed. Flight was fine.*

Less than a minute later he replied. *4362.*

She frowned, fingers typing. *What?*

Minutes till u r back.

She laughed to herself. *LOL Miss u 2.*

The line of people began to move. Rachel pulled her bag from the storage space and entered the stream, shuffling along with the others as they made their way off the plane. She bid her seatmate farewell as they disembarked and pulled her carry-on behind her through the terminal. She was halfway to the baggage claim when a familiar face came into view just ahead of her.

"Barb?"

Her old friend stopped and turned, and a smile broke out on her face. "Rachel!" With a laugh she ran over and wrapped her arms around Rachel's neck. "I can't believe you're here. How random is that?"

"No kidding. Where are you flying in from?"

"Just got back from a weekend in the Rockies. I met some old girlfriends for a reunion. What are you up to?"

Rachel laughed. "You have no idea how complicated the answer is to that question."

Barbara grinned. "Wanna get some coffee?"

Rachel called her mom to let her know she was taking a detour, then followed Barbara in her rental car to a café near Barbara's house. The glare of the sun was a welcome change from the dreary gray of Chicago's lingering winter, and when she reached the coffee shop she took a minute to change from her sweater and jeans to a skirt and blouse more accommodating for the day's mid-70s. They brought their drinks outside and settled into the chairs that sat under the storefront's canopy.

"So I heard through the grapevine that you went to Chicago."

Rachel nodded. "In June. I don't know if you remember me talking about my friend Daphne—we grew up together, and she'd moved out there. If you heard about that I'm assuming you also heard about Patrick, and my parents?"

She nodded, her face sympathetic. "I can't believe everything that hit you all at once."

Rachel waved it away. "I can't believe how selfishly I acted when you were in crisis. I'm so, so sorry, Barb."

"Nonsense. You had every right to be angry, especially when *you* were in crisis and I basically turned you away."

"But with good reason."

They looked at each other and laughed. "Should we just call it even?"

Rachel smiled. "Sounds good."

"It's funny we should meet right now," Barbara said, stirring her drink. "Just before I left on Thursday I found the letter I'd written to you when I was making amends to everyone. I didn't know where to send it when I'd written it, so I set it aside, and it got swept into a pile of stuff that's been sitting forever in my office. I told myself I was going to track you down when I got home. God's funny that way, eh?"

The phrase "making amends" caught Rachel's attention. "That wouldn't by any chance have been part of step nine, would it?"

Barbara's eyes got wide. "How did you know that?"

Rachel raised her hand. "My name is Rachel, and I'm an alcoholic."

"What?!"

"It's true. Depressingly true."

"What happened?"

Rachel chuckled. "How much time do you have?"

The trees down her parents' street looked bigger than Rachel remembered. Everything on her drive over had seemed mostly familiar with just a bit of change—a store here and there had been replaced by something new, a stoplight put in where stop signs had once stood, a half-completed building where an empty lot had been. Here in the neighborhood where she'd grown up she noticed even the smallest changes—new flower boxes, new landscaping, newly painted trim. A lump sprang to her throat when she saw Daphne's house. It was a different color now, with two unfamiliar cars in the driveway. A tricycle stood near the front door.

She pulled into her parents' driveway and pressed a hand to her chest to calm her heart. The Serenity Prayer sprang to mind, and she repeated it under her breath as she got out of the car. She'd already asked her father about the local AA meetings and had determined she'd attend them while in town. She only had thirteen more to go before she'd completed her "90 in 90." Not only did she not want to break her commitment; she knew she really would need those meetings if she was going to get through the three-day visit intact.

What are you waiting for? She took a deep breath and squared her shoulders. *Okay, God. I'm going to need some serious reinforcements here. Give me grace for my parents. Give me willpower for my sobriety. And calm me down so I'm not so stressed.* She closed her eyes and imagined her heavenly Father wrapping his arms around her—an image an AA friend had given her. The thought was comforting. She took hold of the cross around her neck, zipped it back and forth along its chain, and went inside.

… a little more …

When a delightful concert comes to an end,

the orchestra might offer an encore.

When a fine meal comes to an end,

it's always nice to savor a bit of dessert.

When a great story comes to an end,

we think you may want to linger.

And so, we offer …

AfterWords—just a little something more after you

have finished a David C. Cook novel.

We invite you to stay a while in the story.

Thanks for reading!

Turn the page for …

- **Reader's Guide**
- **Author Interview**

READER'S GUIDE

1. Which character in the book most represents you, and why?

2. Have you ever felt similar temptations to doubt God, like Rachel did? How did you respond to those feelings? In other words, can you relate with Rachel?

3. Have you ever had a friend who took a similar path—or nearly took a similar path—as Rachel took? How did you respond?

4. Is there any legitimacy in the path that Rachel took? Do you feel the path was important for her growth as a Christian or was it a detour?

5. Talk about Daphne's character. How do you feel about her? Do you know anyone like her?

6. Talk about symbolic elements in the novel. What do you see as symbolic and why?

7. Discuss the romantic aspects of *Reinventing Rachel.* Who did you hope Rachel would end up with? Why?

AUTHOR INTERVIEW

What inspired you to tell Rachel's story?

The idea for the book actually started with myself and one of my oldest and closest friends, M. Like Rachel, I was raised in a Christian home, and like Daphne, M has always considered herself fairly irreligious. Our lives took very different paths as we grew, but to this day, thirty years since we first met, we're still close and still involved in each other's lives. I began thinking about how different my life would have been had I chosen to follow the path she'd taken, and slowly that idea evolved into "What might happen if a cradle Christian turned her back on her faith to pursue the life that her non-Christian friend was leading?"

What do you hope readers glean from the story?

That what we see in our world and our lives is only part of the picture. When it comes to how God works, we can never assume that we're seeing the whole story. Our perception is so limited, our understanding so finite—we can't take our experience as a clear indicator that God is or is not protecting us. Experience is given an awful lot of weight and importance in the Christian world these days, and I think that is so damaging. We need to start with what the Bible tells us about God, instead of trying to determine from our experience what he is like. The Bible tells us that we will have trouble in this world (John 16:33), but that God and his works are perfect and good (Deut. 32:3–4) and that we cannot know the mind of God (Isa. 55:8–9), and that God does not let fall from his hand those whom he loves and who love him (Ps. 37:33–34).

Are there any parts of you in Rachel?

Yes, though not many. Her personality is somewhat like mine, her inability to comprehend how people live with their godless worldviews. I'm not a big coffee fan, though I do love a good mocha! And we both share a sense of loyalty to our friends. M and I have been through a lot together in our thirty years of friendship, but we both know that if one of us was ever in need, the other would be there in whatever capacity was necessary, and that has been lived out in practice, not just promised in theory.

Which character(s) in the book are most Christlike, in your opinion?

I think Leah and her house church friends most reflect the kind of love Jesus commanded us to show one another. That's what I wanted them to be—an example of what the church should look like. Church for so many people is just a weekend pit stop, a place where they go to relax and hear some good music and an inspiring pick-me-up of a message. It's not a community. It's not a place they know they can go to when they're in their deepest, darkest moment of need. *That* is what church ought to be, and I think when we're in that place, serving one another on a sacrificial level, that's when we're most reflecting Christ.

Why did Daphne have to die? It made perfect sense with the story, but what was the ultimate reason for her demise?

I think Daphne's death was a symbol of the logical end of a life without Christ. She was adamant in living her life on her own terms, and the Bible is clear that a life void of repentance leads to death (Rom. 6:23).

What themes drove you in writing this story?

The theme of friendship was a big one, seeing as it was the original building block for the entire concept of the book. Freedom was another one—what true freedom is, what a life lived in freedom looks like, or how we can think we're free but we're really enslaved to vices or habits or addictions—or even false thought patterns—that we can't break free from on our own. The theme of God's faithfulness was pivotal to the story as well—despite Rachel's active turning away from God and her attempt to completely cut him out of her life, God continued to guide and protect her so that she could come out the other side to a place where she was willing to consider she may have been wrong about him.

What draws you to being a writer, and what's next for you in terms of projects?

I love starting with a little "what if" and letting that play out. What if someone decided after twenty years of faith that she no longer believed in God? (*Reinventing Rachel.*) What if I got in a wreck on the freeway with a celebrity? (*Worlds Collide.*) What if a widow could reconnect with her deceased husband? (*Violette Between.*) What if a battered woman thought she deserved the abuse? (*The Weight of Shadows.*) I love seeing the little twists and turns that develop, and watching the characters develop and change and make choices that they think are going to lead to XYZ, but really end up leading to ABC. The creativity of it all, of watching something new form and blossom, is addicting.

I have two more "what ifs" coming out in 2011. One of them asks, "What if a prominent Christian teacher became an atheist against her will?" That releases in the spring with Zondervan. My next book with David C. Cook, which releases in the fall, asks, "What if the actions of a pastor's wife caused her husband's church to split?"

What are your favorite novels, and why?

I think my all-time favorite book, the one I pull out over and over again and can flip to the middle of and know exactly what's happening, is *Microserfs* by Douglas Coupland. The picture he paints of community is just awesome. And I'm a geek at heart, so I really love the techie setting. *A Tree Grows in Brooklyn* by Betty Smith is another flip-to-the-middle favorite. I recently reread it for the first time in eight or nine years with my book club, and I was stunned at how much I picked up on that I'd completely missed during those other years of reading. And I think that's the sign of a truly great book—that you can read it in your teens, and in your twenties, and your thirties, and beyond, and enjoy it each time while also seeing things you never saw in those dozens of previous readings.

Those two are my absolute favorites; after those, there are a whole slew of books that hold third place—*A Voice in the Wind* (Francine Rivers), *Anne of Green Gables* (L. M. Montgomery), anything by Lisa Samson or Claudia Mair Burney, any of the books in the Night Watch series by Terry Pratchett, Jodi Picoult's third through twelfth novels ... the podium is a little crowded! I'm in a season of life right now where time to read is really hard to come by, and I miss the days of being able to curl up on the couch and devour a book in one afternoon. But when I find a sliver of unscheduled time for myself, those are the books, the old friends, I grab off the shelf.

MORE GUARANTEED GOOD READS

The Reluctant Prophet
Nancy Rue

One Lane Bridge
Don Reid

Hometown Ties
Melody Carlson

Solitary
Travis Thrasher

The Mailbox
Marybeth Whalen

Learn more at DavidCCookFiction.Blogspot.com

800.323.7543 • DavidCCook.com